P9-CTB-130

CLAIMED

BY SARAH FINE

CLAIMED

SARAH FINE

47NORTH

This is a work of fiction. Names, characters, organizations, places, events, and incidents are either products of the author's imagination or are used fictitiously.

Text copyright © 2015 Sarah Fine
All rights reserved.

No part of this book may be reproduced, or stored in a retrieval system, or transmitted in any form or by any means, electronic, mechanical, photocopying, recording, or otherwise, without express written permission of the publisher.

Published by 47North, Seattle
www.apub.com

Amazon, the Amazon logo, and 47North are trademarks of Amazon.com, Inc., or its affiliates.

ISBN-13: 9781477849590
ISBN-10: 1477849599

Cover design by Cliff Nielsen

Library of Congress Control Number: 2014953643

Printed in the United States of America

CHAPTER ONE

*M*emories are nothing but a collection of electrical pulses and chemicals. Neurotransmitters sliding into receptors like hands into gloves. Acetylcholine. Serotonin. Galena closed her eyes and turned her face up to the spray of lukewarm water. She ran the washcloth over her breasts and down to where the scars lay in raised welts just below her belly button. This was always the toughest part. *My body is a complex machine. A conglomeration of cells, each one with a designated purpose.*

Breaking it down systematically helped her ward off the images and sounds that always hovered at the edges of her consciousness, ready to flood in the moment she let down her guard.

"No," she whispered. "Memories are merely synaptic connections forged through covalent alteration of proteins and—" A knock on the door made her heart pound.

"G? The car is here for you," Eli called.

Galena laid her hand over her chest. "Okay," she said, trying to sound steady.

It didn't work. "Hey, you all right?" he asked, his deep voice muffled by the door between them.

"Sure." She turned the water off and grabbed a towel, her hands shaking.

When she opened the bathroom door, her brother was leaning against the wall. His green eyes met hers. "You're not okay."

She looked away, clutching the towel around her body. "I will be as soon as I get to the lab."

"Have you eaten yet today?"

"I'm a grown-up, little brother."

He poked her shoulder, gentle but insistent. "A grown-up who hasn't been eating much. Seriously, don't you need to feed that genius brain of yours?" He was trying to sound playful, but Galena could hear the concern.

"I'll grab something on my way to work."

He bowed his head. "When I came in this morning from my shift, I heard you having a nightmare. You were reliving what happened, and I can tell it's on your mind."

"But it's at the bottom of a very long list," Galena said quickly. "Two of my volunteers were scheduled to check in today. I'll be too busy searching for side effects of the vaccine to think about anything else." Like the fact that she'd nearly been killed last week and that there were a lot of people—wait, *were* they people? Galena wasn't terribly clear about that—who still wanted her dead.

Eli nudged her chin up. "I know the past week has been horrible. Tell me what I can do to make things better for you. I'll do anything."

She sidestepped him. "Get back to living your life and stop worrying so much."

"Um, you know I'm technically dead, right?"

Yes, she knew. She just couldn't wrap her head around it. A week ago she'd watched him get shot repeatedly and heal in a matter of minutes. And that wasn't even the strangest thing she'd witnessed that day. Eli was something called a Ker now, an immortal servant of death who Marked people fated to die and decided how those people would perish. The leader of the Kere was Jason Moros, who had masqueraded as a plain old Harvard administrator and lured her to Boston, but who, evidently, was actually thousands of years old and the living personification of doom. And then there was Cacy Ferry, Eli's paramedic partner and girlfriend, who was a member of the wealthiest family in Boston . . . a family that was apparently responsible for ferrying deceased souls to Heaven or Hell.

Galena's long dark-blonde hair dripped water down her back as she stood there trying to separate all the craziness into components she could comprehend. That strategy usually worked—it was how she'd survived the past two years—but in this case, said components defied common sense, not to mention the known laws of physics and chemistry. She was at a loss.

"Yes. Technically dead." She reached out and took Eli's hand. His skin was hot, like he had a fever, even though she knew he would never get sick again. Eli had told her it was simply part of being a Ker, but like so many other things, it would take some getting used to. "I guess I should be glad that 'technically' doesn't really encompass what's going on, then. But all I meant was that you should go to work. Spend time with Cacy. And stop hovering. Same goes for all those creepy lurkers in the Veil."

The Veil. Eli had described this supposed in-between world that Kere and Ferrys could enter, and had told her that Mr. Moros had posted some of his guards there, close to her, in order to ensure her safety. And though she wasn't keen on the idea of unseen beings peeking in on her, she knew she needed them.

A week ago, the former leader of the Ferry family had nearly taken her out.

Galena pressed her fingers to her temple, remembering the sensation of unforgiving steel against her skin, picturing Rylan Ferry's finger closing over the trigger as he threatened to destroy her brain. She suppressed a sudden shiver and forced a smile. "I need to get dressed." She let go of Eli's hand and ducked past him, relieved to put a door between them.

It didn't keep her from hearing his sigh. "I'll never stop worrying about you," he called out. "That's the way family works."

"I know," she called through the door. She sat down on her bed and focused on slowing her breathing. "Believe me, I know." She'd experienced the stark, merciless certainty that she'd lost him on more than one occasion. "And I do appreciate the protection. As long as they don't watch me in the shower."

Eli chuckled. "If they tried, they'd have to deal with me. Love you, G. I need to get going or I'm going to be late for work."

"Be safe."

"You too," he said quietly. She heard his footsteps carrying him away from her, then the front door opening and closing a moment later.

Galena sagged on the bed. "Move," she whispered to herself. "Keep moving. Motor cortex engagement is incompatible with rumination."

She got up, pulled on drawstring pants and a T-shirt, and yanked her damp hair into a ponytail. It didn't really matter how she looked. Her only companions at work were her computer, which she'd named Danny, and her lab assistants, Ankita and Jian, who were as focused on the research as she was.

Still mumbling to herself about neurotransmitters and electrical pulses, she put on her shoes, grabbed her bag, and stepped out of her apartment to see the sleek black amphibious limousine parked at the curb. As always, the thickly humid air required a breath or two to get used to. When she'd first arrived in Boston, she had felt like she was drowning, and even now, with the late afternoon sun starting to sink, it was sweltering. Galena flapped her ponytail in an effort to create a breeze against the back of her neck, already prickling with beads of sweat. She didn't miss much about Pittsburgh, the violent, desolate town where she'd grown up, but its desert heat was better than this.

The limousine driver, who had reddish hair cut short like Eli's had been when he was an Army Ranger, stood square-shouldered and alert next to the open back door. He'd driven her to work for the last few days, good-natured about accommodating her strange schedule. "Dr. Margolis," he said, giving her a curt nod.

"Hey, Mike," she said, peeking in the front to see who was sitting in the passenger seat. An armed guard was there, scanning the streets and buildings around them. He was new. She eyed him carefully as she slid onto the supple leather backseat, and she flinched as Mike slammed the door.

It was only a five-minute ride to her lab, along the streets of Cambridge just north of the Charles River canal zone, but Galena used the time to work, looking over initial results from the first human trials of the vaccine. *Her* vaccine. The one she'd been researching and developing for years. It was perhaps the world's only hope of conquering the mutating plagues that had claimed a billion lives since a series of earthquakes and tsunamis had decimated dozens of major cities, and rising temperatures and ocean levels had changed the face of the world. Those environmental catastrophes, as well as shifting climates that had turned half of the US into a desert wasteland and the other half into a swamp, had set technological development back a century at least. That was way back in the 2050s, though, and now, decades later, there was a chance to stem the soaring death rate caused by viruses and bacteria resistant to conventional vaccines and antibiotics. Because if it worked, her vaccine would enable the human body to produce antibodies that mutated right along with the diseases they were made to fight.

But it had also made her a target. Apparently, some of the Kere and the Ferrys, who both made money off death, were not big on delayed gratification—and her vaccine could prolong millions, if not billions, of lives.

". . . said that transit is the most vulnerable time," Mike was saying.

Galena snapped out of her own thoughts, listening.

"Yeah," said the guard. "I'm glad we've got backup."

Galena looked out the rear window to see another black car trailing them. When she turned back around, the guard was looking at her. "That's us, Dr. Margolis. Nothing to worry about."

He smiled. She looked away. It had been her habit for two years now. Returning a stranger's smile could be dangerous. Especially if that person was a man. Especially if—

She stuffed the memories down. "When you say transit is a vulnerable time . . ."

"The Kere who are guarding you can be anywhere in a fraction of a second, but it's not like they can run through the Veil and keep up with a moving vehicle," said the guard. "They'll be waiting at your lab when we arrive. Not that you'll see them."

"What if I want to see them?"

"Can't help you there. They work for Moros, and we work for the Ferrys. They've got their own protocol. But Aislin Ferry wants to make sure you're as safe as possible, so she's doubled the personnel on your transport."

Aislin Ferry was Cacy's older sister and the new CEO of Psychopomps Inc. She was also, apparently, the new Charon, the leader of all the Ferrys in the world. She was the second new Charon in the last month. Her oldest brother, Rylan, had taken over for their father the day he was murdered—and Aislin had seized power when they discovered that Rylan was the one responsible.

Galena wondered if there was some new threat that had prompted this increase in security, but then she decided she didn't want to know. She needed to stay on track—no more distractions. She put her tablet phone back in her bag as Mike pulled up in front of the brick building that housed her lab.

The guard, a looming presence by her side, escorted her to the door. He held his automatic weapon in what Eli had once described as the "low ready position," the muzzle angled toward the ground and a finger straight along the barrel. Galena hated guns.

But she hated knives even more.

She shuddered, and her heart kicked against her ribs. *To increase the likelihood of survival, a body under stress increases production of epinephrine and norepinephrine, which elevates heart rate and blood pressure . . .*

The guard opened the door for her, and she darted inside. "I'll be fine from here. And I'll call when I'm ready for a ride home. Thanks!" she said, her voice hitching as she scooted through the entryway, never once looking back. She was almost running as she reached the stairwell that led to the basement.

Her footsteps were still rapid as she made her way down the tiled hallway, but when the white doors of her lab came into view, her taut muscles relaxed and her skittering thoughts fell into place. She leaned forward for a retinal scan, and then the lab doors slid aside and she strode into her own personal paradise. The chair of Immunology, Dr. Elaine Cassidy, had made sure Galena had exactly what she needed, from equipment to carefully controlled room temperature. She smiled—the department chair had been her rock for the last month, checking in nearly every day to ask if Galena needed anything else. As a prominent researcher herself, Dr. Cassidy understood the implications of Galena's work and seemed determined to help her succeed.

A row of nanopore DNA sequencers took up most of one side of the lab. In the middle of the room was Danny. Behind the computer sat the temperature-controlled cases that held the samples of her meticulously tailored antigens. To create each, she holographically manipulated the antigen macromolecules, and then Danny punched out information on stability, synthesis, and other immunologic biometrics for each configuration, which enabled her to test them in culture and tissue samples. She loved working with the holographic projections the most. It was like dancing with atoms. Waltzing with cells. Wrestling with lethal single-celled organisms that she was determined to defeat. She couldn't believe how lucky she was, that *this* was her job.

Jian came out of the supply room, carrying a metal box of wires and data chips. His black hair was neatly parted but sticking up in the back, and under his lab coat, his button-down was sloppily tucked in to his khakis. He jerked back in surprise when he saw her. "I didn't expect you until later."

"I wanted to get an early start tonight. What are you up to?"

His brow furrowed. "You know what I'm up to." He inclined his head toward the sequencers.

"Oh no—is one of them acting up?" Damn. She hoped it didn't interfere with her analyses.

"Yeah," he said slowly. "One's acting up. I'm on it, though." He turned and disappeared behind the machines.

Curious, Galena followed and saw Jian sit cross-legged on the floor in front of the third sequencer from the left. He peered up at her. "Do you need something?" he asked.

"Is that the machine we used to sequence V3?" They didn't refer to the human volunteers by name, though Galena knew each one of them. She knew their DNA, too. She'd used their profiles to customize their vaccines.

Jian shrugged. "You'd have to ask Ankita. She headed home about an hour ago, though."

"Did V1 and V2 come in today for their lab tests?"

"We sent you the usual updates, like you requested." Every word was tinged with annoyance, and Jian looked at the floor as he spoke.

Galena watched his fingers clamp tightly over the closed box. "Are you okay?"

"Just trying to get this done," he snapped. "That's what you want, right?" He squeezed his eyes shut. "I'm sorry. It's just been . . . a lot lately."

"I know it has. But we've been making such rapid progress. I think that's something to be proud of."

Jian opened his eyes and looked up at her. For a moment, confusion clouded his face, but when he blinked, it was gone. "It's definitely something," he said, nodding. "I never thought I'd get to work on something this important."

She grinned. "We're going to make history, Jian. I promise." She turned and walked back to Danny, eager to look up the new lab results from her first two human volunteers. Sure, the vaccine had already been tested on rats, but a human Phase I trial was more complex. The work was so urgent that her team at the University of Pittsburgh had pushed through the preclinical trials in half the time. Here at Harvard, the Institutional Review Board had expedited her application, approving her next series of clinical trials dizzyingly fast. There had been constant oversight, but Galena sometimes wondered if, in their rush to create the vaccine, they'd been careful enough. If they hadn't, her volunteers would suffer the consequences. She wanted to make sure they were healthy.

She swiped her fingertips across Danny's wide screen and opened the daily update she asked her assistants to write up, since she usually came in late and worked through the night. In the well-lit windowless lab, she could hide from the darkness; somehow her nightmares were a little easier to handle in the daylight.

Shaking off a chill at the memory of her most recent nightmare, Galena skimmed the data Ankita had uploaded. V1's exam and lab results looked perfect—so far, his immune system appeared to be functioning normally. With any luck, next week they could start the pathogen challenges, introducing a mutated but disabled virus into his bloodstream and monitoring the system's response once the automutating vaccine was present.

Satisfied that things were on track, Galena turned her attention to V2's results. But they weren't there. Instead, Ankita had entered a short note: *V2 a no-show. Sent messages through all available contacts. Will try again tomorrow.*

Galena frowned. Each vaccine had to be customized to a person's cellular HLA profile, and she had only five human volunteers at this stage. Her research team was still developing methods for more systematic customization so that the vaccine could be mass-produced. Because these initial volunteers were so important, she'd made sure each was compensated well and they'd all been given a clear appointment schedule for lab tests. And one of them was already flaking out?

Or maybe something's happened to her.

Galena swallowed hard. V2. Her name was Nadya Odrova. She was graduate student at Tufts.

You were a graduate student when it happened. You didn't show up in the lab the next day. Or the day after that. You—

Jian cursed quietly from behind the sequencers, pulling Galena from her spiraling thoughts. Her chest was tight as she rose from her chair. *Purposeful mental calculations are incompatible with episodic memory recall.* She tapped her fingers on Danny's screen to generate the holographic projection of her automutating antigen, the tiny cluster of molecules, delivered as a vaccine, that would teach billions of immune systems to deflect any new pathogen. As soon as it arose in front of her, detailed and real, her heartbeat slowed. She poked at it, turning it in midair, already spotting a potential area of instability that might need an additional disulfide bond.

At the sound of a loud beep, Galena looked down to see a light flashing on Danny's screen. Someone was requesting entrance to the lab. Galena grinned. Her volunteer had finally showed! Normally, she didn't do the lab tests herself, but her relief was so great that she was happy to make an exception, especially since Jian had his hands full with the sequencer.

When she checked the view screen, however, she saw that it wasn't V2. Galena's heart skipped as she stared at the man standing at her laboratory doors. She hadn't seen him in several days, but he'd crept into her thoughts many times since. She pressed the "Unlock" icon to let him in.

Declan Ferry strode into her lab carrying a plastic bag. And despite her habit of avoiding men's eyes, she couldn't look away from his. She didn't know him well, but she had already started to trust him, and not just because Eli did. Dec had nearly died in the fight to stop his brother Rylan from killing her. He didn't look any the worse for wear now, though. He was dressed in jeans and a T-shirt, plain clothes that only accentuated his tall, muscular frame. His black hair was charmingly messy, and his eyes were the kind of blue Galena had seen in history files, in pictures of the last of the arctic glaciers before they melted. Ice blue.

"Hey," he said with a friendly smile. "I wanted to see how you were doing, and Eli said you'd be here. I hope it's okay that I stopped by."

Normally, it wouldn't have been okay at all. Galena hated interruptions. But as she looked at his face, she felt a faint, foreign excitement fluttering within her rib cage. "It's f-fine," she stammered. "You didn't have to, though."

He glanced over at her antigen holograph, floating a few feet away. "Looks like you're busy."

"Thank you," she blurted out. She'd wanted to say that for a week. She'd been meaning to call him, but nervousness and embarrassment had kept her from hunting down his number. "For everything you did for me."

He gave her an adorably crooked smile. "You're welcome. It's good to see that you're back on track."

"Totally back on track." Galena's cheeks were burning. The thing was, she'd been *this* close to asking Eli about Dec before everything had happened. She'd noticed him at the Harvard fundraiser a week and a half ago, strikingly handsome as he'd walked in with Cacy on his arm. She hadn't been able to keep her eyes from straying toward his table that night. But their first *official* meeting had occurred the morning after his brother had attacked her, which obviously wasn't ideal. She'd come stumbling out of her room—eyes swollen from crying, thoughts weighed down with sedatives—and Dec had been sitting on her living room couch. The way he'd looked at her . . . it was as if he thought she were about to shatter. She hadn't been able to spare it much thought at the time, but in the days since, the regret had set in. Did he have to be right there to see her at her worst?

She bit her lip and turned to face her antigen so he wouldn't see her blush. "You traveled all the way from Chinatown to check in?"

"Um . . . yeah. I might have asked Eli how you were doing, and he might have mentioned he didn't think you had eaten yet today. And I had just finished my shift, so . . ."

She looked over her shoulder, and he held up the plastic bag.

"I got you some dinner."

Galena accepted the bag and peeked inside to see a sealed container full of real lettuce surrounded by clear boxes filled with cut-up vegetables, various meats and cheeses, and a few different kinds of dressing. It was more than she could eat in a whole day. Some of the foods she'd only ever seen in image files—plump little tomatoes, emerald-green peppers, shiny black olives, a crumbly white cheese. This stuff had to have been shipped in from the Arctic Circle colonies or Siberia, or maybe grown in the private agri-labs that supplied food to wealthy buyers. She came from the land of nutrition bars and rationed water, and Declan Ferry had just casually handed her a feast. For the first time in days, she actually felt hungry.

She glanced up to find his eyes on her. "I didn't know what you liked," he said quietly.

That strange giddy feeling inside her intensified. "Thanks," she murmured, setting the bag on her desk.

"Well," he said slowly, taking a step toward the door. "I guess I should go. I don't want to stop you from doing your thing."

She did indeed need to do her thing. Except . . . she suddenly didn't want him to go. Not yet. "Do you want a tour of my lab?"

He raised his eyebrows, clearly surprised. "Yeah?"

She couldn't help her smile. "Yeah."

She'd just turned toward Danny when a curse and a clatter brought her wheeling around. Dozens of wires and chips scattered across the tiled floor beneath the sequencer Jian had been working on. Dec moved to the side, placing himself between Galena and the row of machines. *Shielding* her, she realized.

"It's all right," she said, moving beside Dec so she could see Jian. "He's my research assistant." She leaned down and picked up a few parts just as Jian stood up, allowing her to see him over the top of the sequencer. "Jian, this is Declan Ferry."

Jian's eyes darted to Dec, who said, "It's nice to meet you" just as Jian said, "We have so much work to do," in an almost pleading voice.

Galena looked down at the parts she'd just picked up. She didn't recognize any of them. But then again, Jian was the mechanical expert in the lab. She made her way past Dec to hand the pieces back to Jian, who had little beads of sweat at his temples. "Here you go."

He snatched them from her and cradled them in his hands. "I'm sorry for being clumsy." He glanced at Dec again. "Do you really want other people here right now?" he asked Galena in a low voice. "I thought you wanted to keep everything under wraps."

"Here, you missed this one," said Dec, coming around the side of the row and offering a small component with a screen, on which there was a numeric display. "Is that a timer?" Dec smiled. "It's the only thing that looks even remotely familiar to me in this whole place."

Galena peered at the component as Jian grabbed it from Dec's outstretched hand. "Dr. M," Jian said, the pleading back in his voice.

Galena touched Jian's shoulder. "Go home," she said gently. "Come back and finish this tomorrow."

Jian stared at her. "Are . . . are you sure?"

"Completely," she replied. "No more work tonight. Spend some time with your wife. Get some sleep." She needed him to be efficient and productive, and instead he looked like he was about to detonate.

Jian looked down at the component Dec had handed to him. "Okay," he whispered. He dropped the reclaimed wires and parts into his metal box, shut it, and walked away. Galena watched him go. *He's human,* she reminded herself. *We all have our limits.*

She turned back to Dec, and her breath caught when his eyes met hers. Was *he* human? Eli's explanation about the Ferry family hadn't been totally clear on that. But as she looked at him, all she could feel was curiosity. And for the first time in a very long time, her desire to explore went far beyond the scientific.

CHAPTER TWO

*H*e seemed kind of stressed," Dec said as the lab doors slid shut again. He pushed down a twinge of guilt—he wasn't sorry to see the guy leave. Dec didn't mind being alone with Galena at all.

She was gazing at the row of machines. "It's been an intense few weeks, and the last week especially." She sighed. "I think I've been kind of hard on both of my research assistants."

"I can understand that. I go out there and do the calls, same as all my medics, but I'm still the one who has to set their shifts and discipline them when they screw up. It's not fun."

She had the most astounding green eyes, and right now they were searching his face. "I try to be nice," she said. "But things have to be done right or—"

"People die." At least, that's how it was in his line of work. Of course, if those people were fated to die, nothing a medic did could save them.

"That's it," she said. "I know it might seem dumb, because I still have a few years of research to go before the vaccine is approved for the general population, but I have to do this right." Her expression was so intense that he couldn't look away. And then, just like that, it disappeared—or, maybe more accurately, submerged—beneath a friendly, casual smile. "So," she said. "Do you want that tour?"

"Lead the way."

Dec watched Galena's face as she touched the screen of her computer and awakened the holographic projection of some über-complex molecules, which hovered between them like a jumbled wire sculpture. The very first time he'd seen her, she'd had the same look in her eyes as she did now, this eager, adorable excitement. It was such a relief to see again—the last time he'd seen her, she'd looked devastatingly different. "So this is part of the vaccine?" he asked, hoping it wasn't a stupid question.

"Yes, this is the antigen, but it has to be altered based on certain genetic markers for each person." Her slender fingers touched the molecules, rotating them in midair. Her full lips curved into a satisfied smile. "I alter the amino acid residues, and Danny makes sure the resulting peptide bonds are stable."

"Danny?" Dec looked around.

Galena gestured behind her as her cheeks suffused with pink, which made his heart beat a little harder. "My computer. Since he does so much of the work, I figured he deserved a name."

She walked Dec around the lab space while she continued to talk, rapid-fire and full of enthusiasm, about her equipment, the samples and serums, the antigens, the cell cultures. Dec understood maybe a third of what she was saying, and he tried to concentrate, but he kept getting distracted by the movements of her hands, the lilt of her voice, the grin on her face. It wasn't just that she was beautiful that got to him. It was the way her eyes lit up and her whole body came to attention as she talked about her work.

It had been one of the first things he'd ever noticed about her. He'd been sitting in the audience at that fund-raiser, expecting to be bored out of his mind, when she'd stood up and headed to the front. She was slender but curvy, strikingly tall for a woman, especially in the heels she'd been wearing. He remembered smiling as she'd wobbled slightly on her way to the podium. Dec could have stared at her all night. She was the first woman in a long time to intrigue him. She wasn't like the jaded, wealthy ones who flocked to his family like flies to a corpse, eager to fortify their own family's power, nor was she like the salt-of-the-earth medics he worked with every day. She had this open innocence about her, this almost childlike glee that made her shine from the inside out. He'd been so captivated that it had taken him several minutes to figure out who she was.

It took him only a second longer to realize how many supernatural beings wanted to kill her.

Protect her and you protect the future.

Those were his father's last words to him, a week before he'd even met Galena. But as he'd watched this brilliant, gorgeous, fascinating woman talk excitedly about her scientific discoveries, he'd known for sure that she was who his father had been talking about. She was working on a vaccine that would cut the death rate by at least a third, if not more. Since his entire family, and all the Kere, made a profit off of every dead soul they delivered to the Afterlife, that meant she was a major threat to their income.

The whole thing reminded him of why he wanted so little to do with the Psychopomps empire. Yes, he was a Ferry. He bore the Mark, the tattoo of the raven that covered his back. He wore the Scope, the window to the Afterlife that hung from the platinum chain around his neck. And he did his duty, guiding dead souls to their eternal reward or punishment. But he hated the politics and the greed. Always had.

Now, though, he couldn't avoid it. Not if he wanted to honor his father. And though he and Patrick Ferry had never exactly seen eye to eye, though Dec had always been the rebel son who fought all his father's attempts to draw him into the corporate world, he would obey his father this time.

It was why he'd come here tonight. He'd been happy to do Eli a favor, but it hadn't just been about bringing Galena dinner. That afternoon, he'd overheard Cacy on the phone telling Eli that

Galena's transport security was being doubled. He'd felt an urge to go and see her for himself, to make sure she was all right. She felt like his responsibility.

"And these are my nanopore sequencers," she said proudly, patting one of the squat beige machines at the end of a row.

"Nanopore?"

"Tiny holes made of protein. We force the DNA through them in a single, long string, and because each nucleotide blocks the hole in a specific way, we can detect its composition by measuring the current passing through the nanopore in that instant." She looked fondly at the machine. "It's a little old-fashioned but pretty precise—and very versatile." She eyed him with a hungry sort of curiosity.

Dec arched an eyebrow. "What?"

Her eyes focused on his Scope, which dangled from the chain around his neck. "I'm just wondering what *your* DNA looks like."

"You want to see my DNA?" He smirked. "Shouldn't we get to know each other a little better first?"

She ducked her head and chuckled. "Sorry. That was sort of presumptuous."

But I liked it. He was opening his mouth to say exactly that when a loud beep made Galena tense. "Someone's at the door," she said.

Dec followed her around the row of sequencers and back to her computer. "Can you see who it is?"

She nodded and tapped her screen. "Oh! It's my volunteer." She unlocked the door, and a young woman with a head full of wild corkscrew curls walked in. "I was getting worried!" Galena said to her.

"Sorry I'm late," the young woman said. "My apartment was broken into, and I was waiting for the police to show up all afternoon, and then my AC unit went on the fritz, and now it's making this weird clicking noise." She threw her arms up. "Basically, the worst day ever."

Galena blanched. "A break-in?" She wrapped her arms around her waist, folding in on herself. "Are you okay, Nadya?"

Dec wondered if Galena was remembering when *her* apartment had been invaded. It made him want to go visit his older brother in the cell where Aislin was keeping him and punch him in the face . . . again.

Nadya smiled. "I'm fine. It's just a pain—they didn't take anything, from what I can tell. Just made a huge mess." She glanced at Dec. "Hi. Are you another volunteer?" Her eyes focused on his Scope, and he hastily tucked it into his collar, but not quickly enough. Her eyes went round. "Oh my God," she said. "You're a Ferry."

Galena looked back and forth between them. "You know about the Ferrys?"

A crease formed between Nadya's eyebrows. "Doesn't everybody?"

Dec cleared his throat. "Of course she does," he said in a friendly, *loud* voice. The last thing he needed was for Galena to spill his family secrets. "Psychopomps Incorporated is a major Harvard donor, and in particular we're supporters of Dr. Margolis's research. She was just giving me a tour of the lab. But I'd better be going."

Galena's eyes were so wide and guileless that he could see the moment the puzzle pieces dropped into place. "Yes! Oh, yes. The Ferrys are definitely patrons of the sciences," she said breezily. Then she bit her lip, and Dec found himself staring at her mouth again. "Thanks for dropping by, Mr. Ferry."

He didn't really want to leave. He'd actually been enjoying himself, which was kind of a rarity these days. But there was no way he'd interfere with her work. "Thanks for the tour, Dr. Margolis."

He returned her grin, then had to force himself to walk away. He paused and looked over his shoulder at Galena before he walked through the doorway. "Don't forget your dinner."

"I won't," she murmured.

Mission accomplished, he strode out of the lab. Suddenly, he was in a damn good mood. As he climbed the steps to the first floor of the building, he pulled out his phone and called Trevor. It had been a few weeks since they'd gotten together to shoot pool and have a cold one. Yeah, the guy was a Ker, one of the fiercest, but he'd also been Dec's best friend for years. Trev's phone rang a few times, and then the man himself appeared on Dec's screen. "Hey, Trev, I—"

"Kinda busy now, man," said Trevor, his dark features clear as he stood beneath a streetlight. He was in front of a shabby building decorated with a jumble of graffiti. Dec could hear the slosh of water—Trevor was in a canal zone. And he looked pissed.

"What's up?"

Trevor's lip curled, revealing a stark-white canine. "Just taking care of some business."

He'd probably just Marked someone. "Got it. You want me to come and help out?" Dec often worked with Trevor, guiding the souls Trev had doomed.

Trevor shook his head. "I'm all set."

"Who's that?" asked a female voice, somewhere offscreen.

"No one," snapped Trev. "Talk to you later, man."

Then he hung up. What was up with him? The device buzzed in his hand, and Dec hoped it was Trev calling back, but it was Aislin. Dec answered.

His sister's pale face appeared on his screen, her blue eyes shadowed with fatigue. "Declan," she said by way of greeting. "How are you?"

"I'm good. I was actually just checking in on Galena Margolis. What's up?"

She gave him a weary smile. "Honestly? I wanted to spend three minutes of my day talking to someone who doesn't want something from me."

Dec exited the building and sat on a low brick wall next to the sidewalk. "Rough day, huh?"

"Exceedingly. Cleaning up after Rylan is going to be much more difficult than I anticipated. Our contacts both in the human world and the supernatural one have certain . . . expectations."

Bribes, probably. Dec had always suspected Rylan was crooked as hell, even before he'd taken over as CEO. "Are you going to meet those expectations?" Aislin had taken the reins, which meant all the pressure was on her—including from creatures who wanted Galena Margolis dead.

Aislin's eyes were like chips of ice. "As always, I will do what I think is right. But I wish Father were here," she added quietly.

Dec's chest ached. He'd never had that kind of relationship with their father, but he knew Aislin had been much closer to him. "Hey, can I ask you something? What did he say to you, before he walked into the Afterlife?"

Aislin took in a sharp breath, and she paused just long enough for Dec to realize what a private question that was, especially for her. Aislin had always played things incredibly close to the vest. "Never mind," he said. "You don't have to tell me. It's just been on my mind lately."

She tilted her head, her gaze taking on a familiar calculating glint. It reminded Dec of Rylan. "Then maybe we should have dinner soon and discuss it," she said, her voice soft but level. She sat up a little straighter. "Anyway, I should go. I just wanted to—"

"Wait, Aislin," he said, knowing she was about to hang up. "Have there been more threats against Galena?"

Aislin smoothed her already-smooth hair. "There have been whispers. Nothing specific."

"What kind of whispers?"

"This is of particular interest to you?"

"Maybe."

Her eyes narrowed, as if she were trying to see into his brain. "Like I said, nothing specific. And Dr. Margolis has all the protection we can reasonably provide."

"Cavan and the ambassador from the Lucinae have arrived for your dinner meeting, Ms. Ferry," said a male voice on Aislin's end.

Aislin sighed. "Send them up." She returned her attention to Dec. "I hope you're well, Declan. Thank you for talking to me."

"Always a pleasure. Good luck."

Her face disappeared, and Dec shook his head. He wouldn't trade places with her for anything. She was scrambling to keep everyone either happy or cowed in order to keep the gold flowing and the empire under control.

Dec looked back toward the building behind him. Galena was in there, doing her lab tests or DNA sequencing or whatever. She was happy and focused. It had been magnetic. Riveting to watch. He gripped his phone tightly. *There have been whispers.*

He'd hoped the threat to Galena had been eliminated when his brother and Mandy, the rogue Ker who'd been working with him, were stopped.

But he'd worked on the streets for too long to be that naive. *Protect her and you protect the future.* What was he supposed to do, though? He was just a paramedic, for God's sake. He'd wanted Aislin to tell him that their father had told her to protect Galena, too. It would have made him feel a little better to share the responsibility. Aislin had a different kind of power.

As it stood, the weight of his father's last request was still heavy on his shoulders—and Galena's face was still bright in his mind.

He wasn't sure which was more motivating, but as he sat outside her building, sweating in the heat of the early evening, he decided it didn't matter. No matter who or what was coming after Galena, Dec was going to make sure she was safe.

CHAPTER THREE

Galena got up in midafternoon and made herself some coffee. She'd worked through the night but she'd been distracted—except this time, it hadn't been with the past. Declan Ferry's face had kept floating through her mind.

It was both exciting and confusing. Last night, when he was in the lab, next to her, she'd felt the attraction. Undeniable and real. It had made her feel light-headed. But she hadn't been with anyone since the attack. She'd buried herself in her work and avoided coming up for air. And she wasn't even sure what would happen if she tried to go out with someone. What if he expected more than she could give? What if he pushed? What if he—

She set her coffee cup down so hard that the bitter brown liquid inside sloshed over the rim. *They took so much, and they just keep taking.* Her eyes stung with unshed tears as she looked down at her body, a puzzle she might never solve. How could she simultaneously want something *and* be so terrified of it?

"This is irrelevant," she whispered, smoothing her hands over her face. "He probably isn't interested anyway." And she didn't have time for it, either. "Move. Keep moving."

She grabbed a quick shower—she took advantage of running water whenever she could. It was a luxury she'd never had before moving to Boston, unless you counted the running water in the University of Pittsburgh's privately funded laboratories, but that had been carefully monitored and available only for experiments and with prior authorization. As she got ready, she ran over her plan for the evening. The three remaining volunteers should have all checked in while she was sleeping, so she'd be able to compare all five sets of results before moving forward. God, she loved data. It was real and certain. Comforting.

As early as next week, she'd be starting on the next phase of the study. And that meant there was a lot of work to do to prepare, not only for her, but also for Ankita and Jian. She pulled her hair into a ponytail. Hopefully, Jian had come in well rested and ready to roll today. When he'd first come to work for her, he'd been full of energy. He'd seemed elated to have been selected as her research assistant. But yesterday, he'd been a mess.

Mentally adding a pep talk for Jian to her to-do list, she hopped into the limo. Mike and the guard with the big gun chatted in front about the latest news from the Arctic Circle colonies—they had officially declared independence from Canada this morning, and there was probably going to be a war in the north. Seeing as how the colonies were now North America's breadbasket, there was concern it might impact the food supply for the whole continent. Despite that potentially earthshaking news, Galena focused on checking her messages, including one from Dr. Cassidy, saying that Galena had been nominated for some kind of early career achievement award. That was nice. The car stopped, and Galena got out. As the guard escorted her to the door, she felt a little ungrateful hoping that if she won the award, she wouldn't have to give a speech.

"Hey, Dr. M," called Ankita, poking her head out from behind one of the sequencers as Galena walked into the lab. Her research assistant's long black hair was in a knot at the back of her head, and her dark skin stood in elegant contrast to the beige paint of the machine. "This big guy has the flu, I think. He's been making some weird clicking noises, and he was spitting out some awfully funny data earlier."

As if in response to that accusation, the machine emitted a few rhythmic clicks. Galena had never heard a sequencer make that kind of noise. "Is that the one Jian was working on?"

Ankita shrugged. "He took off early today. Seemed pretty stressed, actually. He said to tell you he had an appointment and he'll be in early tomorrow to make it up. Unfortunately, the machine didn't start acting up until after he left." She let out an irritated sigh.

Galena frowned as the sequencer clicked a few more times. It almost sounded as if some of the mechanical parts were smacking against something. Maybe a blockage of some kind. She was pretty sure it was the same one Jian had been working on yesterday. And he'd promised to fix it today. Clearly, something was still going on with him. She was going to have to talk to him before it really started to impact their work . . . unless it already had. "That's the one we used to sequence V3, isn't it?"

Ankita nodded, coming out from behind the machine with her tablet in her hand. "Yes. V3." She gave Galena a shy smile. "I thought he was cute. Nice eyes."

Galena rolled her eyes playfully and awakened Danny's screen with a friendly caress. V3 had brown hair and hazel eyes. He was twenty-eight years old, the same age as Galena. He had some genetic markers for depression, but apart from that, his DNA was gorgeous, with no mutations. He had smiled at her while Ankita injected him with the customized vaccine Galena had created. She'd looked away at first and then forced herself to look back and smile in return.

Thank you for volunteering, she had said. *We're going to take good care of you.*

That had been just a week before. "How did his check-in go?" she asked.

"We haven't heard from him or V4," Ankita said. "V5 came in earlier. I've already uploaded her results. Looking good so far."

V4. Twenty-six. Black hair so curly and poofy that Galena had wanted to touch it, just to watch it spring back into shape. DNA that whispered to Galena of future diabetes and Alzheimer's. Because she was a woman, it had been easy to meet V4's eyes, to smile and assure her that she was in good hands.

"Have you tried calling V3 and V4?"

"Twice. No answer from either one. Do you want me to try again?"

Galena checked the time on the screen. It was nearly five, and all the volunteers knew to come in by four for their blood work. "No, I'll take care of it. Go ahead and focus on getting that sequencer running smoothly again."

"I'll see what I can do."

Ankita headed over to the temperamental machine, and Galena brought up the personal information for V3 and V4. V3 lived up in Medford, but V4 lived near downtown Boston on West Street. A quick perusal of the computer map showed V4 was on the east side of the dangerous swampland of the Boston Common. Galena rubbed her palms on her thighs. She hoped V4 wasn't having the same kind of day V2 had yesterday, but—

Home invasions are tragic but so common these days.

Galena flinched, rubbing at her temple. That was what Rylan Ferry had said right before he pressed his gun to her head. Her fist clenched. The last thing she needed was for him to join the dark monsters already lurking in her brain, eager for the chance to ambush her in a weak moment. It was so draining, trying to keep them caged. She sifted through the information on Danny's screen, trying to calm her churning stomach as poisonous fear wound through her.

This was the reason she ate so little. She was *sick* with this fear. Every day. All the time. And no matter how far down she'd tried to push the memories that caused that fear, they were always waiting.

She heard her phone buzz with a text, and she pulled it from her bag. It was Eli.

Already at the lab?

Yep.

Did you eat?

Stop worrying.

I'll take that as a no.

She let out a quiet breath of laughter. He knew her too well. *I will. I promise.*

Good. Love you.

Love you too.

She was about to put the phone back in her bag when it rang with a call. The number wasn't in her contacts, but she recognized it anyway, because she'd just been looking at it on Danny's screen. She'd given all the volunteers her cell number in case they had any questions or concerns, including V4. And now she was calling Galena.

"Hello?"

The sound of rapid breaths made Galena's throat tighten.

"Hello?" she repeated.

"He said . . . he did this . . . to me . . . because of you," a female voice finally whispered, her breathing agonized and wet. "He . . . said you . . . had to stop."

Heat and horror swept across Galena's skin. "Are you all right?"

The woman moaned softly. "Your research . . . stop."

Galena's knuckles went white as she gripped the phone. With her other hand, she called up her tracking program and entered V4's phone number. The tracker told her the woman was calling from her own apartment. "Are you hurt? Do you need an ambulance? I can call one for you right now."

A choked, gurgling sob was the only reply.

CHAPTER FOUR

Dec leaned back and ran his hands through his hair. He could hear the other paramedics laughing and joking in the locker room down the hall, but he was glad to have his own office. He was used to taking care of other people, always being the one responsible for solving everyone else's problems, but he needed to be alone to unwind. No demands. No pressure. No expectations.

It had been a long shift. Trevor had stormed out of Dec's office half an hour ago, ranting about how his new partner couldn't navigate his way out of an insta-cold limbsack, let alone the narrow canals near the edges of Chinatown. Dec had suggested maybe Trev needed a vacation, but he'd just flipped Dec off and left. Dec grunted. He felt ready to do the same thing. Five calls, three casualties, two souls shuttled to Heaven while his partner, Carol, cleaned their rig. As for the third soul . . . well, that one had been destined for Hell, and the guy had figured it out before Dec even had a chance to pull his Scope open and loop it over the guy's head. He'd run. But there was no way Dec would be responsible for yet another Shade in the Veil.

Dec had tackled the guy right before he'd reached the edge of the canal, probably thinking he could jump in and swim away. He'd been pretty speedy for a recently dead soul. Already annoyed,

Dec had zero patience for the man's frantic bargaining and semi-coherent snarls—a signal that this dead soul was already becoming rabid. Dec had punched him into submission and shoved him through the portal to Hell in less than a minute. The gold coin, payment for his hard work, had flown out a moment later, and Dec, winded and distracted, had reflexively caught the red-hot hunk of metal still blazing from the fires of Hell. The burn on his palm was already nearly healed, along with his bloody knuckles—thank God all Ferrys healed ridiculously fast.

But the fatigue remained. It was a bone-deep tiredness mixed with boredom. Same routine, different day. Every day. Every fucking day.

Well, maybe not every day. For a brief time the previous evening, he'd felt himself waking up, coming alive. The drudgery of today had pretty much erased his excellent mood, though.

Once again, he considered retiring. He'd fantasized about it for years, but he had never pulled the trigger. He never spent his money, so he had plenty of it. He could hand over his paramedic badge and his Scope. He could move to his little cabin on Baffin Island, surrounded by mountains on all sides, where everyone would leave him the fuck alone, where no one knew who his family was. Where he could live a normal human life.

It was pretty damn tempting.

His computer screen lit up, and Dec leaned forward.

"*One EMS unit to number three West Street, apartment twenty-four,*" droned the dispatcher, her words simultaneously appearing as text on his screen. "*Suspected assault. Number of casualties unknown. Injuries unknown. Police and fire notified. They have advised that it'll be a minimum of thirty until they're on scene.*" Her voice echoed down the hall, where the rest of the crew was probably listening from the garage.

Dec sighed. Most of his guys had just come off a hard shift, and the new shift had barely started. They were probably still cataloging supplies and getting their rigs ready for a long night. He got to his feet. He hadn't changed out of his uniform yet. He had nobody waiting for him at home. And it wasn't like he could show up at Galena's lab for a second night in a row without a pretty damn good excuse. He paused, realizing he'd actually been considering it. "Answer the damn call, Dec," he muttered, entering the garage and looking over at Paula, the new night shift supervisor. A solidly built woman with steel-gray hair and dark-brown skin, she was standing with her arms folded, staring at the videowall. Earlier this week, he'd quietly transferred Len, the former night shift supervisor, to the Jamaica Plain EMS. He couldn't stomach keeping the man around after what he'd said about Cacy—and the fact that he'd tossed Eli into the disease-infested canal. Paula was a veteran paramedic, and Dec trusted her to take a more professional approach. "I'll take this one," Dec said to her.

"I was about to send Manny and Gil," she replied, still looking at the screen. It showed only the outside of the apartment building.

"Any more info from Dispatch? Is the scene secure?"

"There's no info at all," she replied. "We don't have any eyes inside, because the call didn't come from the apartment, so the connection to any security cams inside the unit wasn't triggered." She pointed at her control screen. "The dispatch display says the call came from Cambridge."

Dec's stomach tensed. "Where in Cambridge?"

"One of the university buildings."

"Any info on the caller?"

Paula shook her head.

Dec began to jog toward his rig. "I'm taking it. Eli!"

Eli Margolis jumped from the back of rig 436. "What do you need, Chief?"

"Heard from Galena this evening?"

Eli frowned. "I was texting with her a few minutes ago. She's at her lab, buried in her work. Why?"

"Okay. Good." Something loosened inside Dec's chest. "Sorry, I guess it was nothing."

Eli caught up with Dec and ran by his side. "You sure?" Now he sounded worried, and Dec felt like an asshole.

"I'm sure. A call came in from Cambridge, and I got antsy."

The alert system went off again. A mass-casualty incident—there had been some type of explosion at Fayette and Jefferson. "Eli," called Cacy from the back of the rig they shared, "we're up."

Eli sprinted for his rig. "Keep me posted," he called over his shoulder to Dec.

Carol was still in the back of their rig, scrubbing under the floor panels after their last bloody call. "Up for another trip?" he asked, tossing a biohazard bag at her booted feet.

Carol tightened her bushy brown ponytail. "Sure thing, boss."

"I'll drive."

Carol slammed the last floor panel into place, tossed the bloody rags into the biohazard bag, and flung it out the back. "All set."

Dec activated the siren as the rig roared out of the garage. The likelihood that this had anything to do with Galena Margolis was slim to none.

But Aislin had said, *There have been whispers.* Dec accelerated, barreling up Washington toward West Street.

"Know what we're heading into?" Carol asked. "Canal zone?"

"No. Dry land. It's close to the Common, though."

"I'd already reloaded the tranqs, so we're good."

Dec smiled. Carol was a relatively new paramedic, but she was serious about the job and always thinking ahead. She reminded him a little of Cacy, his little sister, only with less of a foul mouth. When he turned onto West, the street was crowded with late afternoon traffic: buses, taxis, and a few amphibious cars. The glare and howl of the sirens chased a few of the vehicles away, but most remained, stubbornly ignoring the fact that someone probably needed this ambulance pretty badly. Dec double-parked and edged into the back, where he zipped on his antibacterial gloves, grabbed his med kit and a mobile com unit, and holstered a tranq gun. "Listen. We don't know what we've got waiting for us up there. Let me go check it out, and I'll call down if it's safe."

"Are you still treating me like a newbie, Chief?"

Dec laughed. "No, I'm treating you like a serious badass who can protect the rig from canal pirates." He was only half-joking. She'd taken out two earlier this week as they tried to steal the kidneys from a car-crash victim she and Dec were racing to save. "Stay here."

She groaned as he jumped out the back, his boots landing hard on dry concrete. It took him only a few moments to jog through the lobby of the apartment building. The elevator wasn't working, so he took the stairs. The door to apartment 24 was closed, but when he tried the knob, it twisted easily beneath his gloved palm. He drew the tranq gun and poked his head in. "Hello? Someone need an ambulance?"

Dec edged into the apartment. It was a cramped studio overlooking the street. And on the floor next to a small table lay a woman, pale as paste, her curly black hair a cloud around her face, her sightless brown eyes staring at the ceiling. Obviously dead. Dec holstered his tranq gun and got out his cardiac wand. He crouched and waved it over her chest, just in case, but it remained silent. He stood up and looked over the woman at his feet. She'd been stabbed, once in the chest, but it had been enough. Blood saturated her shirt and was slick beneath the soles of his boots.

The only noise in the apartment was the faint sound of a panicked voice, and Dec found its source in the tangled mass of the woman's hair. A phone. He lifted it from the floor.

"*You're going to be okay. The ambulance will be there soon, I promise.*" The woman on the other end of the line let out a strangled sob. "*I'm so sorry. I'm so sorry.*"

Dec's heart slammed against his ribs. He recognized the voice. He lifted the phone to his ear. "Galena."

She gasped. "Hello? Who is this?"

"It's Dec. I'm—"

"Dec," she squeaked. "Thank God. Is she going to be okay?"

He closed his eyes.

Didn't she have the right to know the truth?

Then again, hadn't she been through enough?

Dec knew what had happened to her in Pittsburgh a few years ago. And he'd witnessed what had been done to her the week before. Though she'd seemed fine last night, he'd seen how she'd reacted when her volunteer mentioned the break-in. Like a shadow had flickered in her eyes, the memory of terror and pain.

How much trauma and tragedy could a soul take and still survive intact?

"Dec," she said in a quavering voice. "Please."

He gritted his teeth. "Who's with you right now? Are you safe?"

"I-I'm in my lab, but—"

"Here's what we're going to do. You're going to stay put, and I'm going to take care of this lady—"

"Her name is Luciana Flores."

"I'm going to take care of Luciana, and then we're going to talk again. All right?"

"But—"

"I need to get going, Galena. But trust me, you'll hear from me soon."

"Okay," she whispered. "Thank you."

He waited until she'd hung up, and then he programmed her number into his phone. He shouldn't have touched the dead woman's phone—this was a crime scene. But he couldn't make himself feel sorry. He called down to Carol and explained what he'd observed. He told her to take the ambulance back to the station and promised he'd hang out and talk to the cops, then get a car to take him home.

As soon as that was done, he pulled his Scope from the setting at his throat, brushed his thumb over the raven etched on its surface, and opened a window to the Veil. He stepped through, shivering a little as the cold air surrounded him. His boots squelched on the now-cushy floor; solid objects in the real world were merely gelatinous structures in the Veil. Dec looked around the frigid gray room. Luciana's soul was sitting on the single bed near the wall, smoothing her hair. Her clothes were bloody, but it didn't seem to bother her. She looked at him with surprise. "What are you doing here?"

"I'm here to show you where you go next," he said gently. "But first I have some questions."

Her gaze flicked to her transparent body lying on the floor near the table. "About what?"

"Your name's Luciana?"

She nodded.

He gave her a friendly smile. "My name's Dec. Can you tell me what happened to you?"

Luciana frowned. She wrapped her arms around her ample chest, as if trying to protect herself from what had already happened. "He stabbed me."

"He? Just one guy?"

"He had a ski mask over his face. He had dark eyes. Red. A little bit red. And a knife." She shuddered.

"How do you know Galena Margolis?" Dec asked, trying to force his voice into steadiness.

"I volunteered to help test her vaccine," Luciana said. "I needed the money."

Someone had targeted and killed one of Galena's research subjects. Dec could barely hear the woman's voice over the alarm bells sounding in his head. "Can you tell me anything else about the guy who attacked you?"

"He had dark eyes," Luciana whimpered. "Red. And a knife. He said she had to stop."

"Who had to stop?"

Her face crumpled, like she was about to start sobbing. "Dr. Margolis. He said her research had to stop."

Dec knew he wasn't going to get anything else out of her. He might look midtwenties, but he'd been ferrying dead souls for nearly forty years. When they started repeating themselves, it was time to send them on. He flipped his Scope and brushed his thumb over the set of scales etched onto that side. He let out a sigh of relief when it sparked with the white light of Heaven. "Luciana, I'm sorry for what happened to you, but now you're going to a wonderful place. Trust me on that." He pulled the Scope wide and lowered it over the woman's body, and the last thing he heard from her was laughter, light and cheerful.

He held up the Scope and caught the gold coin that came flying out of it a second later. Fortunately, coins from Heaven were blissfully cool. With it held in his palm, he compacted his Scope and clipped it into its setting, then turned in place.

"Anyone want to come claim this bounty?" Dec shouted, his voice rising with the heat of rage and suspicion. He held up the coin. "Come on, now. You did the dirty work. Come get paid for it!" Normally, the Ker who had Marked a soul was either waiting or appeared as soon as a Ferry had gotten a soul into the Afterlife, palm outstretched, fangs bared. They wanted their half of the gold.

Not this time.

The silence was as oppressive as it was cold. Dec wasn't chilled, though. His anger was more than enough to keep him warm. This was an unauthorized Marking. An unsanctioned kill. Solid evidence there was another rogue on the loose. And whoever it was, he or she was trying to punish Galena.

"I won't let you hurt her," Dec shouted, though he knew full well no one was listening. He bowed his head and drew a deep breath through his nose. He needed to calm down and think straight. Before he got back to Galena, his priority was notifying Aislin there was another rogue. He needed to let Eli know, too. One of them would give Moros the news: the Lord of the Kere wasn't in control of his creatures. *Again.* And only he could put this right.

Too restless to wait for a car or the cops, Dec decided to take a page from Cacy's playbook and break the rules—by using his Scope as a means of transportation. Well, he'd broken the rules before, too, like the night he'd discovered Galena was the one his father had meant him to protect. He'd sneaked into her apartment, just to make sure she was safe. And then he'd been so ashamed of spying on her that he'd left immediately. Although they were supposed to use their Scopes only to ferry souls, his Scope would take him wherever he most needed to go. He reached for it and pressed his thumb to the raven again, expecting it to open a portal to his apartment.

But when he pulled his Scope open, he gaped in surprise. Lab equipment lined the walls, and a slender transparent figure sat alone in front of the giant computer in the center of the room. Though she was just a shadow in the Veil, Dec could read the tremble in her shoulders and the defeated bow of her head. She was hurting. Scared. Her fingers were closed around her phone. She was waiting to hear from him.

Though he had no right and no good reason, though he'd thought he had other, more important things to do, he stepped through the intra-Veil portal and stood in the in-between, only a few feet behind Galena. Immediately, two Kere appeared, their eyes glowing red and their claws extended, ready to rip him to shreds. Galena's personal guards, handpicked by Moros himself.

Dec held up his hands. But they had already stepped back; they had recognized him.

"Has something happened?" asked Nader. He had a stern face, olive skin, and long black hair pulled back into a ponytail. Dec knew him to be a fierce Ker who tended to kill with sudden bursts of violence.

"I think so," said Dec. "One of Galena's research volunteers was murdered. And I believe a Ker was involved. The dead soul said her attacker had red eyes, and no one came to collect the bounty."

Nader tensed. "You think there's another rogue."

"Looks that way," said Dec. "Stay vigilant."

"We're always vigilant," said Tamasin. She had her dozens of ebony braids tied back at the base of her neck with a colorful scarf, but that was the only thing whimsical about her. Dec had worked with her only a few times, but on those occasions she'd killed with heart attacks or strokes. Quick. Trevor was like that, too. The guy worked all day as a paramedic so he could balance out the lives he took at night. Dec respected that in a Ker. He hated when they drew it out and savored the suffering.

"I'll be updating your boss and mine as soon as I talk to Galena," Dec said.

Tamasin nodded at Galena's shadowy figure. "She seems fragile. Do you have to tell her?"

Dec had no idea. All he knew was that Galena was waiting. For *him*. Like his fingers were on autopilot, he flipped his Scope and opened a swirling window into the warm, messy real world. He pulled the edges of the Scope wide.

And found himself staring right into Galena's green eyes.

CHAPTER FIVE

Galena spun around at the strange slurping noise behind her and found herself staring at the angular gray face of Declan Ferry. With a gasp, she shot back until her chair hit her desk. She had seen the Ferrys use their pendants to open a sort of window into this Veil place, but it was still surreal to behold—especially right here in her lab. Dec lifted the round window up and then lowered it over himself, so that his body was revealed inch by inch, from his head to his boots. He then stepped over the silvery hoop at his feet, picked it up, and pressed at its edges until it shrank back to its normal size. He clipped it to a setting in the platinum chain around his neck.

And then he raised his head and met her eyes again. It took several seconds—during which the silence was broken only by clicks from the malfunctioning DNA sequencer—for either of them to speak.

"Hi," Dec finally said, his voice hushed. "I need to let the powers-that-be know what's happened, but I wanted to tell you first." He eyed her tense posture, her hands gripping the edges of her chair. "I didn't mean to scare you."

"Is Luciana in the hospital?"

She knew the truth before he spoke it. It was in his eyes. "Luciana didn't make it. By the time I got there, it was too late. She's in Heaven now, Galena. I guided her there myself."

The laugh burst forth from Galena's mouth, hysterical and loud. "I've never believed in Heaven or Hell."

"Whether you believe in them or not, we all end up one place or the other in the end." He tucked his Scope into the collar of his uniform, which looked like a cross between a wet suit and military fatigues. He had some sort of gun holstered at his belt. Galena's stomach tightened. Dec's gaze slid from her face to his waist. "It's a tranq gun, Galena," he said gently.

Galena bowed her head. "Luciana suffered," she murmured. "I *heard* her suffering. She called me right after she was attacked. And she said it was because of me."

"But you know it wasn't. Someone attacked her. Someone who wants to get to you. I don't know exactly what's going on yet, but I'm going to make sure we figure it out. I just wanted . . . I wanted to tell you. In person. Luciana's okay now. She's not suffering anymore, and she never will again."

"I couldn't help her," Galena whispered. Her agonizing minutes on the phone with Luciana replayed in her head. She'd felt so helpless. As if in sympathy, the faulty DNA sequencer across the room made more clicking noises.

"I think I know how you feel," Dec said. "I feel it every day on the job. But trying to help matters, even if you can't save someone. I wouldn't be able to survive being a paramedic if I didn't believe that. And you tried, Galena. I'm sure Luciana heard your concern. She knew she wasn't alone."

Galena swiped stupid tears from her cheeks. She supposed he would know. Like Eli, he was dedicated to helping people, even when it was dangerous to try. He was far braver than she was. Knowing he was with her, helping *her* now, gave her the strength to share the news that had been plaguing her ever since Dec had ended their phone call. "I've tried to reach my other volunteers. I haven't gotten ahold of a single one."

"How many?" he asked.

"Five in all. Two of them were fine yesterday, and a third checked in this afternoon, but it's been hours since she left here. The fourth didn't show up today. I've called and messaged all of them several times. I don't know what else to do."

Dec pulled a phone from his belt. It had interactive holographic capability, which had been cutting-edge right before their world had collapsed. Since then, phones like Dec's had become as rare as on-demand hot water. It must have cost him a fortune. He began tapping on its surface, and then held it up to show a projected display like the ones Danny provided. "I've got access to Central Dispatch records. Give me your volunteers' addresses and we'll see if any of metro Boston's emergency services were at those locations tonight."

Galena blinked at him. "Okay." She gave him one last glance before turning to her computer. His black hair was disheveled, like he'd run his hands through it. When he approached her desk and set his phone down next to her so they could both see what it projected, it was all she could do not to scoot away from him. Dec smelled of some subtle herbal cologne and masculine sweat. A warm, almost *hot*, kind of scent. It was making her heart race. It was overwhelming, and after everything that had happened tonight, all her coping mechanisms had worn away. "Um . . . here they are. The addresses," she said, waving at Danny's screen.

Dec was silent as he entered the address for V1, a young man named Andrew Bolcher, but then he cursed as a few paragraphs of information scrolled in front of them. "He was DOA at the North Boston Medical Center at sixteen thirty-four," he said. "Home invasion. Multiple stab wounds."

Galena shuddered and put her hand over her mouth. "Try that one," she choked out, pointing to V2's address. Nadya Odrova.

She'd been there just the night before, and after Dec had left, they'd talked about how lucky she was, that she hadn't been home when her apartment had been broken into.

After a manipulation of the data floating in front of him, Dec cursed again. "I'm sorry. She's gone, too. It was reported about two hours ago. There was an explosion of some kind. It's not clear yet what happened."

"Oh God," whispered Galena as a silent sob made her chest convulse. "This is all my fault."

Another minute was all it took to determine that V3, Mitch Hanson, was also dead, another stabbing. "Try V5," she whispered, dread consuming her.

V5. Katsumi Phillips. Galena remembered how the young woman had shyly reported that she was going to use the stipend provided to the volunteers to buy her mother and younger brother bus tickets to join her in Boston, how they currently lived in the lawless swamplands of Mississippi and needed a better life.

"Damn," muttered Dec as the cold black letters were projected into the air above Galena's desk. "Katsumi Phillips was DOA at the Central Medical Center at seventeen hundred. This one was an explosion, too . . . corner of Fayette and Jefferson. Shit. Cacy and Eli took that call. The police are thinking it was a bomb."

Galena didn't hear whatever he said next. The horror had swamped her, sending her swirling down a deep inky hole. She doubled over, hugging herself tightly, the tears streaking from her eyes. Five innocent people with bright futures ahead of them. Gone. And the only reason: because they had volunteered to help her test her vaccine. "I can't do this," she whimpered. "I can't."

He caught her as she began to slide to the floor. Galena normally hated uninvited touch, but right now she welcomed the steely warmth of his arms, because she felt like she was about to fly apart. "I've got you," he said quietly.

He didn't pull her closer to him—he was simply keeping her on her chair, preventing her body from hitting the cold tile. This steadiness made it possible for her to breathe again. "Why would someone do this?" she asked.

"My first guess is because they can't easily Mark you—you're too protected—so they're going after anyone who might help you with your research."

"Anyone? Dec, what about Jian and Ankita?"

His arms stiffened. "When was the last time you talked to either of them?" He released her as she jerked upright, reaching for her phone.

"Jian was in earlier today, but he'd gone home by the time I came in. And Ankita left maybe half an hour ago." She hit Ankita's name and sagged with relief when her lab assistant picked up. "Ankita! Where are you?"

"Home." Ankita blew a sharp breath into the phone. "Dealing with the usual hassles of living in this town. My apartment was broken into."

Galena shot up from her chair and put the phone into speaker mode. "Say that again."

"It's okay, Dr. M. They didn't take much. Sure did mess everything up, though."

Dec's blue eyes were hard on Galena. He raised his eyebrows as if asking permission to speak, and Galena nodded. "Ankita, this is Chief Declan Ferry of the Boston EMS. Have you contacted the police?"

Ankita let out a frustrated laugh. "Sure, but do you think they're going to show up anytime soon? They told me—"

With a crack and a whoosh, the line went silent. From somewhere out in the city came a deep *boom*.

Dec's eyes flew wide. "Ankita?" he asked sharply. Both of them looked at the phone. The connection had been dropped. It was so quiet in the room that a loud click from the DNA sequencer made Galena jump. Dec frowned and looked in the direction of the annoying machine, and then turned to Galena. "Call her back."

Ankita's number went straight to voice mail. Dec walked over to his own phone, on Galena's desk. "Do you know her address?"

Galena closed her eyes, trying to get herself to focus and picture Ankita's personnel file. "It's . . . uh . . . six Berkeley Street." She couldn't stop shaking. She couldn't concentrate, couldn't hold one single thought in her head. A hard chill raced down her spine. Suddenly, this lab didn't feel safe. *Nowhere* felt safe.

Dec entered the address, and the words that projected in front of him this time were bright red instead of black. Dec grimaced as he read a bunch of codes and symbols Galena couldn't decipher. "It's an active call," he said in a hollow voice.

"What happened?" Dec gave her a pained look. "Please," she whispered. "I need to know."

"Massive explosion. Uncontrolled fire. Fire and EMS requested."

"Explosion."

The glitchy DNA sequencer clicked once more, and her questioning thoughts from earlier about the source of the machine's malfunction came back to her all at once. Mechanical parts, smacking against something. A blockage.

Something inside the machine was keeping its components from moving correctly.

My AC unit went on the fritz, and now it's making this weird clicking noise, Nadya had said.

Galena looked into Dec's eyes and said the only words instinct allowed. "Get me out of here."

His brow furrowed. "You don't want to—?"

The sequencer clicked again, and Galena flinched. Dec's gaze lasered over to the faulty machine, and then he looked once more at the words scrolling through the air between them. His eyes widened. "It *was* a timer," he whispered.

He grabbed her hand and yanked her toward the exit, pushing her in front of him as they burst through the doors of the lab. As they jogged down the hall, she glanced over her shoulder to see he had his phone to his ear. "Eli," he barked. "I want you to call me as soon as you—"

The roar of the explosion silenced him. The lights in the hallway went out as the world shook and began to fall apart. Galena was thrown forward and crushed to the unforgiving tiles. As hunks of plaster and ceiling panels rained down, Dec landed on top of her, his arms around her body and his head bent over hers. "Nader! Tamasin!" he shouted. Was he speaking some foreign language?

Deafening cracks and the hiss and crackle of flames filled her ears, and then another, smaller explosion had Dec arching over her, holding her head to his hard chest. "Hang on," he said, bracing his other palm against the floor.

She gasped as his body lurched, like he had been hit from above. *The building,* she thought, *it's coming down.* She coughed as dust filled her lungs. Dec held her tighter as his body shuddered, but then collapsed, boneless and relentlessly heavy. For a moment, all she could hear was the stumble and stutter of his heart. It didn't sound normal at all. "Dec?" she wheezed. "Dec?"

She needed to get him off of her. She couldn't breathe. The air was stiflingly hot, and his weight was crushing her. In the pitch black, she reached up to touch his face. Her fingers slid through something wet on the firm ridge of his cheekbone. She didn't have to see it to know what it was. The memory came on hard, her trembling fingers sliding over her own belly, the grinding pain, the slick crimson mess.

But this isn't you. This is him. He's hurt.

Slick crimson mess.

Not you. Him. Hurt.

"Galena Margolis," called an unknown female voice from somewhere nearby. "Help us locate you." The voice sounded calm and in control. A rescuer? Or her would-be killer?

Galena flattened her palm over Dec's cheek. "Dec." He was her only ally now. He couldn't be gone. "Please."

He moaned. Her thumb stroked across his jaw, a reflexive gesture of pure relief.

"Declan Ferry," shouted the female voice. "Confirm your presence."

"H-here," wheezed Galena, her thoughts going fuzzy. "Here." *They can't see you. They can't hear you.* She forced herself to let go of Dec and stuck her hand out, digging through debris. They were completely buried. Dec's weight didn't allow her chest to expand. Each breath was shallower than the last. Her fingers wouldn't obey her now. The debris was too thick, too hard, too much. Like trying to swim in an ocean of stones. She drew as much air into her lungs as she could and then forced the word out one more time, with as much volume as she could muster. "Here!"

We all end up one place or the other in the end, Dec had said. Where would she go when it was her time? She closed her eyes. Dec's heart was still thumping unsteadily in her ear. She prayed he'd get through this. She liked that idea. He seemed like a nice man. A good man. She would have liked to have gotten to know him better.

Thank you, she thought as everything faded to black. *Thank you for trying to save me.*

CHAPTER SIX

Dec was swimming in an oily black sea, his lungs screaming for air. He couldn't move his arms and legs. He tried to open his eyes, but it was impossible. He tried to say Galena's name, but his tongue and lips wouldn't obey.

But he could see her face in his mind, wide green eyes fixed on him. Trusting him to protect her. With that thought, he fought to find the surface, to draw a single lungful of precious air. He struggled to raise his head.

"Dec," she whispered. "Please."

I'm trying. His muscles tensed. She needed him.

"Dec," she said again. But she sounded different this time. Different . . . but familiar. "Can you open your eyes?"

"Aislin?" The word came out thin and shredded, but he was rewarded by a squeeze of his hand. It was enough to bring him back. His eyelids fluttered open. Blue-and-green wallpaper, custom blown-glass light fixture. *Rylan's office.* He bolted upright.

His older sister, the Charon, sat in a chair next to the couch where he'd been lying. She was wearing a pale-blue suit that matched her eyes. Her platinum-blonde hair was in its usual elegant twist. Her hand, fingernails perfectly manicured, stroked his hair. "You're safe, Declan. Calm down."

Dec relaxed a little as he reminded himself that Aislin was in charge now. This was her office at Psychopomps headquarters, not Rylan's anymore, and before it was his, it had been their father's.

But how did he get here? He looked around. He and Aislin weren't alone; in fact, the room was pretty crowded. Tamasin and Nader stood near one of the windows, looking more human than he'd ever seen them. Moros himself stood next to them, millennia old but looking no more than thirty-five, dressed impeccably in a suit, his dark hair slicked back, his eyes metal gray. Cacy was sitting on the couch across from Dec, still wearing her paramedic uniform. Eli was next to her, covered in dust and blood, probably from the explosion he and Cacy had responded to.

Eli's arm was around Galena, whose hair was gray with dust. Her eyes were bloodshot. Her cheek was scraped and swollen.

"Are you—?" Dec began.

"A little bruised," she said quietly, grimacing at the rasp in her throat, "but not hurt."

"Because of you, Declan," said Nader, his hard-edged voice slicing through the room. He bowed his head. "Only because of you."

Tamasin bowed her head as well, but not before Dec caught her glancing anxiously at Moros's gloved hands. His touch meant doom, and all the Kere feared it. Hell, everyone feared it.

But Moros merely shifted his steely gaze from Galena to Dec. "It seems we owe you our gratitude, Declan. How is your head?"

Dec frowned and ran his hand over the top of his head. "Fine. I think?"

"You had a depressed fracture to the parietal," Eli said, then he looked down at his hand, which Galena was gripping tightly.

"In other words, you got your head bashed in," said Cacy. "Do you remember what happened?"

"I went to Galena's lab to let her know her research volunteer had been killed," Dec said slowly.

"You should have let me know immediately," Aislin interjected. Her pressed lips conveyed pure disapproval.

"With all due respect, Ms. Ferry," Galena said, her voice faint and difficult to catch, "I really appreciate that he came to tell me in person."

Eli shifted in his seat and gave Cacy a sidelong glance. "So do I. Especially because Galena wouldn't be sitting here if she'd been there alone when the bomb went off." An explosion wouldn't have killed her unless she were Marked. But it might have put her into an irreversible coma, her brilliance destroyed, her body broken.

Dec tried to recall exactly what had happened, but all he came up with was a rush of heat and a deafening roar. His gaze met Galena's. "Your lab."

She didn't look away. "Gone. Everything is gone."

"Not everything," he said, fighting the urge to cross the room and take her hand. She seemed beyond tears, shell-shocked and almost numb. "You're still alive."

She tucked her head against Eli's shoulder and nodded, but it was clear Dec's words had done nothing to comfort her. It bothered him more than it should have.

Moros stepped forward. "Obviously and unfortunately, there is another rogue Ker, possibly more than one." The glint of red in his eyes faded slightly as he looked at Aislin. "I will do all I can to determine who is responsible."

"So will I," Aislin replied, holding her head high. The ornate Scope of the Charon glinted at her throat. "Tonight has been costly. None of the deceased were sanctioned Markings."

"Incorrect," said Moros. "The Marking of Jian Lee, one of Dr. Margolis's assistants, was authorized."

Galena raised her head. "What?" she asked, her voice cracking. "Jian's dead?"

Moros tilted his head. "Mr. Lee was Marked by Trevor. He committed suicide by jumping into the Charles."

Galena's shoulders hunched forward, like she'd been punched in the chest. But then she went very still, and her brow furrowed. "Did he leave a note?"

Moros's eyebrows rose. "I don't know, as that is a mortal concern, one for the police and the young man's family."

Galena shook her head. Dec wondered if she was thinking the same thing he was. Jian looked awfully guilty from where he was sitting.

"Despite Mr. Lee's sanctioned death," Moros continued, "it is true that we have a crisis on our hands. Not only because of the unauthorized Markings."

"No, because someone was able to plant a bomb in Galena's lab," growled Eli.

Nader and Tamasin stepped a little closer to one another, huddling. "We were within thirty feet of Dr. Margolis at all times," Tamasin said. "We couldn't have seen anyone in her lab beforehand—we weren't there until she was."

"And our guards dropped Dr. Margolis off at the door of the building, thinking she was well protected," said Aislin.

"If Dec hadn't shielded Galena with his own body, that would have been it," said Cacy.

Dec shuddered. He could heal, even if his skull was caved in. But Galena couldn't. "We need to do a better job," he said. "We were lucky tonight."

"What if I quit?" Galena said.

All eyes in the room fell on her, and she shrank back a little but kept her head up. Dec could see that her eyes were shiny with tears. "What if I halted my research?"

"That's not an option."

"I don't want anyone else to die because of me!" She rose from the couch, shrugging off Eli's protective arm. "I'm serious. Seven innocent people died tonight. And whoever killed them made sure each of them knew it was because of my work. I had to listen to one of them take her last breath, knowing she was in terrible pain and I couldn't help her." Galena swiped her hands across her cheeks to wipe away the tears. "I've had enough of people coming after me, after my family"—she put her hand on Eli's shoulder—"and after the people I work with. I can't do this."

Moros cleared his throat. "Galena, my dear, you cannot turn away from what fate has in store for you. In the scheme of things, seven deaths is nothing compared to the millions of lives you will save."

Galena rounded on him. "They weren't nothing to *me*, Mr. Moros."

Eli stood up and took her hand. "G, we know that. But I know you. You're upset tonight. You've been through hell. You're hurting. Tomorrow when you wake up, though, you're going to want to continue your work."

She pulled her hand away from him. "With what? My lab has been destroyed. All my equipment, all my samples, all my trial serums. *Gone.*"

"But your data wasn't destroyed with your computer, right?" asked Cacy. "Wasn't it saved to the cloud?"

"Some of it," admitted Galena. "But some of it was so sensitive that it was stored in servers on-site."

"You should call Dr. Cassidy first thing tomorrow," said Eli. "She'll know how the salvage operation is being handled. And I bet she'll be glad to know you're all right," he added softly. "She really seems to care about you."

Galena bit her lip and looked away. "I know, but . . ." She grimaced.

Dec's brain was a sea of conflicting thoughts. On the one hand, it would be an utter tragedy for Galena to give up her research, not only for her, but for the world. On the other hand . . . "Getting back her data doesn't help us with the fact that someone tried to take Galena out tonight," he said. "The Kere couldn't keep her safe. Neither could our guards."

None of them said it aloud, but Dec was sure all the immortals in the room were thinking the same thing: as an ordinary human, Galena was painfully vulnerable. Sooner or later, the enemy would get to her.

Cacy looked up at Galena from her position on the couch. "There may be something we can do about that."

"If you're planning to lock me up in some—"

Cacy put up her hands. "I'm not suggesting that at all."

"Then what *are* you suggesting?" asked Aislin. "Because despite what Moros just said"—she tossed him a cool, assessing glance—"ultimately, it is Galena's choice whether she continues her research."

Moros gave Dec's eldest sister a knowing look. "And wouldn't it be convenient if she didn't, my dear?" he said quietly.

Aislin glared at him.

"I have something to propose," Cacy said. "We could make her a Ferry."

Dec's heart seized in his chest, so tight he couldn't speak. She couldn't be serious. Aislin looked like she felt the same way he did, but probably for an entirely different reason.

"You can do that?" Eli asked, his voice suddenly full of hope.

"It's not that easy," Cacy said, giving Galena a hesitant look. "Since she wasn't born a Ferry, she'd have to be married into the family."

Galena took a step closer to Eli. "What?"

"If you marry into the family and become one of us," Cacy replied, "you will be officially protected from being Marked or harmed by a Ker."

"That won't stop a rogue from attacking," Eli argued. He turned to Moros. "Would it?"

Moros ran his tongue over one of his unusually sharp canines. "It wouldn't. Though when I discover the identity of the rogue, his or her existence is over."

"But that might be too little, too late," said Eli.

Cacy put her arm around his waist. "But Eli, remember that Ferrys heal. *Really* quickly. We can't be killed unless the Charon wills it. I mean, look at Dec. Two hours ago his head was cracked open, and now he's good as new."

Dec ran a hand over the back of his head. His hair was crusted with his own blood and dusty with chipped plaster and grit. He couldn't wrap his barely healed brain around what Cacy was suggesting. Couldn't accept it, and couldn't understand the ache in his chest. He looked over at Galena, expecting her to turn the idea down cold, and was shocked to see her looking at Cacy with her eyebrows raised, interest and hope in her eyes.

"That's all I have to do?" she asked. "If I marry into the Ferry family, I can withstand a complex depressed skull fracture and go on with my research the next day?"

Moros chuckled. "Perhaps one of these esteemed Ferrys should explain some of the . . . complexities." He was looking right at Aislin, a distinctly amused glint in his eyes. Aislin remained silent, her arms folded at her waist and her lips pressed tightly together.

Galena turned away from them to look at Dec. His gut clenched. He could read the request in her eyes. She wanted *him* to explain it. He cleared his throat. Galena deserved to know everything before she considered this path. Dec just wished he could figure out whether he wanted her to take it or not.

It was true that it might save her. It might enable her to complete her research.

It could also destroy her. Maybe not physically, but certainly emotionally. And wouldn't that be the same thing as killing her?

"There are two rituals," he said slowly. "One formal and one . . . informal. But both are mandatory for becoming a true

Ferry." He ran his hand over a smear of blood on the thigh of his uniform, feeling everyone's stares. "The first is the Mark of the Ferry. It goes on your back. You've probably seen Cacy's." At the Harvard fund-raiser, she'd worn a dress that had put it on full display, much to Aislin's chagrin.

"Yeah," Galena said quietly. "A raven."

Dec nodded, keeping his head down. "Accepting the Mark and the Scope allows you to walk in the Veil. Regular humans are only shadows there. Ferrys are solid, able to enter and leave it at will, using their Scopes. Able to open a window to Heaven or Hell when it's called for. So that's the formal ceremony. Our version of a wedding." He licked his lips. His mouth was so damn dry.

"So what's the informal ceremony for?" she asked.

He couldn't look at her. His chest and face suddenly felt very hot. He couldn't push Moros's words out of his mind, when Moros had told Dec what had happened to Galena a few years ago. But he forced himself to keep talking. "The informal ceremony is what makes the person truly immortal, and what makes a regular human body able to heal quickly and completely under most circumstances."

"Sounds important. Why is it informal, then?" Eli asked.

Dec raised his head. "Because it's very private."

Eli became very still. "Private?"

Dec nodded. He couldn't go on, and Aislin seemed to sense that. Her voice was smooth and merciless as she explained. "We do not marry for appearances. You would have to commit to the choice with body and soul."

"Body and soul?" Galena's eyes had gone a little glassy. It was clear that marrying "for appearances" was what she had been hoping for. "So what you're saying is—"

"The marriage must be consummated in order for the ritual to be complete," said Aislin.

"Oh," whispered Galena. She slowly sank onto the couch cushions. Her lovely face glinted with pinprick beads of sweat.

"Is this something you would sanction?" Moros asked Aislin. "After all, you are the Charon."

Aislin unfolded her arms and let them fall to her sides. Her movements were controlled, so poised, but Dec knew her well—she was at war with herself. She let out a slow breath. "I would not stand in the way if this were the path Galena chose."

Moros smiled before turning to Cacy. "This was your idea, Cacia. Who from your family would you volunteer as a worthy partner for Dr. Margolis?"

Filled with both curiosity and dread, Dec looked at Cacy to find her staring back at him. Her turquoise-blue eyes were filled with both apology and pleading. "What about you, Dec?"

CHAPTER SEVEN

Dec's mouth dropped open. "You . . . I . . . I don't think . . ."
He was frowning. And though he'd sought out Galena's
face first as soon as he'd woken up, now he seemed willing to look
at anyone *but* her. She rubbed her sweaty palms on her jeans as
Dec made a move for the door. "I have to go," he mumbled.

"Dec, you can't leave!" Cacy called after him. "We have to figure this out."

Dec whipped around, looking so much stronger than he had
when they'd been brought here by the two Kere who had been
guarding her. "I'm done for tonight," he said in a ragged voice.
For the briefest of moments, his eyes strayed to Galena, turmoil in
their icy depths. "I just . . . can't. I'm sorry."

He was out the door a second later.

Mr. Moros chuckled. "Who knew Declan was so commit-
mentphobic?"

"Shut the fuck up," Cacy snarled at the same time Aislin said,
"Jason, for goodness' sake."

He held his hands up. "Ferrys, please keep me apprised of the
outcome of your latest family drama. I actually have interest in seeing how this one turns out. Tamasin and Nader, cooperate with the
Ferrys, and do not fail me again." His eyes met Galena's. "Galena,

good luck, my dear. We will respect your decision, but I advise you to follow the path that leads to your fate." He inclined his head. "I will take my leave of you now. I have other business that requires my immediate attention."

He disappeared. Just like that. No sign he'd ever been there. How was that even possible? How was *anything* these people could do possible? And now they were offering her the chance to be one of them—but the price was nauseatingly high. Not just for her, either. Dec had looked so upset when he'd stormed out. But she couldn't blame him, not really. They didn't know each other at all. Her shoulders slumped. "What if I say no?" she asked.

Eli sank down next to her and touched her shoulder. "We'd still protect you." He looked at Aislin. "Right?"

Aislin nodded. "Of course." She let out a weary sigh. "But as much as I hate to admit it, Cacia, this idea of yours is the most safety and certainty we can offer Galena. And that is crucial given the number of unsanctioned Markings that have already occurred. Someone or something is trying to unravel the fabric of fate, and this might keep that from happening."

Jeez, when she said it like that, it sounded so . . . big. But then again, Galena knew her research *was* big, or had the potential to be. All she needed was another year or two, enough time to test the vaccine and develop the processes to mass-produce an antigen that required specific genetic tailoring for every individual. Her heart beat a little faster, but in a good way, like it always did when she thought about tackling something new, taking it apart, and solving it in ways no one else ever had. That was what got her out of bed, every single day. It was why she lived, why she breathed—to see the work she'd done touch the lives of people around the world. And it could. It could give them a chance to live, a chance to dream their own dreams.

If she gave up, millions of people, some not yet born, were destined to die needlessly before their time.

Eli was right. She couldn't quit.

But could she take the chance of continuing down this path as an ordinary mortal? If Dec hadn't been with her tonight, she would have been crushed. Burned. Broken. But if she'd been a Ferry like he was, she would have walked away.

Didn't she owe it to the world to do everything she could to stay safe and whole and working?

Galena gazed down at her trembling hands. "But I'd have a choice about who I married, right?" she asked in a shaky voice. "Could I have some time to think about it?"

"Of course," said Aislin.

"But the sooner, the better," Cacy said quietly. "Because then you'd be safe."

"Right," Galena whispered. "Safe."

Eli looked over at her. "I want to take you home."

"Eli, your apartment might be targeted," Cacy said gently.

"Cacy is correct," said Aislin. "Several of the attacks tonight were bombings."

Standing next to the couch, Cacy stroked her hand through Eli's dark-blond hair, and he leaned his head against her hip, his eyes closing in something like relief. "Eli and Galena can stay with me," she said.

Aislin inclined her head. "That's kind of you, but we have living quarters here as well, for visiting dignitaries. They're quite comfortable. Galena, if you'd prefer to—"

"I'd rather stay with Cacy and Eli."

"Done," murmured Cacy. She looked at Aislin. "And you'll ensure protection for her until she makes her decision?"

"I'll try," said Aislin. "Given tonight's events, it seems that the rogue is determined to carve out a wide path of destruction. We have resources, but not enough to cover every possible place they might strike."

"And more innocent people could die," said Galena. "Because of me."

Eli took her hand. "Don't think like that. You have enough to worry about as it is." He stood up, pulling Galena to her feet. "I'm taking them now. Aislin, we'll talk to you tomorrow."

Eli's hand suddenly went from warm to blazing hot, and with a rush of cold air, the Psychopomps office disappeared, replaced by an open living space with plush couches, shelves of real paper books, and quirky antique furniture. Galena wobbled on her feet, and Eli caught her. "Sorry. I know it takes some getting used to."

"I think you do it with style," Cacy said. She rose to her tiptoes and kissed Eli's cheek. "And your control is a lot better."

He grinned. "I've been working on it."

Cacy touched Galena's arm. "I hope I didn't massively overstep back there. I just want to make sure you're protected."

"I know," Galena murmured. "I appreciate it."

"You can stay in my guest room, okay?" Cacy gestured toward the hallway. "And we'll be in my room. My guess is that Nader and Tamasin will be skulking around tonight, too, so you're totally safe."

Galena swallowed and nodded. "I think I need to wash myself off. I'm pretty dusty. Do you have some extra water?" She hated to be greedy, but every time she moved, she felt the grit, and the suffocating memories of everything and everyone she'd lost tonight pressed in on her.

Cacy smiled. "We've got running water twenty-four-seven, lady. You can take a nice long shower if you want." Cacy glanced at Eli as she pulled Galena toward the hall. "Can you pop over to your apartment and grab Galena's clothes and toiletries?"

"Sure thing." Eli gave Galena one last searching look, then vanished.

"You must be ready to fall over," said Cacy as she led Galena into a huge bedroom with floor-to-ceiling windows bedecked with flowing drapes. A large four-poster bed piled with pillows drew Galena's eyes. It was like something out of an ad for a luxury hotel. She'd never seen anything like it.

Too bad she probably wouldn't be able to sleep.

"I'm used to being awake at all hours," Galena mumbled. Her whole body hurt, a dull ache. Her skull felt like it had been stuffed with agar—smooth, gelatinous, and free of any intelligent thought. And that was kind of nice, actually. Except . . . "I guess I have a lot to think about."

Cacy sighed. "Yeah. I'm sorry that Dec bombed out of there like that. I didn't think he'd freak out."

Galena laughed, sudden and high-pitched. "Are you serious? He'd just been asked to marry a total stranger." Her throat grew tight. *And have sex with her.*

"Well, when you put it like that, I guess I shouldn't be so hard on him. But seriously, Galena, I know this is a completely bizarre situation. Eli was right when he said we'd protect you regardless of what you decide."

But if they tried to protect her, would they be hurt, too? And how many more mortals would die? "I know," Galena murmured. "I'm just . . . well . . . this kind of thing isn't easy for me." Even now, she couldn't really think about it, because she was too busy trying to bolster the fence around all those dangerous memories.

Cacy's delicate face pinched with sympathy. "I know, Galena. And I know this must be scary. But if you did want to go through with it, we'd find someone good for you."

Galena ran her hand over her throat. "Okay. Thanks. I think I need that shower now." Anything to get away from this conversation. Someone good for her? Could *any* man possibly be good for her? She shuddered. But then Dec's face flickered in her mind, accompanied by a pang of sadness.

Cacy gestured toward a door on the other side of the room. "You've got your own bathroom. Towels are in there. Enjoy. If you need me, I'm close. Just give me a shout." She patted Galena's arm and left her alone, shutting the door behind her.

Galena trudged to the shower. It was the size of the entire bathroom in her and Eli's apartment. And it had glass walls and colorful mosaic tiles. More luxuries. She stripped down quickly, turning her back to the giant mirror that took up most of one wall. She hated looking at herself. Once she was naked, she turned on the water, delighted to feel the warm spray caressing her fingers. She stepped into it gratefully, letting it wash away all the leavings of this terrible night. She wished it were possible to do the same with her memories.

And her fears.

Going through with this marriage would mean willingly putting herself at the mercy of a man. How could she possibly do that, especially with a stranger? She grabbed a washcloth and soaped it, her nose filling with the scent of lavender. And as her hands moved automatically, scrubbing her skin, her mind wandered, back to the days before she'd been broken, when she'd had a boyfriend, when she'd enjoyed touching him and letting him touch her. It was hard to reach past all the blackness for images of his face, for the times they'd been skin to skin, for the way it had made her feel. It was so vague, a shadow of something that had been good, that she'd craved.

Last night, when she'd been with Dec in her lab, she had felt a ripple of desire within her, the hum of hope, for the first time in two years. The fear hadn't stopped her from thinking about his touch, from wondering how it might feel, from wanting to try. But what would happen if she did?

The washcloth skimmed over her breasts, leaving her nipples hard and sensitive. Galena shivered despite the hot water. Could she let someone touch her again? The washcloth dipped lower, and she gritted her teeth and moved it around the scars, stroking down her hips instead. Her fingers brushed the soaked curls between her legs. Her thighs tensed, and anger rushed through her. She could barely even touch *herself*. A rare sort of rage burned through her, eating away at the thick cloak of numbness she usually wore. They'd taken everything. They'd made her own body her enemy. She was housed in a cage of bone and flesh and weakness, and it hadn't been able to keep her safe. She was stuck inside this fragile mass of blood vessels and electrical charges, and what used to be hers felt foreign.

"I want it back," she whispered. She dropped the washcloth and slid her fingers between her legs, running them over the slick folds of skin, the entrance to her body. Her fingertip trailed up and circled the little nub, gentle and tentative. It made her feel dizzy, and she braced herself on the tile with her other hand. As the water rained down, she rubbed herself, exploring something that still felt like a strange, forbidden place. Part of her mind was trying to pull her into the ordered, clinical space where she spent most of her time, but another part was having none of it. *Just feel. And own it. You can be safe within yourself.*

She'd avoided this for so long that it didn't feel safe at all. But it didn't feel bad, either. Her heart was thumping steadily, not racing. Simply knocking fiercely against the wall of her chest, reminding her that it was still there, still beating. Her breaths whooshed from her lungs. Tiny zings of pleasure began to emanate outward from that sensitive spot, and her fingers grew slick, not with water, but with her own arousal. And once again, unbidden and startling, Dec's face appeared behind her closed eyelids, his broad shoulders and muscular chest and narrow hips and—

"Galena? I—"

She screamed at the sound of the voice and clutched at the walls. Spots floated before her eyes, and her feet slipped over the tiles. "Cacy?" she called, her voice breaking over the name.

"I'm so sorry for scaring you!" Cacy said from the other side of the door. "I just wanted to let you know Eli's back, and I've put some clothes on your bed."

"Thanks," she said with a strangled laugh. "Give me a minute." Her hand rested on her belly, over the thick welts and criss-crossing scars. Her body was still throbbing, her heart racing. But her nerves were jangling, the feeling of being caught off guard too overwhelming. She turned off the water and leaned her head on the warm tile, focusing on controlling her breathing. "It's a start," she whispered to herself.

A few minutes later, she exited the bathroom to find a small neatly folded pile of clothes on the end of the bed. There was a knock at the bedroom door. "Yeah?" she called.

"It's me, G," came Eli's muted response. "Can we talk? I'm worried about you."

"I'm worried about me, too, to be honest." She grabbed some clothes and walked behind the beautifully painted dressing screen that was set up near the closet. "Come on in."

The door opened and closed again. "Our apartment hasn't blown up yet, if it's any consolation."

"I'll take anything I can get right now." She bit her lip as she fastened her bra. "What do you think I should do?"

Eli sighed. "I want you to be safe."

Her stomach churned as she tugged on a pair of sweats. "You think I should do it. Marry some random guy from the Ferry family." God, that sounded horrific—

"I didn't say that."

Galena pulled a T-shirt over her head and wrapped the towel around her dripping hair, then emerged from behind the screen. "So you don't think I should do it?"

Eli rubbed the back of his head and winced. "I didn't say that either."

"You're not being very helpful." She climbed onto the bed and couldn't help but smile as the soft pillows flopped around her.

Eli sat on the edge of the bed. He was still wearing his paramedic uniform—he hadn't even taken the time to change yet. It had been a long night for him, too. "I don't know how to be helpful, G. You've been given some god-awful choices. You're the only person who can make them, though."

"I have to keep working on my vaccine. And I have to do everything possible to complete that work." She let out a shuddery sigh. "But I can't imagine it, Eli. I can't imagine letting some man I don't even know—" She bit back the rest, having to focus on pushing away the razor-sharp memories that wanted to cut her down.

He took her hand. "What if you trusted him?"

She gave him a cautious look. "Easier said than done. To me, it feels like walking through a minefield. And now I'm expecting someone I barely know to be my partner in that? I mean . . ." She swallowed the lump in her throat. "You saw how Dec responded. He couldn't even stay in the same room with me, let alone . . ."

Eli squeezed her hand. "I doubt it was *you* he had a problem with. I know Dec. He's a good man."

"I think so, too," she whispered. "I think I would have been lucky if he'd said yes."

Eli sat back, the tiniest of smiles playing on his lips. "Yeah? You hit it off with the Chief?"

"Don't look at me like that. I'm saying that he seems nice." She bowed her head as her cheeks got warm. "He seemed really aware, I guess. I don't know how else to say it." All she knew was that, from the moment she'd met him, he'd given her space when he sensed she needed it. He'd touched her without making it about him. He'd been nothing but respectful and gentle. Oh, and also gorgeous. She could have sworn, for a few minutes last night, he'd been flirting with her. "Yeah. He just seemed aware. Of me," she said lamely.

Plus, he was a *known*, and all the other faceless men were not, and that made them a lot more terrifying.

Eli ran his thumb along the back of her hand. "Okay. Fair enough. He seemed aware."

"But he also said no."

Eli stared at their joined hands for a few moments, and she could tell he was thinking about something, but she was afraid to ask what. This was awkward enough. Finally, he patted her hand and edged off the bed. "If you want to do this, I'll support you. Every step of the way. I just want you to be careful with yourself. You've been through enough."

Tears burned her eyes. Eli had been through it right along with her, and he was still by her side. "I'm so lucky that you're my brother," she said in a choked voice.

She opened her arms, and he hugged her, accidentally knocking her towel turban off in the process. He stepped back and grabbed it, then laid it flat over the top of her head. Like she was a nun or something. "Love you, Sis," he said, his eyes shining, determination set in his square jaw. "We'll get you through this. Trust me."

He disappeared.

Galena lay back on the pillows. If trusting Eli were all that was required, this would be a piece of cake. Too bad that getting through this required entrusting herself, body and soul, to someone else.

CHAPTER EIGHT

Dec poured himself a few fingers of Jameson and set the bottle back on the counter. He'd gone through half of it in the last hour but still didn't have the numbing buzz he needed. In fact, his thoughts were sickeningly lucid.

Walking out on Galena and the rest of them had been a dick move, but he'd been short-circuited by Cacy's suggestion that he marry Galena. What the fuck. He wondered if Galena was actually considering it, just to have the immortality that would make it possible for her to save the world.

He didn't know whether he would respect her for that or not. On the one hand, it was so unselfish. On the other, it was *too* unselfish.

A knock on his door had him glancing over at his entryway, cluttered with a couple of pairs of work boots. He reached over and tapped the door monitor, fully expecting to see Cacy, all pissed off, on the screen.

But it was Eli. "Hey, Chief, can I come in?"

Dec sighed and hit the "Unlock" icon. He held up the Jameson bottle as Eli walked into the apartment. "Drink?"

Eli shook his head. "Rough night, I guess."

Dec chuckled, bitter and low. "What can I do for you?"

Eli looked around, and Dec did, too, trying to see his place with a stranger's eyes. His weights and gym equipment took up about half of his massive living room, along with a couch and a videowall. The kitchen was about as basic as it comes: sink, stove, fridge, stainless steel counters. No pictures on the walls. The massive windows along the far wall offered a nice view of downtown, but they were tinted, no drapes. Dec wasn't really into decoration.

"I wanted to talk to you about what happened tonight," Eli said as his gaze returned to the counter, to Dec's glass.

Dec took a long sip. "I can't remember half of it, and I'm trying to forget the rest."

"That's too bad." Eli sank onto a barstool next to him. "Because I really need your advice."

Dec gave him the side-eye as he emptied his glass, the whiskey burning in his throat in a vaguely pleasurable way. "Shoot."

"Galena's determined to do this marriage thing."

"Will she be able to go through with it?"

"It seems better to her than being maimed or dead," Eli said. "Which is why Cacy suggested it in the first place, even knowing about Galena's past."

Dec's shoulders sagged. "Yeah. I guess she was right. But still. Galena seems . . . I don't know. She looked pretty overwhelmed at the idea of being with someone."

"Probably because she is," Eli said, his voice taking on an edge. "She's been hurt worse than any other person I know." He cleared his throat and looked away. "And I admire her more than anyone else, because in spite of everything that's happened to her, she's still on her feet." Eli looked over at the bottle. "Actually, I think I *will* have one, if you don't mind."

Dec grabbed a glass from the dish rack and slogged in a few fingers of whiskey, then slid it over to Eli. "I'm sorry that you guys have been through so much," he said quietly.

"You know, don't you? About the attack. About what happened."

"I know it did happen, and that's all."

"For weeks afterward, I thought I was going to lose her. I seriously thought she was just going to curl up and die on me. She wouldn't talk or eat or get out of bed."

Dec's chest ached at the thought. "But you got her through it."

"Not really. She did that all by herself. I wasn't around as much as I should have been. I was so full of rage that I was afraid it would scare her."

And Dec knew, because Moros had told him, that Eli had taken matters into his own hands. He'd stalked and killed every single one of Galena's attackers, and that was why it had been possible for Moros to make him a Ker—he'd already taken human life. Not that Dec blamed Eli. As he pictured Galena's tear-streaked, bruised face, he thought he probably would've done the same. "You must have been there for her somehow, though. You guys are obviously close."

"I tried. But it was her work that saved her. One day, she just got up and went back to her lab. And that was it. I rarely saw her afterward. She dove back into her research and never came up for air."

"So if she stops her research—"

"I'm afraid for her. I think it's how she keeps everything at bay."

Dec closed his eyes. "She'll get tired, though. Eventually." Dec felt tired even thinking about it. Or maybe that was him. Tired all around.

"I think you're right," said Eli sadly. "But for now, the possibility of saving even one life is what keeps her going."

"It seems like it does more than that." It lit her up inside. And God, it was beautiful to watch.

"It does. It always has. And that's why she'll do anything to keep *it* going."

Including what she would have to do to become a Ferry. Dec refilled his glass and topped off Eli's. This was what had gotten to him. He'd been intrigued by Galena Margolis from the first moment he'd laid eyes on her. Sure, he didn't really *know* her, not yet, but he knew enough to want to know more. He knew enough, he realized with embarrassment, that he wanted her to *like* him. Which was stupid. He was a grown-ass man, not a schoolboy. But that hope, that she would like him, that she would trust him, had been smashed when Cacy suggested that he be the one to make her a Ferry—right after he'd seen Galena nearly faint when she found out what it would take. If he agreed to this, he'd be bound to Galena forever, but would he ever have a shot at her heart? Because she wouldn't be choosing *him*. She'd be choosing protection. Two different things.

Why the fuck am I even thinking about this? Dec groaned and drained his glass. He must be drunk. He wasn't usually quite this stupid. The idea of being bound inextricably to another person, especially one who didn't actually love him, didn't sound appealing at all, no matter how intriguing Galena might be.

"So who in your family do you think would be the best match?" Eli asked casually, interrupting Dec's brooding. "Cacy had a few ideas, but I wanted to run them by you."

"Yeah?" he asked, his voice strained. "Like who?"

"She mentioned someone named Bradan. A first cousin?"

"Bradan? He's a total player. Treats women like tissues. Cheap and disposable." Dec had once gotten in a fistfight with the guy on the deck of Bradan's yacht after Bradan had "playfully" chucked one of his drunk girlfriends over the side and into the harbor. Dec had ended up having to give the poor woman mouth-to-mouth, and Bradan had protested loudly when she vomited up water and gin all over his polished deck. It had been the last straw. Dec had pulverized the guy and gotten himself barred from several family events as a result. Not that he minded. How did Cacy not remember that? "He's the last person on earth who should be allowed near Galena."

Eli frowned. "How about Hugh? Another cousin . . . works with Aislin?"

Dec snorted. "Hugh's a pompous, greedy asshole with the sensitivity of a numbing agent."

"Um. Carrick?"

"I'd rather spend time with a Shade."

"That bad? How about Riordan? Cacy told me he's a nice guy."

"He is. And he has the personality of a cucumber."

"Okay . . . Davin? Cacy said he's into science."

Dec grimaced, feeling the anger rise inside him. "Only if you consider all the weird cosmetic procedures he's had done!" What was Cacy thinking?

"So . . . who would *you* suggest we go to? Who might be willing—and able—to be a decent partner for her? Because of all the admittedly shitty options, this is the one she's choosing. I'd like it to be as unshitty as possible." Eli threw back his remaining whiskey in one long swallow. He sighed. "I just want her to be okay. That's all I want."

Dec looked away from him. "Me too," he muttered.

"Then give me a name. Because you're her first choice, and if you won't do this for her, then—"

Dec swiveled around so fast he nearly fell off his stool. "She actually said that?"

Eli opened his mouth to respond, but then winced and looked down at his arm. "I have to go. Duty calls."

Dec was dying to ask more about what Galena might have said to her brother, but he knew that Eli was probably reading a list of names scrawled on his arm, people he was supposed to Mark for death tonight. "Understood. Get going." If he delayed too long, the pain would set in.

"Dec," said Eli as he took a few steps back, "I know it's too much to ask. I know it comes with a lot of heavy consequences. But it could save millions of lives. Including Galena's. It can't happen at the expense of her soul, though. She's really strong, but she's been through hell and she needs someone who's going to be gentle with her. Someone who understands what it will take for her to go through with it."

And with that, Eli vanished.

Dec groaned. It *was* too much to ask. Way too fucking much. He had a decent life. Sure, he was bored to tears and basically trudging through each day, but that didn't mean the solution was to hitch himself to a woman he barely knew in order to make her immortal. He'd been engaged before, when he was a lot younger, but he had realized, as the months wore on, that his fiancée was more entranced with his money than she was with him. She'd wanted him to take a corporate job and quit the EMS, right when he was about to be promoted. She wanted to rush the wedding, because she was twenty-four and dying to get locked in looking fabulous for several decades, since Ferrys aged more slowly than regular humans once they hit their twenties. And when Dec had finally seen through the haze of infatuation he thought had been love, he'd also seen that she'd only ever wanted what he could give her—she'd never just wanted *him*.

And in a way, Galena was the same. Sure, she had a better reason for wanting to become a Ferry, and she didn't seem like the type who'd be interested in his money, but *still*. He hadn't dated much over the last twenty years. He'd given up on finding a woman who could love a regular guy who liked to drink beer with his friends and save people for a living. He didn't own a yacht or expensive furniture or fancy clothes. And he didn't give a fuck that his extended family thought he was a disappointment because he'd never bothered to go to college or do anything other than the one thing he'd wanted to do since he was a little boy. He lived the life he'd chosen. He didn't change for anyone.

Yeah, it was lonely sometimes, but it seemed better than fitting into someone else's box.

"*Fuuuck*," Dec said. His limbs were heavy and tingling from all the whiskey, but he was too restless to lie down. And he couldn't get Eli's words out of his head.

It could save millions of lives. Including Galena's.

When it was put that way, Dec felt like a total asshole for wanting to hold out for someone who loved him for himself. He'd given up on that a long time ago, anyway.

Besides, the idea of *any* of his cousins putting their hands on Galena made Dec want to put his fist through a wall.

He had to make a decision. He had to make it now. The stakes were brutally high.

His heart tapping out a jittery cadence, Dec pulled his phone from his pocket.

CHAPTER NINE

Galena was staring at the ceiling when her phone rang. She started at the noise and scrambled for the device. She paused when she didn't recognize the number. "They can't get you here," she whispered as her thumb hovered over the "Answer" button and then flicked downward. "Hello?"

"Hey, Galena. It's Dec."

Galena blinked at the sound of his voice, deep and slightly raspy. "Hi," she murmured. "How are you feeling?"

He chuckled, and it sent a little shiver down Galena's spine. She wasn't sure if that was a good thing or a bad thing. Her body couldn't tell the difference. "Back to normal," he said. "How about you? Sore, I bet."

"Only a little. Thank you for saving me. Again." She couldn't believe she hadn't said it to him earlier. He'd used his body as a shield. He'd held her head to his chest. He'd taken all the hits so she didn't have to.

He was quiet for a few moments, then said, "You're welcome. Did I wake you up?"

"No. I don't sleep a lot. Especially at night."

"Where are you? Back at your apartment?"

"No, actually. I'm at Cacy's."

"Oh. Um . . . I know this is weird, but can I come over? I want to talk to you, but I'd like it to be in person."

"You want to talk?"

"Yeah. I was an asshole earlier. So is this an okay time?"

"Yes," she said, and it came out without thought. Complete reflex. But it felt right. "Yes," she said again, just to feel in control of it. "I think Cacy and Eli might be . . . er . . ."

She'd heard their voices earlier, and she was guessing they wouldn't want to be disturbed.

"I'll be there in a minute," said Dec. "We can go to the roof for privacy if you want." He paused. "There are guards posted there."

Galena squeezed her eyes shut. He seemed to know how to make her feel safe, and it lit a little spark of warmth inside her. "Okay. I'll be waiting."

She ran a brush through her hair and put on some shoes. And then, cautiously, she poked her head into the bathroom and looked in the mirror, the first time she'd actually done that on purpose in a long, long time. She was surprised at the sharpness of her cheekbones, and the dark circles under her eyes. She drew back, smoothing her hands over her face. She wished she hadn't bothered.

She texted Eli so that he would know where she was, then tiptoed out of her room as she heard the elevator outside the apartment ding. Not wanting to disturb her brother and his girlfriend, she opened the door just as Dec raised his fist to knock. Her breath caught in her throat. He'd changed, too. He was just wearing jeans and a T-shirt, but few people could look quite that good in such a basic outfit. His black hair was boyishly messy, and he had a day's worth of dark stubble on his cheeks. He gave her a sheepish smile. "Ready?"

She nodded. They rode the elevator up to the roof in silence and, when the doors opened, were greeted by an armed guard. "Mr. Ferry," he said, bowing his head in respect.

"Hey, Adam," Dec said as he and Galena stepped into the humid night air. "How's it going?"

Adam's serious face softened a little. "Good, Mr. Ferry. Quiet night. We're on alert, but no sign of trouble."

Dec put his arm around Galena's back but didn't touch her, just guided her over to the thick knee-high wall near the edge of the roof.

Galena smiled as a breeze lifted a few loose tendrils of her hair. "It's cooler up here," she said.

"I like coming up here for exactly that reason. One of the few places in this city where it's actually bearable to be outside." He sat down, and Galena did too, and then he cleared his throat. "Eli came to talk to me earlier. He said you were thinking about going through with this marriage thing."

"Yeah. I think I need to." She gazed out over the city, which looked beautiful from this height. But she knew, down in the alleys, in the canal zones, in the tenements near the Common, there were people who weren't living in this kind of luxury. Like Galena had when she was young, they were dwelling in a dangerous world where death could come through violence or illness, where life was cheap and easily lost. "I don't think I could live with myself if I let my stubbornness get in the way of completing this vaccine." Who was she kidding? It wasn't stubbornness; it was fear.

"That makes sense," Dec said, crossing his arms over his chest and leaning back, keeping his eyes directed at the city. "But it doesn't look like an easy decision."

Galena pressed her lips together. "This marriage-arrangement thing is a little tricky for me on a number of levels."

"It would be for anybody."

"But I still need to do it, Dec." She looked over to find his eyes on her, and it made her whole body feel warm. His gaze was its own kind of haven, like he was making her some silent promise she couldn't yet hear.

"Have you thought about what actually marrying someone would be like?" he asked. "Marriage between two Ferrys isn't the same as marriage between two regular humans. It lasts longer, for one. It's more . . ." He bowed his head and ran his hand over his thick hair. "The two people are more connected."

She stared at his hands as they came to rest on his thighs. "So I guess it's pretty important that I choose the right guy. Assuming he'd be willing to take me on, that is."

"Take you on? I think you might be selling yourself short." Dec's eyes narrowed. "Wait. Is there something you're not telling me?"

Galena froze. "Wha—?"

"Like, are you a dangerous sleepwalker?"

"No."

"An obsessive neat freak?"

"Only in my lab."

"Are you one of those people who alphabetizes their spice rack?"

"I've never even owned a spice rack."

"Sounds like you need a husband who knows his way around a kitchen."

She arched an eyebrow. "I'd never thought of that."

Dec leaned forward. "I bet I make the best Dublin coddle you've ever tasted."

Now both her brows rose. "Dublin what?"

"Coddle. It's made with sausage and potatoes. My mom taught me." His voice took on a note of sadness, but then he seemed to brush it off like a cobweb. "Maybe I'll make it for you sometime. Okay, what else?"

"Huh?"

"What else do you require in a husband?"

Her chin trembled. "Um, I haven't really ever thought about it."

"Nice car? Does he need to have a nice car?"

She stared at him. "No."

"Yacht?"

"*What?* No! I can't swim."

He nodded solemnly. "So you'd need someone who could save you if you fell into a canal. I happen to be an excellent swimmer."

Galena shook her head. "Dec, I don't really understand—"

"Anything else?" he asked. "Hobbies? Habits? Will you get pissed if he leaves his shoes lying around? How do you feel about pool?"

"Pool? I've never—"

"Would you be willing to learn?"

"I guess."

"If he invited his friends over in the evening to play cards, would that cramp your style?"

"I'd probably be at work. I wouldn't want him to be lonely."

"What if he asked you to go with him to a fund-raiser or a gala?"

She wrinkled her nose, and he laughed.

"That is the best response you could possibly give to that question. Okay, what about—?"

"Dec," she said, "I just want someone to *get* me. I just want us to understand each other."

His expression became utterly serious. "That's what you want in a relationship?"

She nodded. "It's all I want. It's the foundation for everything."

Dec looked directly at her with his ice-blue eyes, and she felt like there was an ocean inside them, vast and mysterious. "Well then, I'll do it, Galena. If you want me to."

Her mouth dropped open. "What?"

He gave her a half smile. "Will you marry me?"

All she could do was blink.

Dec edged off the wall and knelt in front of her. Carefully, like he was afraid to startle her, he took her hands in his, holding them loosely enough that she could pull them away if she wanted to. "Galena Margolis, will you marry me?"

She couldn't help it—she started to laugh.

"What, no ring?" she said, giggling.

He groaned and ran his hands over his face. "Would you believe me if I told you I lost it while doing valiant battle with a Shade in the Veil?"

"A 'Shade'?"

"Evil ring-stealing fuckers. They love shiny things."

"Darn. No ring. Well . . ." She looked down at him on one knee, holding her hands in his, and felt a pang of sadness. His playful expression told her this was a joke, and really, she should be glad, because it pushed away all the fear and made it possible to take this step forward. He was offering to let her, a near stranger, into his life, and somehow, he was doing it on his knees with a big grin on his face. Gratitude and admiration glowed in her chest, accompanied by a tiny hopeful spark of excitement. "Okay. I guess I can get over the ring thing. I'm not much of a jewelry girl, anyway."

Dec's smile softened and became something more wistful. Slowly, he lifted one of her hands and drew it toward his mouth. Galena's stomach did a funny little swoop as he kissed her knuckles, his lips soft and warm with the slightest scrape of stubble. "Then let's do this," he said. He stood up as his phone buzzed with a text. He let out an irritated growl.

"Who is it?" she asked.

"Aislin. She wants to talk to me." He looked down at their hands, and Galena was shocked to see that they were still joined, and that it hadn't bothered her at all. In fact, she liked it. His hands were hard but warm, safe but powerful.

Dec pressed a spot on the screen and held the phone to his ear. "Hey. Yeah. I'm fine. I'm with Galena." He paused, and Galena heard the low, steady cadence of Aislin's voice. "Shit. You're sure?"

He rubbed his hand over his face, then gave Galena a concerned look.

"Has something happened?" she asked quietly.

Dec grimaced and nodded. "No, I understand," he said to Aislin. "And it's what I was calling about, actually. I talked to her, and we've decided to do it." He paused again, his jaw clenched. "I hear you," he said in a hollow voice. "I understand." He hung up.

"What is it?"

He sat down next to her. "Another bomb went off. This one was in your apartment building."

"But Eli was just there—"

"He may have set off a timer as he moved through the space. The explosion happened less than ten minutes ago."

Galena's whole body went tight with dread. "Was anybody hurt?"

"Paramedics and fire crews are on scene. We'll have more information tomorrow." Dec sighed, and he looked down at her hand, the one that might have borne a ring if this had been real, if they were actually in love, if this wasn't a tragic joke on the both of them. "But it's obvious that whoever's after you isn't giving up."

She was glad he was holding her hand, glad for his solid strength. "What does this mean?"

His fingers curled over hers, and he pulled her to her feet. "The risk to you—and to the fabric of fate, the future and everything that's meant to be—is too great for us to wait around and get to know each other," he said. "The wedding has to take place tonight."

CHAPTER TEN

Dec stood on the sidewalk outside Psychopomps headquarters, scowling at the text he'd just gotten from Trevor:

Sorry, not up for it.

"What the fuck, Trev?" he muttered, then hit Trevor's number.

"Dec, my answer is no," Trevor said as soon as he answered.

"I need you to be there," said Dec. "What is up with you?"

Trevor sighed. "I've just been off lately, man, and I didn't want to bother you with it."

"Bother me? We've been friends for thirty years. You helped me reattach my arm a few weeks ago." Motherfucking Shades had almost torn it clean off.

There was a long, heavy pause. "I know, man. I know." Trevor's deep-bass voice rumbled with regret. "What's the occasion, though? Your messages were awfully cryptic."

Dec gritted his teeth. Aislin had insisted that no one outside of immediate family know about the wedding before it happened to prevent last-minute desperation-driven attacks on Galena. But she'd agreed to let him have Trevor as his witness, and Dec had been counting on him being here, a steady presence at his side. "It's a pretty big deal," he finally said. "Can't say more than that until you're at HQ."

"Psychopomps headquarters. Yeah. No, thanks."

Dec frowned at the uncharacteristic contempt and anger in the Ker's voice. "At what point are you going to tell me what's wrong? Has something happened? Are things with Greg okay?"

"We broke up last week. And good riddance. All we did was fight."

Dec's eyebrows shot up. Trevor had really liked the guy, and up until a week or so ago, he'd told Dec they'd been getting along great. "Are you sure you're okay?"

"Remember when you told me I should consider taking a vacation? That's what I'm doing. I just need to step away from it, man. I'm tired. I'm pissed at Moros. I need to get some distance. Can you let me do that?"

"Sure," he said. But it stung. "Before I let you go, I need to ask you something. It's important."

"Shoot."

"Moros said you Marked a guy named Jian Lee, and he was a research assistant for Galena Margolis. Can you tell me anything about him?"

Trevor grunted. "You know I also Marked your father's killer, right? This felt like the same thing. Justice."

And Trevor had willed Jian to commit suicide, something he hadn't done in all the years Dec had known him. "That bad, huh?"

"This is exactly why I need a break. I'm fed up with the whole game, and my part in it." There was a long pause. "Good luck tonight. I gotta go." Trevor hung up.

Dec cursed. Something was up with Trev, but he had absolutely zero time to deal with it. The last several hours had passed in a haze. He'd taken Galena back to Cacy's apartment and gone back to his place to crash for an hour. His dreams had been filled with her face—the way it had looked when Aislin had told her that the marriage must be consummated for Galena to become immortal. He'd woken up feeling sick. What the hell had he agreed to?

Last night, he'd acted on impulse, out of a pure, compelling desire to make this easier for Galena. He'd joked with her and generally made an ass of himself, but it had worked, for a few minutes. She had laughed and smiled, and, goddamn, she was gorgeous when she smiled. But after she'd found out that tonight was the night, she'd withdrawn.

He couldn't blame her. Right now he wanted to do the same thing. And that's why he was here. Maybe there was another way to keep her safe—by ending the threat completely.

Dec strode into the soaring lobby of the Psychopomps tower and walked straight to the central desk. Walter was the receptionist on duty, his fingers tapping lightly at one of the many screens arrayed in front of him. Dec leaned on the counter. "How's business?"

Walter smoothed his hand over his thinning auburn hair. "Steady. But your sister's been tightening security and clearances, and a few of our cousins are a bit irritable about being left out of whatever's going on."

Dec was glad to hear it. The less his gossipy aunts, uncles, and cousins knew, the better. "So am I on the list?" He'd been pacing his apartment nonstop all morning—and then this idea had occurred to him. Now he just had to follow through and manage to keep his anger under control while he did. "I want to see my brother."

A line of concern appeared between Walter's brows. "Yeah. You and Cacy have clearance to see him, but Aislin asked that she be notified."

Dec gave Walter a wry smile. "Then let her know. Which elevator?"

"He's on Level Four, so last one on the right. I'll let the guard know." He pressed a button on his earpiece and began to talk to someone else as Dec walked away. In his faded EMS T-shirt and old jeans, Dec got a few disapproving glances from the suits who were coming in for meetings, but he didn't give a fuck. It was one of the privileges of the being the Charon's brother.

The guard at the elevator nodded in greeting. "Mr. Ferry."

Dec nodded in return. "Level Four, please."

The guard ushered him inside and accompanied him up to Level Four, which was a black hole of mystery to most employees of Psychopomps. But Dec knew it for what it was—the prison for Ferrys who had abused their powers. The Charon presided over their hearings, reviewed the evidence, and pronounced the sentence, which could range from death to a few days in a cell. Whenever possible, they preferred not to surrender family members to the police—too much risk of disgruntled Ferrys blabbing their secrets to the wrong people. It did happen sometimes, but their father had been a master of keeping Ferry business within the family. Dec imagined Aislin would follow in his footsteps.

The elevator door slid open, and Dec was greeted by two more armed guards standing in the entrance area to the corridor of cells. It wasn't a long hallway; there were only eight cells and two interrogation rooms at the end of the corridor, with a separate exit. The overhead light bounced off the white ceramic tiles. "I'm here to see Rylan."

Walter must have called ahead, because no one asked any questions. Dec followed one of the guards, who was armed with an electroshock baton, to a door halfway down the short corridor. It was solid metal with a video screen set into it.

It showed an image of Rylan, his dark hair neatly combed, sporting a short, thick beard that told Dec he hadn't shaved since he'd been imprisoned. He looked youthful—he was fit and broad-shouldered, about the same height as Dec—but in reality, he was well over a hundred years old. He was sitting at a metal table bolted to the wall, playing chess by himself.

"When he's not sleeping, he's playing," commented the guard. "Never seems to get tired of it."

When he'd been young, Rylan had taught Dec how to play. Dec had idolized his older brother in those days. "He's nearly unbeatable," Dec said sadly.

The guard chuckled. "What does that really mean, though, if you're playing yourself?"

Dec stared at the screen as Rylan slid his rook across the board. "No idea."

The guard stood in front of the screen to let it read his facial biometrics. "Mr. Ferry. You have a visitor."

Rylan looked up at the camera, his brown eyes sharp. "Who?"

"It's me, Ry," said Dec. He'd expected to feel fury at seeing his brother again. The last time they'd been together, Rylan had shot him in the neck and left him to die. If Aislin hadn't showed up and assumed the power of the Charon, Dec wouldn't have made it. He shuddered at the memory of those few desperate moments when he felt his grip loosening, when he'd stared at the ceiling of Galena's apartment and wondered where he'd go—Heaven or Hell. "I want to ask you about some stuff."

Rylan rubbed his knuckles along his unshaven jaw. "Come on in."

The guard drew his finger across the video screen, and the door clicked, swinging open. "Ten minutes. That's the Charon's policy," the guard told Dec. "Press the emergency button if you need us sooner than that."

Rylan was standing next to his table, smiling. "That's not going to be necessary, Charlie. I think Dec could handle anything I threw at him."

The guard nodded at him. "Sure, Mr. Ferry." He gave him a polite smile and closed the door, locking Dec in.

Dec turned to find Rylan watching him. "I didn't expect you to come," Rylan said quietly.

"I didn't expect to, either. I pretty much thought I was done with you. Turns out I'm not."

Rylan pulled out the chair at the table. He pushed it toward Dec, its metal legs scraping along the floor, then backtracked and sank onto the single bed, the only other place to sit in the room.

Dec sat down in the chair. "How's mortality treating you?" Aislin had stripped Rylan of his immortal status in the aftermath of his murderous scheming.

"I haven't been this achy since I was a teenager with growing pains."

He hadn't been a mere human since then, either. "Has she sentenced you yet?"

Rylan tilted his head. "I figured she'd keep you in the loop, Declan. She always seemed to trust you. What's changed?"

"Don't try that mind-twisting shit with me. Aislin can tell me when she's ready."

Rylan held up his hands. "I wasn't twisting anything. I just thought the two of you were close."

Dec didn't feel that close to Aislin right now. He wasn't quite sure where she stood when it came to Galena and the potential repercussions of her work. But he wasn't about to admit that to Ry. "I have some questions."

Rylan leaned back, looking totally relaxed. All his desperation from last week seemed to have melted away, replaced with his usual smooth veneer—and the barely perceptible cunning underneath. "And you think I have answers? I've been locked up in here since Aislin took over." He raised his eyebrows. "Wait, has something happened?"

"I do think you might have answers," Dec said, avoiding his brother's last question. "Did you choose Mandy, or did she choose you?"

Rylan had worked with Mandy, a Ker, to kill seven people, including Dec and Ry's father. They'd hurt countless others—including Galena—in the process.

Rylan pursed his lips. "Why should I tell you that?"

Because Luciana had said her attacker's eyes had glowed red. "I thought the Kere couldn't make a move without Moros knowing. Aren't they all psychically connected to him or something?"

"More like soul-connected. But Mandy realized she could get around that. She came to me after learning about Galena Margolis. She said she'd resented Moros for decades and was dying to take him down, and she'd finally found the way to do it." He shook his head. "She seemed to really hate the guy. Anyway, she showed me that she could kill by choice, not just by command, and she offered to help me become the Charon—for a price."

"And it was that easy for you, to betray our father."

Rylan bowed his head. "No. And I wish I'd never been that weak. I'm ashamed of what I've done."

"I hope you don't expect me to buy this little remorse act you've got going on. The only thing you're ashamed of is getting caught."

"It doesn't matter anyway. When Aislin takes me before the Keepers, I fully expect the Keeper of Hell to claim me immediately. I'm sure that'll make all of you happy."

It didn't make Dec happy, but he felt there was a certain justice to it. The summit had been Rylan's idea—he'd set it as a trap for Moros, hoping to frame the Lord of the Kere and get him removed from power completely. It had almost worked, too. "When is the meeting?"

"The Keepers move slowly, luckily for me. They've agreed to the meeting, but they haven't given Aislin and Moros a time." Rylan raised his head, the curiosity alight in his eyes. "I wonder what would cause them to delay."

Dec stared obstinately at his older brother, knowing he'd use any information to his advantage. In fact, Dec was taking a risk being here at all, but his determination to find a different way to protect Galena drove him forward. "You said Mandy came to you. Did she mention whether any other Kere had slipped their leashes?"

Rylan smiled. "There's another rogue on the loose, isn't there?"

Dec folded his arms over his chest. "Do you know *how* Mandy managed to hide her actions from Moros?"

Rylan's eyes went wide. "There *is* another rogue. Has he gone after Galena Margolis again? That's it, isn't it?"

"If you're as remorseful as you claim to be, you'll tell me what I need to know."

"But why are *you* here asking me these questions? Why would you be particularly concerned about Galena and her research?"

"None of your fucking business."

Rylan's eyes narrowed. "If I give you information, you will give me some in return. I have just one question."

"Depends on how forthcoming you are."

Rylan's smile was chilling. "Fair enough."

"Tell me how Mandy fooled Moros."

"No idea. She said she could feel it when she had her freedom back, and then she tried to do as much damage as she could. But that freedom obviously wasn't permanent."

"What do you mean?"

"At the end, she was under Moros's command. Otherwise, she would have escaped before she was punished. So whatever she'd managed to do, it didn't last." Rylan laughed quietly. "It was shortsighted of Moros to kill her before asking her these questions himself."

Dec couldn't disagree. He was guessing Moros had been pissed—and also pretty eager to show that he was in control again. Too bad it didn't seem to have been true. "Who else were you working with?"

"Because it didn't end with Mandy," said Rylan, nodding like he heard all Dec's thoughts. "The Lord of the Kere is in a weaker position now than he ever was. I wonder if Aislin is bold enough to ask the Keepers to punish him. I should talk to her. I could help."

Dec rolled his eyes. "Give it a try." He stood up abruptly from his chair. "But you killed our father, Ry. If you think she'll ever forgive you for that, you don't know her at all."

Rylan smiled. "Oh, I know her very well. Better than you do, I think. She's as ruthless as I ever was. Maybe more so." There was a glint of admiration in his eyes. "But she's also more cautious. With me helping her, though, we could take Moros down and fold the Kere into our empire."

"What makes you think you can control them any better than Moros has? Be careful what you wish for, Brother."

There was a beep, and then the guard's voice filled the room. "Ten minutes is up, Mr. Ferry."

Rylan shook his head. "Now you answer *my* question."

"What is it?"

"Tell me what Father said to you right before he entered the Afterlife."

Dec's heart kicked fiercely against his ribs. "No."

Rylan *tsk*ed. "You said you'd answer my question. I thought you were an honorable man."

"I guess I'm less honorable than you thought."

"But it's why you're here. It's why you came to me. You've never been interested in our business, Dec. You've always stayed as far from the politics as possible. So the reason you're here now . . . it's because of whatever Father said to you."

The door opened, and Dec took another step backward. "Good luck, Ry. I hope the Keeper of Hell has mercy on you."

Rylan's dark stare was piercing. "It's *her*, isn't it? Galena Margolis. He told you to protect her."

Dec took a quick step forward, cocking his fist. Rylan jumped to his feet. "Guards! Help!" he cried.

A firm hand closed over Dec's shoulder. "Come on, Mr. Ferry," said Charlie. "Give yourself some space."

Dec shrugged him off but walked back to the door. As he stepped into the hallway, Rylan called out, "Wait."

Dec turned back to him.

"Good luck, Dec," Rylan said quietly, his pretense at fear gone. "You've been given an impossible task. I don't envy you at all."

And with that, Charlie put a closed door between Dec and his brother.

CHAPTER ELEVEN

Galena clutched Eli's hand tightly as they came to a stop in front of the building that had once housed her beautiful lab. It was still standing, but that was all that could be said for it. Construction workers were clearing debris, and the police had cordoned the place off with crime-scene tape, but Galena was hoping they'd let her take a look at what had been salvaged, to see if any of her equipment had been spared.

"You up for this?" Eli asked.

"No," she said quietly. "But I need to do it." She looked around. "I thought Dr. Cassidy would be here by now." She had called this morning and asked to meet Galena here to discuss next steps. Galena was eager to see a friendly, sympathetic face.

Eli frowned and looked uneasily at the bombed building. "When was the last time you heard from her?"

Galena put a hand to her stomach, which threatened to rebel at the caution in Eli's voice. "Only an hour ago." She pulled her phone from her pocket and dialed, her fingers shaking. *Not her too. Please not her too.* The phone rang several times but then switched to voice mail. "Oh God," Galena whispered, tears burning her eyes.

Eli's arms closed around her. "Hey. Calm down. We don't know that anything's happened."

"You know it has," squeaked Galena. She felt like she was being strangled. First, all her volunteers, and then Ankita and Jian. Her poor neighbors who had been home when her apartment exploded. And now Dr. Cassidy? "Eli, when is this going to stop?"

His only answer was in the protective tightening of his arms, the way his hand held her head to his shoulder. Galena closed her eyes. Eli had died because of her research. He'd been hurt over and over again trying to keep her safe. And now Declan Ferry was about to offer himself up, too.

Was it worth it? Was she worth it? What if her vaccine didn't work? What if it was all for nothing?

She had to make sure it wasn't. She owed it to all of them.

"Galena?"

Galena gasped and turned toward the voice, relief flooding through her. Dr. Elaine Cassidy was walking toward them from the direction of the tent the police had erected about a block away, her silvery-gray hair cropped close to her head, her heels clicking on the sidewalk. She looked more like a businesswoman than a scientist, but she'd done brilliant work in identifying the ways in which certain viruses mutated, and without her research, Galena wouldn't have made some of her own discoveries. "I'm so glad to see you," Galena said, wiping tears from her eyes.

Dr. Cassidy's brow furrowed as she took in Galena's appearance: her pallor, the circles under her puffy red-rimmed eyes. "Galena, I'm concerned about you."

Galena shook her head. "No, I-I'm okay." She pulled away from Eli's embrace and let him greet her boss, who gave him a perfunctory hello and a brisk handshake.

Dr. Cassidy's mouth set as she looked up at the building. Through the glass front doors at the entrance, they could see the construction workers dragging damaged equipment up from the basement. "The police confirmed this morning that the bomb had been placed in one of the nanopore sequencers," she said. "The damage is in the billions."

Heat suffused Galena's face. "I'm so sorry."

"G, why are *you* apologizing?" Eli asked. "You're the victim here." He looked down at Dr. Cassidy. "Any hint of who did this? What about that lab assistant—Jian Lee?"

"Well, it's innocent until proven guilty, but his movements over the last week are definitely making him a target for investigators. Unfortunately, the surveillance videos were scrambled by someone with a high level of technical expertise," Dr. Cassidy replied. Her eyes met Galena's. "Jian is dead, but he's not the only suspect. The detectives are making their list of persons of interest. They'll be bringing them in for questioning as soon as they finish collecting evidence from the crime scenes."

Galena clasped her hands in front of her. She was glad to hear about the investigation, but she had little doubt Jian was responsible. She would never have thought Jian capable of this kind of evil, but the moment Moros had announced Jian had killed himself, a feeling of dread had settled deep in her gut. He was dead now, though. If he *was* guilty, he'd already punished himself.

"I just want to salvage what's left and rebuild," Galena said. "I'm eager to get back to work."

And after she got through tonight, she'd be able to do exactly that, and with a lot less fear. Too bad it felt like she was made of fear right now, *especially* at the thought of what she had to do tonight.

"Well, that's something I need to discuss with you," said Dr. Cassidy. "It's why I asked to meet you here. I met last night with the university's administration, and we agreed that you should take a leave."

Galena stared at her. "What?"

"Your lab, the one we constructed to your exact specifications, has been destroyed. It's going to take a few months to rebuild it." Her voice took on a frustrated tone as she gestured at Galena's face and body. "And with all due respect, you don't look prepared to return to work. We think you should take some time."

Eli looked back and forth between the two of them. "Isn't her research time-sensitive? I thought you guys wanted it to move forward as soon as possible."

Dr. Cassidy looked annoyed. "The world has been waiting decades for this vaccine, young man. It can wait a few months longer."

"But I *need* to work," said Galena, her voice rising in desperation. "It's the only thing that'll help me feel better."

"Research isn't about making you feel better. It takes precision and total focus," said Dr. Cassidy.

"I know that," Galena snapped. "I'm pretty damn good at it."

Dr. Cassidy gave her a pitying look. "Of course you are. That's why you're at Harvard. But we need to work with police to figure out who is responsible for last night's tragedy, and then we need to make some decisions about rebuilding. I trust you to cooperate with the police. Once the investigation has concluded, we'll make a decision about your future here."

Galena suddenly felt hollow. "My future here?"

Dr. Cassidy's heels scraped against the sidewalk as she shifted her weight. "After a devastating event like this, one that took many lives in our community and destroyed one of our most recently constructed facilities, the administration must carefully evaluate the psychological profiles of anyone involved and—"

"Wait. Do you think I actually had something to do with this?"

Dr. Cassidy met Galena's eyes. "You've been under enormous pressure."

"I've been under enormous pressure for years!"

"That's a pretty backhanded way of making an accusation," Eli said, his voice hard. "And it's totally unfair to Galena. She's busted her ass every day since she got here, trying to get this vaccine ready. How can you—?"

"I'm sorry, Galena." Dr. Cassidy stepped back, shaking her head. "I know this is disappointing. I wanted to do you the courtesy of telling you in person, but now I need to get back to work. Like I said, please cooperate with detectives on this case. They're eager to get to the bottom of it."

"Dr. Cassidy?" A young woman with brown hair and glasses poked her head out of the police tent and called out in a hesitant voice, "The detective has a question, and I'm not sure how to answer it."

Dr. Cassidy's stern face melted into a smile. "I'll be right there." She turned back to Eli and Galena. "My new assistant. This isn't exactly how she'd planned to spend her second week on the job," she said, and Galena didn't miss the accusation in her tone. "Please excuse me."

And with that, she turned and walked back in the direction of the tent. Galena stared after her, stunned. "She thinks I did this," she whispered.

Eli put his arm around her. "She didn't say that. It's going to be easy to prove you didn't have anything to do with it, G. I'll be surprised if they even label you as a person of interest."

Galena watched as one of the construction workers carried Danny's shattered screen into the lobby and dropped it onto a pile of broken equipment. "If you say so."

He took her hand and pulled her toward a bus stop. "What would you say to something to eat? We don't have to be at Psychopomps for another few hours."

Just the mention of it sent Galena's heart rate skyrocketing. "I'm not that hungry."

Eli tugged her hand as an amphibious bus turned a corner and rumbled toward the stop. "Come on. Humor me?"

She squeezed his fingers and let him pull her onto the bus. The ride to Chinatown was about twenty minutes, first through the Charles River canal zone and then across the river into Boston.

Galena leaned her head on her brother's shoulder and stared out the window as the bus chugged through the chaotic waterway. She'd been so excited to move here from Pittsburgh, so ready to leave all the misery of that place behind and start over in this new city. And now it was all falling apart.

It was hard not to want to give up, just to lie down and do nothing. Arrogant belief in her own ability to save lives had kept her going. Sheer determination. It's what would get her through the night to come, what would enable her to take off her clothes and—

"Hold her legs," the blond one snapped. Iron fingers grabbed her ankles and wrenched them to the side.

Galena shuddered. She couldn't let herself remember. She wouldn't survive if she did. *Dec is a good man. He won't hurt you. He's handsome and sensitive, and you're lucky.* She chanted silently to herself all the way to Chinatown, trying to convince herself it was true.

Eli got to his feet as the bus rattled to a stop. She followed him as he got off onto the crowded street and walked half a block to a noodle place. From the sidewalk, Galena could smell roasted meat, alluring and mysterious. Eli grinned. "Cacy brought me here a few days ago. They have the most amazing food. The Szechuan noodles make your mouth feel like it's been lit on fire."

She smiled in spite of her dark mood. She and Eli had been raised on canned protein slurry and stale carb bars, with the occasional can of real green beans or peaches as a special treat. And now Cacy seemed determined to expand Eli's horizons. "I could give it a try."

He got them a tiny table at the back of the restaurant, reasonably private. Once they'd ordered and had little cups of tea sitting in front of them, Eli gave her a searching look. "How are you feeling about tonight?"

Galena let out a half-hysterical burst of laughter. "Must you ask?"

He shrugged. "You're my sister. I care about you, and I know this is scary. I wish you weren't in this position."

"I guess I should be glad Dec agreed to it."

Eli smiled and looked away. "Yeah. That was a nice surprise."

"Wait. He said you went to talk to him. What did you say?"

He gave her this wide-eyed innocent look. "I just told him what happened after he left Aislin's office."

She was certain he'd said more than that. She'd thought Dec had proposed all on his own, that perhaps he even liked her enough to be willing to give it a try, but now she knew her brother had guilted him into it. "Thanks," she murmured.

Eli frowned. "What's wrong?"

Galena stared at a loose tea leaf in her little cup. Drowned. "Eli, is there any other way to make me immortal?" She looked up, struck by sudden inspiration. "Do you think Moros would make me a Ker? Would that work?"

Eli's eyes half-closed. "No, Galena, that's not possible. Not for you."

But Galena's blood was suddenly pumping with the same excited urgency she always felt when she was on the verge of a breakthrough. "Why not? I mean, you're bulletproof. Even stronger than Dec or any of the Ferrys. And you didn't have to marry anyone to become that way."

"But I did have to give up my soul," Eli said quietly. "Moros reached inside me and pulled it right out. It still hurts, even though it's not there." He grimaced and rubbed his hand over his chest. "It's how he controls us. All of us."

She leaned forward. "But he doesn't control everything you do."

"As long as I'm doing what he wants."

"But he wants me to finish my research. He said so himself. If it's so important to him, why can't he make me like you?"

"You're saying you'd give up your soul to finish this research?"

She sat back, that hollow feeling growing inside her. "I already feel like I am, Eli. That's what tonight feels like." What made it even worse was that Dec was having to do the same.

"But Dec really cares about you, G. He won't hurt you."

It's not him I'm worried about. Her memories were there, always there, just waiting to break free. "Do you think Moros would talk to me? Would he even consider it?"

Eli's jaw clenched. "No. He wouldn't. Because you're not qualified."

"Why not?"

"Do you know what I do every day? I Mark people for death. I touch them, and then, just with my thoughts, I determine how they'll die. Heart attack. Car accident. Gunshot wound. You're all about saving lives."

"So are you! You're a paramedic, for God's sake!"

"I do try to save lives, G. But I've also taken them. A lot of them."

"Well, yeah, when you were in the army, but—"

"No, G. Not when I was in the army."

Galena stared at her brother. "What are you talking about?"

Eli let out a slow breath. "Nothing. I'm just saying that Kere have to take lives, and it's not the kind of thing I want *you* to have to do."

The waitress came and set down two bowls in front of them. Eli thanked her while Galena gazed down at the thin noodles floating in orange-red broth, already knowing she wouldn't be able to take a single bite. *It's not the kind of thing I want* you *to have to do.*

She looked at her brother as he hunched over his meal, slurping up the fiery noodles. She couldn't bear to tell him what she was thinking. She didn't want him to hurt more for her than he already did, but she couldn't help the swirl of betrayal coiling inside her.

Eli didn't want her to have to end people's lives.

What he didn't realize was that it felt like she was sacrificing her own instead.

CHAPTER TWELVE

Shit," Dec said as he took in what lay before him. In the center of the room was a massive wooden table, its unusually tall legs decorated with images from Greek mythology of Charon, the ferryman of the dead. In the center of the table was etched the symbol of the Ferry: the raven, wings spread for flight. Their family motto, *Fatum Nos Vocat*, was carved along the edges of the table. And at the head of the table was a chair. His chair.

He looked down at himself. He was wearing a suit, minus the tie. He couldn't stand ties. But now he wished he'd gotten over himself and worn one, if only to give him something to tug at when he felt the invisible noose tightening.

Every time he thought about tonight, he felt a completely confusing mix of excitement and guilt. He didn't know whether he was looking forward to being with Galena—or dreading it. "It's what she wants," he told himself. "She chose this."

But only because her other choices were even more hellish.

"I chose it, too," he mumbled.

For him, there really was no other choice. Not one he could live with, at least.

The door to the room opened, and Cacy walked in. For once, his little sister was dressed conservatively. Her black hair was loose around her shoulders, and her dress was a simple deep-purple sheath. Her eyes met his. "Eli and Galena are going to come down in a minute. I wanted to see how you were doing."

He laughed weakly and ran a hand through his hair. "How should I be?"

Cacy gave him a sympathetic look and then came over and hugged him. "You're doing a good thing, Dec. I know it's weird, but it's still good."

"I hope Galena agrees with you," he muttered, staring at the table. "Does she know what's going to happen?"

"Aislin and I explained it to her." She made a pained face. "She's pretty nervous."

Dec turned as the door opened again. "Me t—" His words died in his throat as Galena walked in, accompanied by Eli, who was wearing dark slacks and a white button-down, and Aislin, in a black skirt and emerald-green top.

"Seamus is preparing his materials," said Aislin, gesturing at the door at the rear of the chamber. Dec remembered the first time he'd met Seamus—he'd been sixteen and nervous as hell. Climbing up on that table and exposing his back had been the scariest thing he'd ever done.

Dec blinked as Galena walked forward. She was wearing a simple black dress with a V-shaped neckline, and it fit her body like it was made for her. It probably *had* been made for her. His gaze traveled from her slippered feet to her face, and he couldn't help the primal pulse of desire that throbbed inside him. But then their gazes locked, and her green eyes betrayed her fear. He walked forward, drawn by the plea he saw there. "Hey," he said gently. "You look beautiful."

"Thanks," she said, eyeing the table. "Is that where I'm supposed to go?"

Dec nodded. "You ready?"

"That's a really complicated question."

He took her hand and looked over her shoulder at Eli, who nodded at him, a silent thank-you. "Come on," Dec said. "I'll talk you through it."

Her fingers were cold in his as he guided her to the table. Usually during a Claiming ceremony, this room, which was in one of the basement levels of the Psychopomps tower, was filled with people. For people born into the family, it was a coming-of-age ritual. Dec had attended Cacy's and had stood by his father's side. Patrick Ferry had sat in the chair at the head of the table and held his youngest daughter's hands while she was Marked by Seamus Ferry.

Today Dec would sit in his father's place. He hoped Galena could take it. When they reached the table, she kicked off her slippers and looked down at the surface, her eyes tracing the wings of the raven. "How long will this take?" she asked in a small, quiet voice.

"Six hours," Aislin said. "We'll be done by midnight."

Galena's shaking hand gripped his, a tremor vibrating through Dec. He had the urge to put his arm around her and hold her close, but he didn't know how that would feel to her.

The door at the back of the room opened, and Seamus walked in, pushing his cart ahead of him. On the top rack of the cart was his equipment: the tattooing needle, a bowl filled with black ink, and a knife. When Galena saw it, she went very still. "I," she began in a choked voice. "The knife. I—"

"It's not for you," the old man said as he plodded forward, his gnarled hands and thick knuckles protruding from the sleeves of his long black robe. Seamus Ferry was one of the oldest Ferrys alive, though no one knew exactly how old he was. He hadn't retired yet, just aged very, very slowly.

"A Claiming today, is it?" he said in a gravelly voice, his beady brown eyes focusing on Galena. "Mmm. Good. A Claiming."

Dec could feel Galena's horror through their joined hands, and suddenly it was too much. He wrapped his other arm around her waist and sighed with relief when she leaned into him.

Seamus pushed his cart against the table and gestured at it. "Well, get up here, dear. When you're laid out, we'll begin the Marking."

Galena looked back at Eli and then up at Dec. Silently, she sat down on the table and scooted back, then turned onto her stomach. Cacy strode to the side of the table and straightened Galena's skirt so it covered the back of her thighs. The soles of her bare feet, white and soft-looking, faced the ceiling. Dec tried not to stare at her body, but it was pretty much impossible.

"Who Claims this human as a Ferry?" Seamus asked in a loud voice, his Irish accent thick and lilting.

Dec cleared his throat and said his line, though it felt like it was coming from someone else. "I, Declan Cian Patrick Ferry, Claim her."

"And who will witness this Claiming by your side?"

Dec felt a pit in his stomach. He'd wanted it to be Trevor. He looked around. "I . . ."

"I will," said Cacy. She came to stand next to him, and he gave her a smile tinged with sadness. She linked her arm with his as Eli edged closer to the table where his sister lay before them. He looked a little pale.

"And what does the Charon say about this pairing?" asked Seamus, looking at Aislin.

She was silent for several seconds, and Dec's jaw clenched. But then she said, "I offer my blessing." Aislin lifted a flat wooden jewelry box she'd brought with her. "And a Scope, forged by the Keepers of the Afterlife."

Seamus nodded. Then he looked down at Galena. "And you, my dear. Give us your name."

Galena's cheek was pressed to the polished wood of the table. "Galena Rachel Margolis," she said, her voice barely above a whisper.

"And do you consent to be Claimed by Declan, to be linked to him by blood and body, to affix your fate to his until death?"

She nodded, her lips pressed tight together.

"Speak, dear. We need to hear your voice," chided Seamus.

Galena glanced at Dec, then looked away. But then she looked back, and their gazes held. He felt the oddest swooping sensation, like the floor had dropped out from under him. "I do," she said, her voice a little louder.

"And do you understand the blessings and limitations of this bond? Do you understand that, should Declan choose to relinquish his Mark and Scope, or should he become incapacitated and unable to perform his duty as a Ferry, or should he be deprived of his title by the Charon, your status as a Ferry will also be voided, until such time as he returns to his duties?"

Every one of Dec's muscles was knotted tight. This was it. She would be stuck with him, and he would be stuck, too, unable to retire even if he wanted to, unless he wanted to make her vulnerable again.

"I do," said Galena, still looking at him, her eyes wide and trusting. Something about her expression loosened the tension in his body the slightest bit.

Seamus gestured at Galena's back. Her dress was fastened by a row of small buttons from the nape of her neck to the base of her spine, a long, elegant line. "Declan, do the honors."

Slowly, Dec reached down, and he caressed Galena's cheek with his fingertips. "Yeah?" he whispered.

"Yeah," she whispered back.

Her consent allowed him to move his feet, which carried him to the side of the table next to Eli, who stepped out of the way for him. This had to be weird for the guy. He was watching someone undress his sister. Dec purposefully did not meet Eli's eyes as his fingers began to work the buttons, revealing Galena's smooth, pale skin. She was so slender that the wings of her shoulder blades stood out sharp and fragile in the terrain of her body. Her flesh rippled with goose bumps as it was exposed to the cool air in the room. Dec fought the urge to run his palm down her back, just to connect with her, to offer her some warmth. It seemed to take forever for him to reach her waist, and he took a moment to look at her.

His bride.

Damn, she was beautiful. Dec returned to the head of the table, where he met her eyes once more. "Still yeah?" he murmured as he looked at the buttons that held this specially made dress together at her shoulders.

"Still yeah," she said, her voice a little raspy.

Dec's hands trembled as he undid the button on her right shoulder, then her left. He held his breath as he pulled the fabric away and tucked it under her arms, his fingertips only inches from the swells of her breasts pressed to the unforgiving table. Galena's back was bare. The bumps of her spine, the faint ripple of her rib cage as she breathed . . . He could see so much, and the desire to see more tugged at him, a restless hunger he hadn't felt in a long time.

Seamus leaned forward and poked Dec in the shoulder. Dec reluctantly tore his eyes from Galena's body. "Take your seat, Declan, and surrender your blood."

Galena blinked. Dec slipped off his suit jacket and handed it to Cacy. He undid the buttons at his right wrist and rolled his sleeve up to his elbow. As Seamus pushed the cart within his reach, Dec took his seat in the wooden chair at the head of the table, so he and Galena were face-to-face.

"G . . ." Eli said nervously.

"You are not authorized to speak, Ker," snapped Seamus.

"It's all right," said Cacy. "He's her brother."

"Then feel free to stand there and look menacing, but don't interrupt again."

Eli's eyes briefly glowed red, but he didn't say another word. His gaze kept darting between the knife and Galena, who was now staring at the blade as Seamus lifted it from the cart and handed it to Dec.

"Surrender your blood, that she may be Claimed," said Seamus.

"You don't have to watch," whispered Dec. "Close your eyes."

She did, tightly, and Eli gave him a grateful look, confirming to Dec he'd done the right thing. He looked down at the knife in his hand. This was the most sacred of commitments, and he'd only just learned his intended's middle name. He didn't even know how old she was or whether she was a vegetarian or what made her laugh or . . . if she could ever grow to love him. This was fucking insane.

Protect her and you protect the future, his father's voice whispered in his head.

Dec brought the knife down and sliced the length of his forearm, the blood welling immediately as he held his arm over the bowl. It hurt like a motherfucker, but the pain came with an odd sort of elation. The decision had been made. Now he just needed to see it through. Dec stared as the shining red drops fell from his skin and into the bowl of ink. Galena flinched at every tiny *plink*, like they were gun blasts.

After a few minutes, the ink glowed bright, his blood slicking in luminous, shimmering swirls within the ebony puddle. "Ah, that's enough," said Seamus. "Very good." He handed Dec a cloth, which he held over his arm to stem the flow. The wound would be healed long before this ceremony was over. Still, Dec could sense that the knife and the blood upset Galena, so he wound the cloth tightly over his forearm and slid his arm beneath the table, out of her line of sight. Eli nodded, and Dec nodded back.

Seamus stirred the bowl with the tip of the knife, then smiled. "Let's begin."

Dec took one of Galena's hands and interlaced their fingers as Seamus turned on the needles, which hummed with promise. Galena closed her eyes and tucked her face into her shoulder, and it made Dec's chest ache. During other Claiming ceremonies he'd witnessed, the Ferry sitting in this chair would murmur quietly to his or her intended, planting soft kisses on the beloved's brow as Seamus did his work.

Dec lowered his head and spoke quietly into Galena's ear, words only for her. "I'm in this with you, and I'll do anything you need. If you want me close, let me know. If you want me to give you space, push me away. But you're not alone."

Galena let out a soft, desperate whimper as the needles pierced her skin, as Seamus began to draw the raven, not from a stencil, not from a pattern, but purely from memory. He'd done it thousands and thousands of times before.

"I'm here," Dec whispered again.

She squeezed his hand. Hard. And then her other hand slid over the table and rose to touch his face. Her fingers threaded into his hair and pulled tight. She was keeping him close. The world shrank down to the few feet around him. He was only aware of her.

Dec closed his eyes as the needles hummed, as he inhaled Galena's honey-warm scent. It wasn't much. It was only a beginning. But to him, it felt like a miracle.

CHAPTER THIRTEEN

Galena," Dec whispered, "it's finished." His eyelashes fluttered against her cheek as he lifted his head.

"We're done?" she croaked.

"Your Mark is complete," said the old man. "Congratulations, and best wishes for a happy life together." And then she heard the tinny shriek of the cart wheels retreating toward the back of the room.

She raised her head, blinking as her vision swam and blurred. But then they landed on the man in front of her. His dark hair was sticking up in places, and his blue eyes were shot with concern. She'd spent the last several hours clinging to the sound of his voice. Her fingers were still tightly entwined with his, and she didn't want to let go.

"You did great," he said, his thumb stroking over her knuckles.

A glass of water was placed in front of her. Cacy smiled and stepped back. "Thought you might need that. You're all bandaged up and ready to go."

After she took a sip, Galena looked down to realize her dress had been buttoned over her shoulders once more. She reluctantly released Dec's hand and pushed herself up to sit on the table. Eli was leaning against it with an arm clutching his stomach. He looked like he was about to throw up. "You okay?" he asked, his voice tight.

"Are you?" she asked.

"Eli, she's fine. Go," said Dec. "I've got this."

Eli gave Dec a hard, searching look, then disappeared. Galena rubbed her eyes. "There is no scientific explanation for that," she muttered.

Dec chuckled. "You aren't kidding."

She glanced at Cacy. "*Is* he okay?"

Cacy nodded. "He just needs to attend to something urgent, and he's put it off for the past few hours, which made him not feel so good. But he'll be fine now. It's part of being a Ker."

"Ready to go?" Dec asked.

Galena forced a smile onto her face. "Ready." *So very not ready.* She kept her head down as she slid off the table. Dec stepped forward and steadied her with a hand on her elbow. The bandage over her back rubbed against the fabric of her dress. "It doesn't hurt that much."

"We put some numbing cream on it," said Dec.

Aislin stepped in front of Galena and offered her the flat wooden box she'd been holding. "This is the Scope, the Window to the Veil, to the Afterlife. It's your responsibility to safeguard it and keep it on your person at all times." She arched an eyebrow and looked over at Cacy, who scowled. "When there is a soul to be guided, you'll feel it. Dec will show you how it's done."

She opened the box to reveal a pendant exactly like the one Dec and the rest of them wore, a thick platinum disk perhaps an inch or so across with a raven etched into its surface. It was attached to a setting and a shimmery platinum chain. Dec reached around her and took it from the box. "May I?"

Galena nodded and lifted her hair. His fingers were warm against the nape of her neck as he fastened the catch, and the heavy Scope nestled in the hollow at the base of her throat.

Aislin turned to Dec. "We'll be making the announcement in the morning, once you have finished the Claiming."

Dec tensed. "All right. We'll talk to you tomorrow." He took Galena's hand and led her out of the room.

The ride back to his apartment was silent. Dec seemed distracted as he stared out the window at the amphibious vehicles and boats that zoomed by in the canal. In the distance, a siren screamed, and Dec frowned, leaning to try to see where it came from. Galena felt a pang of guilt. She knew he was a dedicated paramedic; Eli had told her as much. Did he resent being kept from his job?

As the amphibious limousine roared up the canal ramp and onto dry streets, Galena peered at the dark skyscraper in front of them, the apartment complex owned by the Ferrys. Her new home. It was farther from Harvard than she would have liked . . . but then again, was there anything left for her there? Everything felt so out of control.

And when the limousine came to a stop in front of the building, Galena's heart kicked into a frantic rhythm. This was it. After tonight, she'd be able to return to her research. Assuming Dr. Cassidy and the Immunology Department welcomed her back. But how could they not? They'd already invested so much in her, and she planned to deliver. She would consult with the university as her lab was rebuilt and get the vaccine trials back on schedule, perhaps in just a few months. It was possible. Especially because she'd only need one hour of sleep per day! When Cacy had told her that before the ceremony, Galena had been thrilled. Maybe the nightmares would disappear, too. It would be worth it.

She just had to get through the next few hours.

As they walked through the lobby toward the elevator, she glanced at Dec from the corner of her eye. His head was bowed, and his eyes were focused on a spot on the floor about six feet ahead. Very soon, she'd be closer to him than she'd been to anyone in years. A horrified thought occurred to her—that meant he'd see the scars. He'd see what they'd done, how damaged she was. She imagined a look of disgust on his handsome face. Now it felt like her heart was in her throat.

Dec took her hand as they stepped from the elevator onto his floor. He led her into his apartment and kicked his shoes off at the door, then cringed and placed them neatly next to a pile of boots. "We'll . . . uh . . . I'll clean it up a bit."

Her brow furrowed. His place wasn't that messy. In fact, it looked like no one lived here at all. It reminded her of her and Eli's apartment in Cambridge, actually, merely a stopping point for essentials—sleeping, bathing, eating—while the rest of life was lived somewhere else. "It's fine," she said. "I don't need much."

Dec looked at her with a half smile on his face. "You're serious, aren't you?"

She tilted her head at his bemused expression. "Why? Did you expect me to whine that you don't have fancy rugs or chandeliers or something? Do you know where I come from?"

He took a step closer to her. "I think I want to. Tell me about when you were a kid."

"Let's see. I went to Allderdice High School, and it was this massive crumbling old building at the top of a hill of cracked dirt. There used to be over a thousand students, but at that point, most kids didn't bother—it was more about surviving each day than planning for the future. There were maybe twenty people in my graduating class. And I remember there was this group of squatters that had taken over the whole rear wing of the building. We had to walk to class in packs, because we were afraid of being mugged."

"In the halls of your school? Why did you go, if it was so dangerous?"

"My dad said it would be a waste if we didn't." She smiled at a memory. "He walked us there every day and was waiting outside to walk us home when we got out of class. He was a big, gruff guy.

A veteran of the Texan Secession War. No one wanted to mess with him."

Dec's ice-blue eyes scanned her face. "Sounds like he recognized your potential."

Galena's heart ached at the memory of him. "He used to say that I owed the world something great."

"That's a lot of pressure."

She looked down at her hands. "It didn't feel that way, though. He had so much confidence in me that it was easy to believe he was right. It was also easy to believe I could do it."

"And you have," Dec said softly.

"Not yet."

"But you will."

She raised her head. The look in his eyes took her breath away. It was so solid, so steady, so certain. Just as confident as her dad had ever been. She smiled. "I think I will." *Assuming I can get through tonight.*

He must have seen the shadow of doubt flicker across her face, because he gave her a playful grin. "So do you prefer Mrs. Dr. Margolis-Ferry, or Dr. Mrs. Margolis-Ferry? Or just Dr.? Because your name is going to be on all the gossip sites. I've heard that I'm an 'inveterate bachelor.'"

"So they'll all want to know who snagged you?"

"Oh, yes." His black hair fell across his forehead. "I'm quite the catch."

Yes, you are. The thought came like a reflex, an easy, indisputable truth. "So they'll all be shocked when they find out you didn't marry a society beauty?"

His face became utterly somber. "No, I don't think they'll be shocked at all."

"But when they find out you've married a dry hard-core academic?"

His crooked smile returned. "They'll wonder why on earth you chose me."

Not really. They'd probably think she married him for his money. *Is marrying him for immortality any better?* "Dr. Mrs.," she said quickly.

"Dr. Mrs. it is," he murmured. He knew the score. He was too smart and too aware not to. But would he ever feel anything real for her? Was that possible?

"Dec . . ."

"Yeah?"

"I just . . . I just want you to know . . . I'm so glad it's you." She reached for his hand.

He laced his fingers with hers. "I wouldn't do this with just anyone," he said. "I hope you know that."

A breath shuddered from her as he caressed her face with the backs of his fingers. The touch made her heart skip and her body tighten.

But Dec frowned, looking at her with concern. "Do you want a drink?" he asked. "Whiskey, or a beer? It might help."

"Help?" She found herself staring at his mouth as he talked. He was the perfect height, so that his mouth was right at the level of her eyes. It had a nice shape: full bottom lip, a delicate curve in his upper lip, a hint of softness in his angular face.

"To relax you?" His thumb slid along her jawline, but there was uncertainty in his eyes.

She closed hers so she didn't have to see it. "No, thank you. Maybe . . . maybe we should just get it over with. Where should we do it?"

"Um. Okay." His hand fell away. "Where would you be most comfortable?"

"A bed, I guess."

She followed Dec into his bedroom. It was as plain as the rest of the apartment, just a wide mattress on a low platform, a bedside table, a videowall, and a set of floor-to-ceiling windows like the ones in Cacy's guest room. The view of the city was breathtaking.

This was it. This was the room where it would happen. *Move, Galena. Keep moving. You can do this.*

She turned, folding herself into Dec's side and feeling his body against hers. Within her mind, the memories shook the bars of their cages, a warning. But she shoved them back—tonight they needed to stay where they were. "It's been awhile since I've done this," she whispered, shifting so that her breasts were pressed to his chest, only thin layers of fabric between them. Conflicting signals cascaded through her, a subtle tightening, a craving, as well as a raw, instinctual fear.

"It's been a while for me too, actually," he said, taking her face in his hands. "And I know we don't know each other well. That'll have to come later. But I will tell you now—you are so beautiful, Galena."

His forehead touched hers. His nose skimmed her cheek. Galena's fingers curled into the sleeves of his shirt, feeling the rock-hard curves of his biceps. His scent was in her nose, his herbal cologne and a hint of sweat: masculine, hot, and dangerous. *Dangerous.*

No. She lifted her chin and her lips touched his. Dec tensed, maybe in surprise, but then he drew her closer, melding his mouth to hers. His lips were soft. The kiss was an act of pure sensuality, slow and restrained. He cupped her face as he slipped his tongue between her lips, not invading her but teasing and pulling back. Her hands slid up his shoulders to his neck. She wanted to laugh. This was okay.

It was better than okay.

It felt good.

She teased him back. The next time he touched her lip with the tip of his tongue, she met it with her own. Dec groaned softly and deepened the kiss, sliding his tongue along hers in one long delicious stroke. She weaved her fingers into his hair, over the spot where he'd been so badly injured protecting her. She was lucky to be here with him. How had she gotten so lucky?

Dec's breath rasped from his throat as their kiss grew more intense. A shiver of delight coursed down her spine—he liked kissing her, she could tell, and it gave her more confidence. Her hand skimmed down to his chest, smooth beneath his shirt. His heart was pounding just like hers. Between her legs, Galena felt a surprising warm slickness, and it felt like victory. Who knew this would be so easy? She arched, rubbing her chest against his.

Dec's hands fell to her hips, and he pulled her close.

Against her abdomen, she felt the long, hard jut of him.

"Grab her arms, fucker!" shouted the blond one as he slammed his pelvis against hers, ripping another scream from her throat. "She's scratching the fuck out of me!"

"I'm sorry," Dec said, panting.

Galena blinked. She was shivering, and she realized Dec was standing three feet away from her, watching her warily. His shaft stood out against the front of his pants, and she stared. "Why are you sorry?" she asked in a tremulous voice. *Oh God, what did I just do?*

Dec ran a hand through his hair. "Obviously, I did something wrong."

Her fingers flexed at her sides, buzzing with cold, tingling numbness. "N-no," she said. "You're fine."

His brows rose. "Are you joking? You just shoved me away."

Frustration sliced through her. "I didn't mean to," she said, trying to keep her tone soft and calm. "You just . . . startled me."

He looked down at the erection tenting his pants and chuckled. "Again . . . sorry?"

"Don't be." *Just push through this. He's ready, and so are you.* She walked forward and drew him near again, and he melted as her lips touched his, though the kiss was more cautious this time.

She pulled up his shirt, untucking it, and slid her palm along the rigid muscles at his waist. God, this man was made of muscle. Her fingernails scraped lightly along his side, and he shuddered, deepening their kiss again.

Galena's mind was a stormy sea of confusion. Low in her belly she felt a hunger, a compulsion to touch him. She couldn't recall being this attracted to anyone in her whole life. But her memories were trying to break free, and it was taking more and more effort to keep them caged. She forced her mind into blankness once again and started to unbutton Dec's shirt.

When her knuckles slipped over the taut ridges of his abs, Dec's hands dropped to her hips again. He slowly started to tug at her dress, inching it up her thighs. His hands had begun to tremble. Was he scared? Angry? Holding back?

Galena didn't want him to hold back. She wanted to get this done, because—

The black-haired one pulled her hair as he crushed her with his body.

Galena let out a choked whimper, and Dec stepped away from her again. "This is *not* okay," he said, turning his back and adjusting his pants.

"I'm fine," she said, her voice cracking. She cleared her throat and mashed her hands against her sides, imagining grinding those memories to dust. *Get out of my head,* she wanted to scream. But she knew they would just laugh. It was their territory, after all. They'd made it their home.

She wouldn't let them take this from her, though. She walked over to Dec and placed her unsteady hands on his broad back. But the memories had broken loose, and now they were stabbing at her, strikes of agony in her mind. *"Hold her down,"* they sneered. *"Hold her down, hold her down."* Tears burned Galena's eyes. *"Hold her down."*

Dec turned around, his blue eyes piercing. She stared up at him, waiting for him to kiss her again, bracing herself for it. She'd been enjoying it, and now those memories had turned it around, made her feel shaky and sick and desperate to hide. But she couldn't. She needed this to get her life back on track. With a desperate lunge, she reached for Dec, trying to bring him close again, but he caught her wrists and held them away from his body. "I'm sorry, Galena," he said, his voice heavy and low. "But I can't do this."

CHAPTER FOURTEEN

What?" Galena's green eyes were huge and filled with tears, but those had been there *before* he'd put a stop to this disaster. In fact, they were one of the reasons why he'd had to.

Dec held her wrists gently but firmly. "I don't think I can stand it."

She yanked her arms from his grip. "I'm sorry the task is so repulsive to you."

Dec laughed bitterly. His cock was throbbing with need, and his heart was still pounding. His entire body was alight with hunger, with the desire to bury himself inside her. "You're the scientist. I think you've got plenty of hard evidence that I don't find you repulsive at all."

She looked away. "Then why can't we keep going?"

He rubbed his hand over the back of his neck. "What was going on for you just now? You were remembering your attack, weren't you?"

Her eyes squeezed shut. "I was trying not to. I was doing my best!"

"But you were thinking of that while you were kissing me."

"Look, I can't help that, all right?"

"Galena, have you ever talked about what happened with anyone?" he said. "I mean, *really* talked?"

She recoiled. "Why the hell would I want to do that? I want to *forget* what happened, Dec, not spend more time remembering it!" Her voice had risen, shrill and breaking.

He held up his hands in surrender. "Fine. Do what you do. But I'm telling you now, I can't go through with this, not . . . not the way things are now." He didn't know how to say it without sounding like he was blaming her. "I don't think you're ready for this, Galena."

Her mouth was tight, every inch of her trembling with tension. "This is *my* choice," she said. "Don't patronize me. I get to decide when I'm ready."

"You get to decide, huh? *Only* you? And what am I, just a dick for hire?"

She blinked at him. "N-no . . ."

"Then what is this bullshit about it being your choice alone? 'No' is your choice, Galena. But it takes both of us to get to 'yes.'"

Her nostrils flared, and she waved a hand in the direction of his pants, where his cock was *finally* getting the message from his brain that this whole thing was a no-go. "You seemed pretty willing."

He rolled his eyes. "Has it occurred to you that I don't let my cock make my decisions for me?" He raked both hands through his hair, mad at her—and himself. He'd signed up for this, and he'd known full well that it wasn't exactly a love match.

"You're confusing me," she said. "You said you'd do this. You knew—"

"I didn't know how shitty it would feel."

"Shitty? That's how it felt to you?" She angrily swiped her hands over her eyes.

Dec let out an exasperated sigh. "Not all of it. Not *most* of it. But I felt you tense up when you remembered the attack. Do you have any idea how you look when that happens? How you *sound*?" Lost. Terrified. In agonizing pain.

"I can't help it!"

"I know. It was obvious."

"But you're holding it against me. And now you're refusing to do the one thing that would allow me to be safer."

"Because it would make me feel like a goddamn rapist!" he shouted. "What do you want me to do—ignore the fact that you're crying, that you're obviously terrified, and just fuck you anyway?" He shook his head. "You must think I'm a helluva guy."

"I'm sorry," she murmured. "I didn't think of it like that."

His frustration cooled, but only slightly. "I know. You were too busy trying to push yourself through it. But there's something I don't think you understand, Galena." He waited until her eyes met his. "It's not only that I want this to be good and *wanted*. It's that it won't work the way it is right now. For our connection to be complete, you can't just endure it. You have to enjoy it." He moved closer to her, his gaze on the fluttering pulse in the hollow of her throat, just above where her Scope lay against her skin. "You have to come."

It was the ultimate surrender, and both of them had to give in to it. Galena's face crumpled, and she bowed her head. "I hate this," she whispered.

Dec stared at the top of her dark-blonde head. He hated it, too. All of it. This whole situation was fucking unfair. And he'd let her down. He wouldn't have been able to live with himself if he'd gone along with it, but now she was nearly as vulnerable as before. She'd gone through the Claiming, had his blood inside her, had her Scope . . . but had none of the true benefits of being a Ferry. Dec exhaled, his anger deflating completely and leaving nothing but exhaustion and regret in its wake. He forced himself to walk over to Galena. He touched her arm. "I'm sorry."

"What do we do now?" she asked in a choked voice. "If you won't . . . I mean, if I can't . . . if *we* can't . . ." Her shoulders sagged.

Dec couldn't take it. He took her hand and tugged her toward him. She didn't resist as he coiled an arm around her waist. Her head came to rest on his shoulder. It was a cautious, hesitant embrace, but she closed her eyes and put her arms around him, holding on. "We'll figure it out," he said, and as he did, the hope rose up inside him that they actually could.

"I can figure out how to tailor a multidomain antigen to an individual human leukocyte antigen system, but I can't figure out how to do this," she mumbled.

Dec fought a smile. "This is more complicated."

"Nothing is more complicated than that."

"Wrong," Dec murmured. "Your mind is more complicated. Your heart too."

She pressed her cheek into his shoulder. "Why are you so nice to me?"

"I like you." From the moment he'd first seen her. "I want this to be okay for you, complicated or not."

She sighed. "I wouldn't know how to find *okay* if I had a GPS and a tracking beacon."

"Then I guess it's up to you and me to hunt it down."

She raised her head. "I don't know where to start."

He looked down at her hand on his waist, her fingers balled in the fabric of his shirt. "Let's start by getting comfortable with each other. There's no way we can go further until you feel safe with me."

She gave him a faint, sad smile. "How should we do that?"

"You're going to take a hot shower and change into something more comfortable. And then we're going to sleep."

"Don't you only need an hour of sleep each day?"

"Yeah, but I can feel it coming on, and at some point, I'm going to pass out. And it might be one hour, but it's like the deepest sleep you've ever experienced. You could rob me blind and toss me over a balcony, and I still wouldn't wake up."

Her smile brightened. "So I guess you'll have to trust me, too?"

Dec blinked, distracted by the curve of her mouth. "I guess I will." He walked over to the bag Cacy had dropped off with Galena's clothes and toiletries. He offered it to her and gestured toward his bathroom. "Take your time."

Galena accepted the bag and disappeared into the bathroom. When he heard the shower running, Dec changed into sweats and a T-shirt. His limbs were heavy with the weight of the day. More than if he'd worked a double shift. He lay down on his bed and stared at the ceiling. His life had changed drastically in the last twenty-four hours, and he was still reeling from it. And after all that, Galena still wasn't immortal.

Failure to consummate a Claiming was grounds for severing the bond. It was easily done. It had happened to his cousin Gael— she had the bond with her new husband nullified the day after the wedding, and Psychopomps guards had to reclaim the guy's Scope by force. Turns out he'd wanted to use it to commit corporate espionage by spying on his business rivals while in the Veil. Because he and Gael hadn't consummated the bond, that was it.

The guy's body was found in a canal a week later. The case was never solved.

If Dec wanted to get out of this, he could tell Aislin he tried, but the thought of Galena's face, her eyes on him while she lay on the wooden Marking table, crushed his urge to escape.

Protect her and you protect the future.

Dec folded his arm over his face. Aislin would be pissed it wasn't settled. She'd been hesitant to make Galena a Ferry in the first place, but she'd agreed to stick her neck out anyway. If it didn't work, she'd have to deal with the fallout.

But did she need to know?

Tomorrow, word would be spread far and wide that Galena was a Ferry. Kere and Ferrys alike would assume she was immortal. So wouldn't that incorrect assumption offer her a little bit of protection, at least until he and Galena were able to fumble their way through this?

Dec's head began to swim, threatening to plunge him into the black ocean of sleep. He fought it, wanting to be awake when Galena came out of the shower, wanting to gauge her level of comfort with sleeping in his bed. But it was too strong, and the last thing he heard before letting it take him was the water in the shower switching off.

CHAPTER FIFTEEN

Galena dried herself off and changed into a pair of pajama pants and a tank. She stared at herself in the mirror and tried to slow her racing heart. She was in Dec's bathroom. On the other side of that door was his bedroom.

Her head buzzed with fatigue, but her thoughts were chaotic. She'd embarrassed herself and managed to insult him in the process. He was, based on all the evidence she'd seen thus far, a thoroughly decent, unselfish, good guy. And then Galena had treated him like—what had he called it?—a "dick for hire." Like a prostitute, basically. She hadn't considered that he might feel conflicted about getting physical with her, because she was so focused on her own needs.

She silently reminded herself that he was going through this, too, and wordlessly promised him she'd try harder. Then she grabbed the doorknob and flung the door open, determined to make a fresh start.

He was lying on his back on the bed, his arm folded over his face, his chest rising and falling slowly. "Dec?" she asked as she cautiously approached.

His only response was a twitch of his fingers. She padded to the other side of the bed and sat on the edge, then got brave and crawled onto the mattress. He'd said he slept deeply, and he hadn't been kidding. She inched closer. He was wearing sweatpants, and they were low on his hips. His T-shirt had ridden up a tiny bit, and Galena could see the deep V-shaped indents of muscle at his waist. Her gaze skimmed over his chest, his muscular arms, his angular jaw, his soft mouth. Gripped by a powerful curiosity, she reached out with unsteady fingers and took his hand, carefully shifting his heavy, limp arm off his eyes. She laid it over his stomach and looked back to his face. She *liked* looking at his face.

His eyes moved beneath his lids. He was dreaming. His brow furrowed briefly and relaxed again. She smoothed her fingertips across his forehead. His skin was warm, inviting. Would he mind that she was touching him like this? Didn't he want her to feel safe with him?

Unable to stop herself, she drew her fingers down his straight nose, then over his cheekbones. There was something about the shape of his eyes, slightly upturned at the outer corners, that Cacy had, too. A family resemblance they didn't share with Aislin. Or Rylan, the one who had tried to kill her. At least, she didn't think he had the same eyes as Dec. She could barely remember his face. But she did remember how hard his hands had gripped her and the sharp smell of his cologne. Galena shuddered.

Then she leaned close and inhaled Dec's scent, mellow and earthy and comforting. She almost laughed—only hours ago it had signaled danger, but now it was like a "Reset" button, clearing her head. She moved until her nose was only a few inches from his neck. As her eyes skimmed over the dark stubble on his jaw, she drew his smell into her lungs. Her body responded instantly, but in an utterly confusing way. Parts of her tightened while other parts relaxed. What was that? Was she scared or excited? She bowed her head. She'd tried so hard to shut down her body that now it was a stranger to her.

And that was going to have to change. She'd been stunned when Dec had told her that to achieve the bond that would make her a Ferry, she had to climax, too. Was that possible? She'd been close the other day in the shower. She'd felt the waves of tingling pleasure, the clenching, the craving. But that had been her, touching herself. She'd been in control. Could she do the same with Dec?

If it was just him and her, maybe. But it wasn't. Her head was full of vicious men trying to carve her up and destroy her. Too bad she hadn't decided to research memory modification instead of immunology. What she wouldn't give to erase her recall of what had happened.

It wasn't fair. She'd had to endure that night—did it have to ruin the rest of her life as well? Because this should have been easy. Effortless. Dec was gorgeous. Undeniably, objectively, astoundingly attractive. Funny. Sensitive. *Aware.* This might be a miserable situation, but she couldn't think of a single person she'd rather be trapped with. And yet she was still struggling. So much so that he probably was dreaming of escape right now.

She owed it to him to get them through this. Maybe once they did, he could return to his old life if he wanted to. She hadn't heard anyone say they had to live together once their bond was consummated.

Galena sighed and got off the bed. Poor Dec. While he breathed, slow and quiet, getting the rest he needed, Galena absently wandered his room, then went out into his living area. It was a huge open space, with a kitchen and bar on one side and a large amount of exercise equipment on the other. A couch huddled in one corner, in front of a large videowall. She was struck by the fact that there were no pictures on his walls, not a single one. No paintings or sculptures, no trophies, no knickknacks on his shelves and side tables. He lived here, but he wasn't collecting things. Like he was walking lightly on this earth, letting his actions define him, not his possessions.

That was why the box caught her eye. It was sitting on an end table next to the sofa and was made of dark polished wood. She walked over to it and flipped the lid open, expecting to see cigars or something like that, but it contained a single antique digital picture frame. She picked up the frame, and as her thumb brushed the surface, it came to life.

She recognized Dec immediately. He had his arms around two people, one a woman and the other a little girl. An older man stood on the woman's other side, his arm around her shoulders. They were standing in front of a waterfall, the kind that Galena had seen only in history files. Except the image must have been recent, because Dec looked no different than he did now: tall, black hair, glacier-blue eyes, and wearing a smile that took her breath away. It was weightless, pure happiness. In the brief time she'd known him, she hadn't seen him smile quite like that.

The other people in the picture looked vaguely familiar. The little girl had black hair like Dec's and looked to be about nine or ten. The woman was hauntingly beautiful. She had blonde hair and hollow cheeks, and her eyes had the same upturned corners as Cacy and Dec's. Come to think of it, the little girl's did, too. The older man had a few gray hairs, but apart from that, he looked almost like an older version of Dec. Slightly leaner, and his eyes were a different shape, but . . .

"That was taken right before she got sick."

Galena let out a yelp and dropped the frame back in the box. It hit with a clatter and went dark. She spun around to see Dec standing behind her, his hair sticking up, his eyes on the frame where it lay in the box.

"I'm sorry," she said. "I didn't mean to snoop."

"It's all right." He closed the distance between them and picked up the frame. It came to life again at his touch. He tilted it toward her and pointed to the man in the picture. "That's my father." He touched the little girl's face with his fingertip. "That's Cacy. She was nine."

Galena blinked down at the photo. If Cacy had been nine . . . "How old were you?"

His eyes met hers. "In this picture? I was forty."

Galena's mouth dropped open. "Which would make you . . ."

He grinned. "Fifty-six. I guess I should have told you that."

She let out a hoarse laugh. "You've aged *really* well."

"It's part of the deal. Aislin is turning a hundred next year. And Rylan is—" He shook his head, obviously not wanting to talk about the brother who'd betrayed them all.

Galena pointed at the woman. "And is this your mother?"

He drew his finger across the screen, lightly caressing the woman's image. "Yeah."

"You said she got sick."

Dec nodded. His eyes were focused on his mother's face.

"She wasn't a Ferry?"

Dec sat on the arm of the couch, close enough for Galena to feel his warmth, for his scent to wrap around her once more. "She was. By marriage. But women who are active-duty Ferrys can't get pregnant. Their bodies wouldn't allow that kind of upheaval, and so if a woman wants to have a child, she has to relinquish the Scope and Mark until after she's given birth. It's a vulnerable time."

"But worth it, I imagine," Galena murmured. The woman had her arm around Dec, who looked only a few years younger than she did. But Galena could read the fierce pride in her expression. Her own mother had looked at Eli like that as he left for Ranger school. It had been the last time the four of them had been together. Her mother had cried for days after he left. "She looks really proud of you."

"She was. I'd just been promoted to chief at the station. She insisted we go on this vacation to the Arctic Circle colonies to celebrate. I hadn't taken a vacation in ten years, and she said that with the promotion, she was pretty sure I'd never take one again." He sighed. "She was right, too."

"If Cacy was nine, why hadn't your mother become a Ferry again?"

"Oh, she had, but they were trying to have another child." Dec's chin trembled. "She wanted another baby. She was a really good mom. She had a hard time getting pregnant, though, and then we got the news that she was sick. Cancer. It set in really quickly, like it had been waiting to pounce."

"But couldn't she just go on 'active duty' again? Wouldn't that have made her immortal like she was before?"

Dec shook his head. "Becoming a Ferry doesn't heal things that are already broken. It wouldn't have worked. My dad must have tried. He was desperate to save her, but the course had already been set. She was fated to die, and so she did. Less than a year after this picture was taken." His voice had become tight.

Galena put her hand on his arm. "I'm sorry, Dec. I can tell you still miss her."

"Yeah. She was the only one in my family who was proud of my decision to become a paramedic. My dad was pissed. He had a position all set up for me in the corporate office. My older brother and sister thought it was a joke. My extended family thought it was embarrassing. But she . . . she . . . I could tell that she wasn't just being nice or motherly. She was genuinely proud. It meant a lot." Dec pressed his lips together. "I never expected to lose her like that."

"It must have seemed so unfair." Galena knew the feeling.

"I was so angry when I found out she was sick, that there was nothing anyone could do. I threw myself into my work, even more than I had before. I didn't want to think about what was happening. I'll always regret not going into the Veil to say good-bye to her, but I couldn't face it. I didn't think I'd be able to let her go, and I didn't want to make her feel bad for leaving. It wasn't like she had a choice."

Galena stroked her thumb over his skin. "I miss my mom, too. She and my dad died a few years ago. I can still hear her voice in my head sometimes, telling me I could do anything."

"Isn't it funny how, when your mom or dad tells you that, it's easy to believe?" Dec set the frame back in its place and carefully closed the lid. He gently smoothed his palm over the top of the box. It was a gesture of reverence, of love, of pain.

Galena had never thought of dealing with grief in this way. When her parents had died, she'd put away all their things, sold the house, and moved into a campus apartment. She'd turned her back and walked away. She'd even deleted their pictures, because the sight of them felt like being stabbed in the heart. Now, though, she had nothing of her parents.

But Dec had handled his sorrow differently. Galena suddenly understood why this picture was in a box. He probably looked at it a lot, but it was too painful to have sitting out, in full view even when he wasn't ready to look at it. So he kept it near and took it out when he felt strong enough. She looked down at her fingers on his arm, her pale skin over the firm ridges of muscle, the dusting of dark hair. And then she looked up to see him staring, too, a bemused expression on his face. Slowly, he laid his hand over hers.

They sat like that for a few minutes, barely moving, just breathing. Galena felt no desire to break it down, to analyze it. Because it was so simple: two people and one touch, no demands, no domination, no fear. *No fear.* God, that was an utter miracle.

Then something stirred inside her, the oddest sort of pull. Almost like a rope had been tied around her spine and someone was leading her forward. Galena found herself leaning, unable to resist. Her chest brushed Dec's arm, then pressed against it, then started to push on him. Dec frowned. "Galena?"

She moved suddenly, like the person who held the rope had given it a sharp tug, and Dec slid right off the couch arm. His hand fell away from hers, but her fingers were clamped over his forearm, balancing her as she crawled over the side of the couch. "Dec," she gasped. "What's happening?"

"What do you feel?"

"A pull." She walked in the direction of the yanking sensation, toward the wide windows that looked out over the city. "But I . . ."

Dec started to laugh. Galena gave him a scared, questioning look. He was wearing an amused grin. She took another halting step toward the windows. "What the hell is happening to me?"

"There's a soul in the Veil that needs to be guided," he said, touching his Scope. "And now that you bear the Mark of the Ferry, you're up."

"I'm up?"

He pulled his own Scope from the setting at his throat. "Yeah. Sometimes you'll feel it because a Ker has summoned you specifically. One of my best friends is a Ker, actually, and we work together all the time." Dec paused, and Galena swore he looked troubled for a moment. Then he scrubbed his hand over his face. "But even if no Ker summons you, sometimes it's just your turn. And since you're new, that's what's happening now. You can ignore it if you need to—another Ferry will usually feel it, too, and everybody's in this for the gold. But if you wait, you risk allowing the soul to go rabid. And trust me, you do not want to deal with that."

"I guess I should go, then," she said, looking down nervously at the pendant in his hand.

He walked over to her and brushed his thumb over the face of the Scope. Its center glowed white. Cold air wafted across Galena's skin. She looked into Dec's eyes. His smile was magnetic, drawing her to him while pushing away her fear. "All right, Dr. Mrs. Galena Rachel Margolis-*Ferry*—ready for your first trip into the Veil?"

CHAPTER SIXTEEN

Dec watched Galena closely as she stared at the Scope in his hands. "It's easy to open your Scope," he explained. "Just slide your fingertip over it, and it'll respond to you."

Her slender fingers rose to the small platinum disk at her throat. "I don't know how to understand what I'm seeing."

"Then wait until you see *this*." He pulled at the edges of his Scope, stretching it to become a hoop about two feet across. Within its boundaries swirled the bubble-thin barrier between this world and the Veil. Cold rolled from it, raising goose bumps on their arms.

"Oh my God. I can see . . . what is that?" She walked around to the other side of the Scope and peered at him through the ghostly gray portal between them. Then her head popped up, and she viewed him over the top of its rim, her eyes round with shock. And then she ducked again and stared at him, like she was playing a baffled game of peekaboo. Dec held back a chuckle as she returned to his side, her trembling fingers moving forward to touch the edge of the real world. Dec felt a strange sort of pride as her fingertips traced across its delicate surface. Any fear she felt seemed to be submerged beneath a hungry sort of curiosity. She let out a gasp as her hand sank through to the other side. But instead of yanking it back, which would have been the normal response for first-timers, she merely stared unblinking at her own palm, now gray and faded.

She swallowed hard. "If the universe is infinite, and the ways matter can configure are finite because of the limitations in its components, then there must be repetition somewhere. This is proof."

A surprised laugh burst from Dec's throat. *"What?"*

She pushed forward until she was up to her elbow in the Veil. "Multiverse. String theory. I-I just . . . oh my God. It doesn't seem adequate." She muttered something about mathematics falling apart under certain hypothetical circumstances.

"This isn't hypothetical," Dec said, hoping he didn't sound like an idiot. "This is very real. Come on." He yanked the Scope wide enough to cover both of them and looked down at her. Once again, he was struck by the fierce eagerness in her eyes. He'd known she was into her work, but he'd never really considered the aggressive single-minded thirst for knowledge it must have taken to get to her level, to be at the forefront of science before she'd even reached thirty, to be capable of saving millions of lives when she'd barely had time to live her own. But now he could almost picture her brain, gears whirring, the most complex machine imaginable. A weird sort of protectiveness grew inside him, different from what he'd felt before. He'd known she was important, but mostly he'd felt compelled to protect her because she was vulnerable. Now he wanted to protect her because she was, well, *special*, he guessed. He couldn't think of a better word.

Oh, wait. *Amazing*. That one was good, too. "You ready?"

She nodded, her eyes narrowing as she wiggled her fingers. "Let's go."

He lowered the hoop over them, and Galena let out an adorable little yip as the Veil engulfed her. By the time the wide ring had reached their feet, she had hopped over its edge and was standing on the now-soft floor of his apartment. Dec scanned his space. No sign of Tamasin or Nader, but that made sense. Tonight, Galena was supposed to become immortal. She wouldn't need as much protection. Besides, he was sure the two Kere had been instructed to give him and Galena some privacy.

He turned to Galena, but she'd disappeared. Then he heard a squelching sound near his feet. She'd dropped to her hands and knees, and her palms were skimming over the gelatinous hardwood. "Matter is in a different state," she mumbled. "Except not. Still solid. But the molecular density has changed." She tried to scoop it up, but it wasn't possible.

"We can't affect objects in the real world," Dec said. "In the Veil, these structures—all the buildings, the vehicles—they're more like suggestions. They bounce back no matter what you do to them. They only change if the actual object changes or moves in the real world."

Galena poked her finger straight down into the floor and drew her hand back in surprise. "The surface tension . . . it's a solid with the properties of a liquid, molecules drawn inward by cohesive forces." There she was, nearly flat on his floor, jabbing her finger in and out of it like she'd never seen anything more fascinating. And then she moaned softly and slid forward, pulled by the need of a soul nearby.

Dec bent down and put his hands on her shoulders. She looked up at him with these huge, innocent eyes, and the bafflement on her face drew another laugh from his mouth. He was so used to the Veil that it held little interest or mystery for him anymore, but now he was filled with an eagerness to show his world to Galena. "Come on, Einstein. There's someone out there who needs you." He helped her to her feet.

"Where, though?" she asked, looking around the gelatinous gray world of his apartment like she expected the dead person to be sitting on his sofa.

"You have to use *your* Scope." He tapped it lightly. "Take it off the setting and just hold it for a second. Think of the soul that's calling to you right now. Then open the Scope like I showed you."

Galena obeyed him, unclipping her Scope and holding it in her palm. "It's warm now," she said. "Ever since I put it on, it's been cold."

"You were feeling the Veil inside it," Dec explained. "Now you're feeling the real world."

Her fingers closed over the Scope. "But this actually feels good," she said in this wispy, drifty voice, and Dec felt a pang. He wondered how long it had been since the real world felt good to Galena. He brushed her hair across her shoulder and moved close to her.

He flipped the Scope in her palm so the raven was faceup. "That's the side you want whenever you're trying to get somewhere," he said quietly. "Now press your thumb on it and concentrate."

She bit her lip, and Dec felt his groin tighten. *Not the time,* he reminded himself. He let out a long breath as she smoothed her thumb over the raven's body, opening an intra-Veil portal. "This will take us where the soul is?"

Dec nodded. "It never fails."

Galena smiled and pulled her Scope wide, then cautiously peered inside. That was smart. It was always good to know what you were getting into. She stuck her hand through the boundary in the center of the hoop. "So I just—"

"That's it. Go ahead."

She looked up at him. "But you're coming, too, right?"

He skimmed the back of his fingers across her cheek. "Wouldn't miss it for anything."

She blinked, but then held the Scope above their heads and lowered it over them. When she was done, Dec looked around. They were in Cambridge, of all places. Right in the middle of Cambridge Common, a large weedy park dotted with scraggly trees. Dec could see the high-rise of the school of government several blocks away, and he knew that Galena's lab was less than half a mile from here. Galena didn't seem distracted, though— she was completely focused on doing what she'd come here to do. She glanced behind her, searching for the soul that had called to her, and then marched off to her left, her Scope clutched in her hand. Dec jogged over to keep up with her, pleased at her lack of hesitation.

"Hello?" she called out.

"The soul probably won't answer," said Dec. "Between the two of you, the recently dead person is always going to be more confused about what's going on."

"That makes a lot of sense. This wouldn't be what I expected, either."

They found the soul sitting at the base of a tree, right next to the shadowy shape of his own corpse. He was in his late teens, maybe early twenties, skinny as a pole, with lanky light-brown hair that hung greasy around his face. Galena slowed down as she caught sight of him.

"Um," she said in a quiet, shaky voice. "He won't hurt me, right?"

Dec eyed the soul. "He looks pretty mellow to me." He figured now wasn't the time to tell her that sometimes souls *did* get feisty. "But if he makes any kind of move, just know I'm here, all right?" And he would crush this guy if he so much as twitched toward Galena.

Galena nodded, and Dec wondered if she realized that she'd inched closer to him, like he was her haven. Once again, that odd sense of proud protectiveness washed over him. "Go ahead," he told her. "Talk to him. Just tell him you're there to show him where he's supposed to go."

Galena stepped forward. "Hi there," she said loudly.

At the sound of her voice, the soul looked up. "Who are you?"

"My name is Galena," she said gently. "How are you doing?"

"I don't know," the guy said. "I don't know how I got here." He glanced at his transparent, lifeless body and looked away just as quickly.

Galena looked back at Dec, and he nodded at her. She turned to the soul again. "I know it must be disorienting. You're being very brave."

His face brightened. "You think so?"

"I do," she said.

Dec tensed, praying she wasn't about to have to send this boy to Hell. He moved close and touched her Scope. "Turn it over so the scales are faceup," he instructed.

Galena turned her Scope over. Her gaze traced the scales, and she frowned. He wondered if she'd realized what they stood for. The Afterlife was not a place of mercy or pity. It was a place where the balance of one's life was weighed. Ferrys didn't get to decide—all they did was mete out justice. "Dec . . ."

"Brush your thumb over it," he told her, preparing to help her follow through if necessary. "It'll open the door."

Galena looked at the young man before her. "I'm going to help you get to the right place, okay?"

The guy's brow furrowed. "How do you know where I'm supposed to go?"

She slid her thumb across the scales, and the center of her Scope flashed white. Dec relaxed. "It's Heaven," he whispered to her. "Go ahead. Use it just like we did when we stepped into the Veil."

Galena grinned. "I'm going to put this over you, and you're going to be in a wonderful place."

The guy stood up, his dirty jeans sagging from his bony hips. "You promise?"

She pulled the Scope wide, and the young man's eyes lit up when he saw what lay inside. As always, Dec felt a quiet yearning, knowing his mother was somewhere within that happy, peaceful world. What he wouldn't give to see her face one more time.

Galena moved forward and carefully lowered the ring of the Scope over the young man's head. "Bye," she said quietly as the guy disappeared. She stared at her Scope on the squishy gray grass, still stretched wide, then started to push on its edges to compact it again.

"No," Dec said, putting his hand on her arm. "Hold it up. Now you get paid."

"I get paid?" She plucked the Scope from the ground and peered into its sparkling bright-white center.

A heavy gold coin flew out of it and hit Galena in the belly before plopping to the ground at her feet. "Wow," she whispered. She knelt to pick it up.

"Need some help splitting that?" The silky voice came from just behind them.

Galena jumped up and whirled, and her mouth dropped open. She let out a cry and stumbled backward, landing on her ass. Dec stepped between her and the new arrivals, already irritated.

Two Kere stood just a few feet away. Luke was leaning against a lamppost, his close-cropped platinum hair gray in the Veil, his eyes glowing red. Dec had worked with him dozens of times. He was quite the voyeur when it came to death—he loved watching his victims as they struggled to take their final breaths. Next to Luke was a young woman Dec had never seen before, her deep-brown hair twisted into an elaborate knot high on the back of her head. She was cute. Round cheeks, big eyes fringed with long lashes, a few freckles dusted across her pert little nose. She wore a patterned sundress. Apart from the fangs and claws, she looked more suited for a garden party than Marking the doomed.

"Luke, who's your friend?" Dec asked.

"I'm Erin," she said.

"She's new," said Luke. "I'm showing her the ropes."

Dec stared at Erin. The Kere were killers. All of them. They had to have murdered at least one person during their human lives for Moros to even consider allowing them into his ranks. This new Ker didn't look the type. She bit her lip as she saw Dec watching her. "I'm expecting to get my first assignment soon. I'm kind of nervous."

Luke smiled down at his charge. "You're gonna enjoy it, honey. I promise."

Of all the Kere to be teaching a newbie, Luke would not have been his choice. The blond Ker looked down at the transparent shape of the dead man lying on the grass, and his lip curled with contempt. "Took him long enough. He hung on so long I got bored."

"Luke," Erin chided. "Don't be mean."

Dec looked over his shoulder at Galena, who was on her feet now. He should have warned her about how the Kere looked in the Veil. She looked down at the coin in her hand, and then up at Luke. "You're the one who did this? You . . . Marked that guy? You decided how he would die?"

Luke nodded. "Classic, no? I thought it was time for a little rat-bite fever outbreak."

Dec groaned inwardly and took Galena's hand, wishing that, of all the Kere in the world, Luke had not been the first one she had to work with.

"What did you just say?" she asked.

Erin frowned when she heard the shaking anger in Galena's voice, but Luke gave Galena an amused look. "Rat. Bite. Fever," he said, giving her a poisonous smile.

Dec remembered that Luke had been there the night Galena gave her speech at the Harvard fund-raiser. *He recognizes her. This is a challenge.* His suspicion was confirmed a second later as Luke said, "Some of the smallest predators are the most dangerous, right, Doc?"

Galena stared at the Ker, her face blank, but because Dec was holding her hand, he felt the rage kindling inside her. "That doesn't mean they're invincible," she muttered. "You enjoy this, don't you?"

Her gaze was so steady that Luke's arrogant smirk disappeared. "It's what I am, honey. I don't apologize for what I am."

"Yes, I can see you're nearly as insightful as the *Streptobacillus moniliformis* itself. Congratulations."

Luke's brows knit together in confusion. "The what?"

"Rat. Bite. Fever," Galena said, mimicking his condescending tone. "If you respect it so much as a predator, the least you could do is learn its proper name."

Erin grabbed Luke's hand, like she was trying to calm him down, even as the claws on Luke's other hand elongated, as if he wanted to strike. "I don't need to know what it's called to start an epidemic," he growled.

Luke was an asshole, but he'd never seemed this aggressive before. Dec edged closer to Galena, who didn't appear the slightest bit cowed. "Enjoy it while it lasts," she said.

Dec couldn't help his bemused surprise. He'd been prepared to tell Luke to step the fuck off, but if anyone looked like a predator right now, it was Galena.

Luke snarled. "Moros has gone soft. Or maybe weak. I don't know why he's protecting you."

"Don't talk about him that way," Erin whispered, her fingers clutching his. "It's dangerous."

Luke looked down at the young Ker. "I'll talk about that bastard however I want," he snapped.

"Galena, you have to give Luke half of your coin," Dec told her as Luke shook off Erin's restraining grip and paced toward them, his eyes flicking greedily to the gold in her hand. "Toss it at him and let him split it." The sooner, the better. He wanted to get Galena away from Luke right *now*.

She held up the coin. "This is solid metal. How is he going to—?"

"Not a problem." Luke grinned, showing his fangs. "Hand it over."

She flung it at him like she couldn't get rid of it fast enough, and he caught it. With a nasty sort of relish, he snapped his jaws down over it. The coin split with a quiet metallic crunch. Erin's eyes went wide, and she ran her tongue over her fangs. "Whoa," she whispered.

Luke spit into his hand and held out the two halves to Galena. "I cut, so you choose."

Galena looked down at the two halves of her Afterlife coin. One was glistening with Luke's saliva. She chose the other, even though it was a little smaller, which was probably exactly what Luke had wanted her to do. Luke kept his red eyes on her as he stepped back. "Nice working with you, Doc."

Galena smiled, a glittering grin that was almost as intimidating as Luke's. "Same to you," she said in a tight voice.

Erin waved. "I guess I'll be seeing you. I'm still getting used to all of this." She gestured around her, indicating the whole of the Veil.

Galena's glare softened. "Me too."

"Enjoy it while it lasts," hissed Luke, bearing his fangs as he imitated Galena's challenge. He grabbed Erin's arm, and the two of them vanished.

Galena shoved the half coin in her pocket. Her hands were shaking. Dec took them in his. "You were amazing." He cleared his throat. "I mean, the Kere are experts at intimidation, but you didn't seem scared at all."

"Because he pissed me off. The other one was much nicer." Galena rubbed her temple. "She looked familiar, but I couldn't place her."

"For all we know, she's a Harvard student or something. Or she was. Hopefully, she'll find a better mentor than Luke." Dec nodded toward Galena's pocket. "And next time, take the bigger half of the coin. He didn't deserve it."

She shook her head. "I don't care about the money. I swear, Dec. I'm going to make that Ker's life a lot harder. Soon. Rat-bite fever." She made a disgusted noise.

Dec squeezed her hands. "I believe you. And remind me not to piss you off. He—" A thought occurred to him.

"What is it?" she asked.

He replayed the encounter with Luke in his head. "He didn't seem surprised."

"Huh?"

His eyes met hers. "He didn't seem surprised you were here. In the Veil. With a Scope. Even though he obviously knew who you were. The news that you're a Ferry doesn't go out until later this morning."

Galena frowned. "What does that mean?"

A screeching wail made her jerk, and her eyes went wide as she looked at something behind him. "Oh my God," she shrieked. "What is that?"

Dec spun around as the wail was answered by several others. Rotting skin, long broken fingernails, oozing eyes. Everywhere he looked.

They were surrounded by Shades.

CHAPTER SEVENTEEN

Panic coursing through her, Galena reached out instinctively, and Dec's hand was right there, reaching, too. His cool fingers locked around hers. "They're Shades," he said, backing up slowly. "Souls that ran from Ferrys in the Veil. If they don't enter the Afterlife, they go rabid. This is the result."

The Shades were shambling toward them from all sides, and the smell of decay was enough to make the bile rise in Galena's throat. Some of them were barely more than walking skeletons, with bits of sinew still clinging to slimy bones, while others were mostly whole, with oozing eye sockets and mouths. Some of them had jagged, torn fingernails, and all of them had their teeth bared—though many of them were missing several, leaving gaps through which they poked their black tongues.

"What do they want?" she whispered.

Her only answer was another shrieking growl. The Shades charged, and Dec shouted, "Run!" He yanked her arm as the creatures lurched toward them. "Get into a building and stay there!" He shoved her ahead of him.

Galena's head swiveled around as she tried to choose a direction through the vast expanse of parkland. The nearest building was hundreds of yards away. She slid on the gelatinous grass and twisted in time to see Dec slam his fist through a Shade's rib cage and sidekick another. When one skeletal Shade grabbed his leg, he took hold of its head, twisted viciously, and tore its skull from its body. Instead of dropping like dead weight, the thing merely grasped at the place where its head had been while its disembodied skull screeched in Dec's hands. Grimacing as another Shade jumped on his back, Dec hurled the skull toward the scraggly branches of a nearby tree.

She was watching it arc through the air when one of the Shades dove at her, growling. Its rotting fingers scraped at her shirt, and Galena automatically brought her knee up, hitting it in the stomach. It grunted and then straightened up—reaching for her neck. Galena screamed as its hands clawed at her throat, but in the next moment Dec barreled into it, ripping it off her. The struggling pair landed on the ground a few feet away, and two more Shades piled on top of them a second later. Dec shouted a curse as one sank its teeth into his leg. Anger shot through Galena, simmering in her veins like a drug. She ran up to that Shade and kicked it in the ribs over and over as Dec punched at the one trying to tear his throat out.

Then another landed on her back, and rending pain tore through her as the Shade clamped its jaws over her shoulder. Arms wrapped around her chest, dragging her.

"Hold her down," the blond one shouted. Hard hands closed over her hips, and cruel fingers squeezed her throat. "You look like you need this," he snarled in her ear.

Galena fell to the ground and looked up to see Dec stomp on the neck of the creature who had bitten her, his eyes lit with rage. "Get yourself into a building," he yelled as another Shade hit him. "And then get into the real world. I'll be right behind you."

Galena fought to stay in the here and now. "I—"

"Go!" he roared as yet another Shade slammed into him. "They want a Scope. You can't let them get yours!"

"Dec—" She couldn't leave him. The Shades were all around them, emerging from behind trees, shambling across the soccer field, sprinting up the roads toward the park. Like all of them had been drawn here. Like they could sense prey.

Dec broke free of the two that had landed on him and lunged for her, grabbing her hand and pulling her toward the street. He stopped briefly to drive his foot into a Shade's leg, which shattered, causing it to fall and trip another that was trying to charge. "We just need enough space to get into the real world," he said, panting.

"Dr. M," called a guttural voice. "Dr. M!"

Confusion swamping her, Galena looked over her shoulder. A Shade was shuffling toward them, arms outstretched. He was wearing a sloppily tucked short-sleeved button-down and khaki pants, just like he'd always worn when he was alive. His black hair had fallen out in places, leaving oily bald patches of rotting skin. His deep-brown eyes, previously full of questing intelligence, were oozing dark fluid and glinting with hunger. "Jian?" she cried, slowing to a stop even as Dec tried to yank her forward.

"Dr. M," he repeated, a pained bleat of desperation. "Dr. M."

"Galena, he's not your lab assistant anymore," Dec snapped as two other Shades descended on them. "For God's sake, get moving!"

Dec ran to the side to draw the two creatures away, but Galena was transfixed, her eyes filling with tears as she beheld her former lab assistant. "Jian, did you have anything to do with the bombings?"

Jian froze. He stared at her, his dark eyes focused on her face. He began to tremble, as if the tension were literally rising inside him. The rest of the world dropped away while Galena waited for his answer. "Jian? It's okay. You can tell me," she said quietly.

"Because of you!" he roared, leaping forward before Galena had the chance to dodge. "You!" He grabbed at her throat, squeezing so tightly that she couldn't breathe. He slammed her head into the soft ground, and the palm of his hand pressed into her cheek, holding her there while he grabbed for her Scope.

Galena punched upward and landed a lucky shot on Jian's jaw. He lost his balance and fell backward, and Galena scrambled up, her bare feet slipping in the slick, forgiving ground. Dec was still battling fiercely with two Shades nearby, but any impulse she had to help was overridden when Jian grabbed her ankle. With a shudder of fear and disgust, she stomped on his face and took off running, determined to do what Dec had told her.

Her breath whooshed from her lungs as she sprinted toward a road that bounded the park. Behind her came the sound of squelching footsteps, and a quick glance over her shoulder revealed that Jian was only a few paces behind her. "Dr. M!" he growled. *"You did this."*

She had to get back into the real world. Had to. Adrenaline drove her forward as she increased her speed, putting more distance between her and Jian. She raced across the street and ran straight for the nearest building, which happened to be an old church, wood with a narrow facade that rose about four stories, a small cross perched on top. She stumbled across the lawn and grabbed for the handle to the thick arched door, but her hand slipped right through it. A surge of terror welled up inside her as Jian scrambled across the street. She ripped her Scope from the setting at her throat and pressed her thumb to the raven etching. It glowed, and Galena yanked it wide.

Right as Jian reached her. He grabbed the Scope's edges and pulled, creating a hoop at least six feet in diameter. He let out a screech as the warmth hit him. Galena tried to rip the Scope from his grasp, but his rotting fingers were clamped hard over its edges, and it only became a wider gateway. From all around her, the echoing shrieks of the Shades told her they saw it. They felt it. They were coming. Thinking she could close it from the other side, Galena made a lurching dive into the center of the Scope.

Jian landed on her as warm air enclosed them. Her Scope was still in her hand, and Jian had a grasp on it, too. Cool air flowed from the other side of the ring as they struggled on the front step of the church, which was now hard and unyielding beneath Galena's body.

Jian twisted, still holding the Scope. His fist collided with the side of Galena's face, making light and dark explode inside her mind. As she jerked back, he wrenched the metal ring of the Scope out of her grip. It shrank down to pendant size as he held it in his hands. He dropped it into his pocket and stared down at her. Here in the real world, he was even more hideous, an oozing travesty of the bright young man he'd been. "You did this to me," he snarled, moving closer. "Everything I did was because of you!"

"Jian, I don't know what you're talking about," she said, even as her head spun with pain. Her blood smeared across the concrete, trickling down her arm from the bite wound on her shoulder. She forced her eyes to focus on the lump in his pocket—she had to get the Scope back.

Jian inched closer, his fingers flexing. "He said you had to die," he grunted. He fell on her, jaws wide. Galena kicked at him frantically while trying to keep his gaping mouth away from her neck. The dark memories swirled in her throbbing skull, threatening to drag her down, but her will to survive was stronger. She managed to plant her feet in his middle and sent him stumbling back, but he was lunging at her again a moment later.

"He said you should die!" he shouted again.

"He can go fuck himself," said a voice just behind them. Dec emerged from his Scope right next to the church entrance, his face tense with pain and striped with blood. He smashed his fist into Jian's nose—once, twice, and then again. As Jian reeled, Dec grabbed him, knocking him back and pinning his arms with his knees. His hand clamped over Jian's oozing throat. "Tell me who *he* is. Who said she had to die?"

Jian flailed and kicked. He seemed beyond reason, beyond words.

"Did he have red eyes?" Dec shouted.

Jian stilled for a moment, as if in recognition, but then he heaved his body so wildly that Galena heard several of his bones crack. It didn't stop him from fighting, though. Dec yelled a few more questions at the struggling former lab assistant, but Jian's only answers were snarls and guttural growls. Finally, Dec seemed to realize it was futile. He tore his Scope from the chain at his neck.

When Galena saw what he was about to do, she put her hands up. "Wait! He has my Scope in his pocket."

Dec punched Jian again and held his arms while Galena dug in the Shade's pocket for her Scope. She sank backward with it clutched in her palm, and its cold burn against her skin was a huge relief.

"You deserve to die," Jian wailed, "after what you did to me!"

Galena opened her mouth to speak, but Dec shook his Scope open with one hand. "No more talking." He shoved a still-struggling Jian back into the Veil and closed his Scope again. His eyes met hers. He was bleeding from scratch marks along his cheek, and his shirt had been torn, revealing scrapes and bite marks on his chest and stomach. He didn't look like he noticed, though. He squatted next to her and took her face in his hands. "Are you okay?"

She stared up into his glacier-blue eyes. "He blamed *me*."

Dec grimaced as his gaze moved to her shoulder. "Shit. You're not okay." He put his arm around her back and helped her to her feet. "And it sounded to me like what Luciana Flores said—like some rogue Ker is going around telling his victims that you have to stop your research."

Galena stared at the place Jian had been, remembering the hatred in his eyes. "No. This was different. He said everything he did, it was *because* of me. He said, 'You did this.' And he was so angry . . ." Her fingers rose to a sore spot on her cheek, the place he'd punched her.

"Shades aren't logical," Dec said. "Maybe he was just angry and guilty about what he did and where he ended up, and the Ker had told him it was because of your research."

"Maybe." She bowed her head, suddenly wanting to lie down and sleep forever. "I'm sorry if I messed up just now."

He pushed her hair back, examining a scrape on her forehead. "You did fine."

"I didn't make it inside a building. The handle—" She gestured at the metal door handle of the church. "My hand went through it."

He gave her a bemused smile. "And you didn't realize your body would have gone right through the door if you'd just kept running?"

Her mouth opened and closed a few times, and he laughed. "It's okay. This was your first time in the Veil, and it takes some getting used to. Plus, we all lose a few IQ points in the heat of battle."

Galena poked his chest. "*You* didn't."

"I've been at this for decades. I barely have to think anymore. Except—" He looked across the street, at the park where they'd found the soul of the young man she'd guided to Heaven. "Luke sure did pick the perfect place to drop that body. Right in the middle of the park, not a single building nearby. Ideal place for a Shade attack."

"Do the Kere work with Shades?"

"I didn't think so," he said quietly, then turned to examine her shoulder again. "We should get you to the hospital."

Galena's entire body shuddered violently. "No." Her fingers pushed against Dec's stomach, trying to get away from him. "I hate hospitals."

He frowned as he looked her over. "Galena—"

"No. Please. Can you just take me home?" Which was *his* place now, she realized. She had nowhere else to go.

"I will, but only if you agree to let me take care of you. You can't just slap a bandage on a wound like this and expect it to heal on its own."

She reached her aching arm up and touched his face. "I'd feel safer with you than in a hospital."

His hand rose to cover her fingers on his cheek. His wounds were already closed, his skin smooth but crusted with blood. And his eyes were riveted on hers. "Okay. I'll take you home."

CHAPTER EIGHTEEN

There was a jittery feeling in Dec's chest as he led Galena down the sidewalk, his arm around her waist. He didn't know how to get over the stab of terror he'd felt as he'd watched her disappear into the real world with a Shade hard on her heels. He only knew everything else went away in that moment, destroyed by his need to get to her.

And now she was bleeding and torn, and Dec knew it could have been a lot worse, and suspected that it had been *meant* to be a lot worse. But he would investigate that theory later. Right now, he had to make sure she didn't succumb to sepsis—Shade bites were fucking nasty.

"I guess we can't use our Scopes to get back?" she asked quietly.

"We can," he said, "but the Shades would still be right there, and I don't know about you, but I've had enough of them for one night."

"So where are we going?"

If he'd thought to put his phone in his pocket, he'd be calling a car for them. But he didn't have a phone—or any money, for that matter, so even public transportation was out of the question. Besides, the two of them were barefoot. They looked like vagrants. Vagrants who had been attacked by other vagrants. "We just need to get into a building. Shades always stay outside. So it'll be a safe zone, and we'll have enough time to get into the Veil and open an intra-Veil portal to my apartment."

She leaned her head on his shoulder. "Please tell me those Shade things don't show up every time you enter the Veil."

He touched her hair, damp with sweat in the humid night air. Her blood was smearing on his already ruined shirt. "You always have to watch out for them. But I've never seen such a large gathering. There had to be at least thirty out there tonight." He didn't want to tell Galena what he suspected—that Luke had intentionally lured her there. Not yet, anyway, because he didn't want to scare her more than was necessary.

"I can't believe Jian was one of them," she whispered.

"Do you have any idea why Jian would have planted those bombs?" Dec understood the stabbings—whichever Ker was responsible had killed the victims himself. But what did that have to do with Jian? How had he been involved?

"Jian seemed so off that night you came to my lab." Galena shook her head. "I guess he'd been quieter for the past week or two, but he was still doing his work. Honestly, it doesn't make sense to me."

"You guys are under a lot of pressure, right? Maybe he just cracked?"

"I guess. But Jian was proud of his work. And he'd just gotten married a few months ago. I know he loved his wife. They were planning their future together. What would have led him to such a desperate place?"

"Somehow, a rogue Ker must have gotten to him. Maybe threatened him. And told him you needed to die. The Ker couldn't get to you directly because you were guarded in the Veil by other Kere, but Jian was the loophole. An ordinary human with access to the lab and the skill to destroy it."

"But why bomb all those other places? Why kill Ankita and the volunteers? It just seems so . . . *elaborate*. Especially since the other victims were killed in a completely different way."

"The rogue Ker would have Marked all of them, though," said Dec. "It looks like he wanted to inflict as much damage as possible, destroying almost everyone linked to your research. I just wish I knew how he did it without Moros knowing."

Galena touched her Scope. "What will happen to Jian?"

"He'll stay in the Veil as a Shade unless a Ferry tracks him down and guides his soul." Dec bit the inside of his cheek. "Usually, the only people who run from Ferrys in the Veil are the ones destined to go to Hell. They either know that's where they're headed or they run when they see the portal opening."

Galena sniffled. "It's hard to think of him going to Hell, even now. I thought he was a good man."

"Sometimes a Heaven-bound soul runs from a Ferry because it's really scared and disoriented, and occasionally I've come across souls that were just determined to get back to the real world because they were convinced they weren't finished."

"Jian did seem pretty determined to get back here."

"Most Shades are, though. It's like a compulsion. That's why they're always after our Scopes."

Galena nodded absently. "I wish he could have told us what happened. If a Ker made him do it to stop my research, why was he so angry at *me*?"

"Like I said—Shades are rabid. Irrational rage is kind of their MO." He pointed at an all-hours convenience store a block ahead. "There's our ticket home."

He nodded at the stocky security guard as they approached the barred storefront. The guy, maybe thirty, with a buzz cut and a dent on the bridge of his squarish nose, scowled. "Customers only."

"I don't know if I'm a customer yet," said Dec, smiling. "I haven't seen what's on sale."

He moved to enter the store, but the guard swished his arm to the side and extended his electroshock baton. Galena let out a strangled whimper. Dec pushed her behind him and continued to smile. "We don't want any trouble."

"Then get away from here," said the guard, clutching his baton tightly.

Dec met the guy's eyes and did something he'd promised himself he would never, ever do. He pointed to the Scope at his neck. "My name is Declan Ferry," he said. "And I want you to let us into the store."

"Ferry?" the guard said, blinking at the Scope. Everyone in the greater Boston area knew the raven symbol—Psychopomps had fingers in every pie from Boston to the canals of New York City. Then his eyes narrowed. "How do I know you didn't steal that from one of them?"

"Do you really want to take that risk?" said Dec, forcing his voice smooth and even. He hated using his family name like that. As if it made him special. But Galena had lost a lot of blood. She'd been through hours on the Marking table, hadn't slept since . . . damn, not even last night. It made it possible to say, "I'd be personally *grateful* if you'd let us use your bathroom."

The guard looked skeptical, eyeing Dec's torn, bloody shirt.

Dec leaned forward. "What's your name?"

The guard took a half step back, still brandishing his baton. "Sanders."

"Sanders, you have a phone on you?"

The guy glowered. "I'm not letting you use my phone."

"Take ten seconds and look me up. Then decide if you want to let me in."

Sanders pulled his phone from his pocket and thumbed in Dec's name. His eyes went wide. "You're the son of—"

"Yeah."

"And you're the CEO's—"

"*Yeah.*"

The guard squinted at a picture of Dec and Aislin that had been taken at a charity event a few months ago. "Hey, didn't I see you on the news that one time when—?"

"*Probably.* Hey. Sanders. My companion and I really need to get cleaned up. Can we come in already?"

The guard looked down at the electroshock baton in his hand, then pressed it to his leg like he was trying to hide it. "Of course, Mr. Ferry. But are you hurt? Were you attacked? You need the police? I can call them for you, no problem. I've got a cousin on the force. He'd be happy to help."

Dec clenched his teeth. *Now* the guard was the picture of compassion. "No. We need a few enzymatic cloths and some privacy. Restroom?"

"Right back there, Mr. Ferry," the guard said eagerly. "Go right ahead." He inclined his head at Galena. "Ma'am."

Dec pulled Galena along the aisle of the cluttered convenience store. The woman behind the counter, who had a bolt gun slung across her back, gave them a suspicious look, but then the guard scrambled in and began to whisper in her ear.

"Fuck," whispered Dec. He had drawn way too much attention to himself. If he'd been alone, he would have risked the Shades and gone back through his Scope right in the middle of the street, or he would have walked as far as he could have to try to get a clear spot. But with Galena here and sagging against him, he had no other choice. He guided her into the cramped bathroom, its waterless toilet giving off pungent fumes that made Dec's stomach roil.

"No enzymatic cloths," Galena said with a weak chuckle as she glanced over at the empty dispenser sitting on the rotted boards that had been laid over the old sink.

"Well, I wasn't really intending for us to spend the night hanging out in here."

Galena pressed her nose into his shoulder as Dec pulled his Scope from its setting and hurriedly opened it. Just as he did, there was a knock on the door and a woman's voice called out, "Mr. Ferry! I have cloths for you! They're the best brand I got."

Dec closed his eyes and prayed for patience. With Galena clutched to his chest, he opened the door a crack and stuck his hand out. The lady shoved a package of Chemiclean cloths into his palm. "Thank you, Ms. . . ."

"Walsom. Sharon Walsom. Honored to have you in my establishment, and if you need any—"

"Sharon, we're all set. Thanks." Dec closed the door again.

"Won't they notice we've disappeared?" Galena mumbled against his shirt.

"No way around it," Dec said in a tight voice. Her face was so pale, and her skin was clammy. She looked like she was about to faint. And that made him willing to deal with whatever fallout came his way. He opened the Scope and lowered it around them. With Galena still leaning against him, he closed the ring and flipped the pendant so the raven was facing up again, then concentrated on his apartment—specifically on his med kit, which was tucked away in one of his cabinets. He was already cataloging which supplies he'd need. He opened the Scope and sighed with relief when he saw his own living room. "Here we go."

He lowered the Scope, and the familiar smell of his apartment washed over him. With his arm around Galena, he closed the Scope and fixed it to its setting again, then guided her to his couch. She sank onto it. "I could really use another shower," she muttered.

"Later. Right now you need to keep your promise to let me work on you."

She closed her eyes and nodded, pulling her knees to her chest. Dec strode to his kitchen and took his med kit from the cabinet. He headed back to the living room and set the kit down on the end table. Galena had a swollen spot on her cheek and scratches on her neck where the Shade had clawed for her Scope. But the worst wound by far was the bite to her shoulder. The motherfucker had sunk its teeth into the pale skin just above her clavicle. "Hey," he said softly. "You want something for the pain?"

"I'm all right, Dec," she said, her green eyes opening and her gaze resting on him in a way he felt deep in his chest. "Do your thing."

He stared down at her shirt. And then he got up and went into the bathroom, grabbed a towel, and returned. "I need to get to the wound," he said. "So we're going to have to take your shirt off." He held up the towel. "But I've got you covered. Or . . . I will."

Her lip curled into the sweetest half smile, and her eyes met his again. She paused, her fingers fiddling with the hem of her shirt. Like she was trying to decide if she was ready for this. He wished he could read her mind. He let the towel unfurl, forming a curtain between them. On the other side, he heard the soft whisper of fabric against her skin, and he shut his eyes tight, focusing on the job ahead.

"Can I keep my bra on?" she asked quietly.

"If you need to. But I have to clean the area, and it might get—"

"It's okay," she murmured. "I'll take it off."

A moment later, her bloody shirt and a delicate lacy bra fell to the floor beside the couch. Dec lowered the towel over Galena's chest, leaving the area around the wound bare. She kept her face turned away.

Dec knew her pained expression and her fear of hospitals must have to do with the attack and what had happened after. Hospitals were cold, bleak places, not nearly comforting enough for someone who'd just lost so much. Dec had transported a few women who had been attacked in the streets, had held their hands and promised them he'd get them somewhere safe. But as he'd delivered them into the emergency department, where they'd be laid out under bright lights and probed by gloved fingers wielding cold metal instruments, Dec couldn't help but wonder if he should never have made those promises in the first place.

He'd do better for Galena tonight. "I'm going to wash my hands and get on my gloves, and then I'm going to clean this."

When she nodded, he went into the kitchen and scrubbed his hands, then donned his gloves. He grabbed a bottle of sterilizing fluid and gently pulled at her wounds, making sure the liquid got all the way into the places penetrated by the Shade's rotting teeth. Galena kept her fingers balled around the bottom edge of the towel. Her face was white with pain, and little beads of sweat stood out, stark on her brow. Dec tore his gaze from her tightly closed eyes and looked at the wound. "Lights level nine," he said, and the overhead bulbs brightened, illuminating the bruising around the bite marks.

Once he'd gotten the wound clean to his satisfaction, he set the sterilizing fluid down. "I'm going to use vascular glue to close these. It won't take long to seal up."

"Thanks for being gentle," she said in this small, quiet voice.

"That's usually what people in pain need, isn't it?" He always softened his tone when approaching a patient, knowing that a comforting presence was as important as solid medical care.

"Doesn't mean they get it."

"They do from me," he murmured, reaching for the glue. "Now, stay really still, okay? This might tickle."

Her tiny, amused snort made him smile. He carefully applied the glue and pressed Galena's wounds closed. She was lucky the edges were even and not terribly deep. It took no more than ten minutes to have all of them closed. When he was done, he loaded an injector pen with an antibiotic and nudged her leg. "I have to shoot this into your hip. The last thing you need is a blood infection."

She sighed and gazed at the injector pen. Then she slowly straightened her long legs and shifted, wincing. The towel at her chest fell forward, allowing Dec to see the bandaged tattoo on her back and the curve of her waist. He swallowed hard. "I'm just going to pull your sweats down a little so I can reach the spot, okay?"

Galena bit her lip and pivoted so she was almost on her stomach. Her head was bowed against the couch.

This was not how Dec had pictured undressing her. With a twinge of regret, he slowly pulled the loose waistband of her sweats down the swell of her hip, revealing her smooth skin inch by inch. *Not the time,* he reminded himself, then he pressed the pen to her gluteus medius and tapped the button. She flinched but remained silent. He pulled the pen away from her skin and tugged her sweats back up. Then he quickly and quietly laid an automatch skin-bandage over her closed wound, adhering it neatly to her skin. "You can take that shower now, if you want."

She nodded and got up. He watched her go with a pang, her naked back exposed and vulnerable, her shoulder blades sharp, that towel clutched to her bare chest. As he listened to the shower switch on, he cleaned up and then grabbed a quick shower of his own in the guest room. He let the water rinse the blood from his completely healed skin, wishing he and Galena had found a way to make her immortal before the Shades had attacked, feeling utterly at a loss for how to get there with her. He dried off and changed. It was nearly five in the morning. Galena must be on the verge of collapse.

He padded into his room and pulled up short when he saw Galena on the bed. She was wearing a clean tank top and shorts, her legs curled beneath her. She gave him a hesitant smile. "I know you've already had your sleep for the day, but I'm exhausted. And I was wondering if . . ." She bit her lip, looking down at the bed. "You said we should work on me feeling safe."

"Yeah, what do you need?"

Her gaze traveled up his body, and Dec felt as if her fingers were on his skin. "Will you stay next to me?" she asked.

Trying to breathe slowly and will away the tightness in his groin, Dec nodded and approached the bed. He slid onto the mattress and lay down on the opposite side from her. "Like this?"

She slowly crawled closer. "Come my way?"

He scooted toward the middle of the bed. "Close enough?"

She shook her head and closed the distance between them, then lowered herself down and tugged at his hand until he raised it and let her snuggle against his side. He blinked at the ceiling as he felt her carefully positioning her sore shoulder. "Are you sure you wouldn't be more comfortable by yourself tonight?"

She sighed. "No, I'm not sure." He looked down at her, and she gave him a wobbly little smile. "But I'd feel safer if you were close."

His breath caught in his throat as she laid her head on his shoulder, as her arm coiled over his abs. She smelled like his shampoo, a minty herbal scent that nearly covered up the warm honey tang that he'd come to associate with her. He leaned so that his nose brushed over her slightly damp hair, and he closed his eyes. His fingers skimmed down her arm, holding her close.

"I'm grateful, Dec," she whispered. "For everything."

Dec lay awake, feeling her warmth against his skin as she relaxed into sleep. This was not how he had imagined the night going at all. But even so, with Galena in his arms, with her body against his, with her feeling *safe* with him, he couldn't help but feel grateful, too.

He didn't know how long they'd been lying there when his phone buzzed on the little table next to his bed. Not wanting to wake Galena, he quickly reached over to silence it. He froze when he saw a text from Aislin:

We have a problem.

Dec frowned and texted back:

?

His heart began to pound as he waited for her response. And when it came, Dec felt the blood drain from his face.

Galena is a person of interest in the bombings. She's expected at Boston PD for questioning.

Dec gritted his teeth. *This is bullshit.*

The detective on the case is a hard-liner. For now, we have to go along with it.

Galena shifted, perhaps feeling the rising tension in Dec's body. He forced himself to relax as he texted:

When?

By noon. Or else they're issuing a warrant. Can I count on you?

To take Galena to the police station, she meant. To turn her over so that this didn't become a scandal that reflected poorly on the family and the company.

Can I count on YOU? he texted back.

As always, I will do what I think is right.

He silenced his phone. It took effort not to slam it down on the bedside table. Then he looked at the woman nestled against him. Her hair partially covered her face, and he smoothed it back and stroked his thumb across her brow. Again, he was reminded of her delight at entering the Veil for the first time, her bravery when facing down Luke, her fragile, hopeful courage as she had asked Dec to stay next to her. He pulled Galena closer, so he could feel her breath against his throat.

"Me too, Aislin," he whispered. "*That* you can count on."

CHAPTER NINETEEN

Galena awoke to the smell of coffee and the sound of Dec's voice. "I know, Manny, but I need you to take my day shift again."

She sat up, her hand smoothing over the large indentation where his body had been. It was cool—he'd been up for a while. She had no idea what time it was, but she hadn't slept that well in years. She stretched happily, then winced as it pulled at her healing wound.

"I understand," Dec continued, his tone level and patient, "and you'll get the overtime pay. Plus some comp time. Come on. I know you had vacation scheduled, but I need this." There was a long pause, during which Galena got out of bed and tiptoed to the door.

"Already tried. Trevor's not answering my texts. Look, I know this sucks, Manny, but it's just another day or two." After another brief pause, Dec spoke again, but his voice had changed dramatically—from conciliatory to razor-edged. "Let me remind you of two things. One, I'm the Chief. And two? I'm the fucking *Chief*. And the last time I took a vacation was before you fucking joined up, and possibly before you started kindergarten. So complain again. Please. Let me hear it." He paused. "Oh? You're okay with it now? Good. Thanks so much for being a team player."

There was a clatter, probably Dec's phone hitting the countertop. Hesitantly, Galena emerged from his bedroom and walked into the living area. Dec stood behind the kitchen counter, his black hair standing on end.

"You don't have to skip work because of me," she said. She'd caused all this disruption to his life, and she was afraid he'd start to resent her for it.

He looked down at his phone. "I guess you heard that, then?"

She nodded, even as her stomach growled. She inhaled, distracted by the delicious scent that was wafting toward her. "What is that smell?"

Dec gave her a sheepish smile and lifted the lid on a skillet. "I made you some eggs and sausage." He gestured at a pastry box that sat on the counter next to the stove. "And I ordered some croissants. Because I think you might not have eaten in the last twenty-four hours, and that is ridiculous."

"It also happens to be correct," she said with a laugh, putting her hand on her stomach. "And I'm starving."

He grinned, but Galena could have sworn his smile faltered before he turned away. She watched his broad hands as he used a spatula to scoop two fried eggs onto a plate. "Do you eat meat?" he asked.

"When it seems safe," she said. "It was pretty scarce and expensive in Pittsburgh, and most of what we got was canned." She shuddered.

"This is good stuff," he said, arranging two sausage links next to her eggs. "I promise."

It was probably from some secret agri-lab and had cost a small fortune, but Dec didn't brag about it. She'd noticed that about him, like last night with that guard at the convenience store. Dec had seemed loath to tell the guy who he was—just like he'd tried to be nice and appeal to his colleague's generosity just now, and only *after* the guy had been a jerk had Dec pulled rank. He usually kept his Scope tucked into his collar, and even though he lived in this heavily guarded enclave belonging to his family, his apartment was relatively humble. *Walking lightly on this earth, letting his actions define him.*

She smiled as she slid onto a barstool and Dec placed the plate in front of her. As he handed her a fork, she asked, "So, are you going to eat, too, or is that not a requirement for Ferrys either?"

"Oh, we eat," he said, pushing the box of croissants closer to her. "I think it's one of the purer joys in life, actually." He snagged one of the flaky-looking pastries and set it on a plate for himself. "Have you ever tasted real Irish butter?" He grabbed a dish from his fridge. "There are still a few functioning farms on some of the islands."

That was a miracle, considering that Ireland had lost nearly 40 percent of its land mass to the sea in the last hundred years, and what was left was a collection of semiautonomous islands fighting over resources. Dec leaned forward, offering her a croissant smeared with the pale-yellow substance. "Try it."

She obediently opened her mouth and then moaned when the salty richness hit her tongue. Her teeth clamped down on the soft layers of the pastry, and she closed her eyes while she chewed. She was overwhelmed for a moment by the velvety feel of it, the way it made the pleasure centers in her brain scream for more. Once she'd swallowed, she looked up to see Dec staring at her mouth.

"I like how you look when you're enjoying something," he said quietly. "Now eat up. It's brain food. Which means you need more than anyone, right?"

She shook her head, laughing, and lost herself in the breakfast for a few minutes while Dec cleaned up. His bright mood seemed a little forced. "Is everything okay, Dec?"

"Hmm?" he asked as he scrubbed the skillet. "Oh. How's your shoulder?"

Her brow furrowed. "It's sore, but fine, really. Like the rest of me. But something tells me there's more than that on your mind." He wasn't acting like himself, at least not the self she knew.

He stopped scrubbing. "Finish your breakfast," he said. "It's not good for you to go so long without eating."

She obeyed, despite the twist of unease inside her. The food was so good that she managed to put away the entire croissant and gobble one of the eggs and both sausages before she sat back, completely full.

"Coffee?" he asked.

"Please." But she touched his wrist as he set the mug down in front of her. "Now tell me what's going on, because you're starting to scare me."

He sighed, staring at her hands as she brought the mug to her lips.

The coffee was like the food—a richer, overpoweringly better version of any coffee she'd had before. It was like she'd never had a sense of what it *should* taste like until now. She set the mug down. "Please, Dec. I can tell something's up. I haven't known you to be quite this cheerful. It looks like it's taking a lot of effort."

"You're way too observant." He lifted his head. His gorgeous blue eyes settled on her. "You've been labeled as a person of interest in the bombing cases, Galena. They want you to go down to the police station and answer some questions."

Galena's stomach turned. "I wish you'd told me before I ate all that food."

"I was afraid you wouldn't eat if I did."

He was right. But now it felt like it was all about to come up. "When do I have to be there?" she asked, her voice tremulous.

"Before noon."

"That's why you took the day off."

Dec nodded.

"I can do it by myself, Dec. I'm actually a pretty competent adult in most respects. You don't have to babysit me."

He leaned on the counter, the muscles of his arms tense. "I'm a pretty competent adult in most respects, too. So when I tell you that babysitting doesn't describe what I'm doing, you can believe me." He looked away from her. "Unless you want to call Eli."

"No," she said quickly. She couldn't bear to burden him with yet another problem. "But Dec, seriously, this has nothing to do with you."

He moved slowly around the counter, and her heart sped as he reached her. Carefully, his fingers skimmed up under her tank, tracing the bumps of her spine, rising higher and higher. She shivered at the look in his eyes as his fingertips smoothed over the strap of her bra to touch the raven tattoo between her shoulder blades. She'd taken off the bandage early this morning when she showered, so there was nothing between his skin and hers as he traced the raven's wings without even having to look. It was like he'd memorized that piece of her already. She felt a new sort of tingling between her legs at that thought, and when she glanced down, she was embarrassed to see that her nipples were hard against the front of her tank.

"This," he said quietly, still tracing the raven. "It might have been purely for your protection, but it connects us. It entitles me to a few things."

"Like what?"

"Like sticking by you when things are shitty," he said. "Like going with you to the police station and making sure you're okay."

His hypnotic caresses made her close her eyes. She would be very happy to let him do this all day—and it was certainly more fun than going to the police department.

Maybe when they got back, though. Once she'd answered whatever questions they had, Galena was eager to see what else

Dec thought he might be entitled to. It was no less scary than it had been last night, but she realized her trust in him had grown with every minute they'd spent together. "All right," she said, leaning her head back on his shoulder and looking up at him. Her breath caught when his gaze slid from her throat to her breasts.

His eyes squeezed shut, and he pulled his hand from beneath her tank. "Good," he said, pivoting quickly to head back to his bedroom. "Leave in twenty?" He shut his door and left her sitting there, her heart racing, her nipples hard, the rest of her utterly confused.

The Boston Police headquarters was in a canal zone southwest of Back Bay, in an area called Mission Hill. Galena stared out the window as their amphibious limo motored past rickety flat-bottomed boats and a few amphibious buses. What used to be a thriving residential area was now block upon block of abandoned, rotting flood-damaged homes mixed with the occasional rebuilt apartment building. A public park had been turned into a shantytown. The people on the sidewalks cast curious, mistrustful glances at the limo. Mud-brown canal water splashed onto the windows when speeding uniboats raced by.

Galena stared at the droplets, thinking of Ankita, Luciana, and all the others who had died two nights ago. Dec sat quietly by her side, but she could tell he was tense. He was dressed in slacks and a navy-blue button-down shirt that looked tailored. She felt a little tattered and frumpy in her maxidress and cardigan, even though it was the nicest outfit she now owned. Her nerves were winding like snakes in her gut, and she absently twisted her fingers together—until Dec took one of her hands and laced his fingers with hers.

They pulled up to the dock in front of the police station, and soon their driver was opening the roof hatch. Dec pulled the ladder down and helped her up. As soon as she emerged into the heavy humid air, she saw a stern-looking police officer with a gun and an electroshock baton at his belt, his eyes riveted on her. "Dr. Galena Margolis?" he asked.

"Yes," she said as he helped her onto the dock.

"Come with me, please."

Dec was by her side a second later. The cop led them through the stone-floored lobby and down a few hallways, deeper and deeper into the building, before guiding them through a bustling room bounded by three videowalls, with desk screens displaying holographic projections of the city. They ended up in another hallway, this one long and sterile.

The cop unlocked a metal door and waved her inside a small white-tiled room with a black videowall on one side and a table in the center. "You her lawyer?" he asked Dec.

"No. Her husband." He stuck out his hand. "Declan Ferry."

The cop's mouth dropped open as they shook hands, but he recovered quickly. "Good to know. The detective will be here—oh, here we go."

A middle-aged man came into the room, his graying hair slicked back. His olive-skinned face could only be described as sad. His lips came to a peak in the center of his mouth, with both sides sloping downward, forming a natural frown. His eyes had a heavy look to them as well. It was like gravity worked a little harder on him than it did on other people. "Detective Amil Botros," he said, nodding curtly. "How are you today, Dr. Margolis?"

"It's been a rough few days," said Galena as she and Dec sat down in two chairs on one side of the table. The detective took one on the other. "For you, too, I imagine."

His eyes narrowed. "Three lethal stabbings, fifteen bombing deaths, one suicide, eight different crime scenes. Yeah, you could say that."

Fifteen bombing deaths? Galena felt sick. Aislin had said that several had died, but Galena had no idea it was that many. Eighteen people killed, plus Jian.

Under the table, Dec nudged her knee, and Galena accepted the silent invitation with gratitude, entwining her fingers with his once more. She felt stronger holding his hand. "Do you have any leads?" she asked.

"A few. Tell me about your relationship with Jian Lee."

"He was my lab assistant. One of two."

"Was he hired for you, or did you pick him?" asked the detective, who was now typing information onto a screen set into the tabletop.

"I was told by my department chair that I needed to hire assistants, even though I prefer to work alone. She said I needed the help." Dr. Cassidy had reminded her that she was one person, and there was no way she could get all the work done herself. "I chose Jian from a group of applicants." There had been nearly a hundred of them, but Jian and Ankita had stood out.

"And he worked for you for . . ."

"Almost a month," she said quietly.

"Was he a good worker? Did you get along?" Botros glanced up at her.

"We did," Galena said. "He was fairly quiet, but his work was solid."

"You never had any occasion to discipline him, anything like that?"

Galena shrugged. "I expect precision, because anything less could interfere with our research results, but generally Jian was very thorough in his work." She leaned forward. "We had no problems, Detective. I liked him. But the night before the bombing, he was definitely off. Irritable and nervous. He was working on a sequencer—the one that turned out to be holding the bomb. And the day of the bombing, he left early, and Ankita said he'd seemed stressed. The sequencer began making noise after he worked on it, and I thought it was because he hadn't fixed it yet, but now I believe it's because he put something in it."

Botros tapped his screen, and it projected a three-dimensional image of a mangled piece of metal, speckled and pitted from the explosion. "That's all that's left of it." He tapped the screen again, and the image disappeared. "He did precise work, that Jian. Not to mention we found receipts in his house for some of the material used to make the bombs."

There it was. Hard evidence Jian had been responsible. But it still didn't explain *why* he had done it.

"So, Doctor, talk to me about you," Botros said, pulling her back. "Your boss, Dr. Cassidy, says you've put enormous pressure on yourself since arriving at Harvard. She said she was worried about your mental stability."

"What?" Galena whispered. Sure, Dr. Cassidy had expressed concern for her, but questioning her sanity?

Botros nodded. "She said the pressure to come up with this vaccine you're working on was too much. She said she was worried you were beginning to break down."

"As I told Dr. Cassidy, I *have* been under pressure," snapped Galena, "but that's no different than when I was at Pitt. I handle pressure well and have the record to prove it."

Botros's eyes traced her face, settling on the swollen patch on her cheek that she'd tried to cover with makeup. "Yeah? You haven't ever dreamed of just letting it all go? Maybe escaping from all that pressure and scrutiny? I hear academia can be tough. And for you?" He blew a breath from between pursed lips. "You've had quite the career so far. Every eye on you. I couldn't blame you if you wanted to get out from under it."

Dec leveled a glacial stare at the detective. "How about you stop the fake-empathy game and just say what you think, Detective Botros?"

The detective arched a thick black eyebrow and put his hands up. "Oh, Mr. Ferry, my apologies." He didn't look sorry. In fact, he looked a little amused and a little angry. Like he would love nothing more than to stick it to the Ferrys. "But since you insist, I'll be honest here. See, Jian Lee left a suicide note. What do you think it said?"

Galena felt a ball of ice grow inside her as she remembered Jian shouting in a guttural voice, *Your fault!* "I have no idea," she said, her voice cracking.

"Well, how about I show you?" Botros tapped his screen, and a typed message floated in front of them.

> *Mei,*
> *I am so sorry for what I have done. I hope you will someday forgive me. Please know that I never wanted this to hurt you. I never wanted to hurt anyone. She forced me to do it. She gave me no other choice. I love you. It's torture to leave you, but I cannot go on like this. Remember me, please.*
> *~Jian*

Galena blinked back tears as she read his note, addressed to his wife of only a few months.

"Sad, isn't it? Now, who do you think 'she' is?" asked the detective. "The woman who he says forced him to do these bad things?"

"Again, no idea," whispered Galena.

"And what would you say if I showed you this?" Botros tapped his screen again, and Galena shivered as she read the projected words, a chat message to Jian dated a few days before the bombings.

> *I'm still waiting to hear from you. Confirm that you're ready to move forward or I'll be forced to follow through with my promise. As you know, the new mutation of the Marburg virus is particularly deadly, and there's no vaccine yet.*

Galena's stomach turned. Someone had been threatening Jian with *disease*? Her fingers locked around Dec's as rage rushed through her. "Who sent that to him?"

"Oh, whoever did it was very clever," said the detective. "Probably thought she'd never get caught. All kinds of encryption and whatnot. Took us awhile to dig the answer up. But here it is." He tapped the screen, so hard that his fingernail made a sharp snap against the surface. And up popped a little box containing an encoded string of information. He tapped another button, which decrypted the jumble of letters and symbols, revealing a system log, including a time stamp and authentication credentials. *Her* authentication credentials. "It came from the central computer in your lab, Dr. Margolis. The one only *you* had access to. And we cross-checked that time stamp with surveillance records. You were the only one in your lab when it was sent."

He stood up from behind his desk, gesturing at the closed metal door. Two cops immediately came into the room—they must have been watching them on camera the whole time. "Galena Margolis," said Detective Botros. "You're under arrest for the murders of Ankita Bhasin, Nadya Odrova, Katsumi Phillips—"

"What the fuck is this?" Dec shot up from his chair as the police approached Galena. "You sneaky bastards. You tell her you're going to ask her a few questions, and instead you ambush her like this?"

Botros glared at Dec. "I have no doubt you can get her a very good lawyer, Mr. Ferry, but the evidence is solid, and it's my job to remove murderers from the streets. Are you going to obstruct me? Am I gonna have to arrest you, too?"

A rough hand closed around Galena's wrist, and she looked up to see a police officer, cuffs out. Too shocked to cry, she searched for Dec and noticed his clenched fist. He looked like he was ready to fight the detective like he had those Shades last night, just to keep her safe. "Dec," she murmured. "Don't."

He whirled around, rage and horror in his eyes. "This is bullshit."

"I know."

"I'm going to get you out of this."

She gave him the bravest smile she could muster. "I know."

Botros stepped between them. "We're going to take you down to booking, Dr. Margolis, and get you settled into a nice cell." He turned to Dec. "She'll be available to meet with a lawyer in a few hours, son. Arraignment will be tomorrow."

"Galena," Dec said.

"Go, Dec," she whispered, unable to force any volume into the words. "I'll be fine. Take my . . . pendant, would you? I don't want to lose it." And they would confiscate it, she knew.

As the cold metal of the cuffs bit into her skin, Dec mumbled something to the detective, who stepped out of the way. Dec came forward, his eyes on hers. "I'll talk to you in a few hours," he said, reaching around to unhook the clasp of her Scope. His fingers slipped along her neck, and she closed her eyes, wanting to cling to the comfort of that sensation for as long as she could.

"Tell Eli you're taking care of it, okay?" Eli would go crazy when he found out about this, and she didn't want him to do anything to get himself in trouble.

"I'll handle this. All of it," Dec said, leaning down and touching her forehead with his. "You're going to be all right." He took her face in his hands and gave her a quick, unbearably sweet kiss on the lips, and then he turned away, stuffing her Scope into his pocket. "Detective, if I find out she's been mistreated in any way—"

"I know, Mr. Ferry. I know what your family can do. Just know that I'm on the side of justice here, okay? That is the *only* thing I care about."

Dec's jaw was rigid as he allowed two police officers to escort him from the room.

"Ready to head to booking, Doc?" asked the detective. "Might as well get used to the idea of being here. No judge in his right mind is going to grant bail."

Galena didn't bother responding. She hadn't felt this out of control and helpless in a while, but it settled on her like a heavy, suffocating blanket. Her hopes that she would be spending the afternoon with Dec, letting him closer, getting to know him, it all seemed like a stupid, naive dream, something from a life that had never been hers, not really. She knew she should be focusing, thinking carefully about how she could get out of this, defend herself, refute their evidence. But as the detective took her arm and guided her out into the hallway, so long that she could barely see the end of it, all Galena felt was numb.

CHAPTER TWENTY

Dec slammed his way through the doors of Psychopomps and stalked over to Walter, whose eyes went wide as he looked up from the screens in front of him. "Mr. Ferry, are you all r—?"

"I need to see Aislin," Dec snapped. "Right the fuck now."

Walter blinked and tapped at one of his screens. "Aislin's in a meeting with the French ambassador at the moment and—"

"*Now.*" Dec leaned forward. "I don't care who she's in with. Call her and tell her I'm coming up."

Walter glanced over at the guards at the elevators, and Dec gave him a hard-edged smile. "They could stop me, Walter, but how would it look? Guards taking down the CEO's brother in the lobby? *I* don't care, but Aislin would. You want to set her up for embarrassment? Go ahead. Because I would fucking love to punch somebody in the face right now, so bring it on."

Dec unfastened the top button of his shirt and then began to roll up his sleeves. He'd had to leave Galena in the fucking police station, in *handcuffs.* The look on her face . . .

Walter, who had gone pale, poked at his earpiece. "Uh, Ms. Ferry? Yes. I'm so sorry to disturb you. But I have your brother here, and he's quite agitated."

"Agitated?" Dec chuckled. "You haven't *seen* agitated yet." He flexed his fingers and rolled his head on his neck.

Walter's lips barely moved as he spoke quietly, like he was afraid the people queuing up behind Dec would hear him. "He's threatening to make a scene, and—okay. Thank you." His eyes met Dec's. "She'll see you."

"Perfect." Dec turned on his heel and strode toward the elevators. The sun shone through the glass facade of the building, stark against the polished granite floor. Outside, the canals and sidewalks were bustling with people, barreling through their lives, trying to survive each day. And somewhere in the Veil, a soul was calling to him. Dec ignored the pull, though. Yes, he was taking the risk that the soul would become rabid while it waited. Yes, he almost never took that risk. But today? There was only one person on his mind, and she was very much alive, and he was determined to keep her that way.

The guards made way as Dec walked into the elevator that would take him to Aislin's office. He folded his arms as he ascended, trying to calm down. Going in hot was Cacy's style, and one of the reasons she and Aislin didn't get along. He was usually mellower. But again, not today. Somehow, in the last twenty-four hours, Galena's well-being had become his number one priority. And not just because he was honoring his father.

Because she was unique. Stunningly smart, dangerously beautiful, and hauntingly vulnerable, all in one. Brave, too. Braver than she gave herself credit for.

He didn't know her well. And he probably shouldn't want to, since they were together only for convenience, to make a physical connection that would provide her with the protection she needed. He couldn't help the longing he'd felt as he held her this morning, though, the pride at being the man who got to put his arms around her, the man she trusted enough to fall asleep with. And he couldn't help the raw rage and panic he felt now, knowing she was going to be locked in a cell and charged with crimes she had absolutely nothing to do with.

The elevator door slid open, and Aislin was standing there with two women and one man, all attired in perfect business suits.

"*À tout à l'heure,* Ambassador Tailler," Aislin said, ignoring Dec as he stepped out of the elevator. "*Encore une fois, je suis désolée pour l'interruption.*"

"*À la prochaine,*" the oldest of the women replied, eyeing Dec suspiciously. Then she and her people got on the elevator.

Aislin waited to speak until they heard the quiet whir of its descent. Her nostrils flared slightly as she turned to Dec, her blue eyes cold. "Threatening to make a *scene*? Really, Declan."

"I've just come from the Boston PD. They arrested Galena. They're charging her with the murders of all those people who died in the bombings."

Aislin went very still. "That is a significant negative development."

"That's an understatement," Dec ground out, heading for her office.

Aislin followed, her high heels clicking. "My contact was unaware—"

"Obviously. The detective's a guy named Amil Botros. Heard of him?"

Aislin moved behind her desk and tapped at the screen embedded in its surface, then spent a moment gazing at the results. "He recently transferred from New York. A distinguished record."

"Yeah. He seemed like he'd be happy to defy us. He produced all this 'evidence' that Galena was threatening the guy who made the bombs." Dec raked his hand through his hair. "As if Jian only did it because she forced him to. And he's dead, so I'm sure the cops would be happy to find a live person to pin this on."

"What kind of evidence?"

Dec rolled his eyes. "In his suicide note, Jian Lee said a woman was forcing his hand. They've also got threatening messages that were supposedly sent from a computer that only Galena had access to."

"What kind of threats?"

"The one I saw seemed to be saying the Marburg virus would be unleashed if the guy didn't take some action."

"So the threat involved a deadly, contagious disease." Aislin's gaze was steady on him. "Are you sure she *didn't* have anything to do with this?"

"*What?*"

Aislin sat down in her chair. "Galena Margolis has been severely traumatized. She has also been thrust into the limelight, a lot of pressure for someone who's been through so much. And she is extremely intelligent. Are you absolutely certain that she didn't arrange this as a way to have this responsibility removed from her shoulders?"

The rage and frustration ran hot across Dec's skin. "Yeah, I'm sure. She was completely distraught at the deaths of her volunteers and her lab assistants."

"Are you sure that wasn't guilt?"

"Of course she felt guilty," shouted Dec. "Innocent people died just because they were connected to her research. But it wasn't because she actually killed them!"

Aislin was silent, and Dec closed his eyes and drew in a deep breath. "All right," he said slowly. "If Galena's so intelligent—and trust me, she is—why the hell would she send messages from a machine *only* she had access to?"

He opened his eyes to find Aislin looking thoughtful. "She didn't try to cover her tracks at all?"

"The detective said there was a lot of security around the messages, but still. Galena would know better."

"Was the message sent at a time that her presence in the lab could be confirmed?"

"Yes. At a time she was the only one there. But—"

"Declan, what do you expect me to do?" Aislin rose from her chair. "It sounds like they've built a fairly strong case against Galena, and although we do have pull within the department, we can't stop Detective Botros from pursuing this right now. People are in an absolute uproar over these bombings, and our board is equally upset over my consenting to make Galena a Ferry. Put those two things together. We'll have to let the wheels of justice turn for a little while."

"You've got to be kidding me. The 'wheels of justice'? The PD is underequipped and understaffed. They're virtually irrelevant. We go around them all the time. Hell, don't we *own* them?"

"I've been the CEO for a *week*, Declan. I'm working to form alliances with all our subsidiaries, including the police, and to earn the board's trust. If I overuse my leverage, especially in a way that draws more negative publicity, there will be consequences. Rylan had many allies, both human and supernatural, and I need to show that I can control both the company and the empire." She clasped her hands in front of her. "And meanwhile, we've had two dozen unauthorized Markings, and any day we're going to hear from the Keepers about the time of the summit. It could go either way. They could punish Moros for losing control of his Kere, but they could punish us, too, for not being able to stop them."

"So you're willing to sacrifice Galena?" Dec asked, his voice shaking.

"Don't put words in my mouth. I consented to her Claiming, didn't I? We took responsibility for her, and now she's immortal. What else do you want from me?"

Dec couldn't help but squirm. Galena *wasn't* immortal, but now didn't seem the time to tell Aislin that he hadn't held up his end of the deal. "She won't exactly be able to do her research if she's in prison."

Aislin tucked a wisp of blonde hair behind her ear. "It is not my responsibility to remove all possible obstacles between Galena Margolis and her mysterious, magical vaccine. Moros has indicated that she is not fated to die in the near future, and now I have done my part in preserving the fabric of what is meant to be."

"That's bullshit," said Dec. "And it sounds a bit like Ry. You want Galena to live, but you don't want her to be able to finish her research?" He studied her face. He'd thought she was done with Rylan. She'd stripped him of his Scope and locked him up. But now . . . "Have you talked to Rylan lately?"

"I've spoken to him. I will not decide his sentence until after we meet with the Keepers. He seems remorseful for what he's done."

Dec shook his head. "It's an act. Don't fall for it."

Her face was blank and her voice was flat as she said, "I daresay I've known Rylan a bit longer than you have, Declan, and I've been here at Psychopomps since I graduated from college. More than two decades before you were born. I have no doubt you are an excellent paramedic, but don't you dare come here and tell me how to conduct my business."

The condescension in her voice made his teeth clench. This was the first time Aislin had pulled that card, and it burned. And it was also the first time Dec wished he *had* joined the corporate world, because maybe he'd be doing a better job of helping Galena if he had. "I'm not telling you how to do your job, Aislin, but are you so certain Rylan doesn't have some rogue Ker buddy on the outside, doing his dirty work?" *Like Luke?* The blond Ker obviously hated Galena, and with disease as his weapon of choice, he had better reason than any other Ker to want her out of the picture.

"If Rylan had communicated with a Ker, we would know. He's closely guarded both here and in the Veil. I think we should assume, therefore, that the rogue is working on its own. However, we should also be willing to consider the possibility that Galena is not completely innocent."

"If you knew her, you wouldn't be saying that," Dec said, his voice gravelly.

Aislin arched a pale eyebrow. "Are you certain that *you* know her, Declan? I acknowledge that the bond has brought you close to her, but knowing a woman's body isn't the same as knowing her secrets."

Dec looked away from his sister's penetrating stare. "She's dead set on completing that research, Aislin. She has zero reason to destroy it. If she did, all she'd have to do was quit."

"Harvard spent billions of private investor dollars to make a lab for her. Her speech at the fund-raiser was in every single news feed in the world within a few hours. It would be a highly publicized and damning humiliation if she even *tried* to quit."

"So is getting charged with murder!"

Aislin nodded. "I regret supporting your Claiming of her. I will do what I can to keep this from reflecting poorly on you."

"I don't give a fuck about how it reflects on me. I need our best lawyer, and I need you to pull every string you can. She shouldn't be in there." His throat suddenly tightened. "She's probably scared out of her mind."

Slowly, Aislin approached him. "I thought you were only doing this out of obligation, Declan." Her face softened into a gentle smile. "After all, you're one of the most honorable men I know."

He didn't feel honorable now. He felt desperate. "You're honorable, too, Aislin. And you know that the honorable thing to do is to help her."

Except—the Ferrys and Kere would be *delighted* if Aislin had found a way to neutralize Galena without starting a war or violating the treaty. It would put Aislin in a doubly powerful position as she faced the Keepers of the Afterlife. Hell, it was even better than Rylan's strategy had been. Dec eyed his beautiful, poised sister. She was one of the most powerful people in the world. And that was no accident. All the heat inside Dec turned to ice.

She put her hand on his arm. "You *care* for Galena."

Damn straight, but he wasn't about to admit that to someone he didn't fully trust and have it used against him. He looked out the window, at the sun reflecting off the high-rises of downtown. "I just think she has important things to do. I want to fulfill my obligation."

She gave his arm a quick squeeze, and then her hand fell away. "I cannot make you any promises right now," she said, returning to her desk, all softness gone. "But you may engage the services of Nan Drummond. She is our best defense attorney."

"Can't you use your contacts at the PD to quash this, though?" It wasn't like the Ferrys didn't do that all the fucking time.

But none of them had ever been charged with murdering fifteen people and destroying several city blocks, either.

Aislin's look said she was thinking the same thing. "If Galena is innocent, then Nan will be able to get her out of this. It may take time, but—"

"She may not *have* time," Dec snapped. "It can't be good for her, locked in a cell in the city jail. Do you have any idea what could happen to her in there?"

"Nothing that could kill her, obviously. But I will call and request additional protection for her. It would cause an uproar if she was hurt and healed right before people's eyes."

"*That's* what you're worried about? Do you know how fucking heartless you sound?"

She glared at him. "I have no doubt Nan will do everything possible to free Galena. For now, that is all I can do."

"Thank you," he forced himself to say. He turned and headed for the elevator.

"Declan?"

He looked over his shoulder at her.

"Do not consider taking matters into your own hands. It would only make things worse. The game is at a critical point."

He met her ice-blue gaze with one of his own, then walked stiffly to the elevator and jabbed his thumb against the "Down" button. *The game is at a critical point.* As he stepped into the elevator and the doors slid shut, he couldn't help feeling he was Aislin's pawn. He stared at his reflection in the metallic doors, the certainty building inside him that he was being used.

Fine. Let Aislin think he was playing by her rules. But if this lawyer couldn't get Galena out, Dec was ready to make a few moves of his own.

CHAPTER TWENTY-ONE

The cell door slid shut with a heavy clang, and Galena winced. She was dressed in the most expensive clothes she'd ever worn, a pink silk blouse and a black pencil skirt, both probably picked out by Cacy, brought to her so she could look the right part for her arraignment.

It hadn't helped much.

Her limbs heavy, wobbling on her heels, Galena took a few steps toward the bed, which was nothing more than a thin mat laid on top of a metal panel bolted to the wall. It wouldn't have mattered if it were the most comfortable mattress in the world, though. As long as she was here, she wouldn't be able to sleep. She stared down at it until its hard edges blurred and softened.

She'd just pled not guilty to over a dozen counts of murder, plus numerous other charges that Galena hadn't even tried to remember. And true to Detective Botros's word, the judge had immediately denied bail. Her lawyer, a tall, stern woman named Nan Drummond, had argued ferociously on her behalf, but the prosecutor had simply stated two facts that seemed to seal Galena's fate: Galena was widely acknowledged as a genius. And she had just married into the most affluent family in Boston. Together, that equaled a flight risk too great to allow, especially in light of the severity of the crimes.

The judge also set her trial date at the arraignment—eight months in the future. With her heart in her throat, Galena had turned around to find Eli and Dec staring back at her. They were sitting together, both dressed up, looking more like businessmen than paramedics. She wondered if the horror in their eyes matched her own. She could read Eli like a book—she knew he didn't believe for a moment that she was guilty. But Dec was unreadable; his glacier-blue eyes were riveted on her face as the guard pulled her to her feet. Did he think she coerced Jian into planting the bombs?

Why wouldn't he? The evidence was damning. And there was more of it than Botros had initially showed her. Jian had apparently received a whole string of vile messages, threatening to unleash a virus, threatening to make his wife victim number one, threatening to find his family and hurt them, too. No wonder he'd been so desperately angry when he'd found her in the Veil. No wonder Botros seemed determined to see her put away for life.

Dec had stood up as the guards led her away. *I'm so sorry,* she'd wanted to say. Not that she'd had anything to do with the crimes. But Dec had been dragged into this, pressured by Cacy, guilted by Eli, and now he was stuck with her. He'd done everything he could for her, too. She wondered if annulment was allowed for Ferrys. He deserved to be free from all this crap swirling around her.

A terrible, writhing frustration had built inside her as she'd stared at the ceiling last night, thinking over all that had happened. She'd known this wasn't fair to Dec. But what made it really, truly hurt? The longer she knew him, the more she wanted to please him, or maybe help him, even once. She wanted to make him smile, a real smile like in that picture he treasured. She felt a connection to him, and she wanted him to be glad he'd taken a chance on her. But there was no way that was happening now.

She was going to be transferred to a women's prison out in Framingham in the morning. She wondered if he'd come visit her, even if just to say good-bye and good luck. Because now that she was probably going to spend the rest of her life behind bars, there was no way she'd finish her research, and therefore her life probably was no longer in danger. Dec could be free.

She bowed her head and wrapped her arms around herself. She wished she could simulate the feel of Dec's arms around her, that she could fool herself into believing, even for a moment, that he was here. She could remember the taste of his mouth, his scent, the blue of his eyes, such a cool color, but when he'd looked at her, all she'd felt was warm. "I miss you," she whispered. "I don't know how you became so essential so quickly, but you did."

Somewhere down the hall, another cell clanged shut. It was such a lonely sound. She'd never minded being alone. Not until now.

Galena skimmed her fingers across her cheekbones, unsurprised when they came away wet with tears. With her eyes closed, she tilted her head back.

And felt a trickle of cold air across her damp cheeks.

Her eyes popped open. Hovering above her head was a growing ring, and within it was the swirling gray world of the Veil. She gasped as it whooshed down over her head, lightning-fast, engulfing her with cold. Enfolded in a steely grip, she instinctively began to thrash and struggle.

"It's me," said Dec, catching her wrist midswing.

"Dec? What are you—?"

"Hang on. I need to focus. More Ferrys will be arriving to guard you at any minute." He closed his eyes as he pressed his thumb to the raven on his Scope. Galena was paralyzed by her surprise, unable to believe he was there, right there. His arm was solid around her, like he had no plans to let her go. His Scope glowed as he brushed his thumb across it, and he shook it wide and peered into the intra-Veil portal. A smile pulled at the corners of his mouth. "Perfect."

He lowered the Scope over the two of them, and Galena found herself in a gelatinous gray version of what looked like an old-fashioned log cabin. "Where is this?"

Dec released her. He lifted his Scope from the floor, compacted it, and then pulled it wide again, creating a window to the real world. "A place to hide." He widened the ring of the Scope and allowed her to step through.

It really was a log cabin. As she walked through, she saw a wood-burning fireplace, a small kitchen, a desk, and a bed covered in an antique quilt. A doorway off the kitchen led to a bathroom, complete with a glass-walled shower. A peek out the window revealed a steep brown-gray mountainside. She turned to find Dec clipping his Scope to its setting. His eyes met hers. "We're on Baffin Island."

Part of the newly independent Arctic Circle colonies, incredibly remote. His Scope had carried them more than two thousand miles in the blink of an eye. Still, that was the least stunning thing about this. "Why did you bring me here?"

He regarded her steadily. "So no one will find us."

"But Eli—"

"He knows. He could find you anyway—Kere can do that, as long as they have a connection to a person. More importantly, he loves you, and I didn't want to keep him in the dark."

She looked around the rustic cabin, which was full of deceptively modern touches and conveniences, like running water, judging by the faucets and the shower, as well as a stove and fridge. "This is yours?"

He nodded. "I've had it for several years, but I've only been here a few times. No one knows about it. I wanted a place that was just mine. In case I ever decided to cut ties with my family." He gave her a sheepish smile. "The last time I was here, I arrived by helicopter. This was much faster."

She touched his arm. He was wearing a jacket, she noticed, and boots. And a large backpack. "Dec, why are you doing this?"

He slid the backpack off his shoulders. "You're being set up, and I wasn't about to let you spend another hour in a cell."

A million questions were tumbling around inside her head, but she settled on one clear, ringing thought. "You don't think I did it."

"I *know* you didn't do it."

She couldn't control the warm laughter that bubbled from her throat. She took two steps forward and wrapped her arms around his waist, leaning her head against his shoulder. The relief inside her was overwhelming, as was her need to be close to him. "I'm a fugitive," she whispered.

"I know. I may be, too, because Aislin will know I had something to do with it. She's going to be furious."

"Why would you risk that?"

He stroked her hair away from her forehead. "Because I couldn't stand to think of you being scared and alone."

And for that, he'd risked *everything*. Galena tilted her head up to his, her lips brushing his jaw. "I'm not either of those things now. Because you're with me."

His gaze dropped to her mouth, and his scrutiny made her tongue dart out to nervously wet her lips. His pupils dilated. And then his mouth claimed hers with a barely restrained ferocity that she met with passion of her own. Her hands found his hair, anchoring him to her as his arms coiled around her. His stubble scraped at her chin, and she surged onto her tiptoes, desire rising inside her.

Galena nipped at his bottom lip, and Dec groaned. His tongue invaded her mouth, gentle but questing, tasting and teasing. Her chest was pressed to his, every part of her pulling tight. She felt the need, low in her belly, pure and strong and heady. For Dec. Only him. Her fingers closed over the collar of his jacket, tugging it away, and a moment later he let her push it off his arms, revealing a long-sleeved T-shirt pulling tight against the muscles of his chest.

Galena closed the distance between them quickly, eager to feel his mouth on hers again. But Dec caught her hips, holding her body away from him. "This," he said, taking a few breaths as he leaned his forehead against hers, his eyes closed. "This is where we hit trouble last time."

She glanced down to see his erection pressed against the front of his jeans. With the way she was feeling right now, she was willing to give it a try, but then she remembered how last time had made *him* feel. *Like a rapist,* he'd said. A pang of frustration and sadness stabbed through her, pushing the truth from her mouth. "I know. But I need you to touch me. Please."

His eyes opened. Slowly, his fingertips trailed up her arm, across her injured shoulder, his touch so light that it left only pleasure in its wake. He traced his way up the column of her neck, and Galena trembled, feeling her nipples turn pearl-hard. Dec's gaze dropped to them like he could sense it. He kissed her again, unhurried and sensual. "Then show me what you want," he murmured, tilting his head and brushing a soft kiss on the underside of her jaw.

He hadn't said it like a challenge, but that was what it was. Galena swallowed hard. *You can do this. You have a right to it.* "I guess you can't read my mind, then," she whispered.

"I'm working on it." He drew his tongue along her throat, and she arched back with the pleasure of it, making her wonder if he was a *very* quick study. But she wasn't about to make him figure it out alone—she needed to own this. She reached up and took his hand, and placing her palm lightly over his, slowly began to move it. His skin was the most sensitive of instruments, completely attuned to her. She guided his fingers down her neck, and he followed with his mouth, tiny kisses tracing the path. Her breath caught in her throat as she kept moving his hand lower, as it crossed over the neckline of her silk blouse.

She watched the motion of their joined hands with wonder as they slid over a breast, but when his thumb stroked her taut nipple, her eyes closed. Slick warmth throbbed between her legs, which nearly buckled. Dec's thumb kept moving in a slow circle as her body pulsed with need. His head was bowed, their cheeks touching, while he kindled the fire inside her. It was the most amazing feeling, frantic but isometric, fraught but completely still. Like she was pushing against some giant unseen force, every muscle in her body desperate to break through.

Full of curiosity and hope, Galena nudged Dec's hand even lower, across her ribs, over her stomach, which quivered at its warmth. Her body was calling for what it needed, and so far, it had been easy to hold back the memories inside her head. But as his hand reached her waist, she realized they had a problem. Her pencil skirt was not going to make things easy. Dec was watching her as she looked up at him, unsure. His angular jaw was hard with tension, but the kiss he planted on her forehead was utterly gentle. "Do you trust me?" he whispered.

"Yes." It came easily. And it was completely true.

"Tell me to stop if you need me to." His hands skimmed down her sides and came to rest on her waist. "Can you do that? One word. 'Stop.' That's all you need to say."

She nodded, tilting her head up to touch her lips to his again. As his tongue slid along hers, his fingers slipped behind her and unzipped her skirt, tooth by tooth, inch by inch, so slowly that it didn't make a noise. It was like he was waiting for her to call it off. But her desire for his touch had pulled her over that edge, and she wanted to feel his hands on her. She silently promised him she wouldn't freak out, wouldn't lose her grip. *You want this. You need this.* And she did. So much that when her skirt slid off her hips and landed on the floor around her feet, her shiver was mostly from the cool air.

Mostly. She couldn't help the tiny snake of fear slithering in her belly, just below the scars. She still didn't want him to see them, worried how he might react. Would her shirt hide them?

She broke their kiss and looked down at herself, the expensive skirt pooled around her high heels, her simple white panties, and the pink blouse that was just long enough to cover all the things she wished she could conceal forever.

"You okay?" Dec's palm was on the small of her back, warm and heavy.

She nodded. "I-I just . . . I'm going to keep my shirt on, if that's all right?"

He nudged her chin up. "Your call." His kiss was unbearably sweet. Hypnotic and hot. Same as his hands, one of which had slipped over her ass and was gently kneading her flesh. His other hand was flattened on her belly, his fingertips caressing the silk of her blouse. He wouldn't feel the scars through it, would he? She put her hand over his again and moved it until his fingertips reached the boundary of her panties. Her body clenched, begging for satisfaction. But as she pushed him lower, as his fingers sank beneath the white silky material and slid over her vulnerable skin, brushing the curls of hair below, a shudder ran through her.

The blond one shoved his fingers into her as his knife pressed to her belly. "Oh, fuck, that's tight."

Dec flinched. Galena realized she'd sunk her fingernails into the back of his hand. She yanked her fingers away. "Oh God. I'm sorry."

His forehead touched hers. "Stop or go?"

She closed her eyes. The last thing she wanted was to put Dec in the position of touching her when it didn't feel right to him. She swallowed, her throat suddenly dry. "I don't know."

His hands moved to her hips. "I'm going to go slow." His fingers hooked under the edge of her panties, and he began to draw them down. His lips brushed a spot on her neck just beneath her ear, and Galena bit her lip, the craving taking her over again. He kissed the base of her throat, his tongue tracing the bony hollow there. She put her hands over his, urging him on as his face slid along the silk of her blouse, his hot breath wafting against her breasts, and gradually skimmed lower. Her heart felt like it wanted to burst from her chest as he got to his knees. "Stop?" he whispered.

Their hands had frozen low on her hips, her panties barely covering her most vulnerable parts, the places where she needed him most, despite the fear.

"You're safe, Galena. You will always be safe with me." His nose grazed her hip, and then she felt his tongue slide down to her thigh. Her head fell back, and she pushed their hands lower, until she could reach no farther. It was a surrender, letting him take over, and he seemed to feel it, because he carefully slid the scrap of fabric down her thighs, over her knees, down to the floor. One by one, he lifted her feet, freeing her. She couldn't help the way her legs were trembling as the air hit her core, making her shake with vulnerability.

Dec took off her shoes, and each movement of his hands was a caress, stoking the flames. He guided her feet a little farther apart, and Galena felt the floor drop out from under her as his tongue slid up her inner thigh. Dec's grip on her tightened, keeping her from falling. "Take a few steps back," he murmured, and guided her, his hands on her hips again.

Galena followed his lead until the soft fabric of the quilt tickled the back of her thighs. His hands skimmed down to her knees as she sank onto the mattress. She couldn't believe this. She was naked from the waist down, and he was right there, pushing her knees apart. She lay back and closed her eyes tightly as he smoothed his hands down her legs and back up, a soothing, gentle motion. He kissed her inner thigh, and she pressed her lips together. He was kneeling between her legs. He could see her. All of her.

As if he heard her thoughts, he reached up and took her hand, locking their fingers together. "Yeah?" he asked, nibbling at the side of her knee, each brush of his lips making her hotter.

She squeezed his hand. "Yeah," she whispered. Her heels came to rest on the hard muscles of his shoulders, her toes curling as his mouth trailed higher, the warm, wet tip of his tongue tracing a delicate path up to the center of her. Galena trembled, eager but terrified. What would happen when he—

With one long, devastating lick, Dec tasted her for the first time. The vibrations of his moan made her inner muscles tighten with need. She whimpered as the soft firmness of his mouth reached her tiny, sensitive bud. He flicked his tongue over it, and she arched back, spreading her legs, offering him more. He started slowly, circling his tongue around it before pressing harder, making her cry out from the tingling pleasure it sent coursing across her skin. Her hips rose, her body moving on its own. Dec drew his tongue up and down, exploring, as Galena lost herself in molten, irresistible throbbing.

He didn't use his fingers—only his tongue, his lips, his breath. But they were more than enough. Galena could feel the slickness of her own arousal, and she knew he must be tasting it, that his tongue was slippery with it. His face was buried between her legs, one hand still skimming up and down her inner thighs, reassuring, calming, while the rest of her coiled tighter and tighter. For a moment, Galena forced herself to open her eyes. She raised her head to find his gaze riveted to hers. As she watched, Dec lifted his mouth from her and licked his lips. And then he leaned down, teasing her clit with his tongue, sending sharp pangs of hard pleasure shooting through her. Galena moaned, and her head fell back again, her hips undulating in time with his tongue as it delivered long, probing licks up and down her folds.

"Still yeah?" he rasped.

"Dear God, yes."

His hand tightened over hers a second before she felt him slowly push his tongue inside her. Galena moaned. Her heels slid to his back. It was exactly what she needed: the pressure, the friction. Her fingers tugged at his hair, urging him on. He wrapped a hand around her thigh and locked his mouth against her, thrusting deep a few times before returning to her clit. She cried out, her pleasure spiraling, her hips canted up and begging for more. *More.* He couldn't stop. She didn't want this to *ever* stop. But she was too lost to form words.

Dec didn't seem to need them. He translated the tensing muscles, her ragged breaths, the urgent bucking of her hips, the tangle of her fingers in his hair. He picked up the pace, fluttering his tongue against her until the wave broke and ecstasy crashed over her, stars exploding behind her closed eyelids and a helpless cry falling from her lips. But he still didn't stop, thrusting his tongue inside her as her inner muscles spasmed, as he tasted her from the inside out. It only prolonged the pleasure, and when she became aware of herself again, her hips were halfway off the bed and she was clutching Dec's face to the center of her, every muscle taut.

Slowly, she sank back, her breaths still bursting from her throat, tears starting in her eyes. She began to shake, feeling it rising up from the lingering pleasure inside her, wringing her out. She'd never thought she'd feel this way again. She'd thought it would never be possible. But somehow, Dec had brought this out of her, coaxed it to the surface and let it spread its wings. Still panting, a tear slipping from the corner of her eye, she propped herself up on her elbows to look at him. His head was bowed against her inner thigh. "Dec?"

"Yeah," he said, a little hoarsely. "You okay?"

"Better than okay," she said. "You?"

"Fine," he said. "Um . . . can you excuse me for a minute?"

"What?"

He sat up and wiped his mouth. "I just . . . I'll be back in a few." He got up quickly and walked into the bathroom off the kitchen.

Galena looked down at herself, her legs still spread wide, the cool air now kissing the slick wetness on her thighs. Shivering, she sat up, just as she heard water switch on, the unmistakable sound of a shower. She frowned. What had just happened?

Had she done something wrong?

A tiny wire of panic crimped inside her, and she put her hand over her stomach. As the water hissed from the other room, she shimmied into her panties and pulled the skirt on again. Her hair disheveled and falling over her shoulders, her body loose, she padded toward the bathroom. The door was open a few inches, and she could see droplets slither down the glass shower door.

A sense of loss and confusion washed over her. He'd given her the most intense orgasm she'd ever had, and he'd managed to do it without awakening a single black, evil memory. And then he'd walked away to take a shower?

Oh no. *No.* Was it because it was terrible? Had it been gross?

She grimaced, taking a few steps closer, drawn to him, terrified to know the truth but needing it all the same. One more step brought Dec into full view.

He had one arm braced against the shower wall, his hand fisted, his forehead pressed to his forearm. Water ran over his muscular, naked body, which was as chiseled and gorgeous as Galena would have expected. She looked him over, her breath catching as she realized what was happening.

His other hand stroked up and down his rigid shaft, which jutted from his body, thick and ruddy. His movements were frantic. The muscles of his back and ass were tense and trembling. And then the side of his fist slammed against the stall. Galena jumped as she heard Dec stifle a groan, pressing his face to his arm. Then he sagged against the wall, his face still hidden, his powerful body slumped.

Galena backtracked unsteadily, stunned and breathless. She'd asked him to touch her, and he had. Selflessly. Gently. Completely aware of what she needed.

But he hadn't asked her to touch him. Instead, he'd taken care of himself. And she suspected she understood why.

Determination rose up inside her. Once again, the black memories had won, and they hadn't even needed to be at the forefront of her mind to do it. Instead, they'd descended like a wall between her and Dec, keeping him from asking for the same kind of pleasure he'd given her. He'd felt alone in his arousal, forced to chase a solitary pleasure for fear of reminding her of things she didn't want to think about. The understanding was both sweet and astoundingly bitter.

Would she ever be able to find her way to him? Was it even possible?

She wiped her eyes and took a few deep breaths as the water in the shower switched off. "I promise, Dec," she whispered. "I'm going to figure this out."

CHAPTER TWENTY-TWO

Dec leaned against the wall of the shower, trying to catch his breath. His muscles were just starting to uncoil after the insistent, relentless tension of the last several minutes. He kept his eyes closed as the water streamed down his body, still savoring the taste of Galena on his tongue. Seeing her laid out before him, her legs spread wide and her head thrown back, with her slender fingers clutching at his hair, all while his mouth had been full of her faint sweetness, the irresistible honey tang of her skin . . . he'd almost come right there. Worse, all he'd wanted to do was to unzip his pants and thrust himself into the soft heat of her.

He'd had to get away from her. She wasn't ready to touch him, to have him inside her. As painful as it would be to know the details, he wished she would tell him what had actually happened to her. That way it might be easier to avoid triggering her. He'd felt her tense as his fingertips skimmed the soft curls between her legs, and it killed him, knowing some guy might have used his fingers to hurt her. Then she calmed down when he'd only used his mouth. He'd felt like he'd been blindfolded and was groping his way toward her in the dark. Luckily for both of them, it had worked. Better than Dec could have possibly imagined.

Except that it made him want to do it again. And again and again. The sound of her moans and whimpers, the desperate buck of her hips, the way she opened herself to him, like she was begging for his touch, like she was *starving* for it . . . it made him want her in every possible way.

He swung open the shower door and reached for a towel. He shouldn't have used so much water—he'd probably just burned through fifty gallons of the two hundred fifty in the tank. It would refill with the next rain, but he should have been more careful. He glanced over and felt his cheeks flush when he saw the door partially ajar. In his wild hurry to release his bottled need, he hadn't been paying attention. He nudged it shut and dried himself off, then put his clothes back on.

He looked back at the closed door. Fuck. He'd gone down on her, then walked away from her like a total asshole without a word of explanation. Except, what would he have said?

If I don't leave this room right now, I'm going to lose control.

Excuse me, I need to go jack off or else my dick is going to explode.

There was no polite way to express what had been going on inside his head and body.

He toweled off his hair and opened the door again. Galena was sitting on the bed looking pale and tousled, and maybe a little shell-shocked. She had gotten dressed again and seemed strangely out of place in her pink blouse and black skirt, which fit every curve of her body in a way that made Dec's dick twitch, like it was begging for another shot.

She watched him emerge from the bathroom, her green eyes wide and curious. "Are you okay?" she asked.

"Yeah. Sorry. I just needed to . . ." He cleared his throat. "Do you want to change into something more comfortable? I brought some other clothes for you."

She gave him a smile laced with sadness. "Why are you so amazing?"

He chuckled. "Your standards aren't very high."

She rolled her eyes and stood up as Dec knelt next to his pack and pulled out a pair of sweats and a long-sleeved shirt. As she took them and headed to the bathroom, she ran her fingers through his damp hair, and he closed his eyes and savored her touch.

By the time she emerged, he was making sandwiches. She laughed when he set one on a plate and slid it in her direction. "Now this is service," she said.

"Did you eat while you were locked up?"

She shrugged. "I wasn't that hungry."

"I *knew* it." He jabbed his finger at the sandwich. "Eat."

They ate in companionable silence. Dec was relieved to see the hunger on her face as she polished off one sandwich, and he quickly made her another, which she finished nearly as quickly. He couldn't help but smile at the protective pride swelling in his chest; she was allowing him to take care of her.

After they were finished, she got up and returned to the bed, scooting over to make room for him. He settled himself next to her. "What now?" she asked quietly.

He sighed. "Now we figure out who actually committed the crimes you're accused of, and we catch them."

"That's all?"

"It's a start."

"Any ideas?"

He turned onto his back and reached for her, pulling her into the shelter of his arms. She melted against him, forcing him to close his eyes and take a few slow breaths, because his cock started to swell at the feel of her body, her warmth. *Concentrate.* "There may be a regular human framing you, or possibly a Ferry, but my money's on the Ker who attacked Luciana, and who maybe got to Jian. And I think I know which one it is."

"Who?"

"Luke. You saw him a few nights ago. He knew exactly who you were. Somehow, he knew you'd been made a Ferry. I think he called you specifically to that spot. And I think he purposefully dropped that guy right in the center of the park. I don't know how he drew the Shades there, but they sense whenever a portal is opened—they can feel the real world when someone steps through."

"But if he knew I was a Ferry, wouldn't he have assumed I'm immortal like you? What could a Shade really do? It can't kill you, right?"

Dec cradled her head on his shoulder, treasuring the feel of her breath skimming over his throat. "A Shade can't kill a Ferry, but they could hurt one badly enough so that he couldn't get back to the real world, especially if they'd gotten his Scope. And wounds don't heal in the Veil. One of my uncles was lost that way, maimed so badly that he was trapped in the Veil for good."

"They just left him there?"

Dec shook his head. "No, we have a special department at Psychopomps that searches for lost or injured Ferrys in the Veil, but the world is a huge place."

"What about the Ker who worked with your uncle last? Wouldn't it be able to say where he was?"

"Yes, but we don't think he was in the Veil to Ferry someone. He was probably using his Scope recreationally." This was why they were never supposed to use their Scopes apart from their duty to guide dead souls. If they got lost or injured in the Veil, no one would know where they were. "Hopefully, we'll find him someday and bring him home." Hopefully, there would be something left of him to find.

"I didn't realize you were so vulnerable in the Veil," she said in a small voice.

"It's not usually so bad." He decided it was better not to tell her that he'd nearly had his arm ripped off a few weeks ago. "What happened with those Shades was unusual. And that's what makes me think Luke is in on it. Maybe he was working with Jian, or working with whoever was threatening Jian and framing you."

"Whoever framed me has an incredible amount of technical knowledge." Galena snorted. "But then again, so do most people at Harvard."

She was absently stroking her fingers along his ribs as she spoke. He wondered if she even noticed. *He* could barely think past the sensation. "Is there any way you could figure out who sent the messages, and how they managed to make it look like you were the one who did it?"

"Maybe, if I could get into the data center that houses Harvard's messaging servers. They would have archived records from the secure chat system."

He nodded, though he had little idea what finding those records would entail. She sounded like she did, so that was good enough for him. "We've already broken plenty of rules, so if you can figure out where this place is, I can get you in." He frowned. "Tracing computer messages isn't going to get us all the way there, though. We have to find proof that Luke was involved."

Galena looked thoughtful. "Maybe Luke tried to intimidate Jian in person? His phone might have a record of contacts between them. Or maybe his wife saw something? The poor woman has had her life turned upside down, though."

"So have you. A few questions won't hurt."

She squeezed him, and her leg slipped over the top of his, her thigh resting on his. "Can we wait a few hours? I'm—" She stifled a yawn.

"Massively sleep-deprived?"

She nodded, snuggling in under the covers and going quiet for a few minutes. But then—"Dec?"

"Hmm?"

"Earlier, right after you . . . um . . ."

Slowly, he turned, propping himself on his elbow over Galena, who was now on her back. The anxious look in her eyes awakened the ache in his chest. "I guess we should have talked about that."

She bit her lip and nodded. "You were so considerate. But I feel a little selfish," she said, her voice breaking.

"Selfish?" He lowered his head and brushed his mouth over hers, his body tightening as she closed her eyes and parted her lips. "Do you have any idea how much I enjoyed that? Tasting you? Feeling you come?" So much that the memory of it was making him hard as a fucking rock. He inched his hips back so she wouldn't feel it.

"But I-I didn't touch *you*. And I know you had to . . ." Her gaze flicked toward the bathroom as her cheeks turned the most enticing shade of pink. It could only mean one thing. She'd seen him in the shower jacking off like a horny teenager.

He chuckled as he shook his head. And although it sent a stab of longing through him, he said, "What I need and what I want— that's not your problem right now. And I'm fine taking care of myself, okay?"

She stared into his eyes, and he would have paid his entire fortune to read her thoughts. "Okay," she whispered, though he could have sworn the word was weighed down with sadness.

He rolled onto his back again and pulled her against him, stroking her hair until her breathing became even and her body relaxed. He lay there, reliving the day, hoping the two of them could figure out a way to clear Galena's name before this mess caught up with them.

Dec chuckled quietly. *What a way to start a marriage.*

The thought slid through his head so effortlessly that he froze as it hit the front of his mind. A few days ago, she'd been nothing more than an enticing stranger at best, a binding obligation at worst. But now she meant something entirely different to him, and it had happened so fast. He didn't completely understand it. All he knew was that being with her here, having her in his arms—it made him feel alive.

She made him feel alive.

A noise from his porch yanked his attention from her. *Creak.* His muscles tensed. Slowly, he slid Galena off him, and she settled into his pillow with a sigh, her hair falling across her face. The sun had long since set, and the night sky was lit only by the stars and moon. Dec padded over to the window and looked out.

Red eyes peered back at him, causing his heart to seize up. Touching the Scope at his throat, an ever-reassuring presence, Dec opened the front door just enough to let himself onto the porch, then closed it quietly, praying he wouldn't wake Galena.

Eli was sitting on a chair, looking out at the dark shadow of Mount Thor in the distance. "Nice place."

"Thanks."

"How is she?"

"Sleeping at the moment." Dec sat down in a chair next to Eli's.

"How . . ." Eli cleared his throat. "Did it go all right? The . . ."

"Claiming?" Dec's gaze ascended the mountain's west face, the largest vertical drop in the world. He thought maybe he knew what it felt like, now, to fall that far and fast. "It went as well as could be expected." Technically, that wasn't a lie. Maybe he should have told Eli the whole truth, but it felt like something between Dec and Galena now, no one else's fucking business.

Waves of heat were coming off Eli. It was impossible to tell his mood, but he seemed content to change the subject. "Aislin is putting a lot of pressure on Cacy to tell her where you are."

"Cacy doesn't know this place exists. No one in my family does."

"And she asked me not to tell her, because she doesn't want to know. She wants you guys to be safe." Eli turned to him. His green eyes, so similar to Galena's, were shadowed, no longer red.

"I'm grateful that you got G out of jail, but it's caused a complete shitstorm in Boston."

Dec shrugged, his fingers tracing the worn wood of his antique Adirondack chair. "I knew it would. But once Galena and I clear her name, I'll come back and deal with it."

Eli sighed. "If Moros asks me to tell him where you are, I won't be able to refuse him. You know that, right?"

"Is Moros in town?"

"Not yet. But Aislin has called him. Hell, he can find you himself, Dec. I don't even think he'd need my help."

"If the Lord of the Kere wants to come here, there's nothing we can do to stop him." Dec's muscles tensed at the thought. He'd fight as hard as he could, but he knew he was no match for Moros.

"But if he wanted to find you, he'd probably already be here," Eli said. "Cacy thinks he's staying out of it, planning to use the chaos as evidence against Aislin when they go to the summit with the Keepers. If it looks like the Ferrys can't manage things, either, he might be able to make a case that you guys aren't necessary, or more trouble than you're worth."

Dec's fists clenched. Moros was playing his own game, just like Aislin. "We're going to try to make this right as quickly as possible. For the sake of all involved."

"Good," Eli said, his eyes turning from green to crimson as Dec watched. "Because I've been sent to give you a message. From Aislin. She knew I'd be able to find Galena, so she sent it to me about an hour ago." He pulled his phone from his pocket and accessed an archived message, then held it up for Dec to see.

Watching it was like stepping into the Veil. The chill crept across his skin until it enveloped him completely. Aislin stared out from the screen, her eyes icy, her mouth hard.

"Declan, you have until midnight to return to Boston and turn Galena in. If you refuse, your status will be revoked, and your

Scope will be decommissioned. It was the wrong choice to cross me, especially now. Fix this. *Immediately.*" The screen went dark.

Dec looked at the time display on Eli's phone. He had twenty hours until she would make good on that threat. He glanced back at the window, just able to make out Galena's sleeping form on the bed. He would give anything not to wake her up, to crawl into that bed with her and hold her all night.

But he couldn't. Now the clock was ticking. And he didn't want to think about how vulnerable he and Galena would be when the time ran out.

CHAPTER TWENTY-THREE

Galena squatted behind the wall that ringed the data center, Dec at her side. He'd awakened her a few hours ago, pulling her from a wonderful dream where she was kissing him, one she'd hoped to make reality. But the grim look on his face had been enough to yank her out of that fantasy. He wouldn't tell her exactly what was wrong, but he had said they needed to get moving. They'd made a brief stop in Boston's Chinatown—in a narrow alleyway that smelled like rot and urine, to be precise—where Dec had been able to get a stable-enough signal on his phone to allow her to access the Harvard system and trace where their mail messaging data center was physically located.

Dec was able to navigate quickly to some places in the Veil, but if he didn't know his destination well, it was hit or miss. So he'd called up a map and stared at the satellite image of the data center so intently that Galena was surprised the screen didn't melt under his scrutiny. And then he'd pulled her close and brought them into the Veil again.

He'd gotten them here. Now they'd have to rely on the Veil—and her technological expertise—to find the information she needed.

"Ready to go back in?" he asked.

She nodded, holding his hand as they stepped through his Scope. "All I need is a maintenance terminal. And a little bit of time."

Dec was busy scanning the area for Shades, but the Veil was silent and still. They jogged along the squishy grass until they reached the door of the center. He grinned. "Want to try the handle?"

She rolled her eyes. "I was being chased by a freaking zombie, Dec. Forgive me for temporarily being scared out of my wits."

He chuckled and led her closer to the door, which was probably made of thick metal in the real world. "You just have to push your way through."

And then he did, disappearing into the gelatinous door. It closed around his body until only his hand was sticking out, still holding hers. His thumb stroked her fingers, and she couldn't help her smile, which she was still wearing as her face plunged into the door. For a moment, she couldn't breathe, and panic surged in her chest. But then her face popped out the other side to see Dec waiting for her. "That was weird."

He nodded. "Always try to go through the thinnest barrier. Cacy got stuck one time when she was new at this. She tried to bust her way through a thick brick wall and ended up with her head and shoulders in the building but her butt and legs on the outside."

Galena giggled at the comical image. "Good to know."

Dec looked around. "So where to? We should get as close as possible before we risk opening the Scope again."

Galena walked down one long hallway and then another, reading the signs on the doors of the rooms that housed specific servers. She'd been able to snag the number range of Harvard's servers, but when they got to the room, it turned out it hadn't been necessary—the seal of the university was right there on the door. "Sometimes I make things too difficult," she muttered.

"So this is it?"

Galena nodded, then barreled through the door a little too enthusiastically and ended up splatting face-first onto the floor of the server room. Dec hoisted her up a second later. In front of them were rows of shelves, each housing dozens of flat boxes about the size of her palm; in the Veil, their little lights shone a watery gray. She walked along one row, searching for what she needed, and finally found it at the end—a small video screen set into the side of the shelf. "This is it," she said.

Dec pressed his thumb to his Scope. "I'm going to—" He turned sharply.

"What?"

"See that?" He pointed down the aisle.

Squinting, she could just barely make out a shadow crossing the other side of the room. "A Shade?"

He shook his head. "A person in the real world. Probably a security guard." Dec jogged to the end of the aisle, peered toward one side of the room, and then scooted back. "He's sitting at a desk in the corner. I'm glad we spotted him. You're not going in there."

"I have to, Dec!"

He brushed his thumb over the raven on his Scope, then swung his arms over her head until the portal into the real world was about two feet wide and right in front of her. "No. You're going to stand right here and stick your hands through. Can you read the screen from here?"

Her back was nestled against his chest, and his muscular arms were on either side of her, surrounding her with safety. Galena slowly stuck her hands through the portal, instantly feeling the warmth of a room full of humming machines. Hesitantly, she touched the screen, and it lit up. Praying the security guard wasn't monitoring the activity of the maintenance terminals, Galena called up a proxy and logged in.

Access denied.

Damn. They must have frozen her account. Frowning, she logged in under Ankita's name. Galena couldn't help that she'd memorized the keystrokes for her lab assistant's password. It had been a habit of hers since grade school, and today she was very glad of it. She used Ankita's account to get to the information for the secure network in her destroyed lab. The data archives for the last thirty days were intact. "I think I'll be able to see when the messages were first sent to Jian," she whispered, staring at the slightly warped display through the swirling barrier between the Veil and the real world.

"Good. Hurry." Dec's eyes were riveted on the end of the aisle. They were at a slight disadvantage—even with a portal open, they could barely hear the guard, and seeing him wasn't the easiest thing, either.

She turned back to the screen, letting everything else fall away. Her fingers flew across the display, pushing through lists of files until she found the catalog of messages sent from Danny's terminal. She couldn't read the messages—she could only see their time stamps and the user account of the person who had sent them. *Her* user account.

The number of secure chats under her name was weirdly high. She scrolled back through the days, finding message after message, until they stopped about two weeks back. That must have been when whoever was framing her started threatening Jian. But it looked for all the world like *she* was the one who sent them. She kept scrolling back through the data files, noting other messages she knew she had sent. Then she noticed a cluster of tech-support chats dated the week she had arrived in Boston. Her brow furrowed.

She couldn't recall contacting tech support. She'd merely gotten her clearance, set her password, and started her work. "Something's not right here," she whispered, preparing to identify all additional entry points to her supposedly secure server. "I just have to—"

Galena's hands were still reaching for the terminal when Dec cursed abruptly and pushed the Scope forward, enveloping her fully in the Veil once more before slamming the Scope shut. "I think he saw your hands," he said, his voice tight.

His arm curled around her waist, and he pulled her back as the shadowy form of the guard jogged down the aisle. His phone was to his ear. They watched in horror as he started tapping at the terminal. "No," Galena whispered. "I didn't log out." She turned to Dec, her eyes wide. "What do we do?"

His eyes were just as wide. "We have to get out of here. Now." He pressed his thumb to his Scope. Without a further word, he stepped close to her, opened a portal, and pulled it down over them.

Galena looked around. They were in the southern part of Cambridge, where its dry streets gave way to narrow, sloshing canals and seedy tenements. "This is close to where Jian lives."

"I know. I looked his address up in the archived EMS records before your bail hearing." When he saw her bemused expression, he gave her a crooked smile. "I might not be a genius, but I use what I've got."

She was not about to argue with that. Dec was one of the more effective humans she'd ever met. He was quick and decisive, but almost never impulsive. In fact, the most impulsive decisions he made seemed to involve her. She knew she shouldn't be pleased by that, but somehow, she couldn't help the little glow of warmth in her chest at the thought.

Together, they approached the apartment building where Jian had lived. Dec paused when they reached it, his eyes tracing over a cluster of graffiti next to the entrance.

"What is it?" she asked him.

He shook his head. "Nothing. Let's go in."

Galena plunged herself through the door and shivered as she reached the hallway. It was nearly eight in the morning now. She'd

been out of jail for about eighteen hours. Plenty of time for author-
ities to mobilize.

And now she and Dec were about to break into a grieving
woman's home, probably scaring the living shit out of her. "Dec,
this doesn't feel good."

"I know. But we're running out of time." He let go of her hand
and stalked through the front door of Jian's apartment.

Galena followed and emerged on the other side to see the
transparent form of a slight woman making coffee in the kitchen.
"Maybe I should go alone. And knock. And ask if I can come in. I
don't want to just appear in her living room."

Dec glared at her. "No way. I'm going in without you."

"What?"

He took her by the shoulders. "Galena, this woman probably
believes you threatened her husband, blackmailing him into killing over a dozen people with those bombs. If you show up at her
door, she's going to believe you're here to finish the job."

"Oh. I guess you're right. But you might scare her."

His expression went from mildly amused to completely blank.
"Not unless I need to. I'm going to tell her I'm one of the detectives
on the case. You stay close to me, okay? And if you see anything—a
Shade, another Ferry, a Ker—you come through and get me. Do
not mess around. Everyone's looking for us right now."

She stepped close and pressed her cheek to his shoulder, and
his arm coiled around her back. He bowed his head, burying it in
her hair. "We're sticking together, do you hear me?" he whispered.

She closed her eyes and wrapped her arms around him. "Yeah,"
she whispered back. "I hear you."

CHAPTER TWENTY-FOUR

Dec smoothed his hair down, tucked his Scope into his collar, and straightened his shirt, wishing he was more nicely dressed. Galena's words scrolled through his head—*You might scare her.* He knew she hadn't meant him personally, at least, he didn't think so. In fact, he was pretty sure she was remembering the last time a strange man had showed up at *her* door.

Dec gave a few quiet knocks, not wanting to alert the neighbors. He put on his most charming smile as he faced the security screen set into the door.

"Who is it?"

"Mrs. Lee? I'm sorry to bother you this early, ma'am. I'm Detective Ferris from the Boston PD. I work with Detective Botros, and I have a few questions."

"Badge?"

Dec yanked his wallet from his pocket and flipped it open. With his thumb over the EMS symbol, he waved his own badge in front of the screen. A moment later, the lock clicked and Mei Lee opened the door. She was maybe five feet tall, with shiny black hair. Her eyes were shadowed with sadness and fatigue, red-rimmed from crying.

"I'm so sorry for your loss, Mrs. Lee," he said quietly.

She pressed her lips together and nodded. "Come in."

He followed her into the cramped apartment. The living area consisted of a couch, a videowall, and a strangely bare, dusty space in one corner—probably where Jian's computer setup had been before it was hauled away by the PD. "Detective Botros sent me over to ask you a few more questions as part of our investigation," he explained as they sat down on opposite ends of the couch.

"He said he'd finished his investigation of Jian," she said, her face crumpling. She dabbed her eyes with the loose collar of her shirt.

"Oh, he has. We're trying to catch the people who Jian was communicating with."

Mei's eyes narrowed. "*Her*, you mean. Have they found her? Have they figured out how she escaped?"

"We're working on it."

"Good. She deserves to rot in prison for the rest of what I hope will be a very long life." Mei's voice cracked, and she covered her face with her hands.

"We're applying all the resources at our disposal to bring the people responsible for these crimes to justice." He leaned forward. "Mrs. Lee, we have reason to believe there's another person involved."

Mei lowered her hands to her lap. "What?"

Dec couldn't believe the esteemed detective hadn't even followed up on any other possible suspects or leads. He'd just singled out Galena and ignored everything else. "Do you know if your husband was receiving threats from anyone else?"

She shook her head. "The detective said all the messages came from Galena Margolis. He said he had proof."

Dec let out a long breath through his nose. "Okay, but did Jian maybe get any other calls or text messages that seemed to concern him?"

Mei frowned. "Jian wasn't himself in those last two weeks. I knew something was wrong, but I had no idea what it was." She rolled her eyes, like she was disgusted with herself. "We were fighting a lot. And our last fight was really bad. It happened the night before he—" She began to cry, but then she took a deep breath and composed herself. "I came home from work and found Jian here with some friends I didn't know. He was already in a bad mood— they were arguing."

Dec tilted his head. "Do you know what the argument was about?"

"They were trying to schedule something. Jian was arguing with the guy, and the guy's girlfriend was trying to hold him back. They quieted down and left when I walked in, but Jian was on a hair trigger. He screamed at me." She sniffled. "But then he apologized. He said he hated his job. That he hated Galena Margolis. I told him he should quit, that nothing was worth that kind of stress." She rubbed her eyes. "He said he couldn't. And now I know why."

Her body shuddered with a sob, but then she wiped her cheeks and eyed Dec. "I already told the detective all this. Didn't he include it in his notes?"

Dec held up his hands. "He may have." But more likely, he hadn't thought it was important. "I've only read the general notes on the case." He had no idea what he was talking about, but it sounded official. "Ma'am, I know you've been through so much, but I was wondering if you could describe this couple to me."

"They were about our age. Midtwenties. The woman was white and had long brown hair. She was wearing a dress and heels. She was much friendlier than her boyfriend."

"Was the guy tall?"

She nodded. "Really tall. I mean, everyone looks tall to me, but he was *really* tall."

"And blond? Pale-blond hair?"

Her brow furrowed. "What? No. Black hair, short black hair. He was African American."

Dec's heart jolted in his chest. "Can you describe anything else about him?"

"He was very muscular. And his voice was deep. His eyes were dark. Except, right as he stopped arguing with Jian and turned to look at me, I could have sworn they looked . . ."

Dec felt like the world had shifted. "Yeah?"

"Nothing. It's crazy. Anyway, I haven't seen him or his girl-friend since that night, and Jian wouldn't say anything except they were graduate students that he shared a class with."

Dec stood up, his thoughts in a whirl. "Thank you for your time, ma'am."

He made his exit as quickly as possible and entered the Veil in a daze, barely able to comprehend what he'd just heard.

Please, let me be wrong. And yet it made a sick, horrible kind of sense. Galena rushed over to him before he'd compacted his Scope. "She told you something? What is it?"

"I think she just confirmed that Jian was visited by two Kere the night before he planted the bomb in your lab," Dec said, shivering from the cold of the Veil and his own icy disbelief. "One of them was Erin, I think. That new Ker we met in Cambridge Common?"

Galena put her hand on his arm. "And was the other Ker Luke?"

Dec's eyes met hers. "No," he said. "I think it was my best friend."

Dec texted Eli: *Meet me.*

He knew he didn't have to say where, because Eli could easily sense Galena and would come straight to her. Sure enough, Eli materialized a minute later in an alcove near Jian Lee's apartment where they were waiting. "What's wrong?"

"I need you to take Galena back to the cabin and guard her," said Dec, forcing himself not to look at Galena.

She wasn't having it. She touched his cheek and drew his face to hers. "You said we would stick together."

He put his hand over hers. "And we will. I just need to look into this first, and it'll work better if I'm alone." He had no idea what he would find when he confronted Trevor, but it seemed pretty damn likely his friend was a threat to the woman at his side. And she was still mortal. His jaw clenched. "You'll be safer at the cabin, and I'll come to you as soon as I can."

"Dec," Eli began, "whatever you're doing, I could come with—"

Dec shook his head. "Make sure your sister is safe."

Eli frowned, looking back and forth between Dec and Galena. His eyes traced over the scratch on Galena's forehead, as well as the ones at her throat. And then his gaze lasered in on Dec. "You told me—"

"Keep her safe." Dec stepped back. "All right?"

Eli's eyes glinted with red. "Someone has to." He grabbed Galena's wrist.

"Wait," Galena said, but then the two of them disappeared.

Dec stared at the place Galena had been. He hadn't gotten to say good-bye. His eyes closed. He needed his concentration more than ever now. She was safe. Much safer than she would be with him.

He pulled his Scope off its chain and focused on Trevor's apartment. He'd spent so many evenings there, just hanging out, drinking, playing pool. Trevor completely understood what it meant to live as long as they did—he was older than Dec, even older than Aislin. He knew the fatigue that came with so many years, so many lost friends, so much of the same old shit year after year. He was a good man. Dec had known something was up with Trevor the past week, and now he might have lost him. Dec slid his thumb over his Scope and stepped into the Veil, then opened a portal to Trevor's place, a loft in the canal zone of North Boston. Dec peered around cautiously, looking for his friend, not sure what he would find.

"What are you doing here?" Trevor had appeared not three feet away. At six and a half feet tall, built from solid muscle, his eyes glowing red, his fangs gleaming and his claws extended, he was intimidating as hell.

Dec stood his ground, even though Trevor could tear him to shreds if he wanted. "You're my friend. I was worried about you."

Trevor looked down at the Scope in Dec's hand. "You could have come to my front door and knocked." He touched Dec's shoulder, and Dec was buffeted by a blast of warm air. They appeared in Trevor's open living area, next to the pool table. Here, in the real world, Trevor lacked the fangs, claws, and glowing eyes that made him look like a monster. Instead, he just looked tired. His broad shoulders slumped as he slowly and deliberately began to rack the billiard balls, corralling them with his long fingers.

Dec was willing to play along. He grabbed a cue and waited, his hands wrapped around its narrow stalk. Once Trevor had the balls in place, he removed the frame and tossed the cue ball at Dec, who caught it. "You can break," Trevor said quietly.

Dec set the creamy white ball on the table and squared up. The familiar movements were easy, but the lump in his throat was making it hard to breathe. With a crack, the cue ball shot forward into the mass of solids and stripes, scattering them. The 2 careened straight into a corner pocket. "I've missed you, man." He lined up for another shot.

Trevor's jaw ridged with tension. "Yeah. Me too, Dec."

Dec took his shot, sending the 3 glancing off a rail. His focus wasn't exactly on the game. "I need you to tell me what's been going on. I came here because I want to hear it from you."

Trevor went to work on the striped balls, taking two shots before he spoke again. "I've been a Ker for a long time, man. I've done Moros's bidding for over a hundred years." He rubbed his hand along his jaw. "And I guess it just wore on me. I've been feeling angry about it. I mean, I chose this. I was all shot up, lying on the street, bleeding out, and Moros gave me a choice. Live forever? Sign me up." He grimaced. "But when I was alive, I killed two people. Now? I've killed *thousands*."

Dec skimmed his thumb over the chalky tip of his cue. "We've talked about this, though. Death is part of life, and you kill as mercifully as you can. And that's why you're a paramedic, too, to preserve life."

Trevor shook his head. "Moros should have left me alone. He made me this. His creature." The muscles on his shoulders bulged with tension. "I wanted to destroy him," he growled.

Dec took a wary step back as Trevor's eyes flashed red. "When?"

"I'd been feeling . . . off. For a few days." Trevor rubbed his chest, leaving a smear of chalk on his shirt. "Just disconnected and strange."

"Disconnected." It reminded him of what Rylan had said about Mandy, how she'd realized she wasn't tethered to Moros, how she could kill at will without him knowing. "For how long?"

"Not sure. The feeling came and went. Then I got this crazy idea when Eli told me Moros was going to have to go before the Keepers." He clutched his head between his hands. "At the time, it felt like something I had to do. But now?" He shook his head. "It seems crazy."

"I just came from visiting Jian Lee's wife. Does that name ring a bell?"

Trevor nodded. "He was supposed to be Marked. I found him coming out of Galena Margolis's lab and followed him home."

"And was Erin with you?"

"You know Erin?" Trevor sighed. "We were hanging out. She was brand-new, and I was showing her the ropes. I don't know what I was thinking, taking her with me."

"So what happened?"

"I Marked him right outside his apartment building, but a few seconds after I did, I got that strange feeling again. This was it—my way to get to Moros, maybe the only way—and I was just going to let this opportunity go? I knew Nader and Tamasin were guarding Galena, but if I could stop her research, do so much damage that she couldn't continue, then the Keepers would destroy Moros. And so I pretended like I recognized Jian. Asked him if he worked for her. At first, Erin thought that was just how Kere do things, I guess. She's so new. She played along, said she worked in one of the science departments on campus. We shook hands, all friendly." Trev whistled, a low, melancholy note. "But Jian was almost shaking with hatred for Galena. As soon as introductions were over, he came right out and said she'd ruined his life."

"And you actually believed that?" Dec snapped, more harshly than he intended. He forced himself to stay calm. "She's Eli's sister, Trev."

Trevor pressed one of his knuckles to his temple and closed his eyes. "I know, man. But in that moment, all I could think about was getting to Moros. After we started talking, Erin realized how crazy I was acting. She was tugging on my arm, pulling me away, but the only thing in my head was revenge. So I asked Jian—if I wanted to destroy Galena's research, how would I do that? Because the dude was doomed, man. One thought from me and he'd have a stroke. I just figured I'd get some information first.

"He looked shocked, but then he told me Galena Margolis was blackmailing him, forcing him to destroy her lab and anyone who'd had the vaccine. He thought maybe *she'd* sent me."

"Didn't that strike you as odd?"

Trev's hand fell away from his face. "That night, that moment? I just thought, 'Great. She's making it easy for us.' I didn't care about her. All I cared about was setting Moros up for a fall." Trev opened his eyes.

"When you told Jian you'd help him destroy Galena's work, what did he say?"

"Hell, he invited us inside. He already had the plans. He'd already planted one bomb, even. I said I would help. I figured, the more bodies, the more trouble Moros would be in." Trevor shook his head, staring at the scattered balls on the pool table. "It felt like justice, man. Pure justice. I remember feeling so sure." He looked sick. "Sure that killing people not fated to die was the right thing," he added in a strangled voice.

Dec's gaze rested on the cue ball. It was too painful to look at Trevor's face. "Did Erin go along?"

"Nah, she was trying to cool things down. I could tell she was really freaked-out. She kept stroking my arm, whispering to me that Moros would be angry, that he would kill me, but I just couldn't hear it, not with all the hate I was carrying inside. Then Jian and I started to argue—he wanted me to follow this set schedule he said he had, started making demands like I was his assistant or some goddamn thing. Bullshit. And then the guy's wife walks in. Probably the only thing that kept me from killing him right there."

"So you willed Jian to kill himself instead, Trev? That's not like you."

"I willed him to live long enough to carry out the plan, and then I wanted him to suffer," he whispered. "And that's how it turned out. I was angry, he was angry . . . he was probably wishing the worst for me, too. Erin got between us and pushed us away from each other. I stayed long enough to get the list of research volunteers, and then I was out of there."

Dec's blood ran cold. "But all those people, Trevor. The ones working with Galena. Did you kill them?"

"I don't know why I was so angry, Dec," he said with a groan. "I've been trying to figure it out for days." His deep-brown eyes became shiny with tears. "Everything made sense. Until it didn't."

"What's happened to you?" Dec muttered.

Trevor stared at him as the tears overflowed. "I'm not that person. I swear. I don't know."

"Do you still have that disconnected feeling?"

Trevor shook his head. "After that night, it went away, and I just locked myself in here. The anger faded. Not completely, but enough that now I can't remember why I ever thought any of it was a good idea. I've been sitting here for three solid days, trying to figure out what to do. But now I know."

Trevor set his cue on the table, then trudged into his kitchen. He returned carrying something in a large plastic bag. With a look of disgust and pain, he tossed it onto the pool table.

The bag contained a knife, its eight-inch blade crusted with dried blood. It lay between them, hard proof of something Dec could barely believe. He let out a shaky breath. "We're going to figure this out, Trevor."

"No. There's nothing to figure out. I want you to take me to Psychopomps. I want to make my confession." Trevor's eyes met Dec's. "And then I want you to summon Moros, so he can put me down for good."

CHAPTER TWENTY-FIVE

Galena staggered away from Eli as she was hit by a burst of warm air. She stumbled against the bed, still unmade. She forced herself not to lower her face to the pillow and inhale, just to have Dec's scent in her nose.

When she looked over her shoulder, Eli was watching her. "You're still mortal."

Galena straightened up and smoothed her fingers over her cheeks, which were hot to the touch. "It hasn't even been three days."

Eli's eyes flickered with red. "Three days during which you could have been killed by anyone." His lip curled with disgust.

"You didn't think this would be easy for me, did you? Are you telling me you're surprised that it's taking awhile for me and Dec to get through it?"

"No, I'm not surprised. And I'm not mad about that. I'm mad because Dec didn't tell a soul."

Anger flashed hot in Galena's chest. "Don't blame him for this."

"Who should I blame then, G? Look at you!" He gestured at the scratch on her forehead. "Did you get that when you were in jail?"

Her fingertips touched the scrape. It was healing. It had never been a serious injury. "No, but, Eli, it could have happened anywhere. I've been mortal my whole life. So have you, until recently. And look—both of us are still standing!"

He shook his head. "It seems like half the supernatural world wants to kill you these days, G, and I thought we'd found a way to protect you. I thought *Dec* would protect you." His face twisted with rage, and he turned away. "Obviously, I was wrong."

"Dec has done everything he could," snapped Galena. "He owes us nothing, and yet time and time again, he's saved me. He puts himself between me and any danger. He's doing it right now!"

Eli went still. "What exactly is he doing?"

Galena let out a frustrated breath. "We were trying to find who was really responsible for the bombings and the killings. We know Jian did it under extreme duress, and we also know that I've been set up. We went to visit Jian's widow, and she told Dec something. I'm not sure what." She frowned, recalling how upset Dec had looked when he returned to the Veil after talking to Mei Lee. "We had thought it was Luke, but—"

"Luke the Ker?" Eli turned around again. "Has he threatened you?"

She shook her head. "But he summoned me to guide a soul. He really seems to hate me. And Dec was concerned that he didn't seem surprised I was a Ferry. Then we were attacked by Shades—"

"You were attacked by *Shades*? Why the hell didn't you tell me?"

"We were handling it!" Galena blinked. We. She and Dec were a *we*. She wished they were together right now. "I'm fine."

"No thanks to Dec. He should have told me, so that I could make sure you were guarded. Anyone could have gotten to you."

"But no one did. They found another way to neutralize me, Eli—they framed me for murder. And Dec is helping me clear my name. I have a feeling he's risking more than he's willing to tell me."

Eli looked away, but Galena caught the flicker of knowledge in his eyes. "What?" she asked.

He sighed. "Aislin is threatening to revoke his status if he doesn't turn himself—and you—in."

Galena's stomach dropped. "Revoke his status? Is that like disowning him?"

Eli nodded. "Cacy said it would make him a regular human."

Dec hadn't told her that. He really *was* risking everything. "He should never have agreed to Claim me," she said in a choked voice. "I should never have said I wanted him." Her eyes met Eli's. "And you should never have talked to him about it. We did this to him, Eli. He didn't need to get involved."

"He was already involved, G. The last thing Patrick Ferry said to Dec before he entered the Afterlife was that Dec should protect you. He's honoring a promise to his father."

Suddenly, it all made sense. His dedication, his determination . . . his tenderness. He was doing all of it to fulfill his dead father's last wish. "Oh," she whispered. "That makes everything clearer."

"It doesn't explain why he didn't call for more protection. We all thought you were safe. Immortal. But—"

"Again, not his fault, Eli," she said, suddenly tired. She sank down on the bed.

Eli came a few steps closer. "What happened?" His voice had lost that edge of accusation and melted into pure worry.

"He tried," she said, her throat closing around the words. "And I tried, too. But I just couldn't . . . and he wouldn't . . ." She lowered her face into her hands. "Every time he gets too close to me, these images just plow through my head. I can't control them."

Eli sat down next to her. "Of that night, you mean. You remember."

"I try not to!" she cried, tears trickling between her fingers. "I push the memories away with everything I have, Eli, but they just keep coming. It's not fair. Especially not to Dec."

"Dec? What about *you?*"

Galena sniffled as she recalled what Dec had done for her, the way he'd made her climax, then disappeared into the bathroom. Because it was his problem, he said. Because she shouldn't have to worry about it. "He's too honorable for his own good," she muttered.

"Glad to hear it," Eli growled.

Her hands fell away from her face. "I don't know how to get through this. And Dec refuses to consummate our bond until I do, because he says it makes him feel . . . bad. Because of me, Eli. Because of how I respond."

He touched her temple. "Those memories are holding you hostage."

She looked up at him as he brushed a tear from her cheek. "Do *you* ever think about that night?"

His eyes were steady on hers. "Every day. Every single day."

"How can you bear it?" she whispered.

"It was nearly impossible at first," he said quietly, tucking a lock of her hair behind her ear. "I didn't handle it well." He cleared his throat and stared at her hands, upturned in her lap like she was begging the sky for answers. "But over time, I guess I've gotten used to it, as terrible as that sounds."

It didn't sound terrible; it sounded impossible. "Are you saying the memories don't . . . don't ambush you? Like if you see something that reminds you of that night?"

"It's never pleasant to think about that night, G. But I control when I think about it, and if recollections come into my mind at a time I'm not expecting it, I feel that pain, but it doesn't take me down."

She shook her head in disbelief. "Sometimes I feel like I spend all my energy keeping the memories at bay. Like I have nothing left because it takes so much work. But still, the memories are stronger than I am. They win. Every time."

He tilted his head, his gaze fond. "Remember what Dad used to say when I was stuck on a homework problem?" He chuckled. "I know he didn't have to say it to you, because you never got stuck, but—"

"He'd say, 'The issue isn't with the problem—it's with the strategy. Try to tackle it in a different way.'" It had seemed so basic and obvious at the time. Of course that's what you needed to do to solve a complex problem.

So why had she been clinging, for *two years*, to a strategy that obviously wasn't working?

Because the idea of letting those memories break free, really letting it all come back, was utterly terrifying. If it meant being able to control them, though, wouldn't it be worth it?

She reached for Eli's hand, and he met her halfway, squeezing her fingers. "What do you remember?" she asked.

"I was happy that night. I remember that. For the first time since Mom and Dad died. You and I had just been to see a movie in that restored theater."

"'Experience the twentieth century!'" she said in a deep voice, remembering the slogan on the marquee. She put a hand to her stomach. "My belly hurt from laughing so hard."

"And we were walking back to your apartment. I was hoping your roommate would be home."

She chuckled. "Yeah, you had a crush on her." Jeannette had liked Eli, too, she recalled. But Galena had never returned to that apartment after the attack, and she'd never seen Jeannette again.

Eli's other palm pressed over hers, completely enveloping her hand. "They came out of a bar and walked toward us."

Galena's heart began to bump against her ribs. "I smiled at them. I was in such a good mood. And they smiled back." She had regretted it every day since.

"It wouldn't have mattered if you'd given them the finger, G. As soon as we passed, they started following us."

"I had no idea." She only remembered them stepping in front of her and Eli, blocking the way.

"I did," he said, apology in every word. "I hoped they would leave us alone. I didn't want to scare you." He paused for a moment. "They waited until we walked down that side street. I was hoping we could lose them. It was the exact wrong thing to do."

She leaned against him. "You can't blame yourself."

"I will *always* blame myself," he said in a gravelly voice. "They grabbed me first."

Galena's skin went cold, and her breathing became shallow. "You screamed at me to run."

"But you tried to help me instead," he said bitterly.

She laid her head on his shoulder, his body heat bleeding through his clothes. "I would never have left you there. I couldn't. Not that it did any good."

"There were five of them," Eli said, his voice hushed now. "But I thought we had a chance."

"You knocked one of them out." Her eyes were shut tightly. She began to shake.

"Breathe, G. Slowly."

She nodded, drawing in a lungful of air and holding it, then letting it out. "One of them started to shock you. With the baton."

His arm tensed against hers. "The other tried to hold me. And the other two grabbed you. One had a knife."

Her stomach turned and she bowed forward, saliva filling her mouth. "Eli—"

"I saw them take you down. I saw them yank your skirt up." Black spots floated in front of her vision. Eli put his hand on her back. "They're memories, G. They can't hurt you now. I'm right here. And so are you. You're here and alive. You got through it."

She nodded, a little frantically, and focused on a little tear in her sweatpants, her eyes tracing every tiny torn stitch. "Go on."

"I was fighting with everything I had, but the guy with the baton kept jabbing it into me, and every time he did, it felt like my bones were melting."

Galena pressed her face to their joined hands. She remembered—Eli had arched back, his body jerking. She'd been sure she was watching him die. "I couldn't stop screaming," she said.

"The last thing I heard was you screaming my name. I knew you needed me. And I knew I had failed you." He put his arm around her and kissed the back of her bowed head. "But that's all I remember, G. It's all I've got. I woke up in the ambulance when they brought me back to life."

She wished that was where her memories stopped as well. She wished they'd shocked her into unconsciousness. Instead, her brain had recorded every second with unwavering detail. "I don't know if I can do this, Eli," she whispered. "I'm afraid to lose control of them."

"They're controlling *you*, G. And you know that. You *know* that."

She let out a sob. "I know."

He pulled her up but kept his arm around her, holding her tight. "But what you don't know, what you need to know, is that you're so much stronger than they are. And I'm sorry that I've forgotten that at times."

"Are you kidding? I'm a mess." She swiped her hand over her face.

"You're a brilliant scientist. You're focused on saving people. After what Rylan Ferry did to you, I thought I'd be picking up the pieces for months. But instead, you kept going. And then, when everything fell apart three days ago, again I was afraid you were done. I was so wrong."

"All of that was because of Dec. He's held me together."

"Maybe he helped, but I don't think you give yourself nearly enough credit. If you did, I think you'd tackle the enemies in your head with as much determination as you tackle all those germs in your lab."

She laid her cheek on his shoulder. "You are the best little brother ever."

"Because I have the best big sister."

She closed her eyes again, filled with gratitude that she still had him by her side. But was he right? Could she really conquer those barely contained memories, the ones that were still holding her down?

Dec's angular face appeared in her mind, his blue eyes, his smile. Just thinking of him soothed some of the panic and made her feel braver. She knew, though—her memories were the wall between them. They were keeping her from really touching him, from really knowing him.

But she wanted to know him. And touch him. She wanted to be able to reach out to him in the fragile hope that he would reach back. Yes, he was protecting her out of honor, and maybe it was no more than that. But she would never know if she didn't try.

Which meant she had no choice but to face the past she had worked so hard to forget.

CHAPTER TWENTY-SIX

Dec stood shoulder-to-shoulder with Trevor as they walked into the Psychopomps tower. He glanced at the time projected up on the wall behind Walter. He had less than twelve hours to clear Galena's name before Aislin brought the hammer down. Assuming she would actually give him that much time.

Trevor looked utterly defeated, his eyes downcast. The sight made Dec's throat tighten with sorrow and confusion. What the hell had happened? He put his hand on Trevor's shoulder. "Can you call Erin? Maybe she could help us figure out what's going on." Because the more he thought about it, the more Trevor's actions didn't make sense. Angry or not, Ker or not, the Trevor he knew would never stab an innocent woman in the chest. He wouldn't Mark people who weren't fated to die.

Trevor's eyes went wide. "No! I promised her I wouldn't bring her into this. She was so scared, Dec. And if Moros finds out, he'll probably kill her just for being with me. None of this is her fault. She tried to stop me." He rubbed at the back of his neck. "She didn't tell anyone because she didn't want to get me in trouble, but because she didn't tell, she looks guilty. I can't do that to her."

"Fine." *But I'm going to track her down.* "Are you sure you want to do this?"

"After what I did?" His dark skin was ashy, like he was going to puke. "If I'm capable of that, I shouldn't be allowed to exist." He looked at Dec and gave him a sad smile. "Thanks for sticking by me."

It was finally becoming real, the understanding that he was about to lose his best friend. "Maybe Moros will show mercy."

"If you believe that, you know nothing about him."

But Dec did know. Moros had a reputation for being pretty ruthless with the Kere who didn't obey him. And the Lord of the Kere had made it very clear that he wanted Galena to be protected. If Trevor had done something to endanger her, he didn't stand a chance. Dec's grip tightened over the strap of the duffel bag into which he'd stuffed the sack containing the bloody knife. He quickened his pace through the soaring lobby.

Four guards intercepted him before he had a chance to reach Walter. "Mr. Ferry, we've been instructed to bring you straight to Level Four," said the one whose name tag read "Max." He was fiddling with the electroshock baton at his belt.

"You'll have my cooperation," said Dec. "As long as you call my sister right now and tell her to meet us there. I need to talk to her."

Max frowned. "Sir, her instructions didn't—"

Dec stepped close to him. "Max, what would she do if she knew you'd prevented me from giving her important information about the Galena Margolis case?"

The guard's nostrils flared with annoyance. "You can just tell us, and we'll tell her."

"I'm not talking to anyone but Aislin." Dec gestured at Trevor. "My friend and I need to speak with her immediately."

Trevor leaned forward slowly, not even trying to hide the crimson glow in his eyes. "We're doing you a favor, son," he said slowly, his deep voice rumbling. "If I wanted to leave and take Dec with me right now, I could do that. But we're here. So call your boss and let her know."

Max took a full step back and bumped into another guard. He pressed his earpiece and waited a moment, then spoke. "Ms. Ferry. Your brother is here. There's a Ker with him. They say they have evidence—oh. All right." His hand fell to his side. "She's on her way down."

The guards escorted Dec and Trevor to the elevator. Dec couldn't control the pounding of his heart as they ascended to Level Four. Would they take his Scope? He hadn't been without it for any length of time since he was sixteen years old. Yes, he'd fantasized about dropping it in a canal and moving to Baffin for good, but when he really considered being truly mortal again, he wasn't so sure.

When the elevator doors slid open, they were greeted by more guards, who surrounded the two of them as they were shunted all the way down the hall, past Rylan's cell, and into a large, empty interrogation room with black videowalls on all sides.

Aislin was waiting in the center of the room, her pale cheeks flushed with anger. "Do you understand the position you've put me in?" she snapped as soon as she saw Dec.

"I did what I had to do, Aislin."

Her mouth twisted with contempt. "What utter garbage. I warned you not to take matters into your own hands. You've put us under a microscope and turned Galena Margolis into a fugitive, even though the evidence against her appears ironclad. Meanwhile, apparently you were traipsing around Cambridge two nights ago, flaunting your Scope and disappearing from some convenience store bathroom?" Her voice had risen, becoming shrill with rage. "Do you have any idea how many of your messes I've been cleaning up today? I thought you were better than this, Declan. I thought you were on my side."

"I thought you were on mine," he shouted. "But ever since I Claimed Galena—"

"Wait," Trevor said, his eyes going round. "You *Claimed* Galena?"

"I did," Dec said, softening his tone as that protective pride surged in him again. *She's mine.*

Aislin's mouth drew tight. "And I should never have supported that ridiculous idea. It's drawn way too much attention on all sides, and—"

"Stop," Dec said. "It's done. I don't regret it. And I will *not* abandon her. She's innocent."

"But I'm not," mumbled Trevor.

Aislin's ice-blue eyes shot to the muscular Ker. "What?"

Dec handed Aislin the duffel bag as Trevor explained what he had done. His own shame and bafflement about his actions made the Charon's brow furrow in confusion, but she remained silent as he spoke. When he was finished, Aislin opened the bag and looked inside, then paled and closed it again.

"Guard," she said, and immediately the door to the room opened. "Take this to the forensic lab and tell them to run rapid DNA. Send the results directly to me."

"Yes, Ms. Ferry." The guard accepted the duffel and left, closing the door behind him.

Trevor watched him go, looking hollowed out. Dec knew he was probably dreading the results, confirmation of something that seemed too horrible to accept without hard evidence.

Aislin was staring at Trevor with sharp curiosity in her eyes. "Are you sure you wish to request execution?" she asked, the authoritative edge gone from her voice.

"I'm sure."

Aislin summoned the guards, who arrived to escort Trevor to a cell. Dec put his hand on Trevor's arm as he headed for the door. "I'll be with you," he said in a strained voice. "I'll be with you when Moros comes."

"Thanks, man." Trevor plodded out the door after the guards, defeat rolling off him in waves.

Dec turned to Aislin. "You said I had until midnight. I need you to stick to that."

She folded her arms over her chest. "Where have you taken Galena?"

"I'll bring her back when we've cleared her name."

Aislin's eyes glinted with cold calculation. "The Keepers have contacted me. Our summit is in one week. And you, Declan, are making me look like a fool."

"You're doing that to yourself, Aislin," he snapped. "You're willing to sacrifice Galena and everything she stands for just to stay in control of the empire. But I'm telling you, she's innocent. It would be damn convenient for all of us if she weren't, but she is. I'm going to prove it. And if you don't let me, you're going to have to live with that for the rest of your very long life. You'll have condemned an innocent woman. And kept her from saving millions of others, even though that's what she's fated to do."

Aislin looked away. "Trevor's involvement doesn't exonerate Galena. You haven't proven her innocence yet."

"I know." But Galena had been on to something just before they were discovered at that data center, and maybe, with enough time, she could figure out who had set her up. "Just give me the time you promised. That's all I'm asking."

Aislin lifted her chin, still not meeting his eyes. "Very well. You have until midnight, but after that, you'll leave me no choice. Too much is at stake for me to be lenient."

Meaning she felt like she had to prove her ruthlessness to one and all, and she was willing to use him to do it. Dec smiled sadly. Aislin had built a wall of ice around her, one that kept everyone away. Even people who wanted to be close to her. "Message received."

He took a step toward the door, but her slender fingers closed over his arm. "She's very lucky," Aislin said quietly. "Does she know that?"

"Considering everything that's happened to her, 'lucky' wouldn't be the way I'd describe her."

"Few people have someone willing to sacrifice so much for them."

Dec stared at Aislin, whose eyes were riveted on the black videowall in front of her. "It's not luck," he said, then strode out of the room.

He walked by Rylan's cell just as his dinner was being wheeled in on a tray. Chinese. Rylan's favorite. He peeked in to see Rylan sitting at his chess table. Rylan's dark gaze skimmed right over the tray of food and met Dec's. "Brother," he said quietly. "Still free, or will you be joining me?"

His guard cleared his throat, and Dec suddenly realized that Ry had probably charmed or tricked his jailers out of a hell of a lot of information. "Still on the loose," Dec replied.

"But your friend Trevor's not. I saw the guards escorting him to a cell."

Dec let out an exasperated breath. "Ry, shouldn't you be worried more about your *own* ass?"

Dec's older brother thanked his guard as the man set the tray on one side of the chessboard. Then Ry picked up a chess piece and tossed it at Dec, who caught it. "Ever feel like one of those, Dec?"

He looked down at the piece in his hand. A pawn, of course. "Why, is that how you think of me?"

Rylan's eyebrows shot up. "Me? I'm not running the board. Not now, not ever. But if Trevor's here, I'm guessing Moros isn't running it, either. So that raises the question—who is?"

Dec rolled his eyes. "I'm not here to talk to you about Ais—"

"I'm not talking about Aislin," Rylan said, picking up the white queen and staring at her. "No, she may be a powerful piece, but she's merely a player."

"The Keepers, you mean?"

Rylan shrugged. "Maybe. Someone powerful enough to wrest control of Moros's Kere away from him. Who would that be?"

"Did Mandy ever seem like she was being controlled by someone else?"

He shook his head. "She said she felt free," he said.

Different than Trevor, who said he felt "disconnected." Mandy had enjoyed pain and chaos. She would have been thrilled to engage in unsanctioned killing. But Trevor . . . Dec couldn't shake the feeling that he hadn't been in complete control of himself. The one thing Trevor and Mandy shared, though, was that both had wanted to bring Moros down, and they'd hurt and killed others to do it.

Come to think of it, Luke had been pretty down on Moros, too. *I'll talk about that bastard however I want,* he'd said.

Dec cursed quietly. He needed to know more about how Moros controlled the Kere. If he knew that, then he might be able to help Trevor figure out whether someone had been controlling him. Dec clenched the pawn in his fist. "I hear you're facing the Keepers next week. Ready?"

"Maybe. Right now I'd say a lot depends on how things turn out with Galena." Rylan set the white queen on the board and scooped up the king, holding the piece between finger and thumb. "She's certainly gotten herself in a lot of trouble, hasn't she?"

Dec slowly walked forward. Never taking his gaze from his brother's, Dec set the pawn in the middle of the board. "This isn't a game to me."

Rylan reached across the board and moved a knight, casually knocking the pawn away and setting the piece in its place. "Maybe not to you, Brother." His voice had become tired, no longer edged with cunning. "But I think someone's having a hell of a lot of fun. If we don't figure out who it is and what they want . . ." He swept his arm across the board, and all the pieces clattered to the tile floor. He looked up at Dec. "Good luck out there."

His heart beating faster than he wanted to admit, Dec turned on his heel and walked past the guard, who'd been standing at the door. As he entered the hallway, he pulled his Scope from his collar.

He had less than twelve hours and no plan. But right now, all he could think about was getting back to Galena.

CHAPTER TWENTY-SEVEN

Eli cursed and looked down at his arm. "G, I have to go. But you won't be alone here, okay? I'll make sure you're guarded."

Galena stood up with him. "No one knows I'm here, Eli. And you're the only one who knows I'm not immortal. Don't you think it's safe?"

He put his warm hands on her shoulders. "Can you forgive me if I don't want to take that risk? Dec's not back yet, and for all we know, he's gotten collared by Aislin's guards."

"What would she do to him?"

"No idea. She seems pretty determined to control every variable, and Dec has been a loose cannon."

Because of her. If anything happened to Dec, she wasn't sure how she would handle it. Somehow, over these last few crazy days, he'd become important—no, *necessary*. She had to figure out a way to clear her name, because maybe it would clear his, too.

Eli studied the worried look on her face. "Do you want me to take you somewhere? Or go get Cacy and bring her back here? She'd be willing, G. She's worried about you."

Galena shook her head. "No. I'll stay here." If Dec was free, he'd come here. And she wanted to be here when that happened.

"All right." He rubbed his inner forearm like it was suddenly sore. "I'm going." He kissed her forehead and vanished.

Galena stood in the middle of the cabin's small living space, shivering. She'd cracked open the cage where she'd imprisoned all those black memories, but now Eli was gone, and she was alone with them, feeling shaky and vulnerable. Eli believed she could reclaim her own mind. Her hand skimmed down her stomach to her lower belly, where the scars lay. *A slick crimson mess. Made of pain and terror and grief.* She let out a low sob. How could Eli possibly have thought she could do this?

A faint cold breeze tickled her cheek, and she turned to see Dec climbing out of his Scope. He looked like he'd lived fifty years in the last few hours. His hair was messy, and dark stubble shadowed his jaw. He closed his Scope and fastened it to its setting, and then his eyes met hers. He didn't say anything. He just came toward her, his arms rising from his sides. Reaching for her.

A frantic noise flew from her mouth as she rushed into his embrace, and he wrapped her up tight, lifting her off her feet. His rough cheek scraped against her throat as he bowed his head against her shoulder. Her fingers tangled in his hair. "I was so worried about you," she mumbled.

He placed a tender kiss at the junction of her neck and shoulder, right next to the bandage. "I know exactly how that feels. Where's Eli?"

"He was here until a few minutes ago."

"Good."

"Are you all right?" she asked. He was holding her so tightly, and he'd looked so sad when he'd come through the Scope.

"No," he admitted, lifting his head. She laid her hand on his cheek, and he leaned into it. "Galena, my friend Trevor was the one who went to visit Jian. He's the one responsible for killing some of your volunteers."

"Why would he do that?" she asked in a broken whisper. "Why?"

"I honestly don't know. All he said was that he'd wanted to get back at Moros, and when I talked to him, he could barely remember how he'd gotten so angry. But Erin was with him, and I'm going to find her and ask her. He doesn't want her involved, because he's trying to protect her, but if it means saving his life, then I'll do it."

"Saving his life?"

"He's asked to be executed. Moros would be the one to do it."

On the one hand, execution sounded just, considering this Trevor person had murdered innocent people. On the other, Dec looked so upset about it that she hoped it worked out. "I'm sorry," she murmured, leaning to kiss his cheek. "These past few hours must have been so hard."

He blinked. "Yeah, actually."

She stood on her tiptoes and touched her forehead to his. "I'm really glad you're back."

His hands rose to her hair, his fingers sliding through her locks, holding her face to his as his eyes dropped closed. "Me too."

She stood there like that for a minute, nose-to-nose with him, then her lips were on his, questing and hungry. He went still, maybe with surprise, but then his arms turned to steel around her and his lips parted, letting her in. Galena closed her eyes and inhaled his hot masculine scent as she ran her tongue along his, exploring his mouth. Her body was made of craving, of desperation. She wanted to destroy anything that stood between them. She wanted to see him, and for him to see her.

Dec's thumbs caressed her cheeks before his fingers slid into her hair again. He tilted her head up and made the kiss deep, the slow thrusts of his tongue only growing the need inside her. And then he pulled back, nipping her bottom lip. "Galena, you're not safe here. After seeing what's happened with Trevor, how out of character this was for him, I think there may be something or someone controlling some of the Kere. And if any of them find out you're here—"

"Make me safe, then," she whispered.

His gaze was heavy on hers. "God, I wish I could."

She laid her hand on his chest, then let it slide down to his stomach, moving lower inch by inch. His muscles were rigid beneath her palm. "You can."

He stared at her, then shook his head. "Too soon."

"There's no time, Dec. And if you do this, you won't have to worry about me anymore."

His eyes narrowed. "Is that what you think I want?"

She tried to lower her head, but his hands were on either side of her face, holding her there. "Eli said that your father told you to protect me. That you're honoring his final wish."

"And you think that's all this is." He waited until she looked into his eyes. "You're wrong."

"I shouldn't have done this to you," she blurted out. "It's not fair to you."

"Stop. I made the decision for a lot of reasons, Galena, and one was that I wanted *you*." He chuckled to himself. "At least I can admit that to myself now."

"How could you have wanted this? You don't even know me."

"I probably know more than you think, but I definitely don't know as much as I want to."

Her hands smoothed over her belly, and a chill rode across her skin. "You've risked so much for me, even immortality."

"I take risks all the time. I've never had a better reason than I do now."

Galena wanted to scream in frustration. "Has it occurred to you that I want to protect you, too?"

The hard edge of his jaw softened. "You want to protect me?"

She tilted her head. "Dec, you're the best man I've ever met. You make me feel safer than I have in years, maybe even before the attack. I don't know how to feel worthy of you."

"You realize that's bullshit, right? Everything I do for you, it's because you're already worthy. Of protection and so much more."

Tears burned her eyes. "But I don't know how to be good for you! How's that? I have no idea how to give you what you need, and it feels awful."

"Would you like to know what I need?" he murmured.

She nodded, swiping a stubborn tear off her cheek. Dec's hands skimmed down to her shoulders. "I need to know everything. I need to know, or I won't ever be able to reach you." He leaned his forehead against hers. "And *that* is something I want more than anything in this world right now."

She closed her eyes. "I'm so afraid."

He kissed each of her eyelids. "Me too. But we're together. And I think we're a good team."

She reached up and touched his face, sliding her fingertips over the planes and angles she'd begun to memorize. Once she did this, once she showed him, once he knew, there was no going back. He wouldn't be able to forget, and neither would she. And if he pulled back, if she lost him because of this, that would be it. She didn't think she'd recover.

But if she denied him, she'd be pushing him away. She'd be allowing her memories, those *monsters*, to win.

Her voice shook as she asked, "Are you sure you want to know?"

Dec brushed his nose against hers. "I think I need to."

She inhaled a shuddery breath, and he tucked a lock of hair behind her ear. "What can I do?" he whispered.

Please don't be disgusted by me. "Just . . . stay with me, okay?" Her voice broke, and Dec pulled her into the shelter of his arms again.

She leaned her head on his shoulder and began to speak, halting and quiet. She got through telling Dec about the first part, the terrible moments she and Eli had discussed earlier. But with every second that passed, her heart beat faster, knowing what was coming. Her fingers curled tighter into Dec's sleeves. He was completely still, solid as a rock, just taking it in, it seemed, just listening.

"I was screaming for Eli," she mumbled. "They were hurting him, and I could hear him yelling. I could see him thrashing." She pressed her face into Dec's shoulder. "And then he went limp. And the ones who were holding me . . ." She blew out a shaky breath as she opened the cage and set the memories free.

The blond one, narrow face, slash of a mouth, grinned as he yanked up her skirt. She kicked out hard and hit him in the thigh, and the black-haired one slammed his fist into the side of her head, sending starbursts of light across her vision. A third one, built like a police tank, walked away from Eli's body and grabbed one of her legs, yanking it wide. And then the blond one pulled a knife. Its blade glinted dully in the yellow moonlight. She shrieked and struggled as the blade descended, as he cut her panties away, the knife's edge stinging the skin on the crest of her hip. Her mind was a jumble of terror, her thoughts wordless, full of red.

"He pushed his fingers into me," she whispered.

"Oh, fuck, that's tight." The knife was clutched in his fist, blade flat against her abdomen. His knuckles bearing down mercilessly. Her arms pinioned, rough hands around her ankles. She couldn't protect herself.

Dec's voice was strained as he said, "I've got you, Galena. I'm right here."

"I remember the sound of him pulling down his zipper," she squeaked. "I remember exactly how it sounded. And then he was crushing me, and . . . God, it hurt . . ." She shook violently as the sensations crashed over her. Dark spots floated behind her closed eyelids.

"Breathe," he reminded her. "You have to breathe."

She focused on Dec's voice, her anchor in the storm, and inhaled. "I don't know how long it lasted," she said. She only remembered the weight lifting and her body shuddering as she gulped for air. But before she knew it, the heavyset one crushed her to the ground again.

"The others were laughing," she whispered. "Making fun of him as he forced himself into me, jeering about this being the only way he could get with a woman. And it made him angry. He put his hands around my throat."

Dec let out a low, strangled growl and held her head against his shoulder, his fingers buried in her hair. Her hand landed on his chest. His heart was knocking against her palm, fast and fierce.

"I couldn't breathe. I thought I was going to die. But then he . . . finished and the other one . . ." She let out a sob. "I can't do this."

"You're doing it," he murmured. "And I'm with you."

"The black-haired one, he grabbed my hair. My head hit the cement." *He pressed his forehead against the side of her face as he slammed into her, his grunts echoing in her head.* "The blond one, I think he was in charge. He grabbed the electroshock baton and shocked the guy who was on top of me, and the jolt went through him and into me. My head . . ." Had exploded into a shrieking, hissing mass of shattered thoughts. And when she'd come back to herself, the blond one was between her legs again, laughing.

"The fourth one was screaming that he heard sirens. He was dragging his unconscious friend away," she choked out. "But the blond one, he wasn't done with me." Galena's hands became fists. Now was the time, and if she stopped, if she avoided it, all of this would be for nothing. She pushed away from Dec, and at first he didn't seem to want to let her go. But she persisted, pressing her palms against his broad chest and moving away from him.

She closed her eyes. With shaking hands, she pulled her shirt off, and then pushed her sweats down her legs. Her fingers traced across her lower belly, the hollow of her abdomen, traveling across the maze of scars, two thick and raised, others puckered, the leavings of all the surgery it had taken to repair her shattered body. "He stabbed me." She swallowed hard, shuddering as she remembered the impact, the agony. "Twice. He was going to kill me."

In the distance, a siren wailed again. "Shit," said the heavyset one. "That sounded closer."

The blond one looked over his shoulder, his knife raised for another blow. Then he disappeared, and she heard footsteps retreating down the block. Her trembling fingers traveled to her belly as she stared up at the sky. Nothing but pain.

"There was nothing left after that," she breathed. She'd summoned all her strength and crawled over to Eli. She'd curled herself around him. And that was how the medics had found them.

Galena's eyes fluttered open. Never in her life had she dwelled in a silence as complete as this one. A cold wave of dread rolled through her as she forced herself to focus on Dec, who was now sitting on the edge of the bed. A tear slid down his cheek as he stared at her body.

"I was Marked a long time before those Kere even knew I existed," she said quietly. She felt out of breath, like she'd been running and running, though she wasn't sure if she was fleeing or chasing. All she knew was that she felt emptied out. "Dec?"

"Yeah," he said hoarsely, blinking and dragging his sleeve across his face. But his eyes didn't leave her scars.

"Say something," she whispered as the shaking began again, tears filling her eyes.

He reached forward and took her hand. His felt warm against her chilled, clammy skin. He drew her toward him, until she was standing between his knees. And then he guided her hand to his hair and leaned his forehead against her stomach, wrapping his arms around her waist. Her head fell forward as she felt his breath against her skin, his lips brushing over flesh smooth and scarred with a gentleness that would have brought her to her knees if he hadn't been holding her up.

"You," he murmured. "You are so strong. And so brave." His voice was unsteady as his arms tightened around her body. "And so beautiful. These scars . . ." He let out a trembling sigh. "They're a reminder of how much courage you have."

He raised his head, and the look in his eyes made her ache. "I'm so sorry this happened to you." His hands slid to her hips, and his voice faded to a harsh whisper. "But I am so thankful that you're here now, with me."

Deep inside her, something shifted, powerful and fundamental. She sank onto him, no longer strong enough to remain upright. And Dec caught her, held her, refused to let her fall. He guided her into his lap as she began to sob. Broken, rasping cries for everything she'd lost, everything that had been ripped from her grasp on that night two years ago. She didn't try to hold the tears back. She didn't try to cram the memories down. She let them come, and Dec absorbed each shudder, each teardrop, each clutch of her fingers as she held on to him, desperately clinging to his strong frame as the noises and sensations of the past tried to pull her away and bury her.

He didn't shush her or rock her or stroke her or make promises. He was the ground beneath her feet. Unwavering and unflinching. He tucked his head against her bare shoulder and held on as her body heaved, like it was trying to wrest control from the enemies inside.

She had no idea how long they remained like that, locked together, a tangle of grief. She lost track of time. She lost track of herself. She was aware only of the memories and Dec's arms around her, refusing to relinquish her no matter how hard the bad memories pulled. His arm was laid against her spine, his strong fingers around the back of her head, as if he wanted to siphon the poison right out of her mind.

He couldn't, though. The memories would always be in there. She knew that now; there was no way to erase them. But that didn't mean they should hold dominion over her.

You're so much stronger than they are, Eli had said. *Tackle the enemies in your head with as much determination as you tackle all those germs in your lab.*

She drew in a deep breath, her body relishing the oxygen as if she had been held underwater, deprived of air. Slowly, she lifted her head and looked at Dec.

"I'm still here," he said quietly.

Her fingertips traced across his cheekbones. "I don't know how I got so lucky."

He took her face in his hands. "Luck has nothing to do with it, Galena." Tenderly, he lifted his chin and brushed his lips over hers. "It's you. Just you."

Dec held her as they slowly sank onto the bed. She curled into his body, her arm around his waist, her head on his chest. Her limbs felt like they'd been filled with concrete. They lay like that for a while, until she felt his thumping heart slow. She looked up at him. His eyes were closed. "Dec?"

He was asleep. She inched up to take a closer look at him, his ebony lashes shadowing the hollows beneath his eyes, his lips slightly parted. As she stared, the longing inside her replaced the sorrow. Finally, she kissed the rough underside of his jaw. "I'm falling in love with you, Dec," she whispered.

Slowly, she got up. She took a shower, letting the lukewarm water wash the tears from her cheeks. She felt a little unsteady, but she was still standing. Her hands ran over her body, and for the first time in as long as she could remember, she felt gratitude. She was glad to have it. Her palm skimmed over her arms, over her breasts, along her hips, up her neck to her face. *This is mine,* she thought.

Hope surged inside her. She wasn't done. She knew she had so far to go. The fear was still there, the cruel memories still reaching. But they wouldn't rule her. She wouldn't allow it.

It was time to reclaim her body, her soul, her mind. Inch by inch. Thought by thought.

And touch by touch.

CHAPTER TWENTY-EIGHT

Dec ran down the alley, his heart in his throat as she screamed. "Galena," he shouted. Where was she? God, where was she? It felt as if his chest were being squeezed in a vise. "Galena!"

"I'm here," she whispered, so close.

Instantly, the vise loosened. "Where are you?" he called, whirling around. Somewhere in the distance, she screamed again. His eyes stung and burned. "Please tell me where you are."

"Right here." Her lips grazed his cheek. He felt it. But she was nowhere to be seen.

He was running out of time, and he knew it. If he didn't find her soon, he would lose her.

She screamed again, more faintly, like he'd been running away from her instead of toward her. The horror gripped him. He couldn't lose her now. Not after she'd let him in, not after he'd realized, in those painful, rending minutes, exactly how much she meant to him.

Suddenly, the ground disappeared, and he was falling. Hard and fast, nothing to catch him. *This is it*, he thought. *When I hit, I shatter.* He spread his arms and surrendered to it, using his last few moments to picture her face.

He woke with a shuddering gasp. Galena stood a few feet from the bed, her wet hair pulled over one shoulder, dripping onto the towel she'd wrapped around her body. His breath whooshed from his lungs as relief swamped him. "I fell asleep," he said stupidly.

Her smile was tender and achingly beautiful. "I know."

"And you took a shower." He rubbed at his eyes and looked at her again, his gaze following a glistening drop that snaked down from her neck and disappeared between her breasts.

"You're *very* perceptive." She took a step closer. "Are you okay? It looked like you were having a nightmare."

He leaned back and braced himself on his palms, unable to take his eyes off her. "I was. But you're here." Looking amazing. He could smell her: fresh, sweet, astringent. "Are you okay?"

She nodded. "But I was hoping you'd help me with something." *Anything.* "What?"

Her dark-green eyes were on him, sliding up his body, making his groin tighten. "I want to see you." Her gaze met his. "And I want to touch you."

His lips parted as the air left him, as all the blood in his brain drained south. "Are you sure?" he said, his voice strained as she took another step closer, her bare knees brushing the edge of the bed.

"I'm sure." She bit her lip. "Will you let me?"

He looked down at himself, as if somehow his body had detached from his head. "Yeah," he breathed. "I mean, sure." Already his cock was starting to throb. "Whatever you want." *Oh God, please put your hands on me.*

She sank onto the bed, her eyes on his. "I don't know how this is going to go."

"It's okay," he said, unable to believe it as her fingers crossed the distance between them and tugged at the hem of his shirt. Her knuckles skimmed his sides as she lifted it, and he raised his arms, letting her pull it from his body. He kept his eyes on her as she dropped his shirt at the foot of the bed and turned her attention to him. Her tongue traced her bottom lip. Still clutching the towel around herself with one hand, she used her other palm to meet the heated skin of his abs, travel up the ridges of muscle, over his pec, across his shoulder. Her fingertips trailed along his collarbone and downward again, brushing over his nipple and making him shudder with want.

She watched his face, then ran her thumb over the little nub again. His head dropped back as his cock swelled, squeezed within the confines of his jeans. With horror, he looked at his zipper, remembering what she'd said about the sound. But then she lowered her head, her cool, damp hair slipping across his stomach, her warm breath on his chest.

Her tongue flicked his nipple, and he groaned, his muscles drawing tight, his cock surging to full attention. She'd see it now. She'd notice. He held his breath and stayed completely still as she slowly kissed her way up his chest to his throat, and when he felt her teeth against his skin, he gasped, his fingers balling in the quilt beneath him. She'd let go of the towel around her now and was using both hands to stroke along his chest, his arms, his abs, his throat, like she was mapping every inch.

He wanted to crush her to him. He wanted to grab her hips and feel her soft flesh yield. But he didn't. He wouldn't. Even if it killed him. What was happening was a good thing. That she wanted to touch him seemed like a miracle, fragile and exquisite, like a butterfly sitting in the palm of his hand.

She rose onto her knees and slid her hands over his shoulders, leaning forward to look at his back. "So perfect," she whispered, tracing the raven between his shoulder blades. Her barely covered breasts were an inch from his face, and Dec ached to take one of them in his mouth, to roll her nipple between teeth and tongue, but he held himself back. And soon, she lowered herself down again, legs folded beneath her as her hands strayed south, finally reaching his waist.

Her fingertip slid into the dip of his belly button, and he felt it like she'd reached inside him, caressing something primal and pure. Her thumbs smoothed across the indentations of muscle at his hips, following the V shape as it disappeared into his pants. She let out an unsteady breath, her eyes on the button of his jeans. "You don't have to," he said. "It's okay."

Her fingers rose and touched his lips, but she didn't raise her head. Her concentration was so complete that he suddenly realized this must be what she was like when she was studying something. When she was trying to figure it out.

When she was planning to take it apart and conquer it.

He felt like he'd stepped outside of his body as he watched her fingers slowly undo the button and then slide across the bulge of the erection straining against his fly. She unzipped his pants quickly, suddenly, a sound that ripped through his mind. Galena took a few deep breaths in the aftermath, and she seemed to be staring at a loose thread on the quilt next to him.

Something ordinary and harmless. Something that grounded her in the here and now. He felt a pang of sadness.

But then her gaze returned to his body. His cock was tenting his boxer briefs. She took hold of the edges of his jeans and tugged them down his hips, and he raised them to allow her to draw the fabric down his legs. The friction pulled his boxer briefs down, too, and his cock sprang out, bobbing rigid against his abdomen. Galena slipped off his boots and socks and stripped his jeans from his legs. She sat near his feet, looking up the length of his body while he sat there like an idiot, braced on his palms, his hands fisted in the quilt, his cock hard and hopeful, begging for her touch.

"You have a beautiful body," she murmured.

"You can look at it anytime you want, from now on," he said.

She let out a quiet burst of laughter. "Thank you." Her wet hair swayed between them as her palms stroked up his legs, over his knees, up his thighs, then hooked over the bottom edge of the legs of his boxer briefs and pulled them down as well. A moment later, Dec was completely naked, shaking with need as her relentless gaze traced over him. She was so fucking intent that it was a palpable thing, with weight and power of its own. Slowly, her fingers trailed up his thigh, skimming over his cock, which jerked at the sensation.

"I saw you stroking yourself," she murmured. "I saw what it did to you."

He must have looked crazed, desperately seeking that release. "*You* did that to me," he corrected. "That was your taste. That was watching you come." The memory of it sent a rush of heat through him.

"Well," she said, her fingers slowly wrapping around his shaft. "That makes me feel kind of powerful, actually."

"Because you *are*." He half chuckled, half moaned as she tightened her grip and pumped him, slow and agonizing.

His hips moved in time with her, seeking more. But she let him go, her long dark-blonde hair tickling his abs and chest as she crawled up his body. As she did, her towel fell completely open, and Dec stared at the swell of her breasts as she moved closer. And when he felt her nipples brush his chest, he groaned again. Her hands were on his shoulders. Her eyes were on his mouth. And then she claimed what she wanted, her lips meshing with his in a possessive kiss. As her fingers slid into his hair, she straddled him, and in a moment of pure amazement, he felt the slick softness of her arousal against his abs. Once again, he felt like he was falling, but this time, it was in the best possible way.

She pushed against him, and he sank backward, his eyes still shut tight, his teeth grinding. "Galena . . ."

She took his wrists and moved his hands to her thighs, which was exactly what he needed. Her flesh was warm and smooth and willing as his palms met her hips, his fingers slipping over the curve of her ass, which kept nudging the tip of his cock, making him dizzy with need. He opened his eyes to see her legs spread over him, pink nipples taut and mouthwatering as she bent to kiss him again. Dec's mind narrowed to one point, her body, blocking out everything else. All his worries and fears, the ticking clock, the danger. Right now, this was the most important thing in the world. He wanted to gather every second of it and tuck it away somewhere, so that no matter what happened from now on, he would have this, the honey scent of her, the sensation of her skin on his, her hair falling around them, her hands on his chest.

She edged down his body, slowly, hesitantly, still kissing him fiercely. Her fingers were on his neck, and they tensed as her wet folds slid over the top of his cock. She whimpered, and Dec's ears rang with alarm. He caught her waist and held her still. "Hey," he murmured, kissing her temple. "You okay?"

She nodded, blowing out a breath from between pursed lips. Her eyes met his, and he saw the fear there. He took her face in his hands as she focused on his mouth, tracing her fingers across his lips. "I need to feel you with me now," she said quietly. She closed her eyes tightly then opened them again. "I don't want to get sucked into my own head."

He tenderly kissed her cheeks, the tip of her nose, and then her lips. "I'm in this with you, Galena. Every second. Every breath." *From now on. Forever.* "I won't let you go." *Ever.*

Her eyes shone with tears. "I believe you, Dec," she said, her voice cracking. One tear slipped free and hit his cheek, and she kissed it from his skin. Then she reached between them and caressed him, her fingers brushing over the head of his cock and sending a rush of want all the way down his spine. His balls tingled with it; his muscles pulled taut. And when she guided him to the soft, slick center of her, it felt like something he'd craved for an eternity.

Her lips met his, and she gasped as her tight channel accepted his rigid cock, bathing him with molten, wet heat. Galena moaned into his mouth, bracing herself with her palms against his ribs, then sinking down, taking him inch by agonizing inch. Dec's blood pounded through his veins, and his mind threatened to go dark as every nerve in his body roared with desire. But he forced himself to stay aware, to listen to her panting breaths, to feel her skipping heart when her chest pressed to his. He began to stroke her sides, her thighs, gentle and soothing like he'd done before, because it had seemed to relax her, to remind her that he would never hurt her, to keep her in the present.

Galena pressed her face to his throat as she sank all the way, until his cock was buried to the hilt. He'd never felt anything so perfect. Or so he'd thought. Because then she rose up, her hands on his chest, her eyes on his face.

"Yeah?" he whispered.

She gave him this gorgeous, victorious smile. "Yeah."

She started to move. Slowly, rising up and sliding down, her inner muscles contracting, wrenching a low moan from both of them. His hands returned to her hips. He was dying to thrust, but he held himself still, letting her do the work, letting her set the pace. She bit her lip, and her breasts swayed as she ground herself against him. Dec couldn't help it; his fingers tightened on the soft mounds of her ass and he canted his hips up, seeking *more*.

"Oh God, Dec," she murmured, her eyes falling shut. "Do that again."

She didn't have to ask twice. He kept his hands anchored and moved her hips, pressing them down as he shifted his hips up, penetrating her so deeply that he swore he felt the limits of her body. Over and over, just like that, they swayed together, never separating more than an inch or two. He stayed deep inside her, ecstasy rolling in hard waves up from his groin, through his belly and into his chest. Galena fell forward, reaching for him, panting against his mouth while her breasts smashed against his chest. He'd never been closer to another person than this. Her fingernails sank into his shoulders as he slid into her, as he gave her all of him. She needed more; he could sense it in the tension in her thighs, in the frenzied clutch of her fingers, in the little cries that burst from her throat every time she felt him all the way inside.

So he pulled back all the way and slid into her, watching her face as they collided, her parted lips. "Dec," she whispered.

"Yeah?"

"Again."

He thrust into her body, gentle but sure, watching the friction undo her.

It was certainly undoing him. Her body was unrelenting and hot around him; her scent was overwhelming. His knees fell apart as his hips bucked, as he squeezed her ass and moved her up and down his cock. He needed her to come soon, because there was no fucking way he was going to last much longer. Praying he wasn't about to screw everything up, he reached between their bodies. He knew it was a risk, but then again, everything about this was a risk. His fingers tickled the damp curls between her legs and found her tiny, slick nub. Like he had with his tongue, he circled it as she sank onto him.

Galena's eyes opened, and she looked down at his fingers. Dec held his breath.

"Yeah," she whispered, opening herself to him. Dec stared at her, her head thrown back, hair cascading over her shoulders.

He began to tease her clit constantly as she rode his shaft, clenching around him like a fist, wet and hot and so fucking perfect. "That," he gasped. "More."

Her inner muscles squeezed again, and Dec arched up, helpless beneath her. His obvious pleasure made her laugh with delight. She owned him. His whole body was tingling, chasing release. Her arousal slicked his fingers as he watched himself disappear inside her again and again. "Galena, I can't . . . I'm going to . . ."

She descended on him, her hips still undulating, demanding everything he had. She held his face in her hands. "Me too," she said with a moan.

Dec stared into her eyes, her gorgeous deep gaze, and let himself fall.

CHAPTER TWENTY-NINE

Galena was lost in Dec's eyes as she felt it coming, this unstoppable pleasure that made her whole body bear down. And as she did, Dec seized her hips and bowed his head against her shoulder, his jaw rigid, his eyes squeezed shut. She wrapped her arms around him as her body let go, and then she lost awareness of everything else. The sensation rose inside her, carrying her right over the edge, sending her spinning and tumbling.

"Galena," Dec gasped as his shaft throbbed inside her, dragging her under again, drowning her in ecstasy. Her body spasmed around him. Dec's hands were iron as he thrust into her one more time, his whole body shuddering.

Then a strange, loose feeling rolled over her, pressing her onto him as he sank back, his head falling to the pillow. The sensation traveled from the top of her head, down her spine, along her legs, and then back up again, this time in tingling bursts. She cried out in surprise, and Dec touched her face, his thumbs stroking her cheeks, brushing away tears she didn't know she'd shed. "It's happening," he said quietly.

"What's happening?"

"The bond. It's complete. You're immortal now."

She held his palm against her cheek. Immortal. She knew she should be ecstatic, but it seemed like the least important thing that had happened in the last hour. He was still inside her; she was still plastered to his chest, her legs spread over him. There had been a few scary moments, but she'd focused on staying in the present. Her trust in him had made that possible. Her adoration of him made it worth the risk. "We did it," she murmured.

His gaze roamed her face. "We did." His lips met hers, achingly tender. "But if you want to stay this way, we have to go back to Boston and find proof that you didn't somehow spearhead a conspiracy to destroy your own research and destabilize the future."

Making her immortal hadn't been the "We did it" she was talking about, but it seemed ridiculous to mention that now. Dec was already sitting up, cradling her in his lap as he slipped from her body. Her cheeks heating, Galena climbed off of him. She was still stunned and breathless by what had happened between them, with the brilliant, blinding miracle of having him inside her, of wanting more, of asking and receiving, of relishing his pleasure as she enjoyed her own. The power of it, too. She was dizzy with it. But she needed to focus on other things, because she wasn't the only one whose status as a Ferry was in danger right now.

They took a quick shower, and Galena drew reassurance from the possessive way his hands slid over her skin, the way his eyes fell shut as she soaped him. She wanted to linger, to savor, and she could tell he did, too, but now it was time to fight for a future in which they could. She was ready to do whatever it took to clear her name and protect Dec from the consequences of his loyalty to her. He looked grim and serious as he toweled himself off and dressed, his black hair damp and disheveled. "Ready?" he asked as she pulled her shoes on. He looked down at his phone. "We have six hours left."

"You didn't tell me that!" She waved her hand at the bed. "And all that—"

He took her hand. "Was absolutely necessary."

She bowed her head. "Yeah. I'm immortal now."

He tipped her chin up, eyes fierce. "Necessary in *every* way, Galena."

"For me too." Their gazes were locked, and the moment was heavy with the weight of all the things they still needed to say to each other. *Six hours,* her mind whispered. *Only six hours until he loses everything. Move.*

"I think I know where we need to go," she said. When he raised his eyebrows, she continued. "Before we had to leave the data center, I noticed a lot of activity in my user account, dating back to the first days I was in Boston. A lot of tech-support requests."

"What was unusual about them?"

"I didn't make any. And I was about to check the network for other points of entry, because it was supposed to be extremely secure. But that guard spotted us before I could. So I need to get access to a computer where I can check that." She sighed. "I could have done it from my lab, but obviously that's gone, so I need to get into the Immunology Department itself. My boss, Dr. Cassidy, would have the kind of authorization I need to access that information."

"So we need to sneak into her lab and get on her machine."

Galena nodded, then cursed. "I don't have my phone with me. They confiscated it at the police department. I'd need it to copy any information we find."

He held up his phone. "You can use mine. But after we do this, we need to find Erin, that Ker who was with Luke the other night. She was with Trevor when he met with Jian, and she might be able to give us more information about what was said, and what was going on with Trev." He pulled his Scope off the setting at his neck, brushed his thumb over the raven, and pulled the ring wide. With a smile she could only describe as shy, Dec held it out. "After you," he said quietly.

She stepped into the Scope and entered the cold gray world of the Veil, and Dec followed after her.

"Good afternoon," said a female voice from behind them.

They whirled around to find Tamasin standing near the closed front door of the cabin. The colorful scarf she used to corral her mass of braids was gray in the Veil, but her glowing red eyes made up for it. "How long have you been here?" Dec asked slowly.

She smirked. "Since Eli Margolis contacted me and asked me to guard Galena after he was called away."

Galena nearly choked. "You've been here the whole time?"

Tamasin shrugged. "I've been on the porch. The view is nice. I had no desire to intrude upon your privacy." Except it was dead obvious she knew what they'd been doing. Her crimson gaze settled on Dec again. "Her brother asked me to guard her. And so I will."

Declan took Galena's hand again. "No objections here. We'll take all the help we can get." He turned to Galena. "Do you know where we're going? You've been there before?"

Galena nodded. "I interviewed for the job in her office. I can picture it." She hoped. Her fingers trembled a little as she pulled her Scope from its chain. She closed her eyes and concentrated hard, picturing the antique wooden desk, the large holographic computer screen set into its surface, the elegant wooden office chair with embroidered cushions, the late twentieth-century art reproductions on the walls, one a painting of naked women dancing on a hillside . . . she tried to imagine every single detail. Then she brushed her thumb across the raven etching and opened the Scope.

Relief drew a smile to her face. "I did it!" Her eyes met Dec's, and he grinned. Galena's breath caught at how gorgeous it was, at how much she wanted to put that look on his face more often. "So do we just—?"

"Go ahead," said Dec.

Galena opened her Scope wide. Tamasin stepped through first. Galena knew Kere could appear anywhere, but she guessed they needed to know the place or the person they were looking for in order to move through the Veil accurately. Dec went next, and Galena followed him. She looked around Dr. Cassidy's office.

"There doesn't appear to be anyone in the office," said Tamasin, her gaze scanning along the videowall, the cluster of couches and chairs in the spacious meeting area, and the single shelf of antique books. Galena smiled. She remembered asking about the books in her interview, and Dr. Cassidy had proudly showed them to her, allowing her to hold one in her hands and flip through its fragile pages. It was the first time she'd ever held a printed book in her hands. Then her smile died. Dr. Cassidy now thought she was out of her mind. She and the other tenured faculty were considering firing her; Galena knew it. As much as she wished she could confide in Dr. Cassidy and explain everything, Galena was a fugitive now. She couldn't resurface until she had actual proof of her innocence.

"Can I just step into the real world?" she asked.

"Wait here." Tamasin strode over to the door to the office and pushed through it while Galena and Dec waited, chilled and shivering.

Galena looked over at Dec. "Are you okay?" she asked.

He nodded, staring at the door Tamasin had walked through. "Just thinking about Trevor," he muttered. "I can't shake the feeling that he wasn't in complete control of himself. And if *he* wasn't, then what if—"

"There's some sort of meeting going on in a conference room down the hall," Tamasin said as she walked through the gelatinous door. "There are twelve attending, and no one is in the outer office."

Galena wondered if they were meeting about her. She was not only the suspected mastermind of a mass-murder plot—she was also a fugitive. If they didn't fire her, she would be shocked.

Determination surged within her. She'd worked too hard for too long to let it end here. "I'm going in, then."

"I'm going with you," said Dec. He glanced at Tamasin.

"I'll remain here to guard," said the Ker.

Galena opened her Scope, and she and Dec stepped into the warmth of the real world once more, inhaling the faintly floral scent of Dr. Cassidy's perfume. Galena's heart raced as she approached the desk.

Behind her, Dec cursed softly, and she turned to find him staring at the screen of his phone. "What's wrong?"

"Aislin's been texting me for the last two hours," he whispered. "No reception on Baffin, and electronics don't work in the Veil, so I just received them. She says she needs me to come immediately." He scrolled through the messages, shaking his head. "Something major happened."

"Go, Dec," Galena murmured, hating the worry lines that had appeared between his brows. "Tamasin's here, and I know what I'm doing. We can meet back at the cabin."

He walked toward her, his fingers trailing down her arm, raising goose bumps of pleasure and longing. "You sure?"

She nodded. "Go. It sounds important."

"Okay. But keep your eyes open. And be careful. We still don't know that Trevor is the only enemy we have in the Veil. I'll be with you again as soon as I can."

Dec pulled his Scope from its chain and disappeared into it in less than five seconds. She blinked at the place he'd been, hoping he'd be okay, then returned her attention to the broad screen set into the desk. Time to figure out what the hell was going on. Dr. Cassidy would have "view" access to all her subordinates' user accounts so she could supervise and review the basic data if necessary. Galena wanted to look more closely at the timing of the messages to Jian, and maybe at the tech-support messages. There had been a lot of setup involved in creating the secure network perimeter for her lab, and maybe one of the computer techs had been sending the messages. She'd have to read them to know for sure.

Dr. Cassidy was already signed in, so Galena navigated to her own employee file. The complete history of her cyberactivity filled the screen. Galena swiped downward to access the earlier actions, all the way back to the beginning, looking for anything suspicious like password resets or addition of entry points into the system. Knowing Dr. Cassidy could return at any moment, she entered a search term to refine the results. Tamasin would warn her, but if she left without the evidence she needed, she might not have another chance.

The computer asked her for verification, and Galena tapped "Yes," but instead of giving her the results of the search, an overlay appeared.

Updating . . .

Galena cursed. In her rush, she hadn't been paying attention, and the verification she'd entered had started a file update. She jabbed her finger at the "Cancel" icon, but it was too late—one of the files had already been tagged. It would show that there had been someone accessing the data. She blew out a halting breath and pulled up the file to delete the tag.

And her heart almost stopped. The system update she was trying to delete wasn't tagged with Dr. Cassidy's user identity.

It was tagged with hers.

But her account was supposed to be frozen. And Dr. Cassidy's user icon was clearly visible at the top of the screen. "What the heck is going on," Galena whispered.

Her fingers trembling, she hit the "Command" tab to archive the modified file, and once again, the system recorded that the activity was completed by *GalenaMargolis*.

Suddenly the unexplained tech-support messages made complete sense, even though her lips were tingling with the shock of the betrayal. She resumed the search and finally found the request she was dreading. Twenty-seven days ago, *GalenaMargolis* had requested that tech support allow full remote access for Dr. Cassidy.

Her boss had set up a way to impersonate her. Dr. Cassidy was responsible for all of it. With this kind of shadow access, all she'd had to do was send Jian messages at times she knew Galena was alone in the lab. It would look like they'd come from Galena's secure system.

Her hands shook as she aimed the scanning port of Dec's phone at the port next to the desk screen. She had to upload all the messages and audit logs or she wouldn't have proof. But even as she activated the upload, her mind was a chaotic mess of questions and disbelief. After bringing her to Harvard, after taking such good care of her, Dr. Cassidy had impersonated her and blackmailed Jian into destroying everything connected to Galena's research. Why? Was it jealousy? Had Dr. Cassidy wanted the credit herself, so she'd decided to get rid of Galena and take over? But then why would she destroy the lab? Why wouldn't she just try to discredit Galena? Hell, why hadn't she just killed her?

Was she working with Trevor? Luke? Or Rylan, somehow? He'd been imprisoned for only a week, and the requests for access to her user account had been made weeks ago. Had he set this into motion?

Dec would help her figure it out. She hoped he was all right, that whatever had happened at Psychopomps wouldn't keep him long.

"What the hell are you doing in here?" snapped a harsh voice.

Galena startled, knocking the phone's port out of alignment and halting the upload of the audit trails. She looked up to see Dr. Cassidy standing in the doorway of her inner office, clearly livid.

"Dr. Cassidy," she said. "I needed to talk to you." She leaned on the desk, trying to move the phone's port back in line.

"I have nothing to talk to you about," Dr. Cassidy barked. "You're nothing but a selfish bitch who stole credit from good scientists in her race to the top."

Galena gaped at her, confusion and rage rolling hot across her skin. "Stole credit? What are you talking about?" She made a quick adjustment of the phone. The screen let out a single beep to signal the upload had recommenced.

Dr. Cassidy scowled as she noticed the phone. "Just like you're stealing from me now," she said as she stalked across the room. "How typical. Get away from there."

Galena stood her ground as the woman advanced. "I won't let you destroy everything I've worked so hard for."

Dr. Cassidy shook her head, her silvery hair glinting under the warm overhead light. "Everything *you've* worked hard for? What about me? I worked my whole life for the kind of recognition you got before you were even out of graduate school, only to have you show up, use all the results of my decades of research, and get short-listed for the Nobel!"

She reached the corner of the desk, and Galena braced. Any second, the upload would be complete, and she could grab the phone and find a way to disappear into the Veil. All she needed was—

Dr. Cassidy whipped her desk drawer open and came up with a handgun, a small sleek weapon that she cradled in her palm, one finger curling over the trigger. Galena's vision tunneled as Dr. Cassidy took aim. Right at Galena's chest. "Step away from the desk," Dr. Cassidy said, her voice steady and quiet. "It's time for this to end."

Galena began to raise her arms. Where was Tamasin? Why hadn't she given a warning?

We still don't know that Trevor is the only enemy we have in the Veil, Dec had said. For all she knew, Tamasin was in on this. And with Dec gone, she was all alone. "Why did you do this to me?"

Galena asked Dr. Cassidy, her voice cracking. "I thought you were on my side."

"And I thought you were on mine. Step away from the desk." Each word was delivered from between clenched teeth.

"Dr. Cassidy, is everything—?" There was a gasp by the door, and Galena's gaze flicked in that direction. She registered brown hair and glasses before she returned her attention to Dr. Cassidy, who was also looking toward the door.

"Erin, I want you to call the police," Dr. Cassidy called out.

Galena's gaze swept across the room again, confusion twisting inside her. "Erin?"

It was the young Ker that they'd met in the Veil that night with Luke. The one who had accompanied Trevor to Jian's place. She tilted her head. "Galena Margolis," she said, her voice full of curiosity.

Galena looked back and forth between the two women, a new suspicion poking its head above the surface of her shock.

The system beeped. Upload complete. Panicked, Galena grabbed for her Scope and the phone at the same time. Her fingers closed around both as the shot rang out. Her chest filled with sharp, molten pain that radiated in waves down her limbs. She stumbled backward, her legs failing her. *I thought I was immortal.* Lying on her back, she looked down to see the blood soaking her shirt. *But I guess that doesn't make me bulletproof.*

"You saw her," shouted Dr. Cassidy, her voice breaking. "She was attacking me!"

Galena's fingers clamped around her Scope. Dec said wounds didn't heal in the Veil. Still, it was her only shot at escape. As Dr. Cassidy came toward her, taking aim once more, Galena kicked out, knocking the gun from the woman's bony hand. It landed next to Galena's shoulder. She shoved Dec's phone into her pocket, wincing at the grinding pain in her chest. Her breathing was labored, and her mouth tasted like salt and iron. Blood. But she was still able to think, still able to move. Her body must be healing itself.

Dr. Cassidy lunged for the weapon, and behind her, Galena could see Erin standing, watching. She wasn't calling the police. Or maybe she already had. Either way, the gunshot would have people coming on the run. Galena flailed, knocking the gun farther out of reach as Erin leaned over and touched Dr. Cassidy's leg. "Stop, Dr. Cassidy," she said gently.

Instead of obeying, Dr. Cassidy's face contorted with rage. "You've ruined everything," she shrieked at Galena, who clumsily shoved the smaller woman off of her. Her knee came up and hit Dr. Cassidy in the stomach, and the woman fell against the desk, gasping. Galena brushed her thumb over the Scope as Dr. Cassidy clawed viciously at her leg. "You're going to pay for everything you've done!"

Galena stomped her foot into Dr. Cassidy's face as the woman came for her again. With a crunching snap, the woman fell backward, her hand over her face. Galena flung open the portal to the Veil and pulled it over herself quickly, groaning with the pain.

She lay on the squishy floor of the Veil, her Scope still clutched in her fist. Through the window into the real world, she could still see Dr. Cassidy lying sprawled on her back, writhing as blood flowed between her fingers. Erin was crouched over her, trying to pry her hands from her face. Then the Ker raised her head and gave Galena a calm, unreadable look.

Galena compacted her Scope. The last few minutes had utterly scrambled her brain, but she didn't have the time to figure it all out now. Fresh waves of pain crashed in her chest, and she shivered, her shirt saturated and dripping with red. Her head was spinning. *Loss of blood. You have to get back into the real world.*

Slowly, the ringing in her ears quieted, allowing her to hear noises coming from the other side of the gelatinous desk that shielded her from the rest of the room. Galena flopped over on her belly and dragged herself forward with her elbows, flinching as she heard a growl, then ripping. Wondering if her bodyguard had turned on her, too, Galena carefully peeked around the edge of the desk.

Tamasin, her braids swinging, threw a hard kick at a tall olive-skinned man with glowing red eyes. Another Ker. "Nader," Tamasin shouted. "Stop!"

He didn't listen. As soon as he recovered his balance, he dove for Tamasin, his claws extended. She threw herself to the side to avoid getting torn to shreds, and her red gaze landed on Galena. Her expression hardened with determination. As Nader leaped for her once more, Tamasin lunged for Galena and grabbed her arm. With a whoosh of hot air, the office disappeared.

CHAPTER THIRTY

Dec stepped into the real world, right in the middle of Aislin's office, to find his two sisters standing there.

". . . Moros gets here, he'll have to explain," Aislin was saying.

"Eli said he'd try to find him," Cacy said.

Aislin gave her a curt nod and turned to Dec. "Where have you been?"

"Out of touch, apparently. What's going on?"

"Where's Galena?" asked Cacy, who was wearing shorts and a frilly blouse, looking far more harmless than she actually was.

"Doing what she needs to do," Dec replied, never taking his eyes off Aislin.

"She could be in great danger," Aislin snapped.

Dec frowned. "You're the one who presents the greatest danger to her now that she's a Ferry." It felt so strange and wonderful to be able to say that. Galena was a Ferry. Not invincible . . . but immortal at least. "What's happened?"

Aislin crossed her arms over her chest. "Rylan escaped."

"*What?*"

"He was aided by a Ker."

"Which one?"

"Which one do you think, Declan?" shouted Aislin. "The one you brought here! We gave him the perfect opportunity—he saw where Rylan was. That was all he needed."

Dec's eyes went wide. "Do you have surveillance video? Because Trevor wouldn't—" Wait . . . *would* he?

Aislin must have seen his doubt. "You are a fool, Declan, and so am I. His 'confession' was a ruse so he could get to Rylan."

Dec looked back and forth between Aislin and Cacy, his thoughts reeling. He would have bet his life Trev had been utterly sincere. But Trev had also said that disconnected feeling came and went—what if it had happened again? Why hadn't he thought of that? "Weren't there guards in the Veil? Did they see him? Did anyone talk to him?" A cold tide of dread rose inside him. "Did he hurt anyone?"

Aislin pressed her fingertips to her temples and clamped her eyes shut. She muttered something about her head exploding and walked over to her desk.

"It happened really fast," Cacy said quietly as Aislin's fingernails tapped on the screen set into her desk. "While the guards were distracted."

"You're serious," Declan said.

She nodded. "It's an unpleasant job hanging out in the Veil, and freaking boring, and I guess they were arguing about something stupid, and the next thing they knew, Trevor and Ry were gone."

"More evidence for the Keepers," said Aislin, looking up from her screen. "Somehow, in the ten days I've been the Charon, I've managed to provide them with everything they need to take us down."

"We can fix this," said Cacy. "We just have to find Trevor and Ry."

"Preferably before they strike," said Dec. It was all he could do not to pull his Scope open and race back to Galena's side. If Trev was out of control again and determined to get to Moros, Galena might be his prime target. The only thing keeping Dec in the room was the knowledge that she was immortal and that Tamasin was by her side. "We need Eli or Moros. Did Eli really think he could find him?"

"He said he would try," Cacy muttered.

"We don't know that this isn't exactly what Moros wants," snapped Aislin. "He claims to be trying to track down the rogue Kere, or at least figuring out how they were able to go rogue, but he has been conveniently absent as we deal with the results of his failed control over the creatures he created."

Dec shifted his weight from foot to foot, thinking of what Rylan had said to him right before he'd escaped, about who was powerful enough to take control of the deadly game they were all playing. "I think someone else might be controlling Trevor. Cacy, you know him. Does any of this sound like stuff he would do?"

She shook her head. "I haven't known him for as long as you have, but"—she turned to Aislin—"this is really out of character for him. It would actually make more sense if someone was using him like a puppet."

"I know you two would like to believe that Trevor is innocent, but the only way to influence the Kere is to take their souls," said Aislin. "Moros told me last week that he could guarantee all the souls were present and accounted for."

"What, does he keep them in some kind of carrying case or something?" Cacy asked. "Or pinned and mounted to his wall?" She looked keenly interested—probably because Eli's soul was among them.

Aislin came out from behind her desk. "Moros has always been incredibly secretive about that. However, given the circumstances, I think it's time we demand more information."

"If this isn't all part of some evil double-cross he's got going, then he needs to admit that he's losing his grip," Dec said. "Because Ry told me Mandy could feel that Moros wasn't in control of her anymore, that he couldn't sense when she was acting against his will. And Trevor said he felt disconnected—and he must have been free, if he could complete so many unauthorized Markings without Moros sensing it. Someone else is interfering."

"But Moros said that Jian Lee's Marking *was* sanctioned, Dec," said Cacy quietly. "That order could only have come from Moros and his sisters."

"Then maybe Moros is playing us all."

"Speak of the devil and he appears," said Moros as he materialized next to Aislin, who glared at him.

"Where have you been?"

"Preparing for our summit with the Keepers," he said, his steel-gray gaze sliding over her face.

"Did part of that preparation include getting one of your Kere to bust Rylan out of his cell?" asked Cacy.

Moros's eyes flickered red. "What did you just say?"

"One of your creatures reached through the Veil and took Rylan," Aislin replied.

"Which one?" Moros asked, his pointed canines flashing in the light. Every inch of him vibrated with tension.

"Trevor," said Aislin. "Dec brought him here after he confessed to conspiring with the human Jian Lee to destroy Galena and her work. He claimed remorse and wanted execution. And he brought us a knife that bore DNA from all three unsanctioned stabbing victims, plus his own." She glanced at Dec. "That was one of the reasons I was trying to reach you. One of *many*."

Dec barely heard her—he was too busy watching the Lord of the Kere. He would have laughed at the dizzying array of emotions crossing Moros's face if it wasn't so horrifying. Puzzlement, shock, rage. Moros hadn't been aware of what Trevor had done. "How many Kere exist in the world, Moros?" Dec said.

Moros's eyes flashed red again as he turned his attention to Dec. "I fail to see why disclosing the number would help you."

"I'd like to know how many are going to come at us when you completely lose control!" shouted Dec. "If you haven't already, that is."

"While you all were allowing chaos to reign here in Boston," Moros said, every word delivered with a side of contempt, "I was once again confirming that all the souls of my Kere are present and accounted for."

"Then you need to think outside of the box, or whatever it is you keep them in," said Dec, gritting his teeth as Moros took a step toward him, his gloved fingers twitching. "You need to find Trevor and bring him back."

"When I find Trevor, he won't be coming back."

"He's served you for a hundred years. He deserves more from you than a summary execution. Come on, Moros, think about it. Help us figure out why Trevor, of all your Kere, would act against you like this. Assuming he *is* acting against you, that is."

"Ah. So we're back to this. You think I'm violating the treaty."

"Perhaps it's time to prove you're not," said Aislin.

Moros closed his eyes. For a moment, he went completely still. He glanced over at Aislin. "I cannot sense Trevor right now," he said quietly. "A few hours ago, I could, but now . . . nothing."

Little stress lines had formed around Aislin's mouth. "Are there any more that you can't sense?"

"For me to know, I'd have to try to bring each one of them to mind." He arched an eyebrow as his gaze met Dec's. "And to answer your earlier question, there are as many Kere as there are Ferrys."

"Fifty thousand?" whispered Cacy.

"You can't sense them all the time?" asked Aislin.

Moros sighed. "No. I can sense when they act against my will, though. If they do not Mark when assigned, if they Mark someone who has not been fated to die . . ."

"But not when they break known murderers out of jail," Cacy said bitterly.

Panic rattled inside Dec's chest like a bag full of nails, threatening to shred any calm he had left. "So at any given time, any one of the fifty thousand killing machines you've created could turn on you, on us, on *Galena*—"

"Declan, stop," Aislin began.

But he was past stopping. Beyond anger. "You owe us answers, Moros," he growled. "We're scrambling to deal with the slaughter while you stand back and watch us flail." He didn't care that Moros could destroy him. Galena's life had been torn apart by beings Moros had created and was supposed to rule. He wanted to put his fist through the guy's face.

"Declan!" snapped Aislin.

Because now he was toe to toe with the Lord of the Kere. "Stop thinking only of yourself and help us," Dec said.

Moros didn't flinch. He simply stood there, with his slick hair, his elegant suit, his stupid earring, and his glowing red eyes, staring at Declan's face. "I understand your anger," he said softly. "I've seen how tightly the thread of your life is wrapped around Galena's now. So perhaps, instead of lecturing me about my business, you should make sure that she is safe, my friend. Because with your brother on the loose once more, I would say she is probably in a great deal of peril."

Dec stepped back when he felt Aislin's fingers curl over his arm, the panic still stabbing at his insides. "Rylan doesn't have a Scope. He's a regular human now." It was Trevor he was worried about, but it felt awful to even think it. "Rylan couldn't be in the Veil. He has to be here with us in the real world. You know him well—can you track him?"

Once again, Moros's face went slack and he closed his eyes. When he opened them again, he looked shaken. "I can't."

"What does that mean?" asked Cacy.

"It most likely means his future is tightly entwined with one of my Kere," he said, his brow furrowed in thought. "That must be what it means."

"Moros," said Aislin. "We have to find Rylan and Trevor. For both our sakes. And those of our people."

"Agreed," Moros murmured. "Agreed."

He vanished.

Aislin cursed, sharp and sudden. "If either of us survives the summit, it will be from sheer dumb luck," she snapped. Her eyes met Dec's. "It's time for you to fetch Galena, Declan. Psychopomps is the safest place for her."

"Will you hand her over to the police?" Dec asked.

Her lips became a flat, bloodless line. "The news feeds are full of her name and picture. The police are attempting to acquire warrants to search our apartment building and this tower for her. Our board members are demanding to know why I'm obstructing the investigation, especially because of who she is and what she can do. There is even talk of trying to replace me as CEO. Cousin Hugh has shored up a large number of supporters, and he's threatening to take this conflict public. It's possible we could lose control of the C-suite, and the empire, entirely!" She bowed her head, breathing hard. But when she spoke again, her voice was soft and steady. "I may have no choice but to give her up, Dec. If she's in custody, I would place guards in the Veil."

"Like the guards who were supposed to keep Rylan in his cell?" Dec yelled, pulling his Scope from his neck. "Aislin, do your damage control. Do your *job*. And I'm going to do mine." He brushed his thumb over the raven and pulled the Scope wide. "I'll be back by midnight."

He stepped into the Veil and opened a portal to Dr. Cassidy's office, emerging into cold gray silence. He looked around and went still as he saw the transparent figure of an older woman lying on the floor of the office clutching her face. Another person, a middle-aged man, was standing over her, shouting into his phone.

A patch of color by the desk caught his eye. Red. It was *blood*. A smear of it across the slick gray floor. And Galena was nowhere to be seen. His heart pounding, he opened another portal to his cabin. She said she'd meet him there. He pulled the ring wide and stepped through it quickly.

She wasn't here, either.

A ragged cry burst from his mouth as he forced himself to concentrate. She might be hurt. She needed him. Could Trevor and Rylan already have her? Had Tamasin betrayed her? Where would they have taken her? He opened a portal to his apartment in Boston. Shivering in the chill of the Veil, he went from room to room, his hope cresting as he reached every doorway and crashing to the ground whenever he looked in to see she wasn't there.

He was just brushing his thumb over the raven again, planning to head back to Psychopomps and enlist Cacy's help, when Eli appeared in front of him. Dec sagged with relief. "I can't find Galena," he said, his voice cracking. "And I think she's in trouble."

Eli stared at him. His green eyes glowed red, and his claws were extended. "She is." He grabbed Dec's arm. "Come on."

Dec felt a burst of cold air, and then he landed face-first on spongy concrete. Cursing and confused, he pushed himself to his feet to find Eli standing over him. They were in a narrow garbage-strewn side street, but it was completely unfamiliar. "Eli?" he panted. "Where is she?"

"Welcome to Pittsburgh," Eli growled, bearing his fangs as he leaned toward Dec. "I think it's time you and I had a little talk."

CHAPTER THIRTY-ONE

Galena hit dirt and rolled, coughing, her lungs screaming. Her Scope flew from her grasp. Bright light poured down on her, making her squint and blink. A dark silhouette leaned over her, and Galena flinched, expecting attack.

"How bad is it?" Tamasin asked, ripping Galena's shirt down the middle and revealing a small round wound high on her chest.

The Ker pressed her fingers against the area around the wound, and Galena gasped. "I don't know." They were on a flat, sunbaked plain, cracked earth and brown as far as she could see. No trees. "What happened? Where are we?"

"Iowa, at the moment." Tamasin put her arm around Galena's back and helped her sit up, then pressed her Scope into the palm of her hand. After a few seconds upright, it became a little easier to breathe. "We have to move again. I'm sorry."

"Why?" She wasn't sure she could go very far. Her chest was throbbing, and the rest of her was cold, buzzing, hard to control. All she wanted was for the pain to end.

"Nader will follow us. It won't take him—"

The lean olive-skinned man appeared not ten feet away, but with another whoosh of hot air, Tamasin pulled Galena through space, and they reappeared on a weathered cliff overlooking an ocean. Even through her pain, Galena was fascinated by the waves, the white froth and the churning water. She'd never seen so much water. It—

Tamasin smacked her fingers lightly against Galena's cheeks. "Remain conscious, please." When Galena pulled herself back into the now and focused on Tamasin's wide-set brown eyes, the Ker continued. "Did you get the evidence you needed?"

"Yeah," Galena said, her voice shredded and weak. She closed her eyes and took a shuddering breath as some of the pressure in her chest lifted. "But Erin was there."

"Who?"

"Erin. A Ker? She was Dr. Cassidy's assistant."

Tamasin scowled. "I don't know a Ker named Erin."

"She's new. Newer than Eli."

Tamasin shook her head. "Your brother is the newest Ker in Moros's ranks."

Galena didn't have time to say anything else—she cried out as a sharp pain tore through her. She arched back, her chest feeling like it had been filled with fire.

Tamasin held her tight. "It's the bullet. Working itself out of your body. We have to remain in this world long enough for that to happen."

But as soon as she said it, Nader materialized again, this time down the hill. Tamasin cursed and yanked on Galena, who sucked in a lungful of burning air as she landed hard. Screams came from all around them, and Tamasin heaved her up to her feet. They were in the middle of a crowded city, though Galena had no idea which one. The street signs were in some Asian language, and the buildings were so high she couldn't see the tops. It was daytime here, and people swarmed in the streets. Tamasin wrapped her arm around Galena's waist and dragged her along the sidewalk as bystanders gaped.

Another sharp pain made Galena pitch forward, but Tamasin kept her on her feet. "I'm sorry I wasn't able to warn you that the woman was coming into the office," she huffed as she carried Galena along. "There's something wrong with Nader. He attacked me."

And now he was chasing them. "Why is he doing this?" Galena gasped out. "Isn't he supposed to protect me?"

"He is." She looked down at Galena, her eyes sparking with crimson. "But he does not appear to be himself right now, and he is extremely dangerous." She lugged Galena down a narrow alley, heading for the sound of thumping music and bright lights.

"Will he just keep following us?"

"Probably," said Tamasin. "It's possible we should separate."

"Is there any place we could go that he couldn't follow?"

"No," said a deep male voice.

Galena stumbled to the side as Nader grabbed a handful of Tamasin's braids and yanked her forward. "Nader, stop this!" shouted Tamasin as she shot hard punches to his middle. "What is wrong with you? Moros will destroy you."

"He doesn't control me now," he growled, wrapping his arm around Tamasin's throat. Here in the real world, he had no claws. No fangs. But he appeared terribly strong as he kneed Tamasin in the chest, twice, making the female Ker gasp for air. "Moros has ruled us for too long. I'm tired of doing his bidding. It's time we ruled ourselves."

He raised his arm and elbowed Tamasin between the shoulders. The impact came with a stomach-turning crack. Tamasin whimpered and slumped, her fingers curling into the folds of Nader's shirt, her legs going limp.

Galena staggered back, the pain in her chest nearly unbearable. It felt like her rib cage was about to explode, spewing her heart onto the dirty concrete in front of her. Nader dropped Tamasin like a load of bricks and stepped over her. The female Ker's legs were still, but her arms were moving. It looked like he'd broken her back. And now he was coming for Galena. He held out his hand. "Give me the evidence you retrieved."

Galena pressed herself against the metal railing of a stairwell as the agony reached a crescendo. She lifted a weak, trembling hand to her chest and felt a hard nub protruding from her wound. The bullet. But before her body had a chance to fully push it out, Nader grabbed her wrist and dragged her into the Veil. Galena fell backward through the now-gelatinous metal railing and tumbled down a flight of stairs, bouncing against the walls and steps like a rubber ball. She landed in a heap at the bottom, looking up at the tall buildings, the gray sky, and the brutal Ker who was watching her from above, his eyes glowing. "You're the key to his destruction," he said, his gaunt features contorting with rage. "You're the way we'll take him down."

Galena clenched her fists, wanting to cry out from the pain, which had only intensified now that she was back in the dead gray Veil. Her body had stopped healing. But in her sticky, blood-stained palm, she felt a warm weight. Her Scope. As Nader began to descend the steps, she held it against her side and pressed her thumb to the raven, feeling a tiny, cool portal opening up. She had no idea to where. But anywhere far from here was good, so as Nader reached the halfway point down the steps, Galena flung the Scope wide and dove into the center of it, pulling it shut quickly.

She was in Dec's apartment. His bedroom. Right in the spot she'd first kissed him. Suddenly the ache in her chest wasn't just from the bullet that had carved its way into her sinew and bone. Where was he? Was he okay? She pushed herself to her hands and knees. She needed to open a window to the real world and crawl through so she could heal.

But hands closed hard around her neck, dragging her back in space and time. *The heavyset one grimaced as he pressed his thumbs against her throat, cutting off her air.* Her mouth opened, a prayer for oxygen, as claws tore through her skin. She landed on her back, her thoughts buzzing with voices from the past and the terror of her present. *Stay here,* she reminded herself. *Stay right here.*

She looked up to see Nader's face. Heat filled her mouth, and she coughed and wiped her lips, her fingers coming away bright red. Her vision blurred. "You'll be human again soon," Nader said. "And then we'll kill you."

Human again soon. Time was running out, and this Ker knew it. He knelt beside her. "Now give me the evidence." His long black hair skimmed over his shoulders and hung between them as he looked her up and down. His gaze halted when it reached the bulge in her pocket.

Then a dark shape plowed into him, sending them careening across the soft floor of the apartment.

"Galena, get away from here!" Tamasin shouted as her clawed hand arced through the air, slashing across Nader's chest. Like Eli had when he'd been shot, she'd healed incredibly quickly.

Nader roared with rage and kicked Tamasin away. The two of them charged at each other, slamming together, their fangs bared. They became a blur of blood and claws.

Galena tried to move, but her body felt like it had been stuffed with concrete and wrapped in gauze. She was drowning in blood. Wait. She really was drowning. With a lurch, she flopped herself over, crimson flowing from her mouth as her cheek landed with a smack against the forgiving floor. Tamasin was right. She had to get out of here.

Her Scope was still clutched in her hand. As she tried to summon the coordination to turn it over, she watched Nader twist Tamasin's arm so hard that the bones cracked, leaving the limb hanging limp from the woman's powerful frame. Their blood dotted the Veil, shining red droplets on the dull gray surfaces. *Sticky red mess,* whispered Galena's mind.

Yes, this dredged up her memories, but she wouldn't push them away this time. It had happened, and she'd gotten through it. And that realization made it possible for her to flip the Scope. With halting, clumsy movements, Galena opened it and peered through the center. Dec's cabin waited on the other side. A wave of longing rolled over her, dampening the pain for a moment. Would he be there? Would he be waiting for her?

The hope pulled her through the portal, her knees sliding through her own lost blood, every part of her screaming with pain. She left Tamasin behind, locked in horrific, bloody combat with Nader, who wanted to kill Galena to get to Moros. Who knew she might be human again soon, an easy target. If he defeated Tamasin, he'd follow her here. But Galena didn't have anywhere else to go. She couldn't hide from a creature who could track her with his thoughts.

She compacted the Scope and opened a portal to the real world, crawling out onto the wooden floor of the cabin. In the small space, she could still detect Dec's masculine scent. She smiled as she closed the Scope one last time and clipped it to its setting.

It was a cold, familiar weight on her skin, and the only comfort she had right now. The pain was gnawing at every part of her. Her body might be healing, but it was far from instantaneous.

And at any moment, Nader might appear, ready to rip her to shreds. Galena took a wet, unsteady breath. "Please, Dec," she whispered. "Hurry."

CHAPTER THIRTY-TWO

Dec scrambled to his feet and took a few halting steps back as Eli came forward, his claws curling slightly at their razor-sharp tips. "Eli," he said, keeping his voice level and patient. "What's wrong?"

"Everything." Eli grimaced and rubbed his chest with a sudden agitated jerk of his hand. He looked around, his eyes glowing red. "This is where it happened, you know. This is where I died the first time."

Dec took in the piles of garbage, the broken windows covered in rotting boards, the transparent shadows of random people, sleeping or dead, slumped against the crumbling brick wall of one of the buildings. *This was the place where Galena and Eli were attacked.* The knowledge settled inside him like a ball of shattered glass. "Is she here? Did someone bring her here?"

"I thought you should see it," Eli said, his voice low and rasping. "If things had gone the way they should have, I never would have been brought back to life. I never would have killed anyone. I would have died right here, and I would have gone to Heaven. I would be with my parents. I wouldn't be *this.*" It came out as a hiss.

"And you wouldn't have met Cacy," Dec added, taking another wary step backward. He could feel the heat and the rage rolling off

Eli. Something was very wrong. Eli sounded a lot like Trevor had, as he'd explained his rage toward Moros.

Eli paused for a moment at the sound of Cacy's name. "Cacy," he whispered, his features softening.

"Yeah. And Galena—who knows what would have happened to her without you? She would have been alone."

Eli's brow furrowed. "I could never leave her alone."

"Exactly. So whatever's going on for you right now, whatever existential crisis this is, how about we talk about it over a bottle of whiskey—*after* we make sure she's safe?"

Eli looked down at his clawed hands. "Galena," he murmured. Then he raised his head, and the flame in his eyes had banked, giving way to lucid concern. "Where is she?"

Dec breathed relief. "She's—"

"Oh, thank God. Here you are!" called a female voice. Erin came running up the side street, her red eyes wide. She grabbed Eli's sleeve. "I thought I was going to be too late."

Eli looked at her as her hand skimmed down his arm and found his, then her fingers wrapped over his own. The puzzled look on his face turned to a scowl. "You're not." His eyes flared with crimson, and he looked at Dec. "I was just explaining to Dec why this was the perfect place for us to be."

Dec's stomach dropped. "Eli—"

"No." He slashed his claws through the air as Erin stroked the back of his other hand. "Do you know what Moros did that night? He set me on this path. And then he took my soul!" Eli advanced on Dec with his fangs bared.

"He did that to allow you to stay in this world, so you could protect Galena," Dec shouted, his mind screaming alarm. Erin. She was doing something to Eli.

She was touching him like she'd touched Luke. Had she done this to Trevor, too? With his gaze riveted on their joined hands, Dec said, "Let him go, Erin. I don't know what you're doing, but—"

"I'm trying to help!" she said. "It's not my fault that he's so angry at Moros!"

"Moros is responsible for all of this," Eli roared, looking monstrous, his face contorted with rage. "But he no longer controls me." He rubbed his chest again.

"And who is controlling you, Eli? If it's not Moros, who's got your soul?" He glanced at Erin.

She shrugged. "Don't look at me. Not my department."

"Moros has stolen thousands of souls over thousands of years. He's ruled us. Destroyed us at will, with a single touch." Eli's gaze was slightly unfocused, like he was looking into a past he'd never lived. But then his focus sharpened once more. "I'm going to destroy him. By destroying *you*."

Dec's fingers rose to his Scope. "If you do anything to me, you'll be hurting your own sister. You love her, Eli. You'd lay down your life for her."

For a split second, confusion flickered across Eli's face, but then Erin smoothed her fingers along his brow, and the fury returned. "Moros has to pay for what he's done. It's worth anything I have to sacrifice."

"Eli, get away from her," Dec yelled, pulling his Scope from its setting. He hated to leave Eli here, but he had to get back to Psychopomps and back to Galena.

Erin's brow relaxed, her concerned expression melting away. "Are you sure, Declan? Are you sure you want me to let him go?" She gave him a small, pitying smile. "Okay." She lifted her hands into the air.

Eli leaped at him, and Dec threw himself to the side, slipping along the spongy concrete. "Eli, think about what you're doing!" he called as his shoulder hit gelatinous curb and sank in. "Think about Cacy!"

Eli was crouched where he'd landed, glaring at him. Erin had seated herself on a stoop nearby and was watching them both. "Do you know her?" he asked Eli, waving his arm at Erin.

Eli glanced at her as he rose to his feet. "Of course," he said. "She's new. I'm showing her the ropes."

Same thing Trev had said. Same thing Luke had said. Luke's exact same words, even. How many Kere had she done this to? "Are you sure she's who she says she is?"

"You're standing in the spot," Eli said quietly, ignoring him. "You're standing right where I took my last breaths. Galena was right there." He pointed his clawed finger at the sidewalk a few feet from him. It would have been hard and cold and unforgiving at her back. She would have been gazing up at a narrow strip of sky as she lived the most horrifying moments of her life. Dec's throat tightened thinking about it.

"Maybe she should have died that night, too," Eli continued. "Maybe it would have been for the best."

Keeping his arm at his side, Dec held the Scope between his fingers and slid his thumb over the raven, feeling the cool air of another place calling to him. He had no idea where. Was it where Galena was, waiting for him? If he went through it, would he bring the danger right to her? He pushed the Scope closed again.

"If she'd died, it would have been an even bigger tragedy than it already was," he said. "She was strong enough to live. She was meant to live."

"She can't live," Eli snarled. "Because if she does, Moros does, too. The Keepers are the only ones who can destroy him, and her death would force their hand."

"It would destroy the fabric of fate, too, Eli. That can't be what you want."

"What I want is for him to pay for what he's done to me!"

This time, Dec didn't move fast enough. Eli barreled into him, and the Scope flew from his hand, landing at Erin's feet. Dec threw a hard punch to Eli's middle, but the Ker didn't even flinch. He grabbed Dec's arm, claws scoring his skin, and swung him up and over his head, throwing him across the street. Dec landed on a pile of garbage and sank through it, temporarily drowning in the sludge. But then Eli grabbed his leg and dragged him out. Dec's back slid along the slippery ground.

"Do you know what time it is, Dec?" Eli asked. "Only a few hours until Aislin's ultimatum. Can you feel the minutes passing? Do you know what's going to happen when midnight comes? You'll be human again. So will she. And when we Mark you, you'll die."

"You don't want this, Eli." Trevor's anguish at having murdered innocent people would be nothing compared to what Eli would go through if he came back to himself and found out he'd destroyed his own sister. "Think about Galena. Think about her."

Erin casually leaned off the stoop and rubbed Eli's back. "Yes, Eli. Think about it."

"It's her fault we're even in Boston," Eli snapped. "Her research. Her job. I had a job, too! I had a life. And I gave it all up to go with her. It's her fault I'm a monster!"

Dec rolled to the side as Eli pounced, but he didn't make it far. Claws pierced his leg, shredding fabric and skin and muscle. Pain surged along Dec's bones. He dug his fingers into the road and tried to drag himself forward, but Eli slashed Dec's back, making him writhe. "Just a few hours," Eli was chanting. "It'll be over in a few hours."

Dec flopped onto his back and managed to get a leg up, shoving Eli away from him, but the Ker merely took a few staggering steps back before stalking forward again. "Eli," Dec groaned. "This isn't you. She's doing something to you." He glanced over at Erin, who was focused on Eli with an eerie sort of calm.

"She can't do a thing to me," said Eli. "She's just a newbie." He kicked Dec in the side. Air exploded from Dec's mouth at the impact, his body instinctively curling in on itself. A second kick. A third. Dec wheezed, knowing that his shattered ribs were probably poking holes in the soft tissue of his lungs, his spleen. That blood was spilling into his chest cavity. Eli grabbed him and hauled him up, freakishly strong. "You're part of this, too," he growled, then slammed his fist into Dec's stomach, turning Dec's world red with agony.

Stop, Dec tried to say. *Please stop.* But he couldn't speak anymore. He landed flat on his back, trying to draw air. Eli stood over him, his legs on either side of Dec's.

"Don't do it," Erin said in a bland voice. "Stop."

Eli raised his arm and struck, ripping his claws across Dec's chest. Blood splattered onto Dec's face as he arched back with the impact, his arms splaying out, nerveless. Eli looked down at him. "That should be enough. I'll be back to Mark you when midnight comes." And then he vanished.

Dec lay there, looking up at the strip of gray sky above him, the only warmth coming from his own blood, flowing from his body. Was this what Galena had seen? What had she been thinking?

Erin's freckled face appeared over his. "You poor thing," she crooned, her brows knit together in false sympathy. "This really wasn't personal. I want you to know that."

"Trevor," he whispered.

"He was almost as hard to convince as Eli," she said gently.

"R-Rylan . . ."

"Oh. Are you asking how he got loose? Do you know how easy it was to stoke the resentment of those guards? They were primed and ready. I didn't even have to touch them." She grinned. "Trevor did the heavy lifting there."

"Who . . . are . . . ?"

"Who am I?" She caressed his cheek.

As soon as her skin touched his, Dec's mind flooded with memories: His father rolling his eyes when Dec had told him he wanted to be a paramedic. Rylan laughing, thinking it was a joke.

A parade of stupid fucking parties he'd been forced to attend to keep up appearances, to please other people. All his asshole relatives who cared more about their money than anything else. His obnoxious sister who defied his orders right in front of the other paramedics. His power-hungry sister who used him like a pawn in her never-ending game . . . Every resentment he'd felt, even in passing, came back to him in a roaring tidal wave of hatred and rage. Why hadn't he retired years ago? Because he felt like he had to meet his obligations. Obligations. All these fucking obligations. And why wasn't he able to retire now? Because of *her*. Because she needed him.

Because she needed him . . .

Erin chuckled and pulled her hand away from her face. "I'd work on you a little more if I had time, but I don't need you, so it's not really worth the effort. I need to go make sure Eli follows through. The next part is really tricky. That guy's devotion to his sister was hard to break through, and even harder to keep at bay." She got to her feet, her red eyes glowing. "Don't worry, Declan. I know the next few hours will be awful, but then it'll be over. And you seem like a nice guy. I'm betting on Heaven for you."

She disappeared.

The next part is really tricky. Eli was going to do something to hurt Galena. And she would have no idea until it was too late. She trusted him with her life, but because of Erin—whatever that evil bitch was doing—Eli would tear that life from her with his claws. Dec tried to sit up, but his muscles weren't obeying. His Scope was lying about five feet away. He could see it glinting in the weak light of the moon. With a shuddering heave, he managed to get on his side. His shaking arm stretched, his fingers flexed, as if his need could draw it toward him. All he had to do was get to his Scope—

Erin popped into the Veil again, right next to it. "I can't believe I almost forgot this," she said with a laugh as she scooped it up, then vanished again.

Dec stared at the place she'd been, disbelief and fear winding through his veins. He had no way back to the real world. No way to get back to Galena and warn her. No way to heal.

A wailing shriek sounded a few blocks away and was immediately answered by another. Dec closed his eyes as despair filled him. And for a moment, he held on to what Erin had said—*the next few hours will be awful, but then it'll be over.* He only had to endure a few more miserable hours. Maybe the Shades would tear him apart. Maybe he would even lose consciousness. That would be a mercy.

But then Galena's face appeared in his mind, pushing away his craving for oblivion. She'd fallen into his life, which had felt as gray and pointless as his situation now, lying here in this alleyway. She'd made him feel alive. She'd made him curious. He wanted to know what came next. He wanted to be by her side when it happened.

Another screech tore through the Veil, closer this time. The Shades would be on him soon.

Dec's fingers twitched. He had to move. If he wanted a chance to live past midnight, he was going to have to fight for it.

CHAPTER THIRTY-THREE

Galena was awakened by a tug in her gut, like cool fingers had wrapped around her spine and shaken her awake. She winced as she sat up and looked down at herself. Something small and metallic hit the floor and rolled toward the fireplace. Her body had finally pushed the bullet out. She ran her hand over her chest. Her torn shirt was stiff and sticky with drying blood. But when she pulled the fabric away from her skin, she saw that her chest had mostly healed. The wound was now just a red pucker that was rapidly regaining its previously smooth texture.

She gasped as she felt the tug again. It must be a soul in the Veil somewhere, waiting to be ferried to the Afterlife. Should she try to go? What if Dec came back while she was gone? She wanted to be here when he arrived. She pulled out his phone and looked down at it, a chill riding over her skin. She'd been out too long. Way too long. They only had an hour left.

And she couldn't call Dec, because she had his phone. She put her hand over her middle as the pull increased in intensity. Could the soul wait for her? Hadn't Dec said another Ferry would shuttle the soul if she didn't?

Hadn't he also said the soul might become rabid while it waited?

She pulled her Scope from its setting. Indecision gripped her.

A swirling burst of hot and cold air lifted tendrils of her hair, and Galena looked up to see Eli materialize near the kitchen.

There was dried blood on his hands.

Galena shot to her feet. "Oh my God, Eli, are you all right?"

He looked down at his fingers and then back at her. "I'm fine," he said in a harsh, rasping voice. "I'm almost finished."

"What are you talking about?" Any relief at seeing him was evaporating quickly. He looked so different from the last time they'd been together. His face was pulled into a grimace, like he was in pain. The usual kindness in his eyes was gone.

"I never wanted to be a monster," he muttered. "He never should have made me a monster."

"Eli?" she whispered, taking a step toward him, her hand rising from her side, reaching for her brother.

"Moros. There's no way this can end unless he dies." His green eyes met hers. "And the way to get to him is you. It's the only way."

Her stomach tightened. She could still feel the pull of the dead soul, but it was overlaid by fear. "What do you mean?"

"It's almost midnight." Eli's face was contorted, lines of stress around his eyes and mouth.

"Do you know where Dec is?" she asked, her voice small, strangled by worry.

"He needed to understand, G. I had to show him where it happened, where everything started. I wanted him to know why I had to do it."

Her hand, suspended in air, trying to cross the distance between them, froze. She looked down at the blood on his hands again. "Eli, what have you done?"

"What I had to. And I have to do this, too." It sounded like he was forcing every word from his mouth. His fingers curled, his every muscle taut, he stalked toward her.

Hot hands closed over her shoulders and yanked her backward. Cold air enveloped her, and she staggered, but arms wrapped around her torso, keeping her upright. She craned her neck to see Tamasin, her brown skin streaked with blood, her braids swinging around her face, her eyes glowing. "You have to get away from here," she said in a tight voice. "We've lost Eli, too."

No sooner had she said it than Eli appeared. They were in the shadow world of the Veil, but still in the cabin. "I can follow anywhere you take her." His voice was flat. Dead.

Tamasin shoved Galena behind her. "Eli, this is your *sister*. Your devotion to her is the reason you chose to join Moros."

Eli's claws elongated, and his eyes burned crimson. "I know," he roared. "This is her fault!"

Tamasin launched herself at Eli, right as he charged. Galena fell back. Caught by the murderous look in her brother's eyes, she stared, horrified, as he and Tamasin kicked and slashed at each other. The man fighting Tamasin wasn't her brother. It couldn't be him. Like Nader. Like Trevor. Not themselves.

"Eli, stop!" cried Galena. "Remember who you are. I love you. Don't do this."

Eli flinched, and Tamasin landed a solid kick to his middle, sending him off balance. He crashed into the kitchen counter and sank in. As Tamasin crouched, waiting for his next attack, Galena got to her feet. "Eli, look at me," she said. "Think of everything we've been through together."

He rubbed at his chest and winced, his eyes glittering with pain. "G...I..."

Erin suddenly appeared at his side, her freckled face full of concern. She wasn't wearing glasses anymore, and her long brown hair was loose around her shoulders. She laid her hand on Eli's cheek. "You are so difficult," she said in a gentle but chiding tone.

"Erin?" Galena said. "Why are you here?"

"Who are you?" Tamasin barked at the same time.

Erin turned to look at them. "I'm the boots on the ground," she said, her fingers caressing Eli's face. It contorted with rage, revealing his wickedly sharp fangs.

Anger rose inside Galena, pushing down her fear. Erin's touch . . . she'd touched Dr. Cassidy, too. "You're doing something to him."

Erin arched her eyebrow. "Well, it doesn't take a genius to figure that out—"

With a growl, Eli charged at Tamasin again. The force of his attack knocked Erin to the side, and she bounced off the counter and fell to her knees. A Scope flew from her pocket and slid to the middle of the floor, raven face up, flecked with dark-red droplets. As Tamasin collided with Eli, Galena lunged for it. She knew it had to be Dec's.

She grabbed it and rolled backward just as Tamasin and Eli hit the floor between her and Erin, who looked pissed as she laid her hand on Eli's back. "Finish her and fetch your sister, Eli. Remember what you're here to do."

Eli's head lurched to the side, and Galena felt like his gaze was going to burn right through her. "You have to die!" His voice was guttural. More animal than human.

Galena scooted backward just as Eli flipped so that he was straddling Tamasin, whose face and neck and chest were a mass of red gashes. Eli spread both his arms wide and slashed his claws down, embedding them in Tamasin's chest. Galena screamed and dove for the door of the cabin as Tamasin let out a shriek of agony.

The gelatinous door was no match for Galena's frenzied, panicked strength. She punched right through it and rolled onto the porch. The cabin was set into a steep mountainside that led into a flat, rocky valley. Beyond it was the vertical face of an incredibly tall mountain. No other buildings, no cities, no people.

"You can't run from me," Eli snarled as he pushed through the door.

With a gasp, Galena jumped off the edge of the porch. She fell through the air, arms pinwheeling. Her mind spun with calculations and guesses. *Increase your surface area or you'll get stuck when you land.* She flung her arms and legs out as she landed flat on her back and bounced. She curled into a ball again as she rolled down the hill. She had to get herself far enough away from Eli to have time to open the Scope.

"Trying to get to him, G?" Eli called, striding down the mountain after her. "I'll be right behind you."

She needed to lose her brother somehow. Panting as she rolled to a stop, she looked over her shoulder to see him jump from a boulder and land in a crouch on the floor of the rocky valley, not twenty feet from her.

"What happens when ordinary humans die in the Veil?" he asked. "I bet the Chief's wondering that right now."

She rubbed her thumb over her Scope. Dec's glowed warm in her other hand. He needed it. Eli had trapped him in the Veil, she was sure. And he must be hurt. Time was running out. Tears burned her eyes, thinking about him, alone and in pain. Her jaw clenched as she felt the now-familiar tug inside her. "I'm going to save him right now," she yelled, yanking her Scope wide and diving through it. The last thing she saw was Eli vanishing.

She slammed her Scope shut and looked around. She was in Cambridge, near her lab. And two people were wrestling on the sidewalk at the corner. Galena ran toward them—one of them was the soul she was supposed to guide . . . and one of them was a Ferry, a petite woman with wavy black hair. "Cacy?"

Cacy punched the soul—a middle-aged guy with a generous belly and thinning hair—in the face and looked over at her. "Was this one yours? By the time I felt the pull, he was already going rabid." She punched him again as he struggled and grunted. "Open up your damn Scope and shove him in—I can't hold him much longer!"

Too shocked to do anything but comply, Galena flipped her Scope so the scales were up, then brushed her thumb over it. Searing heat poured from within, and Galena opened it wider to see nothing but cinders and fire. She looked up at Cacy. "We have to put him in here?"

"Now, Galena!" The guy shoved Cacy and kicked her backward, and she stumbled as he jumped to his feet.

Galena didn't question her again. She ran toward the soul, whose eyes went wide. As he turned to run, shrieking, Galena slammed the hoop over his head, sinking to her knees and pulling it all the way to the ground with a smoking whoosh. The scent of sulfur filled the air, and Galena fell forward. Cacy yanked her to her feet. "Where have you been?" She took in the look on Galena's face. "Where's Dec?"

Galena jumped as a coin flew from the ring of her open Scope and landed on the soft pavement. She didn't bother to pick it up. "Something's wrong with Eli," she said as she slammed the Scope shut. "He's hurt Dec, and now he's after me. I fooled him into going to the wrong place, but he'll be here soon. I don't know how to stop him."

Cacy blinked at her, clearly trying to process all the information Galena had just spewed out. "When you say something's wrong with Eli—"

"He wants to destroy Moros. And he says he's going to do it by killing me."

Cacy's mouth dropped open. "Eli would never—"

"He would. There's a Ker named Erin, and she's doing something to him. I've never seen him like this, Cacy," Galena said, her throat closing around her disbelief and pain.

"You said he hurt Dec. Where's my brother?"

Her stomach ached with the old fear. "Based on what Eli said, I think I know."

"Go to him. I'll stop Eli." Cacy's delicate face was hard with determination.

"He's unstoppable, Cacy. I don't want you to get hurt."

Cacy reached up and laid her hands on the sides of Galena's face. "I love him, Galena. I'm going to find a way to bring him back. Can you do the same for Dec? Can you find him?"

Galena stared into Cacy's eyes, usually turquoise blue, now gray in the Veil but no less intense. "I can."

Cacy let her go, already pulling her Scope from her neck. "He's lucky he has you."

Galena looked down at his Scope, heavy and warm in the palm of her hand. "Luck has nothing to do with it." She took a deep breath, preparing to go to the last place she ever wanted to see again. But if it meant saving Dec, if it meant bringing him home, she was willing to face it.

CHAPTER THIRTY-FOUR

Dec propped himself up in the dank, narrow entryway of the broken-down apartment building, his head bowed, his back against the soft, slick wall, trying to find the strength to get to his feet. He'd barely managed to lug himself up the steps and through the door of the building before the Shades got there. There had been a shitload of them, and now Dec understood—it had to be Erin, whatever she stirred up in people, whatever hate and resentment, the Shades had felt it and had come running. Just like they had that night in Cambridge Common.

He'd listened to them, snarling and shrieking, as they'd run up and down, looking for the source of the warmth, maybe for a Scope that could carry them back to the place they'd left. For the first time, he understood what it felt like. He would have given anything to feel warmth on his face, to hear the sound of people all around him, all bustle and chaos and hope.

A few minutes ago, Eli had showed up again, a sudden nightmare. He'd poked his head through the gelatinous surface of the door, and Dec had braced himself for another attack. Instead, Eli's red gaze had swept through the entryway, searching, and then his face had twisted with anger. He'd disappeared once more.

Dec had no idea what that had meant. He could only hope Galena had evaded her brother somehow.

He had to get up. He had to get back out there. His only chance was to find a newly dead soul. A Ferry would arrive to usher it into the Afterlife, and he or she would have a Scope. A ride home. It was a solid plan. The only problem was that it required a huge amount of luck, and it was clear Dec's was running out. The heels of his boots slid against the floor as the muscles of his less injured leg tried to push him up. His other leg was ruined, a mess of torn flesh and exposed bone beneath his shredded pant leg. His fingers sank into the wall as he tried to rise, his broken ribs shifting and stabbing. He gritted his teeth to stifle his cry. He had to try. Galena was depending on him.

He didn't know how much time he had left, but he knew it wasn't long. And when it was up, Aislin would revoke his status. She'd only be thinking of looking strong, of proving to the Keepers and the board and everyone else that defying her brought consequences. She would have no idea he was here, that his injuries were fatal, broken ribs and bleeding insides, blood loss and shock. It wouldn't take that long for him to die. And Galena, wherever she was, would become human again, too. He squeezed his eyes shut, trying to block out the image of Eli descending on her, his claws out.

Stifling moans of pain, Dec hauled himself up to standing, his fingers buried in the forgiving wall. He leaned back, eyes still closed, panting through the agony. His body was begging him to lie down, to give up. The pain would subside. He could drift, it promised him. He might not even be aware when the end came.

But for her, he had to try. He plunged through the soft door and lost his balance, falling face-first down the steps. Cushiony or not, it hurt enough to steal his breath and blur his vision. His mouth filled with the taste of blood, and he spat onto the gray concrete as he pulled himself forward on his belly, every movement bringing fresh lightning strikes of pain.

Up the street, something flickered, and Dec squinted, trying to bring it into focus. A light. Color. Was it . . . ?

"Dec," Galena shrieked as she pushed her Scope closed and sprinted toward him.

He stared at her, blonde hair flying around her face, her wide eyes alight with fear as she raced up the street. He'd never seen anything more beautiful.

She landed on her knees next to him. Her soft hands smoothed over his shoulders and back as she tried to turn him over. He pushed with his arms, helping as much as he could, and together they succeeded; he ended up with his back to her front, her arms around him. She cradled him in her arms, her breaths coming fast. "I knew he'd brought you here," she said as she flipped her Scope like a pro and pressed her finger over it, then opened a window to the real world. "Come on."

She opened the ring and lowered it over their heads, and the two of them struggled to get his body through. She gently lowered him to the pavement and pulled the ring over his torn legs, her mouth tight. She shut the Scope and crawled back up to his head, her eyes scanning up and down the street.

Looking for danger. Her hands were shaking.

But then her fingers were tangled in his hair and her lips were on his forehead. "You'll be okay," she said in a thin, breaking voice. Her mouth was warm comfort against his Veil-chilled skin.

"Eli went after you," he wheezed.

"Tamasin protected me. She's amazing." Her expression darkened, and Dec wondered what had happened to the Ker. It had to be something or she'd be here, still protecting Galena.

"Did Erin—?"

"She's evil, Dec." Galena's nostrils flared. "I don't know how she's doing what she's doing, but she's behind this."

Dec knew how she'd done it, but he couldn't explain it, not really. All he knew was that her touch had made him want to seek revenge for every tiny slight or grievance he'd ever experienced. And it was obvious that was what had been done to the others, too. They were all determined to take down Moros, though any of them in their right minds would have obeyed his orders without questioning. Erin was plotting to destroy Moros using his own Kere. She was trying to control the game board.

"You're right," he wheezed, holding tight to Galena's hands as his broken bones began to knit back together, which was just as painful as having them broken. "She has to be stopped."

"My first priority is you," said Galena. "We have to get you back to Psychopomps. We have to make sure Aislin doesn't revoke your status." She pulled out his phone and let out a panicked moan. "We only have ten minutes left."

"Text her," he gasped out. "We can explain."

She gave him an apologetic look. "There's no network here, not for the past several years. This is Pittsburgh, not Boston."

He gazed at the phone, suddenly remembering why she had it. "Did you get what you needed?"

"Yeah. Dr. Cassidy did it, but Erin made her. I'm sure of it. She was posing as her assistant. Dr. Cassidy wasn't herself, Dec. She kept shouting about how I'd stolen all the credit for her research."

Dec would have laughed if he hadn't been in so much pain. "Definitely Erin. She touched me, Galena. One touch and I was so angry that I wanted to fight and hurt everyone I love."

"But it went away?" she asked, her eyes shining with tears. "Because Eli . . ."

"I'm right here, G," said Eli, who had appeared on the stoop of the building where Dec had hidden. "If you have something to say to me, you'd better say it now." In the real world, Eli almost looked like his usual self. Except for the blood on his hands.

Galena's grip on Dec tightened, her hands covering his chest. "I was only saying that I love you, Eli. I've always loved you, and I'll never stop."

Eli's lip curled as he looked around. "I remember the last time I was here."

"Me too," she whispered.

Dec found the strength to cover her hand with his.

"Do you know what I did afterward, G? I never told you," Eli said. "I was too ashamed."

Dec went cold. His fingers closed over Galena's as Eli sauntered down the steps. Up the street, someone shouted and glass shattered. Galena flinched, her body tightening. "What did you do?" she murmured.

"They weren't hard to find," Eli said quietly. "I went after the black-haired one first. His name was Philip Carver. It took me a little longer to hunt down Jake Waters. He was the blond one. The one in charge."

"You killed them," she said, her voice shaking. "That's what you meant when you said that you'd killed people before."

He nodded. "All five of them. As it turns out, I'm very good at killing." He pulled his phone from his pocket and glanced at the time. "A few minutes left, Dec," he said. "Any last words?"

"Fight back, Eli," Dec said, taking a pained breath and sitting up, his newly healed bones aching. His leg wasn't bleeding anymore, but it still wasn't fully healed. "Erin, whatever she is, has been messing with your mind. She's using you."

Eli shook his head. "Everyone else is using me. She's just a newbie."

Galena rose, stepping between Dec and Eli. She pointed to a spot on the sidewalk, the place where Eli had told him she'd been raped. "When they left me there," she said, her voice strained, her finger trembling, "all I could think about was getting to you. I was bleeding and broken, but I crawled over to where you were. Did you know that? Did you feel it?"

"I was dead," he said quietly. "I wasn't here."

"I didn't care. I wanted you back. I held your head. I kissed your face. I begged you."

Pain flickered within Eli's eyes. "You should have let me go."

She shook her head. "I will never let you go. You're my brother. And you won't ever let me go. You won't do this, Eli. You're too good."

As she spoke to him, trying to remind him how much he loved her, how they'd saved each other, how he was the only family she had in the world, Dec got unsteadily to his feet. His heart was pounding now. He could try to get them into the Veil, but Eli was more of a monster there than he was here. The most he could hope for was getting Eli away from Galena, long enough to allow her to get back to Psychopomps. She had the evidence she needed to clear her name. Aislin could protect her if she understood the threat.

He needed to make his move soon, though. Once Aislin revoked his status and decommissioned his Scope, they'd be trapped here, and Eli would have them Marked and doomed in less than a minute.

"You died protecting me, Eli," Galena was saying. "Because that's who you are."

"Oh, for fuck's sake," snapped a familiar voice. Erin stepped from behind Eli, her cute face pinched with irritation. "Eli Margolis, you are pathetic."

"Don't let her touch you," Galena screamed, but it was too late. Erin grabbed Eli's hand, and his head snapped back, his jaw rigid. His eyes opened, crimson with rage. Everything seemed to move in slow motion. As Eli reached for Galena, Dec lunged between them, jabbing his fist into Eli's throat. Eli's arms flew wide, his eyes bulging. Galena screamed Dec's name.

"Galena, find Aislin!" He threw another punch, slamming his fist into Eli's rock-hard abs, then another right to his face. Eli staggered back, and Dec had a moment of hope, that maybe he'd be able to knock the Ker out or incapacitate him long enough to allow him to escape. But Eli caught himself and shoved off, hitting Dec like a city bus. The breath exploded from Dec, his ribs screaming. A swirl of cold air chilled his skin as he landed on his back with Eli above him. Eli's fangs gleamed as his arm arced through the air.

Every split second mattered, but Dec didn't have enough of them. Eli's claws were a blur as they descended. Dec's entire being shattered with the pain of the impact. His thoughts went white, even as he groped, blind, still trying to reach Galena, still trying to save her. But her face was fading from his mind along with everything else, and so he focused on the one thing he'd wanted to tell her, the one admission he hadn't had time to make, the one thing he'd never get to say.

I'm falling in love with you.

CHAPTER THIRTY-FIVE

Galena tackled Erin as Eli and Dec disappeared. She landed on top of the smaller woman, but as soon as she did, Erin grabbed Galena's hands. Her mind immediately filled with memories: of being made fun of by her classmates, of her father spending more time with Eli than he did with her, of her mother making a huge deal out of Eli leaving for Ranger school but barely batting an eyelash when Galena started grad school, of Eli being gone all those nights when she'd needed him most. On and on came the march of frustration, all the things she'd ever let go, all the things she thought she'd forgiven and forgotten. They were all right there.

"Oh, crap," Erin said. She released Galena and disappeared. Galena fell forward, barely catching herself before her face hit the concrete.

"Where's Eli?"

Galena looked over her shoulder to see Aislin, Moros, and Cacy standing on the corner. "He took Dec into the Veil," she choked out.

Moros's customary smugness was gone. "Meet me there," he said to Aislin and Cacy, striding forward and grabbing Galena's arm. With a gust of cold air, they burst into the Veil.

Eli was on top of Dec, who was nothing but a mess of blood and torn flesh. Everything was red, splattered all around the two of them. Galena knew just from looking that he was gone. She couldn't even recognize his face. The wail started at the base of her spine and surged through her, flying from her mouth as she lunged forward, only to be yanked back by Moros's gloved hand.

"Eli," Moros barked. "Stop."

Eli, his face speckled with Dec's blood, paused and looked up at Moros. "You can't control me." He jumped to his feet, his eyes a lurid, ugly red, dark as all the blood he'd shed. "So I guess nothing's stopping me from doing *this*," he hissed.

He leaped at the Lord of the Kere. Moros shoved Galena so hard that she went careening across the street. He ripped off one of his gloves as Eli flew through the air at him.

And then Eli dropped like a stone to the spongy concrete, gasping and writhing. Moros blinked, clearly surprised, his bare hand still outstretched to meet Eli's attack.

At the same time, Cacy and Aislin stepped through their Scopes, their eyes filled with alarm as they took in the scene. Cacy dove for Eli, and Aislin went for Dec. Galena didn't know what to do. She couldn't take her eyes off the two men she loved, one lying still and limp and destroyed, and the other contorted at the feet of the Lord of the Kere, clawing at his own throat.

"Stop now," Moros said quietly.

Eli's hands fell from his neck, leaving bloody gashes behind.

"Do you have control of him?" snapped Aislin.

"I do now," Moros replied, his brow furrowed as he looked Eli over. "Until a few seconds ago I couldn't feel him at all."

Eli's eyes were empty and stunned as he looked up at the sky. Cacy hesitantly laid her hand on his chest. "Eli?"

He gazed down at her pale fingers spread over his red-spattered shirt. "Oh God," he whispered, his voice strangled to nothing as he looked himself over. He sat up quickly and turned toward Dec, his mouth dropping open in a cry of pure agony. "No!" he howled, scrambling over to Dec.

"Eli, stay back," said Moros, and it was as if he were pulling invisible strings attached to Eli's limbs. Galena watched her brother crawl backward and end up across the street, tears carving their way through the blood on his face.

Galena rushed forward and fell to her knees at Dec's side. Aislin had her hand on the top of Dec's head, the only part of him that seemed intact. Galena's fingers fluttered over the gashes in his forehead, across his angular face, over his neck. "Dec?" she whispered, bending down. Her hair was swishing through the blood that had pooled beneath him, but she didn't care. "Dec," she murmured in his ear. "I'm here with you. Every second. Every breath."

No movement. No response. A horrifying thought occurred to her. She raised her head and turned to Aislin. "Did you revoke his status?" she cried.

"She was about to when I got to her office," said Cacy, who was kneeling on the sidewalk a few feet from where Eli crouched, wearing a look of pure horror.

"But I didn't," Aislin said, her skin so pale that it nearly glowed. Her eyes sought Moros's. "Jason, I want an explanation. This . . ." She looked down at Dec and squeezed her eyes shut. "Come on. I'm taking him into the real world." She pulled her ornate Scope from the chain at her neck and flicked it wide enough for her and Galena to drag Dec through. Moros appeared a moment later with Cacy and Eli at his feet.

Moros looked down at Eli. "This is the second time in as many weeks that you have violated the treaty forged by the Keepers of the Afterlife to keep peace between the Kere and the Ferrys. You have attacked and maimed the brother of the Charon." He sighed. "This is a crime punishable by death."

"No," said Galena, just as Cacy shrieked the same thing. Cacy reached for Eli, but he put his arms up and cringed.

"Don't touch me, Cacy," he begged, his gaze riveted on Dec.

Cacy looked over her shoulder at Galena, her tear-filled eyes full of pleading.

Galena stroked her fingers down the cold skin of Dec's arm and then stood up. "Eli wasn't in his right mind when he attacked Dec." She spoke loudly, trying to chase the unsteadiness away. With her brother looking tortured and Dec unresponsive, it wasn't easy. But her need to protect Eli—and the knowledge that Dec would do the same if he could—drove her forward. "He was being controlled by a Ker named Erin, and he's not the only one she's done this to. Killing Eli won't stop her. She'll probably just commandeer another Ker and come at us again."

Moros arched an eyebrow.

"She was just here—it was almost like she knew you were coming, so she disappeared."

He scowled. "I have no Ker named Erin."

While Cacy sat on the curb, trying in vain to comfort Eli, Galena explained the odd behavior of each of the Kere: Luke, Trevor, Nader, and her brother. She then explained how her boss had framed her, provoked once again by Erin. "When she touches you, all you can think about is getting even."

Moros's mouth opened and then closed, his debonair manner blown away by shock. But then he looked down at his own bare hand with realization. "Her true name isn't Erin," he said quietly. "It's *Eris*."

"And you know who she is?" asked Aislin.

Moros nodded. "Though I thought she was gone. Nothing but a memory. But now, it appears, she has returned to destroy me. And she chose the messiest, most destructive way to do it." His smile was bitter. "I suppose I should have expected nothing less."

Cacy looked back and forth between Eli and Moros. "Who *is* she?"

"She is Strife. She is the personification of conflict, of twisted resentment and petty bickering, of blood feuds and bone-deep animosity." Moros's handsome features softened into sadness. "She is also my sister."

Before, Galena hadn't believed in miracles. Such a thing implied defiance of the laws of science, of the universe. Now, she was grateful to have been so wrong. But perhaps what she was witnessing didn't defy any laws . . . perhaps she hadn't understood them to begin with.

When Moros had brought them to the guest quarters within the heavily guarded Psychopomps tower, Dec had been a shell. A broken version of himself, torn and shattered. Even though Aislin had reassured her that he would recover, Galena hadn't really believed it.

She'd sat in a chair in the corner as one of the Ferrys' personal physicians had worked on him, trying to ensure that his body put itself back together properly, sedating him so that he wasn't in constant, terrible pain as he healed. The nurses had cleaned him off. And then they'd left her here with him. She'd been offered a room of her own, but she couldn't bear to leave him. She knew she should go see Eli—Cacy had sent a message with one of the nurses asking if she would—but Galena couldn't stand the idea of Dec waking up alone.

Aislin had dropped by personally to check on Dec and to assure Galena that the building was safe, that Aislin was working with Moros to make sure the tower couldn't be infiltrated as it had been when Rylan had escaped. But Galena could tell the Charon was worried, about her brother, about her empire, about the future.

Galena knew she should be worried about the same. Everything had been turned upside down. Her research. Her career. Her plans. Her family. Her life. But somehow, right now, she could only worry about one thing. He was lying on the bed, the lower half of his body covered in a sheet, his chest rising and falling slowly. Faint pink streaks were all that remained of the terrible wounds Eli had inflicted, and even those seemed to be fading. She stood up and moved closer, watching his face. His dark eyelashes fringed the hollows beneath his eyes. He looked peaceful but tired. He'd been through so much.

She sat down on the edge of the bed, unable to stay away anymore. She didn't know how to contain the feelings inside her; they were so powerful that they were pushing at all her boundaries, making her heart beat with a new rhythm. There was the fierce tap of devotion, the skipping thrum of curiosity, the need to know everything about him. The thumping bass of desire was ever present. But so was the stutter of uncertainty, throwing off the beat.

The crisis was over for now. Erin had been revealed for what she truly was, and Moros and Aislin were doing everything they could to stop her and protect everyone else. Galena was a true Ferry now, with the Mark on her back, the Scope around the neck, and the ability to take a bullet to the chest and come up fighting. She wasn't as fragile as she used to be. Thanks to Dec, she was less fragile in a lot of ways.

He had done his duty. He had protected her, made her immortal. She owed him so much, but she still wanted more. She wanted his heart. He already had hers.

His eyelids fluttered, and he moaned, and Galena scooted back to her chair, not wanting to creep him out with her hovering. He opened his eyes and stared at the ceiling, blinking. Then he sat up quickly, holding the sheet over his lap. He sagged with relief when he saw her. "You're okay."

She smiled. "I'm fine, thanks to you."

He looked at her like he was trying to read her thoughts. "Eli?"

"Alive."

"Erin?"

"Vanished. It turns out she's Moros's sister, the living personification of Strife."

He rubbed his hand over his face. "Mmm. That makes a weird kind of sense. Moros?"

"Knows Eli was being controlled."

"Aislin?"

"Didn't revoke your status, obviously." She waved at his chest, dusted with dark hair, ridged with muscle, perfect and unmarred.

"Okay." He was still staring at her with a piercing intensity. "Okay. Give me a few minutes."

He got up, holding the sheet around his waist, and grabbed his phone and the stack of clothes that had been left for him. He headed into the bathroom, and a minute later, the shower switched on. Galena folded her arms and fought to hold herself together. Should she tell him, or should she just let him go? They hadn't had a chance to really talk since they'd consummated the bond. Now that she was safer, would it change things?

Dec came out of the bathroom wearing jeans and a long-sleeved T-shirt, his black hair damp and standing on end like he'd rubbed his towel over it and let that be that. "Cacy texted me. She was asking if we could come see Eli."

"I know." She clasped her hands in front of her, fingers twisting. "I was waiting until you woke up."

They stared at each other for a moment. "You didn't have to do that," he said, a small smile playing at his lips.

Yes, I did. She cleared her throat. "I know," she said quietly. "Shall we go?"

"Sure," he said, drawing the word out as he watched her. His hand rose from his side, and Galena took it. The feel of his warm skin against hers made the blood whoosh through her veins in that new, unsteady, ferocious rhythm. And as they walked out of the room, hand in hand, as one simple touch filled her with more yearning than she'd ever felt in her life, she realized they needed to talk sooner rather than later. She had to tell him all of this was real for her. It wasn't about immortality or safety—it was about him, his noble heart and selfless spirit, his fierce devotion and iron will. She had fallen in love with him, but if they were going to be together, it had to be because he loved her back. She couldn't bear to be with him any other way. That meant she had to give him the chance to walk away. Yes, it might break her scarred, barely healed heart. But she could get through that. She was stronger than she'd believed, braver than she'd thought. And Dec was worth any risk she had to take.

CHAPTER THIRTY-SIX

Dec locked his fingers with Galena's as they walked down the corridor that held the guest quarters at Psychopomps. Having her hand in his after all those frantic, fearful moments when he'd thought he was about to lose her was pure relief. There was never a way to make her completely safe, but he'd done his part to protect her. They'd consummated the bond, leaving him in awe of her bravery, leveled by his longing for her, desperate to tell her—she'd made him feel alive again. He had fallen for her so hard and so fast that he knew he was already too deep to recover. But Galena had important things to do, and now that she was safer and stronger than she had been, did she need him anymore?

He wanted to give her everything he had. But in return he wanted her heart, and he wasn't sure she was ready—or willing—to offer it to him.

He pushed away the uncertainty and focused on getting her through the next few minutes. "Are you ready for this?" he asked as they reached the door.

"Are you?" She squeezed his fingers. "I'm worried that he won't agree to talk to me."

"Let's find out." He knocked. "Cacy? It's me. Galena too."

Cacy's face appeared on the screen. Her turquoise eyes were shadowed by dark circles. "Come on in," she said quietly.

Dec opened the door and ushered Galena into the suite. Cacy stood in the entryway. Dec released Galena's hand and opened his arms, and Cacy's face crumpled with grief. She rushed into his embrace. He held her head against his chest as her body shuddered with a sob. "I don't know how to help him," she choked out. "He hasn't moved in hours. He says he wants Moros to destroy him. That it's safer for everyone."

Galena put her hand over her mouth, stifling a cry. "I need to see him."

Cacy pointed down the hall. "The room at the very end. Just . . . be gentle with him, okay?"

Galena touched Cacy's arm. "He's my brother, Cacy," she said quietly, then turned and walked slowly toward the room, her fingers trailing on the wall.

"Is that safe?" Dec asked, aching to go with her.

"He's under Moros's control. Now that we have an idea of what happened, Moros said he can ensure that it doesn't ever happen again." Cacy swiped her sleeve across her eyes. "But I feel like I've lost him, Dec."

He held her steady as she sobbed against his chest. His love for her, his little sister, so young but so passionate and powerful, made him ache. He remembered bandaging her bony knees when she scraped them up as a child. He remembered wiping her tears away and making her smile. But those were simpler problems, solved with a kiss and a dab of numbing cream. "We'll figure this out, Cacy. We'll find a way through it."

"He's been terrified of becoming a monster, ever since Moros made him a Ker. I thought I'd gotten him past it, that he could accept what he is and be okay. But this—"

"Was not his fault," Dec murmured. He closed his eyes, trying to forget the sight of Eli's contorted face as his claws had descended. "It wasn't him."

"Moros told Aislin that he's trying to work with his other sisters, the Fates, to ensure the security of the Kere souls. Aislin doesn't trust him, though. I have no idea what's going to happen at that summit with the Keepers. I can tell Aislin is really on edge."

Dec looked down at her. "Wait—does this mean you actually spoke to her? Like, a real conversation?"

Cacy shrugged. "I'm as surprised as you are. I think she feels bad about doubting Galena, Dec. She'd reviewed all the evidence Galena collected and said it was obvious her boss had set her up. She's already made the Boston PD aware, and the charges against Galena are going to be dropped. Not sure what's going to happen to Galena's boss, though." Her gaze slid down the hall, to the open door. Dec could hear quiet murmuring coming from inside. "And Harvard has frozen the funds for Galena's research. They're just trying to pick up the pieces."

Dec listened to the soft lilt of Galena's voice as she tried to comfort her brother. "I'm going to make this right for her. I'll ask Aislin to set aside space here at Psychopomps. I'll pay for it myself."

Cacy chuckled. "Still taking care of her?"

Dec bowed his head. "I'll give her anything she needs, for as long as she needs it. Father asked me to. Did I tell you that?"

She stroked his arm. "Eli did. And it didn't surprise me at all."

"It sure as hell surprised me. When I found out how important she was, I couldn't help but wonder why he didn't ask someone else to do the job, given what he thought of me."

She pulled away and looked up at him. "I think he respected both of us more than he ever said, Dec. He made me his executor. He asked you to protect a woman who's fated to change the world. If he thought we were both fuckups, why would he give us the hardest jobs?"

He blinked. "I never thought of it like that."

"But you should. He asked you to protect Galena. He chose *you.*" She smiled. "And you did it," she added softly.

"Yeah," he said, his voice strained. "I guess I did."

"Why do you look so broken up about it?"

He gave her a sheepish glance. "I fell pretty hard for her in the process, Cace. But I'm trying not to make a big deal out of it. She's dealing with enough shit already."

Cacy stood on her tiptoes to kiss his cheek. "Are you sure she doesn't feel the same? She was determined to get to you, Dec. She wasn't going to let anything get in her way."

"I actually think that's just how she is." Again, that proud protectiveness swelled in his chest. And even when he reminded himself that she might choose to move forward without him, he couldn't quite suppress it.

Galena poked her head out of the doorway. "Dec?" She came down the hall. "Eli asked for you. Will you talk to him?"

Cacy pulled away from Dec, and both women watched him, anxiety etched into their faces. "Sure," he said, even as his muscles tensed. He caressed Galena's cheek and headed down the hall.

Eli was sitting in the corner of the bedroom, his knees up, his arms resting on them. Dec sat on the edge of the bed a good ten feet away. "Hey," he said. "I'm here."

Eli's eyes met his. The sorrow in them was miles deep. "Hey." He looked away. "Galena said that I wasn't the only Ker that Erin got to."

"Not even close. She got Trevor, too. I still don't know where he is." And it was killing him. He'd lost his best friend, and for all he knew, the next time he saw him, Trevor would be an enemy.

Eli pressed his thumbs to his forehead, like he was trying to crush a knot of stress that had formed there. "I'm so ashamed, Dec," he said, his voice breaking. "I remember everything I did.

Every single thing. I remember what I was thinking at the time." He stared at his knees and shook his head. "Ugly, hateful thoughts."

"She started to do it to me, too. I felt it." Dec leaned his elbows on his knees. "It was all stuff that's real, but stuff that doesn't really bother me most of the time. About Aislin and Cacy. Even about Galena. Stuff that's so outweighed by the good that it's easy to push away. But when Erin touched me, it was all I could think about. And I felt like the only right thing was to get even."

"But you didn't."

"Only because she let me go. I wasn't part of her plan. She said she didn't need me."

"Galena does, though," Eli said softly. He rubbed his eyes and looked at Dec again. "I'm sorry, Dec. I'm sorry for everything. I don't think I'll ever be able to make up for it. But I'm sorry."

"I know, Eli. It's all right." And it was. Eli was so obviously good that it wasn't hard to forgive him. "You're going to have to forgive yourself, though. Because Cacy needs you. She's hurting. You mean everything to her, and she'd do anything for you. And she's down the hall right now, crying her eyes out because of what you're doing to yourself. So unless you want me to punch you in the throat again, I suggest you pull yourself together, go to her, and make this right."

Eli chuckled and rubbed at his throat. "That was a pretty brutal shot." He glanced at the doorway. "I don't want her to see a monster when she looks at me."

"She only sees *you*, Eli. She sees everything clearly. And despite that, or maybe because of it, she's not going anywhere, even when it hurts."

"I love her, Dec," he said hoarsely. "I love her so much."

"Then let her stand next to you, Eli. She's strong enough to do it. And you need her. Why deny yourself something she's willing to offer?"

"I don't want to hurt her. Or anybody."

"We all know that. And if you try, we'll stop you. But I think we're going to find a way to fight back—if we all stick together."

Eli's gaze was hard and shiny, like glass about to shatter. "Thank you. For everything. But most of all, thank you for protecting my sister."

Dec stood up and offered his hand. "You don't have to thank me for that. In fact, I think I should thank you, for playing that little trick on me."

Eli took his hand and let Dec haul him to his feet. "I'd never try to trick you, Chief."

"So the list of candidates for Galena's Claiming—or more accurately, the parade of losers—that was Cacy's idea?"

The corner of Eli's mouth twitched, like he was trying to smile. "We came up with it together."

Dec rolled his eyes. "Then let me tell you, you're a good team."

"You aren't mad?" he asked as they walked to the doorway.

"I'm grateful."

This time, Eli managed a full smile, still tinged with sadness but real nonetheless. "Me too. She's changed, Dec. Being with you has changed her."

Dec looked up the hall, to where Galena was standing with Cacy, her gorgeous green eyes focused on him as he walked toward her with Eli at his side. The sight of her hit him right in the heart. "It's changed me, too."

CHAPTER THIRTY-SEVEN

Every step made Galena tenser as they trudged back to their quarters. Dec was awake and healed. She was immortal and whole. Cacy and Eli seemed like they might be okay. Dec had just told her the murder charges were going to be dropped, and that he would make sure she had all the facilities and resources she needed to resume her research.

He was giving, and she was taking. Yes, she'd wanted to tell him how she felt about him, how she never wanted to leave his side, but it all felt selfish now. She needed to go somewhere and rethink all of this. When they reached the door, she stopped. "I'm guessing you're pretty thrashed."

His brow furrowed. "I was unconscious for several hours. I basically just got a week's worth of sleep."

She nodded, her cheeks heating. "So you must have a lot to do. You probably want to reconnect with your paramedics at the station and all that."

His look of puzzlement intensified. "Yeah, I was going to do that later this afternoon. Are you all right?"

"Fine." She chuckled. "You must be sick of me at this point."

His gaze was piercing; she could almost feel it inside of her, sorting through all her shaky, self-conscious thoughts. Then he took her hand and led her into the small apartment where she'd waited for him to recover. "What if I told you I didn't think that was possible?" he asked, closing the door and turning to face her. "What if I asked you to stay with me?"

"Here, you mean?"

He tugged her hand and brought her closer. "Here. My apartment. My cabin. Anywhere in the world you need to be, anywhere you'd be happy and safe."

"Dec, stop," she whispered. "It's too much."

"Why?" His voice had taken on an edge.

"Because you got your head bashed in and your guts clawed out trying to protect me, and now you're offering to spend a billion dollars of your own money on my research?"

He gestured at his body. "The only reason my head and guts are absolutely fine right now is because *you* protected *me*. You went back to the most terrifying place in the world for you, and you did it to save me. I'd say we're even."

She put her hand on his chest, willing herself to be brave, to stop putting the moment off. She owed this vulnerability to him. He was worth it. "Okay, how about this: I'm falling in love with you." Her eyes met his. "Completely, crazily, beyond logic or reason. And I can't take more from you unless you feel the same way."

"Take more from me?" Dec coiled his arm around her waist. "For a minute, I'm going to brush that one aside, even though every time you accept something I offer you, it lights me up in a way nothing else has in a very, *very* long time." His gaze traced over her face. "Galena, the first time I was in the Veil with you, it seemed like a brand-new place. You saw a wonder in it that I stopped seeing ages ago, that I'd forgotten was even there. You understood things about it that I'd never even bothered to question." His palms slid up to her shoulders, then her neck, and he took her face in his hands. "You have no idea how badly I needed that, how ready I'd been to walk away from all of it, how tired of everything I was.

Being with you changed that. It was like stepping from the Veil into the real world, where things are warm and messy and complicated and confusing, but goddamn interesting at the same time. You brought me back to life."

Now her heart was pounding for a different reason. "So I guess you do feel the same way?"

"Hell, yes, I do." He pulled her face to his. The kiss was desperate, rough-edged and unsteady. Galena's fingers closed over the taut muscles of his shoulders, giving herself up to it. His stubble scraped at her chin as he possessed her mouth, as his hands roamed her body. Her palms skimmed down to his chest to feel the miracle of his heartbeat, then ventured lower to lift the bottom of his shirt. Fierce need for him consumed her as she pulled his shirt off, as he edged her toward the bed, offering no more words, only his actions, which were more than enough.

She undid his zipper slowly, taking control. Dec frowned as she shuddered and placed his hands on her arms, and she stared at his mouth until it felt okay again. And then she dipped her fingers into his boxer briefs, teasing and caressing him as he kissed her with a passion that made her knees weak. She peeled his clothing from his body. Feeling powerful and dizzy with want, she pushed him onto the bed. He guided her on top of him, pulling away from her mouth to nip his way down the column of her throat. Galena gasped at the hard shock of desire that shot down her spine, melting her.

His hands wrapped around her thighs, spreading her legs over him, and then he pulled the collar of her T-shirt aside to nibble at the junction of her neck and shoulder, making her whole body clench. "I just want to make sure you understand—you're immortal now. You don't need to be with me, not really," he mumbled against her skin.

"Yes, I do."

"But only by choice. Always by choice. Because I would never take the immortality away, even if you wanted to leave me."

She looked into his glacier-blue eyes, desperate to read what lay there. "Dec, I know our relationship started in the strangest possible way, but I'm glad it did. And not because of the immortality. Do you understand that? If Aislin took it away tomorrow, or if you decided to retire and give it up yourself, I would still want to be with you."

He paused, staring into her eyes. "Then you're going to have to let me do a few things."

She wriggled against him, letting the hard feel of him stoke her desire. "Like what?"

"I want to make you breakfast and see you eat it. I want to watch your face as you learn something new." His hands stroked across her back and down her sides. "I want to memorize every single inch of your body and figure out how to make it sing for me. All of that. More than that. Everything."

"Me too. Every second," she murmured, touching her lips to his.

"Every breath." His fingers curled under the hem of her shirt and pulled it up, and Galena allowed him to strip it off. He had her bra undone in a matter of seconds. His gaze slid over her breasts as he rolled her over onto her back. His eyes met hers. "Yeah?"

"Yeah." She tangled her fingers in his hair as he lowered his head, tracing his tongue down the center of her chest as he teased a nipple with his thumb. Her palms smoothed over the raven on his muscular back. She arched up as his mouth closed over her breast, sudden and hot, the sensual pull making her whimper. He drew the tight, pearled bud between his teeth, and the exquisite pleasure had her guiding his hand down. He pushed her sweats and panties down her hips, his movements growing more frantic right along with her desire for him. As he sat up and pulled the garments over her ankles, off her feet, tossing them onto the floor, she stared at his body, now fully healed, strong and beautiful, and she felt nothing but hunger. No fear.

It wasn't that it was gone. And she never knew when she'd be reminded, when the memories would rise. But when Dec turned her onto her side and kissed his way up the back of her leg, her ass, her spine, when his hard arousal nestled against her, she knew she'd face it with him, that he would be here, that he wouldn't run. He'd proven that. He'd seen everything; he knew everything. He was aware. She smiled and reached back, pulling his cheek to hers as his hand stroked down her belly, over the scars, between her legs.

His fingers slid through her arousal, and he cursed, bucking gently against her backside. He hooked his fingers beneath her knee and raised her leg, and she reached down and found his rigid cock, hot and silky. She guided it to the place she needed it most.

"Yeah," she whispered, and as soon as she did, he thrust into her. She was so wet that he slid in easily, and both of them moaned. *God, this feeling.* The pressure and friction as he pushed himself inside her body was overwhelming, but not in a painful way. More like every nerve was firing at once.

He released her leg, letting it slide over his as he slowly pumped his hips. He folded his arm over her chest, and his hand closed over her breast. His mouth fastened to her neck, teasing her with teeth and tongue. Galena shut her eyes and felt all of it at once, his hard body wrapped around her, inside her, claiming her. She welcomed every stroke. Another miracle. He gave pleasure while taking his own, his hands steadying her, teasing her, spinning her higher while plunging her deeper into the ocean of her feelings for him.

His palm flattened over her belly, over the scars, possessive and protective. She raised her knee, spreading her legs wider, offering him more. More. She wanted to feel him deep; she wanted him to own her body like he owned her heart. He raised his head and looked down at her, his eyes hazed with need. His lips were parted, his breath bursting from him every time her body accepted his rigid cock. She looked up at him, her arm winding behind his neck. The tightening of her fingers in his hair had an instant effect on him. His hand curled over her hip, and his pace increased. "Yeah?"

"Oh, yeah." She was so close. And when he reached between her legs again to tease her clit, like he knew exactly what she needed, it sent her over the edge. She gasped his name as the ecstasy swallowed her whole, drenching her mind in swirling colors and sparks. She clutched at his hair, at his arm, using him as her anchor while the rest of her spun and danced with sheer, blinding pleasure.

Dec groaned as she clenched around him, rhythmic spasms that carried aftershocks through her belly and up her spine. Galena turned her head, panting every time his hips snapped up, driving his shaft deep. His eyes were closed, his teeth gritted, and his hand was a vise on her hip. Not bruising, just possessive. "I'm yours, Dec," she murmured. "Yours."

He let out a ragged, desperate noise and wrapped his arms around her, burying himself inside. She felt the throbbing heat of his climax as his body shook, the tremors rumbling along her bones. She'd never felt so treasured, so needed, so safe. After a few frenzied moments of their bodies locked together, every muscle trembling, Dec relaxed slightly. His head was bowed against hers, his breath in her ear. "Did you mean that?" he whispered.

She looked up at him, nestled against his powerful body, feeling his stubble scrape at her skin. "Yeah."

His grin was the most profoundly beautiful thing she'd ever seen.

EPILOGUE

Aislin paced her office, her heart thrumming. She felt like a fox, hunted and cornered by dozens of snarling hounds.

The fate of the Ferrys rests with you.

Those had been her father's last words to her. At the time they had both thrilled and baffled her, because Rylan was the Charon. But as his evil had been revealed, Aislin had assumed the role of head of family without hesitation. She'd been certain that was what her father had meant, what he'd intended for her.

Now she wasn't so sure. How many mistakes had she made? She'd lost count. And now she was about to lose everything. In a few days, she might be known as the last Charon, the one who presided over the fall of the Psychopomps empire. Assuming her cousin Hugh didn't find a way to take the Scope of the Charon from her first.

She walked to the window and laid her hands on the glass, looking out over the city. Her city. The haze was rising through the midnight air, steaming the pane, making everything seem unreal.

God, how she wished this wasn't real.

"I've always thought it was a lovely view," said a voice she knew all too well, one that sent confusing chills along her skin.

She whirled around to see Moros standing by her desk. "I've always thought it was incredibly ill-mannered to enter without knocking."

Moros smiled. "You Ferrys do enjoy lecturing me, don't you?"

Aislin took a step toward him, watching his face. He was ancient, thousands of years old, though he looked no older than Rylan. His wavy black hair was tousled, not slicked back as usual. There were faint shadows beneath his steel-gray eyes. If she didn't know better, she'd say he looked tired. Exhausted, actually.

"Did you ascertain the security of the souls in your charge?" she asked.

He nodded. "Though my sisters swear they have been secure all along."

"You don't trust them."

Their eyes locked. His glinted red. "I no longer trust anyone."

Aislin knew what that was like, and for a moment, she felt a pang of sympathy for the Lord of the Kere. Then she reminded herself who he was and what he could do. "Can you ensure that Eli is no longer a threat? He's closer to us than any of the Kere, and my sister will never give him up."

Moros pulled a small object from his trouser pocket. It looked like a cigar case, sleek and polished. "Eli is no threat. He is under my control."

Aislin eyed the case. "You have his soul in there." It was both terrifying and fascinating, knowing that this man carried another man's soul in his pocket, that he did it with the same casualness that most men carried their phones.

"Because of his proximity to both you and Galena, I felt it best."

"You believe that someone has been taking the souls?"

His eyes traced over the case. "There is no other way to control them."

"So Eris stole Eli's soul—and then put it back?"

He slid the case back into his pocket. "I'm not yet certain of that."

"Have you been able to locate the rogues?"

"Luke is himself. Nader has returned to my service, and Tamasin is by his side. Their souls are safe and sound. But Trevor's is nowhere to be found."

"And my brother? Do you have any idea where they've taken him?" It had to be in the real world, since he was no longer a Ferry. It chilled her beyond words to know that Rylan was in the hands of an enemy. "Rylan knows every detail of our business. He could be very dangerous under the wrong influence. But he is also human now. You should be able to track him."

Moros's nostrils flared, and he bowed his head.

"Is it that you can't find him, or you won't?" she asked.

He walked over to the window and stared out. "The fabric of fate is in tatters," he said quietly as Aislin watched his reflection in the glass. She had long since memorized his expressions; she felt as if she'd been watching him her entire life, and yet she'd never been able to figure him out. "My sisters are distraught. If it continues to fray like it has been, it's going to fall apart completely."

"What happens then?"

He looked over his shoulder at her. "Chaos."

Aislin folded her arms over her chest, frustration coiling within. "Our summit with the Keepers is in six days, Moros. They will want an explanation. The stakes are incredibly high for both of us. So I suggest we decide, right now, if we're going to work together or against each other."

Moros tilted his head. "Come now, my dear. We both know that if you were working against me, you'd never say it openly. You're far too clever for that, and so am I."

She forced a superior half smile onto her face. "What a compliment. I have no desire for war, Moros."

"But you wouldn't mind having the dominion of death to yourself."

"What I wouldn't mind is having the business running smoothly," she snapped. "What I wouldn't mind is knowing that there aren't rogue monsters on the loose, threatening my family and trying to destroy the future!" She stalked toward him, too angry to be intimidated. "Stop these petty little games. You're in too weak a position to play."

Moros's eyes glimmered. "Have you considered the risk of allying yourself with me at a time like this?" He sobered, his smug smile fading to nothing. He walked back over to her, close enough for her to feel the heat rolling from his body. "Aislin, I cannot sense your brother. And I don't know what that means."

"Are you actually suggesting that I work against you?"

He gave her a smile tinged with sadness. "No. I'd hate to have you of all people as an enemy."

Her brow furrowed. Her *of all people*? "I am not like Rylan, Jason. I will not sacrifice order for power."

"I believe you. But now we are playing a game with gods. Lesser gods, perhaps, but still gods. Ferrys are the most vulnerable players on the board. You cannot look at what Eli did to Declan and think otherwise."

"And yet Declan is alive and well, and so is Galena, whom he was protecting." She arched an eyebrow. "If you're trying to manipulate me into asking the Keepers to release us from the treaty altogether, you are both arrogant and foolish."

He laughed, and his smile was startling in both its power and its beauty. His sharp canines glinted as he grinned at her. "You remind me so much of your father."

She turned away. What she wouldn't give to have her father by her side now. She missed him so much it hurt. "Stop patronizing me."

"Aislin," he said quietly, "that was a true compliment. Take it."

"Thank you," she said, wishing her voice didn't sound so strained.

His gloved fingers brushed her sleeve, and she faced him again. His eyes were gray once more, with no hint of red. "I don't want to be your enemy," he said.

Aislin stared. She'd never seen him look so human. *He's tired,* she thought again. *He feels hunted, too.* It almost made her reach for his hand.

His gaze was riveted to her face, and he seemed to read something in her eyes, because he added, "But right now, being my friend is a very dangerous proposition."

She lifted her chin and gave him the coldest stare she could muster. She was the Charon, and she couldn't forget that, even for a moment. "We are business associates." And though the idea of ruling the empire alone had its appeal, the thought of having to control the Kere, especially now, was abhorrent. "Our alliance stands for now. But we will never be friends."

Moros's arrogant smirk returned as he opened his mouth to reply, but she never found out what he'd planned to say.

With a rush of hot air, Rylan appeared in the middle of the office. He wore a finely tailored suit and his face was cleanly shaven. His dark hair was combed and neat. "Hello, Aislin," he said, straightening his tie.

Aislin blinked in surprise. "Rylan? What—? How—?"

Moros took a half step in front of her. "How did you get here?" he demanded.

Aislin moved to stand beside Moros. Rylan watched them, a look of amusement on his face. "Look at the two of you, squirreled away in here, trying to figure out how to stop the inevitable."

Moros tensed, ripping one of his gloves from his hand and letting it fall to the floor.

Rylan snorted. "Don't bother. I'm here to deliver a message and nothing more."

Aislin willed her voice into a steadiness she did not feel. "We're listening."

Rylan's brown eyes glowed red, and Aislin couldn't stop herself from recoiling in horror. She looked back and forth between Moros and Rylan. "You're a Ker?"

Her brother grinned. "So perceptive. You stole my rightful status, but I think I negotiated myself a better deal."

"Negotiated." Dread was suffocating her. "Did you really betray your entire family like that?"

Rylan's eyes faded to a dull dark crimson. "I would have taken care of the entire family, sister, if you hadn't betrayed *me*. So whatever happens now is on your head."

"Who made you?" Moros snarled. "Who owns your soul now?"

"Not part of the message I'm here to deliver." His gaze shifted back to Aislin. "But this is: You can join us, or you can welcome your own destruction. This is your chance. We won't ask again. Be a wise leader—choose the winning side. Not for yourself, but for all the Ferrys. Their fate rests with you."

Aislin stared at her brother, trying to read the shrewd look in his eyes as he echoed their father's last words to her. It took a great deal of effort to keep her voice even despite the terror growing inside her. "Join you in *what*?"

"Awakening Chaos, Aislin," Rylan said. "We don't have to be servants anymore, to fate or anything else. And we will not stop until the fabric of fate is nothing but a mountain of tattered thread."

And then he vanished. Aislin sank into a chair, unable to remain upright for another moment. Rylan was a Ker. "Could Eris have created him?" she asked weakly.

"I wouldn't have thought so." Moros glared at the place Rylan had been. He was silent for several moments before he finally spoke. "So what will you do, Charon? Will you join them, or will you remain my ally?" he asked in a low, rough voice.

He turned to her, his eyes glowing as crimson as Rylan's had, and she felt the heat inside her, burning right through to her soul. "Because whether you wanted a war or not, it seems one has found you."

ACKNOWLEDGMENTS

To my editor, Leslie "Lam" Miller: Without you, this book never could have become what I wanted and needed it to be. Thank you for your honesty, your patience, and your willingness to push me until I made you believe in the story and the characters. The someday-drinks will be on me, by the way. Now it's in writing. So there.

So much gratitude goes to the amazing team at 47North. Thanks to Jason Kirk for shepherding the book from the start, and to Britt Rogers, Justin Golenbock, Ben Smith, and so many others for making sure this series has the visibility it needs to reach its audience. I feel so fortunate to have all of you on my side. Thanks also to Elizabeth Johnson, my awesome copyeditor, for fabulous attention to detail and the occasional saucy comment in the margins. Cliff Nielsen gets my deep appreciation for designing me such amazing covers.

My agent, Kathleen Ortiz, gets credit for holding me together. We're way past color-coded schedules, KO, but you still help me stay on the rails, which is no easy feat. I'm also grateful to the staff at New Leaf, including Danielle Barthel, Jaida Temperly, Dave Caccavo, Pouya Shahbazian, and Joanna Volpe, for providing excellent behind-the-scenes support.

A major thank-you goes to Paul Block, who went over and above to make sure I could write this book while staying connected to my other professional role. More thanks go to Catherine Allen, for captaining the ship, and Casey, Chris, Kristal, Bethany, Erica, Anne-Marie, Yerissa, and the entire staff of CCBS for being a fabulous group of people to work with.

Lydia Kang: What to say? Thank you so much for lending your biomedical expertise (and I fully acknowledge that any immunological ridiculousness in this story is my error and mine alone). But beyond that, and even more importantly, thank you for being a dear friend. Thanks also to Jaime Loren for beta-reading at the speed of light, and to Virginia Boecker for cheering me on.

Mom and Dad, thank you for Wednesday morning calls and constant support. Cathryn and Robin, I am so lucky to have you as my sisters. Asher and Alma, you delight me.

And to my readers, thank you for existing. I'll try to keep telling stories that are worthy of you.

ABOUT THE AUTHOR

© Rebecca Skinner

Sarah Fine is a clinical psychologist and the author of the Guards of the Shadowlands series (*Sanctum*, *Fractured*, and *Chaos*), as well as other young adult novels and the adult fantasy novel *Marked*. She was born on the West Coast, raised in the Midwest, and is now firmly entrenched on the East Coast, where she lives with her husband and two children.